T0354506

DEEP GREEN

STONE SPICER

The first in a series of
Kensington Stone
Novels

Watch your bookstores for

HIDDEN

to be published during
Summer 2014

Order this book online at www.trafford.com
or email orders@trafford.com

Most Trafford titles are also available at major online book retailers.

Cover photograph: Kualoa Beach Park, Kaneohe Bay, Oahu, Hawaii with Mokolii
Island (Chinaman's Hat) in background by Andy Beal of GoVisitHawaii.com

Printed in the United States of America.

ISBN: 978-1-4669-8577-3 (sc)
ISBN: 978-1-4669-8576-6 (hc)
ISBN: 978-1-4669-8578-0 (e)

Library of Congress Control Number: 2013904171

Trafford rev. 03/15/2013

 www.trafford.com

North America & international
toll-free: 1 888 232 4444 (USA & Canada)
phone: 250 383 6864 ♦ fax: 812 355 4082

A special thanks to Ms. Pat Ryan for her incomparable editing skills. Without her expertise, this novel would have had far too many words as well as far too many unnecessary commas.

Author's note

Descriptions, backgrounds and mentions of places and areas throughout my novel are, for the most part, only similarly accurate. Some specifics like John Dominis Restaurant, The Tahitian Lanai and Papeete Bar beside the Waikikian and Empire Café, diamonds from the past that have disappeared from view, are temporarily brought back to life in a tribute to Hawaii's beautiful past.

Prologue

The year AD 1269 . . .

> . . . several miles off the southern coast of the
> island of Hawaii, Pacific Ocean

The fire was spectacular against the dark night. It glowed
through the cresting waves like an opaque cavalcade as
one wave curled to its breaking point then rushed to settle
onto the surface and lend way for the next to rise up into
the bright glow. Even from this distance, the fury of Pele, the
fire goddess, was evident in the fountains of red molten rock
angrily bursting high into the air above the waves.

All those onboard, the mix of weariness and fear plainly
evident on each face, breathed easier despite the perils they
had yet to face. Some of their fears were abated knowing they
had finally found the place they were searching for during the
course of their lengthy voyage. The home they had left behind
was slowly but certainly becoming a memory.

Many weeks prior, they had barely been able to escape
pursuing warriors. The high chief on the island of Rarotonga,
their ancestral home far in the south pacific, had sent warriors

to kill Chief Kanoa for having spoken out against many of the customs that the gods dictated, traditions that had been practiced for centuries. Chief Kanoa had called the ancient traditions barbaric and wanted them brought to an end. The penalty for his outspokenness was a quick death for him, his family and his entire village.

With food supplies hurriedly placed on board their voyaging canoe, Chief Kanoa and forty others, both family and villagers, quickly made their way out through the breakers of the reef that protected their island home and set sail north into the unknown.

Now, near the end of their voyage, Chief Kanoa stood in awe as he contemplated the sheer power emanating from the strange fiery red fountains dancing before them. Folklore from legendary travelers told of fiery lands far to the north. Now they were there, having followed a path set out in handed-down stories.

Keani, the navigator, having guided their canoe by stars and currents, carefully guided the craft onto a sandy beach.

Malo, a kahuna, high priest, and advisor to Chief Kanoa, ordered everyone to remain onboard, saying he must first seek communication with the local gods before any of them could set foot on the new land. It was a tense moment for if the local gods took offense and refused Malo's petition to accept them, they would die of starvation as food gathering would not be permitted and their provisions were nearly depleted.

Malo, together with Hanalei, who was a trusted friend of Chief Kanoa's, carrying a lauhala-wrapped bundle under one arm and lit torch in his other hand, made their way up the lava-strewn hill above the beach. They soon discovered and descended into the opening of a large lava tube as Malo, guided by instinct and an innate *knowing*, lead the way. They ventured far into the bowels of total darkness lit only by Hanalei's torch when suddenly Malo stopped and became silent and motioned Hanalei to his side.

The bundle was unwrapped exposing a carving of Keahimauloko, Chief Kanoa's personal god—the god who had guided their voyaging canoe to this land. Wrapped together with the sacred carving was a crystal-clear large green rock the size of a coconut. Malo carefully placed each item on the floor of the cave then looked over at Hanalei and gave an almost imperceptible nod.

Hanalei, without question, took his place on the ground next to Keahimauloko and the glistening green gem. He had the great honor of remaining there and traveling into eternity with Keahimauloko. His duty was to provide a human spirit for this mighty god if the god determined he had a need for one.

The gods of this new island were pleased with Chief Kanoa's arrival and gave Malo the knowledge they were welcome to stay. With torch in hand, the kahuna made his way out of the lava tube and back down to the shore to pass on the good news.

Most onboard glanced in the direction of their friend, tears pooling in their eyes. In their hearts they knew his new path into the future was a great honor, so they were at ease knowing his spirit would forever remain in peaceful stillness.

Chapter One

Three miles off the coast of Oahu, Hawaii,
Pacific Ocean

Viane knew from the very depths of her soul that she would
not survive. It was the sort of "knowing" that flashes through
every cell of your body when certainty merges with reality,
and she had already begun to give it power.

She had no concept of how long she'd been floating but
was certain of the endless hours of having been continuously
battered by waves crashing down over her, each with
unbelievable force. In the dark, every cold explosion of water
came suddenly and unseen, each as crushing as the last, each
claiming its toll on her capacity to survive.

The incomprehensible panic that had nearly paralyzed her
after being left to drown hours before had abated with this
acceptance of her fate. There had been moments in her short
life when she'd pondered her ultimate death, as most people
do to some limited extent, but it was always an imagined,
unreal, or elusive sort of thinking. These morbid exercises of
thought usually followed hearing of a loved one's tragic end

and often took the shape of prayers for a peaceful finale when their time eventually arrived.

She didn't want to die—not here, not now—not as all her dreams and desires were beginning to blossom. She was on the cusp of becoming a geologist. It had been her life's dream, and she could visualize a perfect future unfolding, containing everything she wanted in life. She knew she could become one of the best if given the chance.

She struggled to remain conscious in order to stay alive but, barring a miracle, she could not conceive of a way out of her ordeal. Perhaps losing consciousness was the best alternative, but with her innate "fight to the finish" attitude, she knew she'd keep fighting as long as she took breath. Her faith in God supported her belief in miracles, but she was also a scientist and knew her present predicament just might be pushing the miracle envelope to the extreme.

Her grasp on the life ring, which was keeping her afloat, had become rigid and unresponsive, the muscles of her hands and arms no longer responding to her will. The life ring had become entangled in a seaweed-covered piece of fishing net several hours before which was serving to keep what she believed was a shark she'd spotted earlier at a safe distance. At first, she thought the fish net was like a gift from God, and it had given her the confidence to keep going; but now, after so many long, frigid, wet hours, the net only served as a cruel offering prolonging her drift and ultimate death.

She had been chilled to her core a few hours ago but now only felt the almost-pleasant numbness consuming her as the inevitable hypothermia slowly took hold.

On the edge of total unconsciousness, she failed to hear a boat as it slipped past just a few feet away. Her eyes were closed, her lungs drawing in weak, shallow breaths of wet, salt-laden air.

A sudden intrusion into her numbed world, though, began to rekindle her mental awareness. Something was moving around her with a determination of unrelenting effort and was quickly and roughly engulfing her. Whatever had wrapped itself around her began to tug and pull at her body, ripping the life ring out of her grasp. A vision of huge octopus tentacles wrapping themselves around her body drifted through the cracks of her near-deadened mind. The grip around her chest was compressing the remaining air from her body as the thing continued to pull. An enormous air bubble loudly erupted from her lungs as she was lifted above the water's surface.

Fright gripped her dimmed consciousness once again as the abruptness of force renewed her near-deadened will and strength to survive.

Chapter Two

Also three miles off the Oahu coast

His name was Kensington Stone according to his birth certificate, fishing license and other important legal documents, including his divorce decree. He made a steadfast point, though, of never talking about that latter one, although in retrospect he would reluctantly admit that it had given him the opportunity to buy the beachfront, two-story, A-frame house on the back portion of Kaneohe Bay that he now called home, so in many respects it had worked out well. Besides, he wasn't one to ever hold a grudge.

His driver's license decreed him to be fifty-five with a Scorpio's October birthday. It also stated he was six feet two and 180 pounds, but it failed to recognize just how hard he had to work at keeping that latter number from ballooning—pardon the pun. The license also mentioned the license holder should be wearing glasses, but he was experiencing an enormous struggle accepting that testament to age and usually opted, instead, for squinting his way through restaurant menus.

His love of the Hawaiian Islands and the admiration he held for the ancient builders of the mile upon mile of stonewalls that appear throughout Hawaii led family as well as friends to refer to him simply as Stone, and he liked it. It was different, and it usually drew a comment or two when introduced. He discovered that people generally had an easy time remembering it, and he secretly found women warmed to the name, an observation he was always vigilant to notice.

At fifty-five, he'd had the necessary time to develop a calm disposition to life. That, coupled with an unrelenting positive viewpoint almost to a fault, gave him an eternally rose-colored outlook of everyone he met and of everything he experienced, which he found could be a big irritant to those who thought a good conversation was one that explored all the wrongs in life.

His present circumstance, though, was overshadowing all his positive thinking and rosy-colored outlook, and he only had himself to blame for getting into the current struggle. He'd never bought into a *victim* mentality, firmly believing that each individual was the ultimate ruler of his own life and therefore had to accept his own decisions—good, bad, or otherwise. God set up the canvas and handed out the brushes, but each individual determined what picture got painted, including the inevitable screw-ups and unthinking choices, which were all integral parts of life. How he wished, though, he could change the current picture of the circumstances he was currently painting.

He was grateful no one was close enough to hear all the inventive expletives he'd been mindlessly voicing into the blustery wind for the past several hours. As a rule, he rarely swore but was quickly coming to accept the notion that out of sheer necessity, the combination of boats and water brought out the "sailor talk." Then again, perhaps it was fear attacking him on a level of his understanding that encouraged—nay, required—primal responses. Whatever the reason, he managed to find it in himself to laugh as he thought about all the sisters at Holy Trinity Church and how they would be so certain that their ears were irreversibly damaged were they to hear him right at that moment.

It was after 9:00 p.m. Monday evening, and the only thing he could see in the dim light of night was the white curling tips of huge waves heading his way. Each wave that smashed into his boat gave him what he considered good reason to mutter more choice words.

His day had started quite abruptly a few moments before seven with the alarming sound of the telephone coming to life as it rested close to his bed. It instantly roused him from a deep sleep.

Normally, he was up and running, or at least up and drinking coffee, by 5:00 a.m., but he'd been in his office late the previous night working on a client's account. As a financial consultant, he prided himself on being one of the best; but to achieve that honor, it took long arduous hours. Whenever the markets bounced from good to not good as they often did and his clients became concerned, he felt compelled not to let them down if he could possibly avoid it, which often necessitated working Sunday evenings.

"Is this Mr. Stone?" a man asked after Stone mumbled a greeting into the receiver.

Stone recognized the man's voice immediately. He'd been expecting the call—just not this early. It was the perfect voice for a boat dealer: a soft deep quality, gravelly yet exhibiting a wealth of strength. The first time Stone had heard him speak, offering a brochure to look at, he immediately thought of a Hollywood Mafia character—one of the *Godfather's famiglia*, "I'ma gonna make yous a deal yous shouldn't refuse."

Anticipation is a wonderful emotion, especially when it involves a large new toy. His never-been-in-the-water yacht had been due to arrive from Seattle by barge at a Young Brother's pier in Honolulu Harbor sometime over the past two days. He knew the dealer, Ross, would have been hard at work since then getting it ready for its water test and final delivery, which they had both anticipated would be today. Knowing the immense advertising value of this magnificent machine floating around the island waters, Stone visualized Ross working laboriously to get it delivered and into the water as fast as he could make it happen.

"Aloha, Mr. Stone, this is Ross from the Kewalo Boat Exchange. We got a boat here that's got your name on it." Stone could hear the smile in Ross' voice.

He had been doing a lot of thinking about his new yacht as if he'd been waiting his whole life for this day to arrive. He recalled stepping on to a boat as a nine-year-old when he and his dad spent a day on Wilson Lake on the west-central part of Oahu doing some serious freshwater fishing. It was a thrill then, and he was anticipating an even bigger thrill now.

"So today's the day," Stone replied, fully awake, "and please, Ross, just Stone works for me."

"Great. It'll be ready by noon, Stone," Ross went on. "Kimo, my assistant, and I will meet you at the Ala Wai boat harbor next to the Harbormaster's office around noon if that's good for you. We can go over her operation and answer questions and then take her out for a shakedown cruise. The calm water off Waikiki will be the perfect place for you to get a feel for how she handles."

"Can we make that closer to one, Ross? I have a few things to arrange ahead of time, and a friend wants to be part of the initial run, but he can be difficult to track down at times."

"Fair enough, Stone, I'll see you there. *Ahui hou.*"

"Ross, one more thing before you hang-up: can you arrange to have the gas and water tanks filled for me? I'll write you a check when I see you."

"Actually, that's part of our 'service with a smile.' We just finished topping off all the tanks, and we've thrown in three bumpers to keep you from damaging any piers you happen to nudge along your way."

Stone had talked to his friend, Lloyd Moniz, a few days before about taking the shakedown run together. They had been best friends since attending the University of Hawaii too many years in the past to recount. They met the first week of their freshman year while sitting in the back row of a huge auditorium in Bilger Hall listening to a very boring lecture on world history. They had both quietly voiced their thoughts of how great a cold beer would taste right about then and had quickly left class, downed far too many Brew 102s, which were ninety-six cents per six pack back then, obviously falling short of being a high-quality beer, and had been close friends ever since. Lloyd's love for boats was actually equal to or greater than Stone's. It was, however, a conditional love: Lloyd considered boats a means of conveyance for fishing, which was one of his main outdoor activities in addition to buying and fixing cars and trimming various hedges in his yard to resemble animals. He wasn't an artist so this latter endeavor left a lot to his neighbor's imaginations and wonderment.

"Hey, Lloyd," he said as Lloyd answered.

"Today's going to be some good day, eh?" Lloyd replied, with a touch of pidgin English. Talking with Lloyd was like carrying on a nonending conversation. It could be weeks between contact, but his easy manner made it seem like yesterday. It was an integral part of what made him such a good friend—that and his ability to narrate an unceasing string of jokes.

"You ready, my friend?" Stone asked. "The water's smooth as a fresh bowl of poi and beckoning us out for adventure."

"Eh, Stone, you mind if Kawika tags along? He's been after me to ask since you and I first talked about it."

Kawika was Lloyd's son. He was one of those rare kids who weren't shy or afraid to speak up but also knew, or usually did, when it was in their best interest to keep quiet. He was a good kid, and Stone liked him a lot.

"I'd love to have him along. Besides, he can help us with the docking lines while we figure out what we're doing. You mind stopping at Zippy's on your way down and getting some bento lunches to take out with us? I told the dealer we'd meet at the Ala Wai Harbor next to the Harbormaster's office at one."

"No sweat, Stone. Us and bentos and some fishing stuff will be there waiting for you."

The mention of fishing gear gave Stone reason to pause. He had envisioned hitting deep, smooth water and not slowing down. With a calm ocean, a new yacht vibrating under his feet, and all the horsepower waiting to roar, he'd thought they could run across the channel to Molokai and back. Perhaps pull into Haleolono harbor while they were close. It was a rarely used facility that once upon a time had been the primo spot to harvest sand to replenish a continually disappearing Waikiki Beach. It had been many years since he and Lloyd had been there picking opihi. The thought of slowing down or even stopping to fish didn't fit the plan, though, not to mention the inevitable fish blood all over his new "everything"; however, if fishing gear showed up, he knew they'd stop and drop their lines out on Penguin Banks at some point in the ride. Besides, he couldn't remember the last time he'd caught any nabetta, and the thought of their taste made his mouth begin to water.

As Stone headed over the Pali Highway to the Ala Wai boat harbor, he realized that finding a parking stall could be a nightmare at this time of day. He was prepared for the worst but was also positive that the perfect spot would present itself. *Parking angels, I need your help!* He found a metered stall under the overhang of the Ilikai Hotel, a short walk to the Harbormaster's office. He gladly took it and thanked his angels. He usually had to be conscious of others when he mentioned his parking angels—people who didn't understand often gave him strange looks.

He shoved as many quarters as he could find into the meter and accepted the notion that if a ticket was waiting for him when he returned, he would simply chalk it up as being part of the cost for the day's adventure.

Chapter Three

There's a rush that sweeps over you when you see something of extraordinary beauty for the first time, and your lungs expand to accommodate an enlarged awareness. It's an adrenaline explosion that makes every nerve ending in your body tingle, from the tips of your toes to the frayed ends on your hair, and makes your heart swell in an attempt to become large enough to consume the vision. Ask any guy, and he'll tell you the *rush* his adolescent mind went through when he saw a woman's bare breast for the first time. He immediately knew his life had made a dramatic shift and infinite possibilities suddenly loomed on the horizon.

Stone thought he was fully prepared for what he was going to see since he'd been staring at the yacht brochure so much and so often the color had begun to fade from the pages, but he came to a sudden halt and felt the adrenaline rush rinse through his body as he rounded the corner of the Ilikai heading toward the Harbormaster's office.

There in front of him, resting on a monstrously large trailer was a magnificent white yacht larger than life itself, and she was all his—a*nd the bank's, of course!* It was like that thing about icebergs: you can see a boat sitting in the water or see a picture of it in a brochure, and it looks big, and the numbers "read" big, but nothing prepares you for the actual size until it's up close and fully exposed, with nothing hidden beneath the water. There it was, balancing on a large trailer that, even for *its* enormous size, conjured up the mental image of an elephant sitting on a tricycle.

Ross and his partner were busy doing last-minute prep work as Stone approached.

The purchase was now history—his dream just beginning to materialize. A fifty-two-foot Searay Sundancer boasting twin 480-horsepower inboard Triton engines with MerCruiser outdrives. He'd ordered all the bells and whistles the factory had available—it was loaded from tip to tail. It was white with blue trim, upholstered in UV-protected blue-and-cream Dolphin leather, albeit and thankfully imitation. The flooring above and below deck was finely finished teakwood with a fully equipped stainless steel galley, three staterooms with polished teakwood walls, built-in dressers, and twin nightstands on each side of queen-sized beds. There were two full heads—bathrooms for the land locked—each with a full-mirrored shower. It was everything one could imagine and a great deal more.

They spent an hour going over things in greater detail than Stone needed or wanted. He was anxious to be on his way heading out into open water.

"And this switch will operate the air breather that originates in the bilge. Remember, Stone, this **must** be turned on at least ten minutes before firing up the engines. If a gas leak occurs, which is rare but a very real possibility, the fumes will collect in the engine compartment and would probably ignite when you power up."

The words were not lost on Stone. Long ago, a friend had died because of that very thing. Spilled gas from a fill-up had apparently collected in the bilge, and his friend had forgotten or ignored checking the engine compartment before starting the motor. All conjecture, really, as his friend was never able to tell his story. The explosion had been heard for miles.

"And this group of switches operates the running lights, cockpit and cabin lights, and a stern spotlight. You'll also need to read all the rules of the road. The Coast Guard has an immoveable propensity to come down hard on those who don't follow them."

Stone was quickly reaching the point of information overload. He looked around for Lloyd and Kawika, but they were nowhere to be seen. It was almost 2:00 p.m.

Interrupting Ross' walk-through, he went across the road to the Chart House Restaurant to use their pay phone. *Thank God there are still pay phones in this world.* It was those unscheduled times that he could *almost* be convinced that a cell phone would be beneficial. Lloyd answered the phone on the first ring.

"You know you need a cell phone, Stone. I've been trying to figure out how to let you know that Kawika and I haven't left yet. Pam's using her car, and mine has a dead battery because somebody," he said with exaggerated reference, "and I refuse to incriminate myself, left the parking lights on all night. Kawika's charging the battery right now. We'll be on our way in ten minutes."

"Hey, some things can't be avoided," responded Stone. "Listen, Lloyd, we're about to head out for the shakedown. Shouldn't take much more than an hour. When you get here, wait for me in front of the Harbor Pub at the transient dock, and we'll go out from there."

The launch went smoothly as Ross and Kimo, working in choreographed efficiency, made the effort appear almost graceful as Stone stood off to one side "to observe" at their insistence.

When Ross, Kimo, and Stone arrived back at the dock, there was still no sign of Lloyd. Back at the Chart House payphone, Stone called Lloyd once again.

"Sorry, Stone, looks like today's not going to happen," Lloyd said, the sound of defeat was palpable in his voice. "Me and Kawika had the car running and all set to leave when Kawika's boss called and told him to come to work. Apparently, they had some emergency going on, so Kawika had to take my car since he'll be required to do a few deliveries."

Kawika worked at a fiberglass shop making outrigger canoes. If the truth were known, the boss had probably made some rash promises to a buyer just to complete a sale and needed Kawika to pull him out of his bind.

"Ah man," he said, disappointment quite evident in Stone's voice. "I'm sorry to hear that, Lloyd. You know, there'll be other days. We're going to spend a lot of time out over the banks catching fish. I'll call you when I pull into Kaneohe Yacht Club later this afternoon. How about coming down and helping with the tie-up? Maybe we can get in a short cruise around the bay before nightfall."

It was four-thirty in the afternoon when Stone made his way back out the channel finally on his way toward Kaneohe Bay and the yacht club where he'd become a member and had been assigned a slip. Heavy clouds had been building over the previous hour, and the trade wind was becoming more noticeable. *Nothing unusual*, he thought.

He was pleased that Lloyd and a few other friends would be at the club to help guide him into his new slip. That first time into a new boat slip can make skippers old and gray overnight. The more hands there are to grab ropes, the less likely he'd run into something immovable and cause damage.

The footpath along Magic Island was lined with walkers and joggers. He was pleased to see so many heads turn to look and hopefully admire as he maneuvered out the narrow waterway. He saw a few young toddlers tugging on adult shirttails excitedly pointing and waving. He waved back.

The cruise past Waikiki Beach was a pleasurable one. A renewed awareness of just how fickle the ocean was showed itself as he rounded the Diamond Head buoy and headed east-north-east directly into the face of the trade wind. The calm water had disappeared. The seas were not a concern but were bumpy enough that his thoughts of sipping champagne had blown away with the wind. He was forced to throttle back to avoid taking a pounding and having to face excessive water spray over the bow. He hadn't put the canvas top up as he found the smell of the ocean carried in the trade winds intoxicating, and he loved it—he wanted the full effect.

It is often voiced by many previous boat owners that there are really only two happy days in the life of owning one—the day they buy it and the day they sell it. He was pragmatic enough to know the second line of that tale would someday become reality, but in the meantime, he was in the process of becoming the happy captain of his destiny.

His euphoria, though, quickly evaporated. The waves continued to build in size and were closing in on each other. The sky and clouds became considerably darker and more threatening. Hindsight, always being so perfect, would have had him turn around and steer back to the protection of the Ala Wai Harbor or to its next-door neighbor Kewalo Basin, but a stubbornness he was well known for made him tighten his grip on the wheel and continue into the wind.

It wasn't until he rounded Koko Head heading north that things became turbulent. The waves were huge, running fifteen to eighteen feet. The trade wind had turned more north-northeasterly, pushing the waves higher, making them curl into a white fury towering into the night sky. Turning around, as he now wished he had done earlier when he had a choice, had become a non-option as was abandoning the helm to put up the canvas top for some sheltered relief. With no choice remaining, he steered a course slightly off-center instead of straight up into the rising walls of water, praying his yacht's bow would cut a path over the top. The bow of most boats was designed for taking waves head-on, while the stern, just by its shape, could become a giant soup spoon scooping up water in the following seas so turning around, as he was tempted to do, would spell disaster. He'd throttled back even further, keeping just enough headway to maintain control.

Wailana Sunrise, as he had already named her, handled well, tracking straight on the face of the swells, hanging for an instant at the peak before sliding forward down the wave's backside. He was quickly discovering, though, that his desire to name his yacht *Wailana Sunrise* may have been premature. *Wailana* conjured up visions of calm and peaceful escapes on the open expanse of the ocean—a chance to reunite with nature, so to speak. That coupled with the *Sunrise,* the beginning of a new day, was Stone's most favored time. He was now humorously entertaining the thought of changing the name. *Maybe* Idiotic Chaos *would be more appropriate.*

He told himself everything would be all right, keep calm, maintain that positive thought he always possessed, and keep a prayer in his heart. *And for God's sake, put on a life jacket!*

Chapter Four

Still three miles off the coast of Oahu

Strain and fatigue were evident on Stone's drenched face. His hair was matted to his head, and droplets of saltwater rolled down his face. His arms and hands were cramped from holding on to the helm of *Wailana Sunrise* so tightly. Even the string of expletives he'd been yelling into the wind a few hours ago had ceased—his humor gone.

He had been at the helm for five excruciatingly long hours, and the seas continued to build in height and violence. He judged them to be at least twenty feet—an observation he garnered from the angle *Wailana Sunrise* attained as she powered her way over each watery mountain. The waves reached their peak fury before crashing down over the bow, roller-coasting themselves over the smooth, shiny expanse of fiberglass and up over the windshield, blasting into Stone's face like a fire hose every few dreaded seconds. Everything from wind to darkness was hostile to his attempts to make headway. Everything disastrous had happened so suddenly, but he kept berating himself for not having attempted

something to get the covers up earlier even when he thought
he couldn't chance it. *Hindsight could solve all the problems
in the world*, he thought as he was convinced of this now.
Now it would be certain suicide to release the helm even for a
second. He could do nothing but guide his new love forward
into the barrage of waves.

Hawaii is a frequent victim to passing storms sweeping
their way across the Pacific. Most often, though, they pass
quickly, much to Stone's relief as he became aware that
the ocean swells were beginning their journey back to a
semblance of comparative gentleness, lacking the wind
to drive their fury. A multitude of stars began to open to
the world below, attempting to cast their glow over the
still-agitated water as the clouds dispersed.

He forced himself to relinquish the helm to the elements
and rushed below deck for a dry towel and fresh T-shirt. With
hair dried and warm T-shirt hugging his body, he finally
smiled once again at the thought of his first adventure, his
positive attitude back in place and fully in control.

Now only a couple miles off the Windward Coast, he
began navigating a forest of buoys, putting his trust in the
people who had placed them there. Properly positioned,
buoys kept boats off obstacles that could easily tear holes in
the shining exterior of any that ventured near the gargantuan
coral hazards inches below the surface. Even a slight bump
against one of the razor-sharp coral heads would cut gashes
into the boat's hull—like a scalpel plying itself against an
overstuffed grocery bag. Instead of food packages, though, it
would be him spilling out, directly into waters frequented by

fish that liked to eat things that moved, or didn't move, for that matter. Creatures of the deep weren't all that finicky in what they chose to consume.

The buoys marked the entrance to the Crash Boat Channel, which ultimately led into Kaneohe Bay and the yacht club.

The marine base at Kaneohe had been forced to open up this boat channel through the reef many years prior as their emergency access to downed aircraft, but they made the water path relatively narrow and crooked—they had taken the easy, not the best, way through.

A loud *thunk!* launched a vibration coursing through *Wailana Sunrise*'s hull with an accompanying shock wave rippling up Stone's spine.

It was an unmistakable sound of the hull glancing off something solid. *Wailana Sunrise* slowly and insistently hauled to a stop like a bungee cord reaching the far point of its stretch as the port engine died. He quickly throttled back on the starboard engine and closed it down. All was quiet but for the cresting and breaking of the waves as they rolled past him in their non-ending parade toward shore.

Stone knew it wasn't one of the buoys he had hit. If he had gotten close enough to accidentally glance off one of them, he would most unquestionably have known it. Getting close to those floating islands of steel would be like standing next to a large office building: it would be very difficult to miss noticing.

Below the waterline and sprawling out behind *Wailana Sunrise*, Stone could see the tattered remains of a barnacle-encrusted cargo net with a large assorted collection of flotsam the net had caught along its journey. Part of the net appeared to have tangled in one of the propellers. A clump of something had attached itself to the far edge of the cargo net and was faintly visible across the water looking like a ghostly white blob floating on the surface.

A shudder coursed through him as he thought of having to enter the foreboding water to find his way under the hull to cut his yacht free.

Distant lights from the H-3 freeway and the mountain tunnels had come into sight casting their slithery reflection off the water as the dense cloud cover dissipated. The shapes of the Koolau Mountains on the horizon behind Kaneohe town were silhouetted against the glow of light reaching skyward from busy Honolulu, far on the other side of the mountains. The calming image gave Stone a good indication of where he was. It did nothing, however, to ease the eerie feeling of the task before him. Checking out the bottom side of his new toy was something he hadn't planned on doing this early in the ownership game, nor was having to do it in the middle of the ocean—in the dark.

Being in and under the water was something he had grown up with and accepted without thought. He'd been introduced to the ocean by his free-thinking mother when he was just a few months old. He was an avid scuba diver, and when not suited up with tanks, he loved nothing more than snorkeling the reefs, admiring the beauty that was so abundant below the surface.

He fastened the Velcro of his dive knife around his forearm, thankful for having thought to include it in his backpack, as he moved through the transom doorway onto the swim platform extending out above the water line. Just to be safe, he tied a length of rope around his waist and secured the loose end to the transom railing. Thank God it didn't happen very frequently, but stories surface of solo boaters being left behind in the middle of the ocean, having fallen overboard from their moving boats. If anything were to happen, he preferred to take his chances attached to something solid and trustworthy and not having to hang on to the frayed ends of a barnacle-encrusted cargo net.

He took a few deep breaths as he looked into the dark water and moved to the ladder. An involuntary gasp escaped his lips as he descended the ladder, and the cold water caught the lower few inches of his bathing suit and crotch. The temperature of the water around Hawaii stays fairly consistent, around seventy-two degrees; but with the night air wafting softly over the water, warm as it may seem, it still possessed the power to make a warm heart leap several inches in various directions.

He was about to let go of the ladder when suddenly something silky and clinging floated around him and pulled at the hairs on his chest. A frightening screech echoed across the water—*his*—as adrenaline-fed panic forced him to turn and face whatever it was that had floated around him. His body went into an instant "fight or flight" mode as he instantly turned and clawed his way back up the ladder, white knuckles pressuring against skin, his head banging hard on the ladder in his attempt to create distance from the unexpected sight.

As he stood on the swim platform, his heart pounding like an old drum at a hippie reunion, a surrealistic image came into focus as he looked down at the top of a head of hair and a partially exposed face, gray and ghostlike. The attached body was entangled in the cargo net that had drifted close and surrounded the stern of his yacht; a hand held a death grip on a white life ring. He saw a woman's body serenely floating on her back as if she were in a swimming pool at the Moana Surfrider dreaming of some exotic memory. Her eyes were closed, and she appeared dead or very close to it.

Stone bent and grabbed the net, pulling it closer, and reached for the woman. Wrapping his arm over her chest and down under her armpit, bracing himself, he pulled her up onto the swim platform along with a portion of the blackish-green seaweed dripping net that was tangled around the woman's legs. A loud gurgling sound escaped from her throat from the pressure of Stone's grip around her chest. He worked quickly cutting her legs free with his knife, then half carried, half dragged her through the transom doorway onto the rear main deck and laid her down.

Water trickled out of her partially open mouth as the woman struggled for air. He held his fingers lightly against her neck and was relieved to feel a weak pulse yet strong enough that CPR wouldn't be necessary. By her pale color and labored breath, he knew her internal systems were fighting hypothermia. Looking at her face, he saw how young and exceptionally beautiful she was, dressed in pale green evening attire, which now clung to her like a sloppily plastered wall. He quickly picked her up again and carried her down into the labyrinth of luxury in the interior of *Wailana Sunrise* and forward into the master stateroom. He knew the thing she could use most was warmth and as quickly as possible. He pushed the thermostat to its maximum and felt the warm air quickly begin to fill the room from an undetected vent. He piled the only available blankets that came with the boat over her and tucked them close, the best he could do for the moment. A quick journey to land and a hospital would be the next best thing for her.

A strand of the net had grabbed the port propeller and wound around the propeller shaft, choking off the engine. Despite having to work in the dark, only by touch, surfacing three times for air, he finally freed the yacht from her tether. Nets such as this one occasionally wash off the decks of commercial fishing boats and cause grief and involuntary death to any sea creature that happens to become entangled, not to mention hapless boaters like him who get snarled and ruin expensive equipment. He secured what he could of the net to the swim platform, with the intention of dragging it into Kaneohe and out of harm-creating way.

He went below to check on his guest. She remained as he had placed her and encouragingly seemed to be breathing stronger and with more ease. The warmth she was experiencing was helping.

Back on deck, his damp towel thrown across his shoulders to invite some warmth, he had no clue where he'd tossed his T-shirt. He restarted the engines, feeling once again the euphoria with the responsiveness of his new yacht. Easing forward gently on the throttles, he moved through the labyrinth of buoys, past Mokapu Point, and beyond into Kaneohe Bay.

He felt the nagging reminder of his self-proclaimed resistance to cell phones as he grabbed for the radiophone and went through the arduous task of connecting with 911. He relayed all the relevant facts to the Honolulu Police Department operator, giving his estimated location and ETA at Kaneohe Yacht Club. He asked that they relay the information to Sgt. Mike Kalama, an old friend. He would feel better knowing Mike was a part of any investigation that was certainly coming. When that call was finished, he called Lloyd.

"Auwe! Stone, you still out there? Where are you?"

"I'm just passing the marine base on the inside of Kaneohe Bay, so I'll be at the yacht club within a short time. If your car's home come down and help me tie up. By the way, I happened to find a beautiful mermaid along the way." He told Lloyd the entire, though abbreviated, story. "She must have fallen overboard from a passing cruise ship judging by the evening dress she's wearing." It was the only explanation Stone had been able to visualize.

"Could be she got into bed with the wrong guy, got caught, and was tossed in an attempt to kill her." Lloyd had a flair for the dramatic.

"Kill her! I hadn't thought of that. It's no doubt going to be an interesting story when we get all the details from her."

Below deck, Viane Koa was regaining consciousness and becoming aware of being in surroundings she did not recognize. So much had happened in such a short time, she was confused and knew she desperately needed to clear the fog in her thoughts and figure out what to do. The last thing she remembered was Doc attacking her, then being forced overboard and spending an eternity floating in the cold water. Doc was her friend and colleague. *Why would he have done such a thing?*

Kill her!

The words resounded through her foggy thoughts. They came from a voice directly above. Whoever it was, Viane had had enough intrigue and injury for the day. Getting to someplace familiar suddenly became paramount to her safety and perhaps, survival.

She sat up slowly and awkwardly, her body aching as though she had just finished running a marathon. She felt as if her muscles had been severed from her bones. The air in the room felt chilly against her damp skin, and a mass of goose bumps rose up in protest all over her body as she pushed the blankets to the floor. She shivered violently. Her first attempt at standing hurt too much, and she fell back on the bed—her muscles heavy and stiff, refusing to cooperate. With great effort, she stood and let the blackout dizziness that swept over her pass.

Leaning hard against the wall for a few moments, she slowly opened the cabin door and peered out. There was a short hallway leading aft to a small sitting area. As silently as she could, she tiptoed out and through the sitting area and an adjoining galley to a short group of stairs leading up and out onto a deck. Pausing at deck level, she raised her head above the handrail and looked around. The men's voices were loud, calling out to one another, laughing at one another's antics.

She noticed a tall man standing at the helm, completely immersed in maneuvering the boat into a berth, responding with excited orders for pulling ropes and fending off piers.

She shuddered at the thought of having to get back in the water, but it seemed to offer the only means of escape, other than running for it, and she was positive she couldn't run three steps. She'd probably fall flat on her face right at the guy's feet! She made her way to the stern out of sight of her captor and eased through a small open doorway in the transom onto a swim platform. Her body protested with agony as she lowered herself into the water. Possessing a good knowledge of boats, having a father who was an avid fisherman who had owned many boats over her lifetime, she knew to avoid the propellers that were churning the water someplace below.

There were many boats and small piers close by. With the aid of an old cargo net secured to the yacht, she quietly moved through the water, aiming for the closest pier that afforded cover. She struggled, pulling herself up out of the water. She was safe so far in the shadow of darkness.

Chapter Five

Viane knelt on the small finger pier in the shadow of a sleek large sailboat that was tied up beside her. She was shivering violently. *I've never been so cold—probably end up with pneumonia.* She saw the man still standing at the helm of the yacht she had just deserted, engrossed in the docking fiasco. *He doesn't look menacing, but then neither did Doc!* Looking at him now, she realized she wouldn't mind meeting him when circumstances were back to normal, if and when that day ever came. She could see he had a passion for his endeavors. His smile to those around him appeared genuine, and he moved with ease and confidence. She noticed the First Responders standing waiting to board. *They are obviously there for me.* She felt a twinge of remorse having not stayed onboard—but not sufficiently so to go back.

With everyone fully engrossed in handling a rope or standing around giving directions to anyone who would listen, she quietly moved to the main pier, keeping as low as she could, praying no one would see her. She headed toward land and the clubhouse and quickly blended into the darkness at the end of the pier.

Viane recognized the yacht club right away but couldn't grasp the time frame of when she and Doc had arrived there hours before, looking forward to dinner on a private yacht. A shiver ran through her at the thought of just how anxious and excited she'd been. *Some dinner cruise that turned out to be!* She could see the pier where the *Whiskey Sea* had been tied up. The spot was vacant now.

She moved around to the front of the building to the main parking lot just as a taxi pulled in. *A little unusual, for this time of night,* she thought. A man and woman stumbled out accompanied by a volley of laughter. Yacht clubs always had visiting yachts coming and going, with owner and crew, as well as guests showing up at all hours. Trying to remain hidden the best she could, she moved to the far side of the car. Just as the man and woman slammed the door closed, Viane quickly opened the opposite door and jumped in. The aging taxi driver turned rapidly, borderline fright etched into his face. Scrutinizing her in more detail, he relaxed with the certainty he wasn't going to be choked, stabbed, or beaten as Viane gave him an address in Nuuanu Valley and settled back for the twenty-minute ride, praying her friend Teri would be home.

Teri White was an Italian-American born in Racine, Wisconsin. She stood five feet seven if she stood up on her toes and had a framework of physically fit beauty. She also possessed a deep innate sense of caring for those who came into her life, such as Viane did right when she needed help.

Teri had a master's degree in psychology and up until two years ago had her own practice working in the arena of eating disorders and family counseling. She felt her life unfulfilling and decided to reenter university life to study geology—a childhood passion.

When they met, Viane had been having difficulty creating a questionnaire for her criminal behavior elective class that was due to be handed in the next day. The roadblock to creating the questionnaire was actually her questioning her own sanity for electing the class in the first place.

She opened a conversation in the fashion of a complaint about herself with a woman sitting close by in the university library. The woman was Teri.

Teri mentioned that she had done some contract work for the police department in criminal profiling, and from that point on, the questionnaire evolved with little effort. They immediately hit it off and, in spite of the generation that separated them, became close friends.

Viane's taxi ride was consumed with worry. If Teri was not at home, Viane was not sure what she would do. She desperately needed a change of clothes. The dress she had been so proud wearing before her whole awful adventure started was beginning to get crisp and itchy as it began to dry, and the saltwater began to morph into just plain, crusted salt. She needed some cash to pay the cabdriver, as well as a ride back to her dorm room.

She rode in silence and thought about her dad, who was the rock of her existence. She needed to go home to Hilo and take time within the safe confines of her family to think. She knew she must figure out what happened and why and also what she needed to do about it. *Dr. Margelese, Doc—her trusted friend and colleague—her would-be killer!* There was a whole lot of newfound information to think about as well as a reevaluation of how she arrived at that crossover point of blindly placing full trust in people. She thought about her treasured find and wondered if she'd ever see them again. *Pops will be so disappointed.*

It was an uneventful, albeit worrisome, ride up the Pali Highway, over the Koolau Mountains, and down into Nuuanu Valley to Laimi Road. She had crowded herself up against the left-hand passenger door in an attempt to avoid the driver's constant attempts to check her out in the rearview mirror. He talked at length on his cell phone all the while glancing at her in the mirror. *Darn wraparound taxi mirrors you can't hide from!* He had a very friendly face, and on better days, she would have loved to talk with him and hear his story—but not tonight!

Teri's house was dark as they pulled up the hill and into the yard. She quickly explained her money problem to the suddenly unsmiling driver and got out before he managed any response.

To her great relief, a light came on brief moments after she banged on the door. A doorbell was present, but pounding the door seemed a more appropriate effort considering the circumstances. *This wasn't a social call.* Doorbells often imply pleasantness.

Teri's appearance gave hint to a hurried exit from sleep viewed through the few inches of space of the partially opened door.

"Viane? What on earth . . ." The door swung open.

Teri's dark blond hair was a mass of tangles, looking as if a miniature cyclone had recently swept through her house. Her bathrobe had obviously been hastily tied as one side hung lopsided well below the other, leaving most of her left breast exposed to the air and an observant taxi driver. His face now wore a wide grin, no longer absorbed in trying to figure out whether or not he had been stiffed.

Teri pulled the flap of her robe over her breast and gave the taxi driver as nasty a look as she could summon. She wrapped her arms around her friend and guided her into the house, closing the door after Viane signaled the cabby to wait.

"I'm so sorry to wake you, Teri," Viane said as they released their hug. "Could you loan me $20 so I can pay Smiley out there what I owe him? Then I really need to talk. I hope its okay."

"Of course, Viane. God, you look and smell like you got caught in rising surf and decided to stay for the ride! I want to hear the whole story."

Teri went out and paid the cabdriver and gave him a generous tip and a friendly smile before returning to her living room and Viane.

"You get into the shower and get warmed up. I have a pair of jeans and a T-shirt that'll fit. I'm going to make us some tea, and then we can talk. Is that okay? Are you hungry?" Without waiting for any replies, Teri took Viane's arm and ushered her into the bathroom, turned on the shower, and left, returning moments later with an armful of clean clothes and a towel, placed them on the vanity and went out, closing the door behind her.

Viane emerged twenty minutes later, feeling quite normal despite what she'd experienced. The past many hours now seemed like a bad dream that hadn't actually happened. The smell of noodle broth made her realize just how famished she was. Teri was famous among her friends for her incredible saimin, the noodle soup dish so unique to Hawaii.

As they ate and sipped *mamaki* tea, a local specialty, Viane told the story of her ordeal. Teri wasn't too surprised to hear of Dr. Margelese's actions. "A minor in geology that I took naturally involved several classes from that slime. I was working with him late one night," relayed Teri, "when his attention turned to admiration for my body and his supposed ability as a perfect lover. I think it could have turned to rape if it wasn't for a fellow colleague of his walking in at that moment. Margelese later made it very clear to me that nothing had happened and I better not say anything because it would be his word against mine, as well as a probable failing course grade. I'm so sorry, I should have warned you."

They talked on for over an hour.

"It's very late. Why don't you make yourself comfortable on the couch," Teri suggested, stifling a yawn, understandably quite sleepy herself. "I don't think going back to your dorm room would be a good idea. In the morning, if you still want to head home, I'll get you to the airport."

Relaxed and totally exhausted, Viane fell asleep, comfortably and gratefully wrapped in the warmth of a thick blanket.

The morning came fast. Teri loaned her friend more clothes, a suitcase, and some money and drove Viane to the Hawaiian Airlines terminal. Viane knew it was essential to be with her family and take time to figure out what to do. Her neat, orderly life was suddenly upside down and in need of a new prospective.

The wonderful air that confronted her as she emerged from the airplane into the open-air terminal in Hilo was filled with an "aliveness" that is so very unique to Hilo as she stepped into the open-air structure of the terminal. It was a familiar awareness she always anticipated and enjoyed. Her senses felt as if they were being captured by serenity and security. Coming home was the right choice. She would stay for as long as it took to figure out what needed to be done. Her dad and her oldest brother, Sonny, were there at the bottom of the escalator waving, as she descended into the baggage claim area. Both held beautiful pikake and plumeria flower leis, and the smell was heavenly.

Chapter Six

Hilo, Hawaii

The matchless fragrances of the plumeria and pikake flower leis draped around her neck coupled with the warmth of her brother's arm softly resting on her shoulder were exactly the security that Viane desperately needed, though lingering confusion and a silent fear persisted—unshakable. She tried to relax as she took in a deep breath and willed the sweet fragrances of the flowers to flood her senses. She sat in silence allowing the rich green lushness of the macadamia nut trees along the airport roadway to envelope her. The familiar sounds of Pops' forty-year-old Nissan pickup and his loving pat on her knee was heaven to her. She was home—she was finally safe.

Viane Koa was a typical island girl. She was typical in the sense of having the combined bloodlines of many nationalities, a true cosmopolitan by Hawaiian standards. Her father, Rudy, or Pops as she lovingly called him, was of Caucasian, Filipino, and Hawaiian extraction. Her late mother, Etta, carried a mixture of Portuguese and Japanese as well as a large portion of Hawaiian. The result was a stunning combination. Viane stood five feet seven, with a head-turning slender figure and strikingly flowing long black hair that shone like a midnight sky on a crystal clear night. Her eyes were dark and alive with a constant excitement for life; her skin the light brown color of softly polished koa wood. Fortunately, none of her remarkable beauty detracted from her wholesome, fun-loving spirit, nor had they swayed her from a deep curiosity of life and a strong-willed drive for success. Whenever she saw her reflection in a mirror, she could never see the beauty that others spoke of and admired. She saw only the excitement and adventure of a young woman facing a future that held no limits.

She had grown up in Hilo, a quaint ocean-side town on the east side of the big island of Hawaii. Her childhood home on Kinoole Street, a large two-story structure dating back to 1891, sat on the knoll of a hill with a commanding view of the surrounding neighborhood, the town of Hilo around it and Hilo Bay in the distance. A massive moss-rock foundation gave it an impressive manner. Her grandfather had been the Luna, the boss, on the old sugarcane plantation that existed there many decades before. This had been his home. Viane's parents had inherited it shortly after they married.

Her father, Rudy Koa, was a small-time entrepreneur whose main and perhaps only claim to fame was mixing, bottling, and selling *patis*, a Filipino sauce made from the fermentation of fish innards. A dubious claim at best in most circles, but in his case, a culinary miracle. Pops always figured you had no problem enjoying his *patis* if you were either Filipino, had simply acquired a taste for it, or possibly didn't

know what you were pouring into your bowl of *dinuguan
baboy*, which in itself could be a whole adventure in eating all
on its own.

Etta, her mom, had been born and raised in Hilo in a
picturesque place called Keaukaha, a Hawaiian community
that meandered east of Hilo along the water's edge. She had
died giving birth to Viane's youngest brother, John, leaving
Rudy to raise the three children himself: Viane, John, and her
older brother Sonny. A host of family members lived close by,
so Rudy always had a wealth of support from an abundance
of aunties and uncles.

Like many local kids born in some of the more rural areas
on the neighboring islands, when it came time to head for
college, University of Hawaii in Manoa Valley on the island of
Oahu offered the best choice. It was away from home, away
from parental control, yet close enough that they could come
home for holidays and birthdays or whenever the need arose to
retreat home for some loving support, such as now for Viane.

She had been aware of volcanoes most of her life, a
natural enough occurrence considering she had grown up on
the slopes of Mauna Kea and Mauna Loa, two of the world's
largest. Numerous hikes onto its vast expanses of terrain
with her father and brothers helped pique her curiosity. That
awareness increased as she grew up listening to the tales her
father would tell of weeklong forays to the summit of both
Mauna Kea and the sister mountain, Mauna Loa. That interest
had eventually led her into an encompassing study of geology
in which she would soon earn her doctorate degree.

The requirements of her chosen field of study were not
easy as she quickly discovered. She had enjoyed a straight A

average through high school, but that was a gift of the past
as university-level subject matter dipped ever deeper into
enormous detail. There were numerous field trips in the
blazing heat of the sun, climbing incredibly rough terrain
on the slopes of Mauna Loa, far above the Hawaii Volcano
National Park. There she would study some unique mineral
deposit that had surfaced with an eruption a thousand
years before or find herself rappelling down the insides of a
vertical lava tube to the very bowels of the earth to retrieve
some extraordinary piece of solidified mineral that had
mysteriously been a part of the earth long before the majesty
of the volcanoes surfaced above the ocean's swells. She loved
it all even when it got close to unbearable.

She spent long nights in the desolate and bone-chilling
cold of the cabin on Mauna Loa's summit, having to break
through a layer of ice an inch thick that covered the only
water source available at that altitude. Using the collapsing
outhouse that stood on the edge of the caldera had been an
unexpected thrill as the view was spectacular and also quite
unavoidable since there was no door to the rustic shed to
shield anyone who might not enjoy the sheer drop-off.

It was on a field trip with her freshmen classmates deep in
the heart of a lava tube that she first realized the overwhelming
beauty of olivine, a semiprecious gemstone of clear, deep green
color. It was a gem that was fairly common in the volcanic
areas of the Big Island, albeit in minute sand-grain size. A
ray of sunlight had probed the depths of the lava tube, and
the olivine, interspersed throughout the rock, lit up with
the sparkle of a thousand miniature green diamonds. It was
breathtaking and had almost caused her to lose footing.

She'd seen olivine many times before as almost every kid growing up in Hawaii has, at least those on the Big Island where it was so prevalent because of a lack of urban sprawl. Pops had often taken the family for daylong picnics to the south end of the Island along a rough sandy drive to Mahana Beach. From the high cliff looking down to the beach and the often-crashing surf of this magical place, the beach was deep green in color, the semiprecious gem, albeit in minute size, being so liberally mixed with the black sand.

The previous Friday she had flown home in order to escape classes for a few days. She needed a break from studies, and as much as she loved Honolulu and Manoa Valley where the university was situated, she also needed to find a reprieve from the hectic pace and crowds of Oahu. As they tried to do as often as possible, her brothers had also returned home to be with her.

Pops took advantage of having them all together and arranged an adventure so they could have some family fun, a tradition that was becoming lost as each of them followed their dreams onto their own life's paths. Pops adventure this day was collecting glass fishing floats on Kaahuahu beach, or so he said anyway. Pops was fairly certain they weren't likely to find any glass floats as they were becoming a thing of the past, but the fun was in just being together for the day. Beachcombing usually guaranteed them of discovering something unique, especially in such a remote place.

The road down to the beach from the quaint country town of Naalehu was a seven-mile-long dirt, four-wheel-drive experience that was exhilarating, dusty, and bone jarring.

They had gotten halfway to the beach, having gone through the gates of an old rock wall corral when Pops, smiling with certain intention, abruptly made a left turn and headed up hill over a pasture and away from the beach. The rough ride ended just as quickly as it had begun when he pulled up to the lip of a caved-in lava tube and turned off the ignition.

"A long time ago when I first found this lava tube," Pops told them all, "I wanted to climb deep inside and explore it but just never got to doing it. Now, kuuipo, you can educate us all." Pops always called her kuuipo, sweetheart, and she loved it. At the bottom of the caved in area was a gaping entrance. They eagerly climbed down the slope to the opening. A cold, damp air wafted out of the enormous mouth of the cave giving them all a slight chill despite the heat of the day.

It was obvious that Pops had planned this when he pulled four flashlights and a huge ball of surveyor's string from his backpack.

With flashlights in hand, the four of them made their way into the pitch-black void of the cave. Sonny brought up the rear, playing out the string as they went. They had all done this type of thing before and knew it was all too easy to become disoriented in a cave such as this and be unable to find the way out. Having been in and out of many caves on recent field trips, Viane let her mind wander and her senses absorb the unique feeling of a centuries-old cavern as she navigated over gargantuan lava boulders as they moved deeper into the darkness.

They laughed and joked with each other, turning their flashlights off to experience the utter void of light. Sonny and John kept a barrage of silly questions directed at their sister knowing they would ruffle her serene nature, all part of the fun of having a sister they loved.

An hour's time past as they moved farther into the cave, a silence had overtaken them as they progressed. Viane wandered a little apart from the others to look at something that had caught her eye. It sparkled as she brought it into the beam of her flashlight—her breath caught in her throat. She instantly recognized the object as an extraordinarily large piece of olivine, as large as a coconut, its polished smoothness mesmerizing in its beauty. Beside it, lying on its side, was a wooden carving about a foot in length. It had fiercely carved facial features, wooden eyes vacantly staring out across the rock-strewn ground, through a covering of dust and dirt. Remnants of decomposed lauhala and strands of decayed binding rested close by. She was aware that Pops, Sonny, and John had moved to her side, curious to see what she had found. None could remove their eyes from the gemstone as light from their flashlights danced from its surface.

The two objects were obviously quite old. As she held them, she felt a level of exhilaration she had not known before. She also felt a sense of dread that perhaps this treasure was something they would have been better off not finding. The prudent thing to do would be to put them down and walk away, but she couldn't bring herself to do so. A piece of olivine this size was unheard of and was holding her in its beautiful spell. As for the idol, she could only imagine that it must carry some important significance to have been honored in such a fashion to accompany something so rare. She realized they could be keys to connecting lost pieces of Hawaiian history. She also knew she was most likely rationalizing, but she honestly believed scholars and keepers of such knowledge should be allowed to see and analyze these treasures and discover for themselves what had been hidden from them.

She also had a research paper to write and present before the academic board as part of her doctoral program. What better subject could there be than a semiprecious gem larger than any thought to exist? She was about to place the large olivine gem in her backpack, but as she held it up, it seemed to come alive as a glow from its core appeared to move in the light of her flashlight. It was suddenly both mesmerizing and frightening.

She quickly placed it, together with the carving, in her backpack and zipped it closed, rationalizing that she had probably been moving the light itself, making it appear to be dancing inside the gem. Even so, it left a strange feeling in the pit of her stomach. Pops nor her brothers had said anything since first seeing the artifacts, aware of some unexplainable presence.

Everyone headed back toward the entrance, silently, reverently following the string Sonny had played out.

Settled in the car once again, they continued down to Kaahuahu beach and were finally able to enjoy the rest of the day laughing and playing, all the while hunting the elusive glass floats. To everyone's delight, they found a small rolling pin-shaped glass float just before they left for home. They were delighted with their find.

The remainder of the weekend was filled with laughter as they all celebrated the enjoyment of being a close family. They were together and appreciating the moment and that was most important—no one willing to broach the subject of Viane's find.

Chapter Seven

Manoa campus, University of Hawaii, island of Oahu

Pops called late Sunday evening just as Viane was getting back to her dorm room at Frierdon Hall and was putting her now-empty backpack in the tiny closet. The treasures she found were resting in the center of her desk. He told her how uneasy he was feeling about what they found and said he'd called an old friend who lived in the small town of Waiohinu on the highway above the lava tube they had explored. His friend, an elderly Hawaiian man who went by the name Joe K, had said he knew of the cave and mentioned that legends claimed it to be a burial cave of the ancient travelers to Hawaii. On learning what they found, he had told Pops that the artifacts implied that something of sacred importance must have occurred there and asked if they had also found any bones.

"He says we should put those things back in the cave where they had been, kuuipo."

"How can we be certain it was a burial cave, Pops?" asked Viane. "There were no bones or anything else in the cave that we were aware of. Besides, legends are just that, made-up stories without facts." In reality, she believed in the legends and knew she was rationalizing her decision to keep the artifacts at least a little while longer.

"Kuuipo, don't be so quick to discount this. Joe K said bones could have been farther in or covered by dirt, and we just missed seeing them. There are many reasons for things we may not know. You know what I'm telling you as we've talked of such things many times before. I think we need to replace them, sweetie."

"I'll give you a call in a few days, Pops, after I talk with some people here at the university and at Bishop Museum."

She sat and stared at her treasures. She knew they were not hers to keep—that was very clear in her mind. But where they needed to be was something totally different. They should either be returned to the lava tube or given some prominence in the museum. She felt the fine line between honoring her ancestors' resting place versus opening a further understanding of their past. She brought the olivine gem and carving from her desk and placed them on her bed and began taking pictures. Even in the viewfinder, the gem brought back the eerie uneasiness to her stomach as if it had some power or spirit that was pulling at her. She quickly finished and put the gem and carving into her backpack and placed it back in her closet out of sight. She rationalized that even if the artifacts ended up back in the lava tube, at least she'd always have the pictures of them.

She was sure her mentor, teacher, and friend, Dr. Margelese, or Doc as she called him with a familiarity he encouraged, would be in his office and probably had been since the break of daylight, even on a Sunday, just as he had been for the past thirty years. He was the only one she could think of to talk with.

As she gently pushed his office door open, Doc looked up through the stacks of books and papers that appeared to have consumed his desk and were actually doing a good job of hiding his presence.

Dr. Krivoi Margelese was an undersized man. He had weasel-like small features with an exceptionally sharp appearing nose and eyes set much too close together. His hair was salt-and-pepper colored and thick and sat on his head like an old, well-used mop. He smiled as he looked up at her.

Viane knew that many female students found him somewhat attractive because of his confident manner and the air of importance he surrounded himself with, something Viane admired but failed to find attractive. He surrounded himself with his passion: four walls of fat, old geology books bound in decades-old leather bindings, periodicals and miscellaneous catalogs sliding off deep stacks, and trays of rocks on every available flat surface, some precariously balanced on piles of others. The floor was littered with discards yet to be thrown away, further cataloged, or simply forgotten.

His smile, though somewhat disingenuous, widened as Viane glided through the door. Of all the beautiful female students he had ever had the pleasure to have in his classroom, Viane was by far the most irresistible.

Unknown to Viane and most of his other female students, Margelese was a man with the morals of a clump of dirt. He had long ago decided, after she first appeared in one of his classes, that he'd give his left testicle to get her into bed. With the same token, he knew his place in the hierarchy of the college and valued his job far too much to jeopardize it by making any sort of advances on her—yet: he was working to change that plan. With Viane, he knew his advances would be thrown back in his face as so many such advances on other female students had been over the years. There had been a fair number of successes, though, from the more desperate of those who caved in for promises of higher grades. He was fortunate the dean, although not particularly fond of him, valued his contribution to the teaching programs. Indiscretions, if not too blatant nor serious, had often been overlooked with nothing more than a shake of a head.

Margelese's smile and imagined pleasures evaporated when Viane placed two objects on the small clearing in the center of his desk. He'd been teaching for so long there was very little in the field of geology that excited him anymore. Suddenly, though, his mind began to race. He understood immediately what he was looking at, and his heart picked up the required speed. It was undoubtedly the largest, most beautiful piece of olivine he had ever known to exist. The other object, a carving of some sort, was like many other Hawaiian artifacts, totally out of his realm of interest, thought, or desire to learn more.

"This is worth a small fortune," he blurted in amazement as he looked at it with a puzzled expression, sensing something about it that bothered him. "There are people who would pay a king's ransom for a piece of stone this size and clarity." He ran his hand over the smoothness but rapidly pulled it away, uncertain why he had done so—something about it!

Viane was surprised by Doc's remarks and his rapid reaction to move away from her treasures. She had not given thought to any dollar value but instead had been torn between what her father had said and her desire to talk with Bishop Museum to perhaps negotiate with them to create a display to honor this treasure of Hawaii and its accompanying "keeper." She had hoped the resulting publicity would benefit the UH and the geology department—and her, of course. There was some selfishness in her thoughts as well, and she knew that. The value of a research paper of this magnitude and the benefit that would accrue toward her career in the field of geology were immense. She was merely being a realist, she thought, as her gaze was pulled back to the gem.

Margelese had dedicated his life to teaching. For the past thirty-three years, he had done his best but often reflected on the dullness of his life and the small rewards it had offered. He was approaching sixty and facing a meager future in retirement. All the accolades from the staff and his "job security" as the dean had put it were like anchors that didn't do a thing to brighten his outlook at the prospect of a dismal future.

Thoughts of this had been eating at him. Six weeks ago, with the encouragement of two men whom he'd met in a bar one night, he had devised a way to pilfer Hawaiian artifacts from the local museum. His two new friends had convinced him they were eager buyers willing to quietly feed his personal financial coffer. He was dazzled by the prospect of potential wealth and the thought of creating a new future of luxury away from the mundane existence he had experienced for most of his professorship life. Just a few more priceless objects and he'd be able to find a comfortable place to enjoy some of the good things in life. Perhaps Taos, New Mexico, he thought. He wasn't exceptionally imaginative.

The olivine presently sitting in front of him was making his eyes blurry with imagined dollar signs. This could be his gold mine to the future. If what the old Hawaiian had told Viane's father was true, there may be more treasure to be found deeper within the cave. Perhaps even the sacred bones of Kamehameha the Great, whose burial site had been lost in secrecy as well as history, would bring an untold fortune to the finder.

They talked for an hour as Viane told Doc about the family adventure that ultimately lead her to the find. Margelese offered what he thought the university could do in the way of giving her guidance, which he purposefully minimalized as best he could.

"After all, there are many very influential people here at UH who are well connected with Bishop Museum," he falsely explained to her—he really had no idea if there was or not. He was already formulating a plan to relieve her of the gem and learn the location of the cave, which, by her words, she was not yet willing to divulge. He had no desire to obtain the carving but would certainly look into its worth, nonetheless. He realized that obtaining either or both of them was not going to be a simple matter as she was close to deciding what she planned to do with them, and it didn't include him in any way. He would have to devise a scheme to change her mind.

Chapter Eight

On Tuesday mornings, Viane had no classes on her schedule. She awoke excited with the prospects of the day. She had no way of knowing at that moment that this particular day would end with her having to accept her own death as inevitable as well as being quite close at hand.

Her talk with Doc the day before, although somewhat confusing, had helped clarify her thoughts of holding on to the idol and olivine for a few more days. She was up early and planned to use the time to do some research into the ancient voyagers from Polynesia and Micronesia who traveled throughout the Pacific and what they may have brought with them. She was particularly interested in discovering information on deities they honored during their voyages and in whose hands they placed their lives. The UH library had an extensive Hawaiiana section, so she was confident of finding something that would bring her closer to an understanding of what the items she had found might mean. She needed that understanding before approaching anyone at Bishop Museum and presenting her finds.

As she headed out of her dorm, she noticed a message pinned to the bulletin board inside the building's main door. Her name was prominently written across the front.

Viane,
Come to my office this morning. I have some
information for you.
Margelese

Dr. Margelese looked up from the pile of papers on his desk as the door opened. He beamed with pleasure seeing Viane enter and easily overlooked the fact she had failed to knock to gain his permission to come in, as the sign outside his door demanded. It was a persistent habit of hers and one he always managed to overlook just for the pleasure of seeing her.

"Good morning, Viane. It's such a pleasure to watch you walk through my door," he said. "I'm pleased you found my note. I wasn't sure how else to contact you." He knew he could have gone through channels in the geology department office but wanted to eliminate the chance of anyone else knowing he was meeting with her. "The less everyone knows the better" was his motto.

He took a quick glance at her shapely form barely hidden beneath her T-shirt and tight shorts. *Legs that belong to a goddess,* he thought. He'd had a lot of practice over the years, from his place in front of the classroom, fantasizing about female students when he thought they weren't aware of his gaze.

Viane, though, was aware of a leer on Doc's face that he wasn't even trying to conceal. It made her very uncomfortable, but only for a moment as her excitement overran any concerns she may have had were she to spend time thinking of them.

"Good morning, Doc," she replied and walked to the front of his desk. She eagerly sat on the edge of the chair facing the professor's desk, barely able to contain her enthusiasm. "The note said you have some information for me. Is this about the finds that I showed you yesterday?"

Margelese had picked up a pen and was absently drawing circles around some notes he'd made earlier on the notepad in front of him, his thoughts busily composing his next words.

"In a way, yes," he replied, leaning closer over his desk, putting his pen down, and peering at her through the stacks of papers and periodicals. "I have two colleagues who have extensive knowledge of the early exploration of Polynesian travelers, and they have suggested that we bring your treasures to them for identification and, perhaps, some historical perspective."

"That's wonderful!" she exclaimed with noticeable excitement, moving even farther onto the edge of the chair. "When can we talk with them? Are they here at the university? What is their expertise?"

Margelese smiled at her enthusiasm and eagerness and held up his hands to ward off further questions he didn't want to answer.

"They own a yacht tied up at Kaneohe Yacht Club and have suggested we join them for a dinner cruise this evening. It'll be away from prying eyes since we are trying to keep things quiet for the time being and will afford an opportunity for each of us to be as candid and open as need be. Why don't I pick you up in front of your dorm at six o'clock? We can ride over to the yacht club together."

"This is so exciting I can hardly wait to hear what they have to say. They probably don't need to see the olivine, do they? I'll just bring the carving since it's the most important piece. I'd hate to chance carrying the gem in case something were to happen to it."

"No," said Doc almost shouting, startling Viane. He took a deep breath as if to squelch a hiccup and spoke more calmly than he appeared, saying, "I think it's best to bring both pieces. You'll want to get as much information as you can, so there's no sense only going partway now, is there?" He hoped that he'd smoothed over that small outburst well enough so that she wouldn't feel apprehensive. Seeing her still beaming with excitement, he knew he needn't have been concerned.

"You're right, Doc. You're such a good friend. How can I ever thank you enough for your help." She resisted the urge to go around the desk and give him a hug. Instead, she smiled as she rose from the chair and headed for the door.

Perhaps your repayment will be made tonight, he thought, stealing another look at her shapely legs as she walked out the door.

"One thing before you leave," he quickly added. "Dining on the *Whiskey Sea* is usually a dressy affair, so be warned."

Hearing his words, Viane turned and tucked her head back through the doorway. "It sounds absolutely wonderful, Doc. I'll be looking for you about six o'clock out in front of my dorm." She was still tempted to go back in and give him a hug. *Probably improper to hug one's professor*, she thought. Besides, she was aware there was something else holding her back from approaching him, something in his overly friendly behavior and stare that didn't feel right. She quickly closed his door and headed for the library.

In the sunshine once again outside the geology building, she stopped; and with eyes tightly closed and arms stretched out to embrace the air, she smiled and offered a silent prayer of thanks for having the support of someone as special as her friend, Doc. She was excited to be moving forward, discovering more information about the carving and the olivine and perhaps shedding some light on where the two pieces had originated. She thought of calling Pops and telling him what was happening but decided she'd wait until tomorrow when she had more information.

As she made her way to the library room, she couldn't help thinking of her visit with Doc. The strings of her intuition were tightening as she recalled his nonchalant appraisal of her body when he thought she wasn't watching. *It wasn't the look from a friend or a professor.* She had heard rumors around campus of female students getting into compromising situations with him but had always overlooked them as being reproachful from those who wanted his mentoring but may not have gotten the grade they thought they deserved, and here she was planning an outing with him and two of his colleagues—on a boat yet! She knew she'd have to be a little more on guard than she normally was when alone with him.

After Viane left, Margelese sat in his office quietly thinking of the past few minutes and the thankful, appreciative look Viane had given him. She would be in the right frame of mind for the dinner cruise tonight. Some champagne and a gently rocking boat would be perfect. He would make his advance on her then, and he knew she would consent with gratitude. He felt himself becoming aroused as he thought of their first embrace.

Chapter Nine

As a college student on a very limited budget, Viane's clothing options were not what anyone could call expansive; so on most occasions, her choices were limited. She had one dress, though, that Pops had given to her to be "worn on a special occasion"; and she decided, this certainly was a special occasion. Pops' intention had been to encourage his daughter to go out on dates since she was approaching twenty-eight and so far had shown very little interest in settling down much less even going out on an occasional date.

She looked at herself in the mirror, used to seeing herself in shorts or jeans and pullovers and her often-used, and therefore very comfortable, hiking boots. She was pleased at what she saw but, at the same time, was a little apprehensive of what others must see when they looked at her. Her self-confidence waned at times like this, going into unknown social territory. She knew she had a nice-looking figure, and the pale green chiffon dress that Pops had selected was ideal for her. It was loose fitting on top with gathered straps over the shoulders, leaving just a little cleavage showing—just enough to gain second looks but not enough to overly advertise the goods. It fit snugly around her slim waist and hips and dropped slightly full to just below her knees. *Thank you, Pops,* she thought to herself, making final adjustments in front of her mirror. She didn't want to offend her dinner hosts by being too casual. "If dressy is what they want, well, look out 'cause here I come," she exclaimed, smiling at her reflection, excited at the prospects the next few hours held. She closed the door behind her and headed for the stairs, her excitement at full volume.

Margelese felt an overwhelming sense of delight as he drove up the circular drive to the front of Frierdon Hall and saw Viane standing by a tree waiting for him. The wind had picked up and was blowing the tree branches above her head in a frenzy of motion. He noticed with delight that her dress had molded to the front of her body, delineating her perfect shape, accentuating every beautiful curve. He could almost see her naked form beneath. He smiled at the thought of what tonight held in store as he got out and went around, opening Viane's door for her.

She was pleasantly surprised to see how different he looked. He wore a blue blazer, grey slacks, and a crème-colored polo shirt. A gold chain hung around his neck, disappearing into a tuft of dark chest hair showing above his open collar. She thought he looked quite distinguished and told him so. His smile broadened.

The ride over the Pali Highway and down the windward side of the mountains to the yacht club was a quiet one. Viane's continued excitement overrode all her thoughts and kept her quiet. Margelese was consumed in thoughts of his own.

Driving through the gates of the yacht club, Margelese rolled into the parking lot fronting the clubhouse entrance and found easy parking.

They walked side by side out onto the wooden pier leading toward the bay, passing boats of varying shapes and sizes. The trade wind was strong, blowing sideways across the pier as they walked. An uneasy feeling prompted by the weather had taken hold of Viane, and she tightened her grip on the backpack containing her treasured items with one hand and held tightly to the hem of her dress with the other. She was well aware of the negative effects weather can have on boating, from having grown up with a father who was an avid fisherman and who had owned numerous boats over his lifetime. She knew bad weather was not conducive to pleasure cruising, so figured they would probably remain tied to the pier instead of the planned cruise in the bay.

"There's their yacht," Margelese pointed toward the end of the pier and then waved to two men standing on her deck.

Viane looked up in awe observing what appeared to be amidships portion of a huge wooden yacht seemingly straight out of a vintage 1930s movie. She couldn't help reflect on how things manufactured in that era were so striking in their opulence and absolute attention to detail. Both bow and stern were hidden behind other yachts as it stretched well beyond both ends of the T pier.

The men who stood on deck next to the gangplank waved them aboard.

Margelese took Viane's arm and pulled her close to his side in what he was portraying as a gesture of gentlemanly support as they ascended the gangplank to the deck.

She was a little surprised to meet two men who looked more like aging playboys than the college professor stereotypes she had expected to see. Roland Pratt and Greyson Giani, or Grey as he promptly said he preferred, were both in their seventies, deeply tanned with a physical presence of fitness and outdoor living combined with a widening softness around their middles from too many cocktail-time happy hours. Both were in shorts, T-shirts, and bare feet, and each casually held on to a bottle of Coors. So *much for dressing to a tee*, she thought. There were no polite formalities, neither man smiled nor came close to being pleasant beyond the barest minimum. If she wasn't so eager for information, she would have been tempted to turn around and catch a bus back to her dorm.

At Viane's polite but excited insistence, since neither host had offered, Grey took them on a quick and abbreviated tour of the yacht. Both men were obviously anxious to get on with the evening, and the tour hadn't been part of their plans. However, Grey found it difficult to resist her enthusiasm, not to mention her beauty and charm, and indicated for them to follow, condescendingly as if by no choice.

He led them through four elaborate staterooms below the main deck. Each had large bathrooms rivaling any Viane had been in before.

"These old wooden yachts have an appeal that doesn't come with the newer plastic sort," Grey offered. He wasn't normally inclined to give an opinion about things that were close to him, and he surprised himself by offering one. Viane had her charm, and Grey was finding he was quite susceptible.

"Roland and I found this yacht in a shipyard in San Francisco. We had no intention of buying a yacht but had stumbled on to it by sheer happenstance. It had been abandoned and was falling apart, the bright work mildewed, her interior in shambles as raccoons, feral cats, and who knows what else had made their home in it over the years. Apparently, it had been built and used in a Hollywood movie in the mid-thirties; and when filming was completed, she was put away for safekeeping and subsequently forgotten." The story was fictitious, but Grey liked the history he'd created. He and Roland had actually paid a fortune for it from a yacht broker in Seattle—pristine and ready to go. He had no clue as to its actual history nor did he really care to find out, so he felt quite at ease making up a history people would enjoy hearing him tell—not that he told it very often. Besides, nobody needed to know the truth anyway—the less they knew, the better off he and Roland were.

Far aft on the stateroom deck under the large outside deck that extended above them, they entered a stainless-steel galley. Numerous signs of food recently prepared were visible amid pots left helter-skelter for later washing. It was a galley to rival some of the best of which *Better Homes and Gardens* made elaborate pictorial spreads, yet there were no cooks or dishwashers—there appeared to be nobody else onboard.

They ascended the staircase to the main deck and into a room Viane was told was their lounge. Grey went straight for the bar and retrieved beers for Roland and himself. Roland had been idly sitting there waiting their return. Grey didn't bother offering anything to either of his guests as Margelese, slighted by the lack of courtesy, his eyes filled with contempt, silently appraised his two colleagues. Unfortunately, he knew his future relied on them for at least a little while longer.

Viane noticed and decided to ignore the charade and looked around the room. She was amazed that such an elegant place could be found on a boat. She had become accustomed to the style of boats her father had had over the past, the kind meant for down-and-dirty fishing.

"This room is incredible," she exclaimed as she did another slow three-sixty turn.

An overstuffed brown leather sofa sat opposite the doorway with a wall of shelves containing a beautiful array of antiques that would rival many museum collections. One piece in particular captured her eye. It was a large jade carving of Buddha expressing his well-known, peaceful-heart serenity, establishing a focal point in the room.

A door opposite that which they had entered apparently led out onto the deck on the other side of the boat. To the left was a floor-to-ceiling bookcase filled with volumes of all sizes and genre. Centered on the wall of bookshelves was a floor-to-ceiling smoke-colored mirror three feet wide. It looked oddly out of place. The opposite end of the room held a bar with a full-mirrored background. Odd-looking shelves along the mirror held glasses and bottles of liquor. She assumed the shelves were constructed in a fashion to hold the glasses and bottles securely while at sea. Several stools anchored to the floor gave it the appearance of an after-hours nightclub. The surface of the bar counter was ultra-glossy, rich dark-colored wood giving the entire room an opulent feel.

Three very old-appearing oil paintings of wooden sailing ships at sea hung on the wall adjacent to where she stood. Directly beneath them was a glass-enclosed case protecting a scale model of a ship similar to those in the paintings. The paintings and the model looked to be something that Columbus might have sailed on his voyage of discovery. The model was quite beautiful, and the paintings were exquisite.

Probably worth a fortune like everything else in this room, she thought.

Grey couldn't help smiling, watching Viane take everything in. "We call this room our lounge for obvious reasons. Rol and I spend most of our time here whenever we're onboard and not at sea." He continued watching her as she absently ran her hand over the spines of several books on one of the shelves. He could easily see why Margelese was so taken in by her.

Margelese all the while was impatiently folding and refolding his arms across his chest, anxious for Grey to stop ogling Viane so they could get on with the real meaning of this little get-together. *So I could get on with getting on with some physical pleasures.*

Back on deck, they walked a short distance forward, following Grey into the last doorway along the deck. It was a room filled with instruments like someone would expect to see in the cockpit of an aircraft. It was their control room, as Roland pointed out. He was obviously quite proud of the heart center of their yacht. An instrument panel nestled against a curving wall of glass overlooked the huge bow deck. A buffet of food choices was set against the back wall on what may have been their chart table. Several cubbyholes filled with rolled charts attested to this. Nearby was a cozy-looking wooden table set for four. An ornate porcelain decanter resting over a small flame centered the table. Small crystal glasses were in front of each place setting bordered by forks, folded napkins, and ivory chopsticks resting on ornate ceramic half rings.

Grey impatiently gestured for Viane to lead the way in choosing her dinner fare. She would have liked to take her time to gain a sense of the room but felt urgency in the demeanor of all three men.

She picked up a heavy earthenware plate and began selecting from the numerous platters, with Margelese close behind her. Grey disappeared out the door as Roland went to the center of the instrument panel and started the engines. Apparently, they were going to eat and cruise at the same time.

Grey returned shortly having released the lines holding them to the pier and, without explanation, grabbed a plate and filled it without much discernible thought and sat down. Roland, satisfied they were okay on autopilot, was even quicker than Grey at filling his plate and sitting. Viane noticed he was quite adept at watching their progress ahead through the forward wall of windows while eating what he had placed on his plate. She could see a line of channel markers flashing their red and green warnings leading off into the distance as they headed for the Main Ship Channel that would take them past Chinaman's Hat and beyond to open water.

Their meal was of Japanese flair—yakitori with salmon teriyaki and vegetable tempura—and was delicious in Viane's assessment. She hadn't realized how hungry she was. In anticipation of the events of the day, she had failed to have anything to eat. She stood and helped herself to more tempura. The decanter being warmed in the center of the table held sake, something she had yet to experience.

She was a very light drinker, but not wanting to offend her hosts, accepted the sake that Grey poured into her glass and nursed it in small sips. Doc and her two hosts, however, weren't nursing anything and were indulging with more gusto than she felt comfortable with. Doc already appeared somewhat intoxicated, which surprised her. She didn't expect to see a university professor on his way to being drunk, especially this man who she respected so much.

When the last of dinner was consumed or left untouched, Grey lead the way back to the lounge. Roland, obviously satisfied with their progress into open waters, followed behind, went straight to the bar, and produced drinks for the three men; she declined.

She realized her hosts, given sufficient sake and all the other drinks they were consuming, were quite genuine in their humor and straightforward in admitting their independent wealth and unconsummated desire to obtain artifacts from around the Pacific Basin. Any attempts, though, to determine the source of their immense wealth went unacknowledged. Both Roland and Grey were old friends as they had mentioned, and it became obvious as each helped to fill in the other's stories. *Whatever they did to earn their living, they obviously did it extremely well*, thought Viane. She was pleased to learn they possessed an intimate and very thorough knowledge of Polynesian artifacts and of the collection at the Bishop Museum.

The yacht's motion had become quite erratic, and Roland was examining a radar screen built into the countertop of the bar. He spoke into a small microphone he'd retrieved and began listing numbers. Viane felt the yacht slowly change direction, and their ride smoothed out.

"We have a verbal command center, part of our autopilot equipment," he said, noticing Viane's quizzical look. Satisfied with the settings, he approached her and stood a few feet directly in front of her.

"Now it's time to get down to business and look at the treasures you brought with you," suggested Roland as he sat and got comfortable. Doc poured himself another drink and staggered back to his chair, the movement of the yacht exaggerating his efforts.

Viane reached into her backpack and came up with the bundle she had wrapped in a terry cloth towel. Letting the cover fall to the side, she held up the large olivine gem as its glow danced in the cabin's light.

"That's magnificent," said Roland quickly sitting forward in his chair. "I've never looked at a piece of stone more beautiful." He took it from Viane and turned toward Grey so they could both examine it.

"It's absolutely perfect in clarity and color, and the size . . . it's magnificent," Grey echoed Roland's expression. "It must be close to fifty carats, maybe more!"

Putting the olivine into Grey's hands, Roland turned back to Viane.

"Dr. Margelese mentioned that this beautiful piece of rock was companion to a carving. Where is that?" he demanded.

Feeling somewhat intimidated by a demanding voice and an almost threatening business attitude that had consumed the air in the room, Viane hesitantly pulled the carving from the backpack.

"Ahh!" exclaimed Grey, still holding the olivine in his hands but becoming fully attentive to the revealed carving. "It's definitely Keahimauloko as we had thought," he said, handing the piece of olivine back to Roland and taking the carving from Viane's hands with an air of ownership. "Legend has it that travelers who left islands in the South Pacific bound for these islands carried Keahimauloko with them as a guiding spirit, so to speak, on their voyage. The olivine was probably a gift to the new land in the form of something rare and treasured from their island of origin. We'll have to see about getting them both carbon dated," remarked Grey, addressing Roland directly.

"So we can authenticate a time line," finished Roland.

Viane noticed the mood in the room since they started looking at the artifacts had taken on an abrupt, demanding, and very cold nature. Events and discussions had been taken out of her hands.

"Dr. Margelese told us that you found these items some place down on the South Point area of the Big Island, Viane," Roland said. "Exactly where did you find them?" he demanded.

Viane answered with as much politeness as she could muster. "I don't want to seem an ungrateful guest, Mr. Pratt, but hopefully you'll understand that I'd rather not say at this time. I'm not sure yet what I need to do with these pieces. My choice would be to see them in the Bishop Museum on display as part of our island heritage, but I have also been advised that they should be returned to where they were found and left as they were originally intended."

Roland and Grey glanced at each other, and both turned a questioning, if not actually threatening, look at Margelese. Viane immediately knew she had inadvertently said something that was unanticipated and not in line with expectations.

With a raised and demanding voice, Grey confronted the professor, "You said these pieces were for sale. We agreed on the $1.5 million if both pieces were what we thought they would be. What gives, Margelese? Don't you want your 10 percent?"

Margelese's embarrassment mixed with anger was evident. His thinking was blurred, and he fought for a response that would set everything right. He had specifically told them not to say a word about buying the pieces until he had a chance to talk Viane into letting them go. They must have thought he had already done so. He had also wanted to arrange for a bigger cut for himself. *These two clowns are going to blow all my plans*, he thought to himself.

Viane stood and attempted to retrieve both pieces from her hosts but was blocked as both men stood, each holding one of the pieces out of her reach.

"I don't know what's going on here, but I'd like to have those pieces back, please." Viane's voice shook with unaccustomed anger, as she again attempted to reach around Grey to retrieve the carving.

Ignoring her, Grey turned to Margelese. "Look, Margelese, we had a deal." His voice was threatening. "You talk with your pretty protégé and make sure she understands the nature of things. We'll be forward in the control room." At the doorway, Roland turned and looked at Margelese and then at Viane. "When you both have come to an understanding, find your way forward." With that, the two men went out, closing the door behind them.

"You lied to me, Doc," Viane loudly exclaimed, her anger beyond her control. "What happened to your ethics and our friendship? You can't arrange to sell something that's not yours. How dare you assume I would go along with this? You said your friends were influential at the museum, yet they appear to be just plain crooks." She pushed past him and charged for the door intent on following Roland and Grey.

Margelese staggered to his feet and made a clumsy grab at her. His arms went around her as he pulled her into a tight embrace. Touching her body made his long-held desire suddenly surge. He struggled to pull her down onto the plush carpet, but she was considerably stronger than he had anticipated and broke free of his clumsy embrace and ran out onto the exterior deck and headed aft looking for anything that would serve as a weapon to fend off her ex-friend and attacker. At the aft railing, she grabbed a life ring and turned to take a swing at him with it. He charged toward her, grabbing at her arm with one hand and reaching for a handhold on her hair with the other. He was beyond self-control.

She had backed into the railing and was trapped between it and her attacker. Margelese's hands went quickly beneath her dress, groping and kneading, racking at her panties, trying to pull them down her thighs. Resisting with all her strength, she felt herself being lifted up against him and higher on the railing, a strong wind pushed at her as the yacht rose against a wave.

And suddenly, she was falling . . .

She plunged deep into the cold water and came up still holding on to the life ring. Her frenzied breathing came in huge gasps at the realization of what had just taken place. Instinctively, she released the life ring and began swimming with all her strength toward the stern of the yacht.

Within moments and few strokes, she realized that the yacht was not going to turn around as neither Roland nor Grey was aware of the peril she was in. She knew that the chance of them doing anything to help, even if they knew, was quite slim. They would undoubtedly appreciate that her unexpected swim was a solution to their problem.

She looked up at the receding stern and saw Margelese with both hands resting on the rail in the same spot he had been standing when she went over. He was simply looking at her—expressionless.

She anxiously watched and with all her might willed the boat to turn around, as the name *Whiskey Sea,* so nicely scripted across the stern, disappeared behind a wall of water that rose above her and crashed down with unbelievable force. She caught the words Port Townsend, WA tucked under the boats name as the wave passed. An absurd thought filtered in that it was such a nice-sounding name.

Huge waves were lifting her high into the air before, dropping her down into the trough between. She retrieved the life ring and held it tightly. Turning and looking toward shore and the barely discernible lights, she realized with terrifying awareness how far she was from land. The reality of her situation took a few more moments to settle before a fear the intensity of which she had never known gripped her with crushing force pushing her to the pinnacle of sheer panic. She was alone—a small tree limb in a gigantic forest.

"Please, God, help me," she pleaded, her tears merging with the saltwater running down her face.

Chapter Ten

Yacht club, Windward side of Oahu

Stone slowed *Wailana Sunrise* to barely a crawl and began the intricate maneuver of threading his yacht into his newly assigned moorage slip suddenly becoming very aware of its size. Lloyd had finally arrived at the club and, with a quick *shaka* sign aimed at Stone, immediately took over handling the tie-up. Stone's relief seeing Lloyd's able control of things was palpable, throwing lines to friends who'd shown up as well as any onlookers that were willing to grab one. There were more people there than Stone thought possible considering the late hour. New yachts coming into a yacht club for the first time are always cause for onlookers to gather and admire, although this late at night, the group of onlookers were mostly bar patrons drawn away from their nightly gathering practice. Tonight was no exception as evidenced by the many partially emptied bar glasses placed on any flat surface that happened to be handy, including the deck of *Wailana Sunrise*.

As soon as the yacht was securely tied to her new berth, Stone went aft and, using his dive knife, cut the cargo net loose and pulled it around to the pier.

Lloyd came over and grabbed hold of it. "Hey, Stone, the First Responders are here with a stretcher. I think they want to see your mermaid. Let me secure this net to the pier. I'm sure the port captain will enjoy hauling it away in the morning unless, of course, you were planning to keep it as a souvenir of your journey." He chuckled to himself as he hauled the net to the pier.

Stone made a disguised look of ill humor, but it came out more of a tired grin as he turned to greet the medical crew. A man and woman dressed in the blue uniforms of the First Responders stepped aboard. Both appeared to be in their twenties and obviously quite fit by the ease with which they moved about the yacht. The man carried a rolled-up stretcher under his arm, the woman carried a large medical-looking bag with thick black straps draped over her shoulder as she leaned to one side under the strain of its evidently heavy contents.

Sgt. Mike Kalama, an old friend of Stone's, came aboard following the First Responders. *Wailana Sunrise* gave a little to starboard as it accepted Mike's 250 pounds. He was a big man and at six feet four moved with surprising ease. He was thirty-five years old and was the essence of charm and earthly presence that graced the Hawaiian race. Looking over at Stone, he gave an almost imperceptibly quick eyebrow raise in acknowledgment. They were close friends, so no other greeting was needed.

"There's not much more I can tell you, Mike. She was here when I looked in on her an hour ago," Stone's facial expression mimicked those of the others who stood peering through the narrow doorway of the stateroom. All eyes were focused on the empty queen-size bed, quizzically trying to comprehend the story Stone was telling. Even he had to admit that if it weren't for the damp impression and the two blankets rumpled on the floor, he might begin to think he'd hallucinated the whole affair.

Madame Pele's legend was certainly making itself known. The mythical Hawaiian fire goddess frequently appeared and disappeared at will. Legends can do that but rarely flesh and blood.

Stone couldn't help puzzling over when the woman could have jumped back into the water? A better question, he thought, was why she would want to? The circumstances didn't fit with anyone trying to commit suicide. Stone's intuition said there was obviously another, very serious reason for that woman to be in the water in the first place. To disappear so quickly certainly added to the mystery. He realized it had also planted a compelling seed of curiosity in him to search for answers.

The First Responders talked briefly with Mike and, after being assured they were not needed, headed for the pier and their waiting ambulance.

Mike picked up the blankets from the floor and absentmindedly began to fold them, eyebrows furled in thought. "What I got to do, Stone, is make a report on what you claim to have taken place and file it with HPD and with the Coast Guard. No crime's been committed unless there's a missing person report filed or if the lady herself comes in and files a complaint against somebody." He hesitated for a moment, and then continued in a quieter voice, "Maybe even against you." His eyes met Stone's in a semi-accusing manner, obviously a practiced cop expression.

"That's great, Mike. I've gone from hero to suspect, and it's still the same very long, weary night. Instead of waiting around, maybe we should check with the Coast Guard to see if any cruise ships with a missing passenger might have passed through these waters lately instead of standing there giving me the evil eye."

Mike was still appraising him. His sense of humor was limited to a partial curling at the corners of his lips—the price some police officers paid after years of seeing too much of humanity's ills and deviations.

"When I talk with the Coast Guard, they'll inform me of any ships that might have passed through the Kaiwi channel between Oahu and Molokai in the past twenty-four hours." Mike was "cop-talking" as he laid the blanket down on the bunk. He turned and headed the few feet to the galley and on through to the outside deck. With his height, he never had sufficient headroom in tight places and was obviously uncomfortable, judging by the way his neck had been bent over while below deck.

"Could you pinpoint on a chart where it was that you found her?" Mike asked as he emerged on to the open deck. "It would help plot out the general area that she may have started her odyssey. Perhaps the Coast Guard can help with information about who else might have been out cruising in that neighborhood in the past day or two."

"I think so. At least I can show you the general area. It was just north of Mokapu Point, and all those buoys out there that lead into the Crash Boat Channel."

"I could bring the forensic people in," Mike went on, "but I don't see any reason to mess up your boat that way. For all we know, she may have ended up in the water by accident and decided to get home as quickly as possible to a warm bath and a glass of wine and a loving family and didn't think to say aloha on her way over the transom—weird, but could be."

What he is saying is true, thought Stone. He also knew that any attempt to have the police work on discovering who she is would be strictly for his own personal reasons, and the police department wasn't about to accommodate him like that even with the higher-up connections that he had. They had their collective hands full just keeping Honolulu and the rest of Oahu safe and sound.

"I sure would like to know what happened to her and why," thought Stone, talking to himself, obviously too loudly.

Mike turned and gave Stone a puzzled look. "Are you mumbling to yourself, Stone?"

"Yeah, I guess I am. You know you're right, Mike. Until she comes forth and volunteers information or seeks help, we'll have to let it go.

"On a different subject, I hope you're planning to come to the christening this weekend. It's Sunday afternoon; here at the club at 3:00 p.m. I'm inviting all the Hui guys as well." Hui O'Kailua was a group of friends that Stone had been associated with over the past thirty-five years; twenty fun-loving, poker-playing buddies who were Stone's extended family. Mike had once been a part of the Hui but had to quit because of his erratic work schedule.

"Hey, *mahalo a nui*, Stone. I'll try to make it. Gotta see what duty schedule I pull first. Guess even if I'm on duty, I can still swing by. You going to take me out on this beauty one of these days?" he asked.

"For you, any time," he replied, taking hold of Mike's extended hand. "I'll come down to the station tomorrow morning with a chart and pinpoint where I found her. *Mahalo* for your help, my friend, see you in the morning."

Lloyd appeared at the end of the finger pier just as Mike was turning to leave. "While you guys been standing talking and scratching your respective heads, I've been looking around, kinda doing some of your police work, Mike. Maybe you should think about hiring me as a detective. Anyway, I think you'll find a spot two finger piers down toward the clubhouse where someone climbed out of the water and walked away." Lloyd was grinning, noticeably quite pleased with his detective work. "I'm betting it was our mystery lady."

Both Stone and Mike followed Lloyd to the wet markings on one of the small finger piers. It was very apparent that someone had recently climbed out of the water and headed toward the clubhouse.

"By the size and shape of the print," said Mike, "it was most likely a young local woman."

"How the heck could you figure all that out by just a wet footprint?"

"The spread of the toes and high arch are indicative of someone who's spent a lot of time not wearing shoes as most local kids do, as you know. I'm guessing at the 'young' part," he said as he looked up at Lloyd and smiled and continued, "and it's also too small to be a man's."

"I'm impressed, Mike, and with you too, Lloyd. Detectives first class, that's what you two gentlemen are."

"Gentlemen?" They all laughed at the implication.

Stone watched as Mike walked off the pier and headed toward the parking lot. Their friendship was such that Stone knew if he ever needed help from the law, Mike would be there.

"So we'll just have to wait and see if she shows up again," said Lloyd, breaking the momentary silence.

"I'd like to find her, Lloyd," replied Stone, turning to his friend. "When someone happens to cross paths with me the way she did, I'd find it very difficult not knowing the rest of her story—I need to fill in the blanks."

"Yeah, guess that's true. Listen, Stone, it's late, and I left the house in a rush and probably left every light turned on. Pam will be concerned about where I disappeared to, so I better go."

Pam was Lloyd's wife of thirty-plus years and was a very understanding woman and quite used to the erratic hours her husband often kept. He was a night owl whereas she enjoyed retiring early. She would more than likely be sound asleep, an open book resting close by.

"How about giving me a ride home first since it's on your way? Besides, it would appear everyone else has left already, and I'm not ready to spend the night on *Wailana Sunrise* yet."

"It's the opposite direction, and you know it, but I'll give you a ride anyway," Lloyd replied and smiled as they headed down the pier toward the clubhouse. "I heard you mention to Mike you'd see him tomorrow. Want some company? I got nothing important going on that can't be put off for another day."

"That'd be great, Lloyd. You can drop me off at the Ala Wai afterward so I can retrieve my car, if it hasn't been hauled away by the meter maids yet!"

"What is this? Am I suddenly your chauffeur?"

"What's the matter? It'll be fun, you'll see. I'll even spring for breakfast at Zippy's."

A feeling of total peace settled over him as he unlocked the door to his home and went in. He loved the feeling of coming home. He could finally let go of the built-up tension that had gripped him so firmly during his exhausting, very long day. Thoughts replayed the details of his journey as he descended the stairs leading to his bedroom and much-needed sleep. He knew the memory of blustery weather and raging surf would diminish in importance and become just another story to be told. *But the woman!* There is a reason she had shown up—everything in life has a reason for taking place. An involuntary chill coursed up his spine as he thought about how close he must have come to running over her and mangling her in the churning blades of the propellers. *He may have kept on going and never known what happened.*

"And how had she gotten away?" he puzzled aloud. "By the wet prints on the pier, she must have slipped out over the side during that comical commotion of docking; and at that time of night, without cash or dry clothes and bare feet, she would have had to either walk or hitchhike away from the club. That stretch of Kaneohe Bay Drive was not a great place to be a hitchhiker, especially for a pretty woman who looked like a runaway from a wet T-shirt contest—and why am I talking to myself," he said.

For the time being, he was very tired and needed sleep. There was nothing he could do other than let his thoughts wander aimlessly. *Might just as well be lying down while they wandered loose.*

He noticed Bert patiently sitting outside the sliding glass door of his bedroom meowing for attention. The cement deck overlooking the back side of Kaneohe Bay was Bert's favorite spot to hang out when Stone was not at home. Bert was his buddy. Burt was also his pet: a Bengal with personality, as he referred to her. The name notwithstanding, Bert was actually a she but didn't know the difference, and neither did Stone when he had first named her.

Chapter Eleven

Stone awoke early the following morning, made his coffee, shuffled out through the sliding glass door of his bedroom, and walked the short distance to the seawall. He sat and let his mind wander through its maze of thoughts—it had become an absent-minded morning ritual ever since moving into the beach house. He began each day beside the water relaxing, sipping coffee, and watching the water of the bay lap against the seawall that formed the boundary of his backyard. The bay this morning was *malie*, like a glass tabletop, perfectly reflecting the lush greenery of the hills on the opposite side as if attempting to replicate themselves in a mirror. *Big change from yesterday.* He felt Bert rubbing up against his thigh as she began to purr.

Bert was a feral cat when Stone found her on the Big Island of Hawaii. She was a very tiny kitten then, standing in the middle of the highway outside the small town of Keaau, in the pouring rain, mere inches from the crushing roll of tires from the continuous parade of cars and trucks heading downhill toward the quaint small town of Hilo. She was drenched and totally lost to the world when Stone stopped and picked her up. Wrapped in an old towel, he had cradled her in his lap for the ten-mile ride home. The bond between them was instantaneous. It was as if Bert knew she had been saved from a certain death on the highway. She could always be found close on Stone's heels unless otherwise preoccupied as the resident vermin exterminator. One got the idea that keeping the population of geckos, cockroaches, and rodents at bay around the yard was a duty Bert took as a serious challenge.

When he moved away from the Big Island to Oahu several years before, he had been fortunate to have acquired a beautiful, two-story, A-frame house on a back corner of Kaneohe Bay. It had a small private beach and a long rock and cement seawall that held the ocean in its place, keeping it from consuming the yard. A short pier that he had built the previous year jutted into the bay. The water's edge was twelve feet from his bedroom door but felt as if it were mere inches during storms like the two hurricanes that roared through the islands a few years before. He loved the closeness with nature and the calmness it lent on days when there were too many other events and emotions playing for his attention—like now.

He could see the yacht club two miles across the bay from where he sat and felt a swell of pride knowing *Wailana Sunrise* was safely berthed virtually within sight. It would have been nice to have a private dock attached to his yard and have his yacht within easy reach, but the water in this part of the bay was much too shallow at low tide for the yacht's needed depth. The small pier found its perfect use for launching kayaks and for attracting sea life.

His thoughts shifted to the previous day's intense adventure and the sudden disappearance of the young woman.

"I still don't understand how she could slip away like that, Bert." Bert was a good sounding board. Stone could verbalize his thoughts without making the neighbors think he was becoming unbalanced by talking to himself all the time, although they probably already thought that anyway: who else in their right mind would take a kayak out at midnight to paddle around the bay in the dark just to enjoy the sensation of "being" with nature as he often did, especially on nights when the moon was full?

"How could she have gotten off the boat without me seeing her?" He checked his sounding board as if expecting Bert to answer, but the cat was in pursuit of something moving at the edge of the sea wall. *Who is that woman, and what the dickens was she doing floating around so many miles from shore? Many questions but no answers.* He stood up and climbed the outside staircase of his house and went into the kitchen. Lloyd would be here soon and be in need of a large quantity of coffee for the journey to town.

"What an experience, Stone," exclaimed Lloyd as they pulled to a stop in front of the Maunakea Street police station in downtown Honolulu. Stone had just finished telling Lloyd the story in full detail. "I sure wish things had been different for me yesterday so I could have been there. Of course, had I been there, our timing may have been a little different, and you wouldn't have run across her, pardon the pun." He looked at Stone with a comical expression.

They had talked all the way into town about the previous day's journey, the funny parts as well as the fearful ones when Stone first become aware of a body floating next to him.

"You know the thing that's bothering me most," he explained, "is not knowing what happened to her and how she got to where I found her. It's one thing to pull someone in from the ocean and lend a helping hand, but there is generally some sort of explanation that goes along with it. Helping someone in distress is usually accompanied with knowing what the distressful situation was."

"We may never find out, Stone. She may not want to be found."

"Let's go in and show Mike the chart. He was planning to call a friend of his who is the main radio operator at the Coast Guard station and see if they have received any information on other boats or ships that may have been out in the channel around that time. Are you going to drive me to the Ilikai afterward to see if my car is still there?"

"Unfortunately, the Coast Guard has no knowledge of any other traffic cruising through those waters," Mike told them. The three of them were standing around a marine chart Mike had laid out across his desk showing the Kaiwi Channel, the water off the windward side of the island. Stone made a mark on the chart, showing where he'd been when he pulled the woman aboard. "It's not unusual since most pleasure craft don't give notice of their plans short of major transpacific cruises," offered Mike. "My friend was helpful, though, in mentioning there had been no passenger cruise ships passing through the Kaiwi Channel during the past week, so that eliminates any passenger being thrown or falling off one of them."

"That sort of leaves a grey spot in our nonexistent theory, doesn't it?" Stone and Lloyd had left the police station and were making their way through town in the direction of Waikiki and the Ilikai Hotel and, hopefully, Stone's car.

"Let's think this through for a second, Lloyd. She got off *Wailana Sunrise* at the yacht club, and it was late at night. So she had to either walk or ride away from the club. Of course, she may have had a car parked there and just drove away, but I know for sure she didn't have any keys hidden in any pockets."

Lloyd looked at his friend as if about to make a comment about how he had gone about looking for keys and then changed his mind. "Okay," responded Lloyd in a matter-of-fact tone, "that means if she didn't drive away, so she either hitchhiked, caught a bus, or grabbed a taxi. Since the office was closed, she would have been hard-pressed to get to a phone to call someone, and I can't see anyone who looked the way you described her hitching a ride on Kaneohe Bay Drive. The best possibility that I can see is one of the taxis that frequent the club must have picked her up, or she caught a bus and promised to pay later, since I'm sure you didn't find any money on her when you searched her body for keys."

Stone chose to ignore his friend's ribbing. "That last one about the bus doesn't sound too likely but is something to think about. In the meantime, we may have to dig up some money to get my car out of the pound if it's been towed away. After that, let's each check out the bus and taxi prospects. At least we can start to narrow the choices a bit."

"Let me call the taxi companies to see if something's been logged in about a fare heading away from the yacht club around eleven o'clock," offered Lloyd.

"That'd be great, Lloyd. I'll check the bus schedule and see if I can locate the driver on that route. If she got on a bus, you can bet the driver will remember."

Turning the corner, they found Stone's car, just as he had left it and without a ticket.

"Miracles can and do happen, Lloyd."

"Eh, before you start into a sermon about miracles and we head off in different directions, and since we didn't make it to Zippy's for breakfast, you got time to buy me lunch in exchange for my exceptional chauffeuring service? Let's go to Puanani's Drive-In on Beretania Street for some chicken katsu."

"You talked me into it, Lloyd. Actually, laulau and poi sound really good right about now as well. I'll meet you there."

It took a lot of explaining to the young Oriental woman in charge of scheduling buses to convince her about someone floating around in the middle of the ocean, then having her disappear, and now wanting to find a bus driver who may have picked her up. She finally agreed to check the schedule, probably thinking it was going to be the only way to get rid of this guy and his crazy story as she flipped pages in her scheduling book.

"There were two drivers who had passed along Kaneohe Bay Drive after 10:30 p.m. up until the route shut down for the night," she offered and then promised to talk with each of them when they came back on duty and would give him a call. Stone wasn't too sure that would ever happen as she wasn't exactly enthused about the story or the extra work it would no doubt entail. She probably wasn't paid enough to do any more than bare minimum, but she'd grudgingly agreed to do it nonetheless. Stone wasn't going to hold his breath waiting.

Driving back over the Likelike Highway toward Kaneohe, he was hoping Lloyd had better success with the taxi companies.

There was a phone message waiting when he got home.

"At 72 Laimi Road in Nuuanu Valley, just off the Pali Highway. I lucked out, Stone. Rudy, a high school buddy from Roosevelt, works nights at Island Kine Cab; and when I called, he just happened to be reading through the dispatch log from last night. Apparently, the driver gave a full description of his fare to the dispatch clerk because of 'circumstances.' The cabby had underscored the word. Be interested to know what 'circumstances' he was referring to? Drop off was at 11:36 p.m. Also, without checking with you, I called Mike and found out that a Ms. Teri White, age forty-eight, no arrest record, no traffic violations, lives at that address. Mike says you owe him a favor."

"For that, I'll grant him several favors. What a fantastic job, Lloyd. I stand amazed. I think I'll go see if Ms. White's at home. Want to come along?"

"I'd like to, Stone, but I have a couple of things around the house that need attention before Pam makes me sleep in the living room with Keiko Da Cat. Give me a call after you've talked to her. I'd like to hear about the *circumstances*."

The door opened partway a few moments after Stone rang the doorbell. A very attractive woman with shoulder-length dark blond hair stood looking out through the narrow opening. From what he could see, she wore a red T-shirt with some white lettering across the front that he was unable to decipher, beige shorts, a shapely leg attached to a bare foot was the extent of his observation. He definitely wanted to see more.

He was rarely without words, but it took him several moments to resurrect the reason he was there, suddenly realizing he'd been just standing looking at her. *Like viewing a magnificent sunset that momentarily absorbs all your thoughts.*

"Would you be Ms. Teri White?" Stone finally found his voice and, with effort, brought his focus back to the task at hand.

Her head dropped slightly to the side as she opened the door a little wider. With obvious curiosity and an instant interest in the man standing in front of her door, she replied, "That depends on who's asking and why."

"My name's Kensington Stone. I understand a young woman was dropped off here by taxi last night, and I'm trying to locate her. Is she here?"

"And if that actually happened, why would it be of any interest to you?" she replied, caution edging into her voice as she backed a few inches away from the door ready to close it quickly if the need became apparent.

"I almost ran over her while she was floating in the middle of the ocean last night. She disappeared off my yacht before I had a chance to talk to her and see if she was all right. Since she came straight here, I assume she's a relative or close friend of yours. May I please take a moment to talk to her?"

Teri opened the door, immediately aware this was the man Viane had mentioned who had pulled her from the water. She took a step back and motioned Stone in. "Please come in, and yes, my name is Teri. Would you like a drink or some tea or coffee?" she asked as she led the way into the kitchen and motioned to a stool at the island counter in the center. "I hope you don't mind the kitchen, Mr. Stone, it's my favorite room for informality. Besides, the coffee and tea are close at hand."

"Kitchens are my favorite room of the house as well," Stone replied, relieved to have his brief explanation taken for fact and to have seemingly been taken off the spot of being caught openly appraising her or attempting to read the lettering written across the chest of her T-shirt, which he now saw was for a 5k run to sponsor a foundation for autistic children. He relaxed. "I'm a pretty good cook I'll have you know and spend a lot of time in the kitchen, and yes, tea would be great, thank you. Green if you have it."

A gentle smile of approval creased the corners of her lips as she reached for a teapot already heated. She had been about to have tea when she'd heard someone at her door. She retrieved a second mug from under the counter, filled both, and sat down opposite Stone, looking at him intently. It was her turn to appraise her guest.

"Tell me, Mr. Stone. How did you know someone was brought here by taxi last night?" she asked, her head moving to the side in a quizzical but almost amused fashion. "Are you a policeman by any chance?"

Stone took a sip of tea, put the mug aside, and leaned back as he appraised her. She returned his appraisal, holding his gaze. The room had become silent as he looked deeply into her eyes—hazel eyes that he noticed were exceptionally expressive and incredibly beautiful. He smiled and finally answered her question. "I do have close ties to Honolulu PD, but no, I was never a policeman. I was a detective for a local security company once upon a time not too long ago though, if that helps." He broadened his smile as she gently leaned closer to the table, playing with the handle of her cup.

Stone sat forward as well, which brought them to within a few inches of one another. He began to recite the previous night's tale speaking softly, almost confidentially, since they were so close—he didn't want to speak too loudly and force them to move apart.

"You are obviously good at detective work, Mr. Stone," she said. "Please, just Stone. My involvement in detective work was in the past, but it's like body surfing—once you know how to let your body and the water work together, it becomes an innate part of who you are. As I mentioned, I have some dear friends connected with law enforcement, and they help me fill in any blanks I may have. I take it the woman I'm looking for isn't here at the moment," said Stone, not shifting his gaze.

"I did some contract work with the police department in the past. Who are these 'dear friends' you mention? Maybe I know them."

"It's mainly just one, although I'm on speaking terms with many others including an ex-brother-in-law. His name is Sgt. Mike Kalama. He works out of the Maunakea Street station. He and I have been friends for many years. You know him?"

"No, most of my work was with the missing persons section out of the main station."

Picking up on the sincerity of her guest, she decided to be open with him and trust her instinct—at least open to an extent. Prudence was still important. "Her name is Viane, and she's currently back home on one of the neighbor islands and planning on staying there for a few days. I dropped her off at the interisland terminal early this morning. And please, Teri is fine with me as well. I gain an intuitive sense that you can be trusted, Stone. I like that and sincerely hope I'm not wrong."

He reassured her that trust was a sacred part of him as well.

She proceeded to relay a few events, nothing too specific though, leading up to Viane being in the water and then asked, "I'm wondering, what interest beyond curiosity you might have in this? I don't mean to diminish the fact that you were responsible for saving her life, but what interest do you have beyond that? Right now, I don't know you from a lua salesman and won't put Viane's life back in danger through lack of vigilance."

"I guarantee you I don't sell toilets or any other bathroom fixtures. To be totally honest, up until five minutes ago, it was mostly curiosity. I merely wished to make sure she's all right and to offer any help I can give since she went through quite a traumatic ordeal. It would be very easy to walk away and forget everything that transpired and end the story there, but too many of us in today's culture do just that instead of showing concern for the continued welfare of others. If something is amiss, I'd like to help make it right. I believe events in our lives happen for reasons we don't fully understand and often don't accept or even think about. Hers and my life's paths crossed in a dramatic way, and I need to follow where those events appear to be leading. Besides, there's a small slice of male chauvinism in me that wants to be a white knight in someone's life."

Teri's laugh was gentle and affirmative and encouraged him to continue. "That was 100 percent of my motivation before you answered your door. Now I have other motivations, but that'll have to fall into the 'wait and see' category." He held her gaze until she looked away.

She easily read the intention behind his words and felt herself being irresistibly drawn to him, which surprised her. She had decided at the break up of her last relationship that she would stay away from becoming involved with anyone else for a year or possibly ten or even forever if it came to that. *My resolve could be in serious jeopardy,* she thought, catching the appreciative look in his eyes—*Blue as a crystal-clear ocean.*

They talked for another hour, learning about the things that made them laugh and the things that made them sad. Both were unintentionally hesitant to end the visit, their tea sitting cold and forgotten.

"I'll call Viane later today and tell her about you and about your interest in being of help to her. If she's willing, we can figure out what to do about it. Fair enough?"

He drew something out of his shirt pocket and held it out to her. "Here's a card with my home phone number. Please call me after you've talked to her and let me know what she says. Then I'll know more about how to proceed."

Teri rested her back against the door after closing it and looked at the card held tightly in her hand. "Kensington Stone, Stone. Investment in Your Future." There was a phone number in the Kaneohe area but no cell number nor address.

Investment in Your Future. She stared at the words on the card and smiled. Her spirit suddenly felt as light as a feather.

Chapter Twelve

Kailua-Kona, Big Island of Hawaii

Evening morphed into night as the shore along Kailua-Kona became aglow with light from the hotels and the many open-aired restaurants along Alii Drive. The stonewalled grounds surrounding the nineteenth century Hulihee Palace stood out in the glare by its gentle, soft light. Its historic grounds, shadowed only by the single steeple of the nearby hundred-year-old Mokuaikaua Church, reminiscent of a bygone era, had changed little over the past century and a half: serenity under an umbrella of palm fronds that were gently swaying in the soft breeze. Flickering orange flames from the many torches softly lit the way for the spirits from the past; the flames glow shimmered across the water. Distant sounds of music drifted on the air from the King Kamehameha Hotel as it made its way across the water following a road of light created by the moon leading to the edge of the horizon.

Such serenity belied the emotional turbulence that contaminated the *Whiskey Sea* as she rode at anchor a short distance from shore. The now calm night deceivingly gave only a slight motion to the yacht as it lifted and fell on insignificant swells.

After abandoning Margelese's lady friend in the middle of the Kaiwi Channel, the three men had continued on toward the west coast of the Big Island. Now at anchor a half mile out, they had guaranteed themselves some needed privacy. Recent glitches in plans had to be discussed and resolved.

Roland walked into the lounge and settled into the soft leather of the couch, plumping Grey's favorite leather-encased pillow behind his back. Grey and Margelese, sitting in chairs side by side, were inspecting the olivine, turning it and holding it toward the ceiling light, marveling at its glow. Roland got up and went to the bar along the wall, pouring himself a large glass of okolehao as he noisily threw in some ice and returned to the couch. Since a fellow drinker at Biggies Lounge had offered both Grey and Roland a taste of the Hawaiian home brewed ti-plant whiskey, Roland had taken an immediate liking to it, instantly drawn to its uniqueness.

"I know someone who could facet this green gem for us without asking too many questions," Grey said as soon as Roland had settled. "It would add a lot of value as well as making it unrecognizable, which we really need to consider."

"Nothing wrong with adding more value for each of us," Margelese interjected, tentatively reaching for it. Grey absently—intentionally—moved it out of his reach.

"Are you talking about that strange guy we met in Port Townsend when we dry-docked there, Roger or Robert or something like that?" asked Roland. "I personally think it'd be a good idea to change its appearance. Its unique quality is enough to be very readily recognized as it is if someone who knows about it were to have a glimpse of it. We could then actually sell it through a retail gem dealer and triple our take instead of hawking it through our usual outlet and worrying about someone noticing it and asking too many questions." Their "usual outlet" was the antiquities black market.

They had previously discussed, on many different occasions, the pitfalls of dealing through the black market. Chief among those pitfalls was the real chance of getting caught by someone talking too loudly. *Margelese, perhaps?* He was becoming a burden.

"Speaking of added value, Margelese," Grey said as he turned to face him with an intimidating stare as he spoke. "As far as we're concerned, your *value* has already been set. Truth is, your value has all of a sudden taken a downturn."

"Ryan's his name," said Roland, continuing his earlier thought. "That's that strange guy in Port Townsend who could cut the gem for us. Let's pull in there when we get back to the West Coast and talk to him. He owes us a favor from that deal we put together for him anyway, you remember?"

Grey nodded in affirmation but still thinking of Margelese's drop in value.

A few months before leaving the coast for their trip to Hawaii, they had helped a fellow black marketer by the name of Ryan, no last name, find a buyer for a load of pilfered opals from the mines of Australia that he was stuck with after the deal he had set up collapsed. He was in their debt even after they had extracted a healthy finder's fee. It was the rules of their existence.

Roland dumped an ice cube from his glass into his mouth and started to grind away at it with his teeth. It was a nervous habit of his. For some reason, he thought it helped him think. It irritated Grey listening to the *chomp chomp chomp* of ice being methodically crushed. *It's a wonder he has any teeth left.* He looked at him but withheld comment—anything he would say would later come back to bite his butt.

Margelese was becoming uncomfortable with the direction the conversation had headed, realizing things were swiftly moving out of the control he perceived himself as having. "I hope you two aren't planning to leave until after we complete the deal on these and all the other pieces I brought to you from the museum last month. I didn't put my teaching career on the line for nothing, and you both know that. A lot of money needs to change hands before I get off this boat of yours."

"By the way," Margelese continued accusingly, "where are all those Bishop Museum pieces I got for us?"

Roland rose from the couch ignoring the question and moved to face Margelese. Resting a hand on each arm of the chair, he leaned over, crunching the last of an ice cube, placing his face mere inches above that of Margelese. "Listen, Margelese, and listen well. It's because of you and your idiotic actions between that woman and that little brain you carry around in your pants that we now have to think about leaving the islands quicker than we had planned. Let me ask you, and I want a straight answer, did you do as we told you and not tell anyone you were coming onboard and bringing your young friend with you?"

"Yes, of course. Why on earth would I have told anyone anyway? You think I want to screw up this deal we got going?"

Margelese was getting angry, and he tried to stand, but Roland didn't move, leaving no space for him to maneuver, much less stand up. He rested back into the chair. "Okay, tell you what I want," he said, trying to sound as uncompromising as possible while attempting to avoid Roland's hovering form. He felt fear rising in his throat along with his words. "You pay me for everything I've brought to you, all eleven items, the full amount of what we already agreed on, and leave me here in Kailua-Kona. I know you have the cash sitting in that safe of yours, so there isn't any excuse not to. I'll call the dean and fabricate a reason why I won't be back for a few days. That'll give some time for the air to settle before I go back. They'll find someone to cover my classes until then, so I'll be fine, and I'll be out of your hair."

Roland pushed off the arm of Margelese's chair and stood up. He walked a few steps away and looked at Grey, giving him a slight nod of understanding.

Margelese missed the signal. He was regaining a bit of the composure he'd lost with Roland hovering over him although his fear continued to keep its grip deep in his intestines.

"Maybe you're right, Margelese. Grey and I have to head back to Oahu and make plans." Roland sat back down on the leather couch, gave the pillow a good smack for comfort, and picked up his glass, rattling the remaining ice cubes. "We've got a lot of details to work out. I've put word out to our contact about finding a buyer for these two pieces as well as the other carvings and items you *requisitioned* from the museum."

"It's about time you two Neanderthals saw the way of things and coughed up my money." Margelese's confidence was making a rebound.

Roland looked over at Grey. "I think it's definitely time to dump things and move on. What do you think, Grey?"

Grey nodded. "I agree, and the sooner the better," he said and stood up, quickly grabbing Margelese's right arm and roughly pulling him to his feet. He twisted the arm behind his back, forcing Margelese up onto his toes.

"What do you think you're doing?" yelled Margelese. "Let go of my arm, or this whole deal's off." He struggled to free his arm as a renewed fear began venting its way toward panic. "Listen, with what I know about you two and your operations, a little renegotiation needs to be discussed. In fact, I think I need to demand a bigger cut." Intimidation wasn't working as he continued to struggle, trying to break Grey's hold. Grey tightened his grip. "Let go of my arm, you lummox, you're hurting it."

"Let's go below deck, Margelese," said Grey, winding a length of rope he had been holding for this purpose around Margelese's arms. "I want to show you one of the staterooms you haven't seen." Margelese was propelled through the doorway and out onto the deck. Roland grabbed his glass and wandered after them. All three headed aft and descended the staircase. Margelese was roughly deposited in one of the staterooms, his legs secured with the loose end of the rope that dangled from his arms. Roland stuffed a rag in Margelese's mouth before closing and locking the door.

"He'll be fine down there until we're well away from here," said Grey, as both men headed back up to the lounge for another drink. "Let's head due south for a few hours and get rid of our handicap before turning toward Oahu. We've got to go back to Kaneohe and wrap up plans."

Margelese struggled against the rope tying his arms behind his back. The more he struggled though, the tighter the other end around his ankles became. The pain was almost a relief from the intense fear that was making his heart pound like a busy carpenter's hammer against his chest. *Surely they're just trying to scare me,* he thought. *They wouldn't hurt me, I know too much about them,* but he wasn't convincing himself, desperately trying to ignore the blatant facts that were facing him: he was tied up and completely at the mercy of two criminals, in the middle of the ocean—two men he'd just been stupid enough to threaten exposing. *That probably wasn't very smart,* he acknowledged to himself.

He heard the low grumble of the engines and felt the vibration shake through his bunk and the unmistakable sound of the anchor being raised. The yacht rocked gently as the RPM of the engines increased and then leveled out. They were underway. Any thoughts of going ashore into Kailua-Kona and escaping were quickly fading. He could only hope they were headed back to Kaneohe and would then let him go. That was a lot of hoping that he had little faith in as well as a lot of hours away. The rag Roland had stuffed into his mouth was making his jaw muscles ache.

He guessed he'd been lying on the bunk for at least two hours, maybe longer—the room was so dark he couldn't tell—when the door suddenly burst open, and light from the companionway spilled into the room. Roland and Grey walked in and, without speaking, picked him up head and foot and carried him out and up onto the deck. It was still dark, but he could sense the flow of water rushing past the boat.

In silence, Margelese was lifted up over the railing. His captors let him drop with the motions and facial expressions they might have had were they instead getting rid of a bag of potato peelings.

"Good. That was easy." Grey looked to Roland for agreement.

"We should worry about the sharks getting sick eating that sack of scum."

They headed back to the lounge and their waiting drinks.

Margelese's panic consumed him in his frenzied attempt to gain release from the bonds around his arms and feet. His instinct to take a breath was being pushed to the limit. His exertions, though, quickly caused an involuntary breath, and water rapidly began to fill his lungs as his struggles became frantic. His thrashing quickly subsided as an unwelcomed serenity enveloped him. He felt more than saw the presence of what he could only imagine were spirits gently pulling him into their embrace as his living world drifted away.

Chapter Thirteen

Stone sat on his seawall, steam drifting silently off his mug of coffee, engrossed in watching the beautiful colors of the sunrise brokering their way through the low billowy clouds that hovered above the hilltops beyond the marine base at Kaneohe. The early morning air was cool, caring the intoxicating scent of pikake flowers from his neighbor's yard. The tide was low, exposing rock and seaweed. It was obviously one of Bert's favorite times of day, standing below the seawall in the still-wet sand with an unblinking stare, hunched over something that had no doubt made the mistake of moving from one rock to another and catching her attention.

It had been a whole day since Stone had met Teri. He was anxious to know how her friend, Viane, was doing and was contemplating calling her when his phone rang. Putting his coffee mug down on the adjacent grass, he hurried to the closest phone, which was inside his bedroom, catching it on the third ring.

"I hope this isn't too early to call you, Stone." It was Teri, and her voice sounded happy and cheerful. "I recalled you saying you were an early riser. I think you phrased it 'a sunup kind of guy,'" she said. "I am too on occasion—actually make that *rare* occasion. The sunrise this morning is incredible. I may have to make a habit of rising earlier just to enjoy the benefits."

"Good morning, Teri," he responded to the smile in her voice. "Now this is the way every morning should begin—a call from an attractive woman commenting on the beauty of a sunrise."

"Give me compliments like that, and I'll make sure I call every five minutes. What are you up to this morning?"

"I'm sitting by the water, coffee in hand, watching the morning begin, and nursing a strong desire to talk with you. Your voice is just what I wanted to hear."

Teri blushed, holding the receiver away from her as if he may be able to see her. She had had the hardest time not calling him yesterday just to say aloha and hear his voice. *This is nice*, she thought. She was finding justification for the warming feelings she was beginning to experience.

"Do you often go to the beach in the morning with your coffee, or is today an auspicious occasion of some sort?"

"Actually, I'm sitting in my backyard or front yard depending on your point of view. I didn't mention where I lived yesterday since it didn't enter our conversation, and besides, I was more interested in hearing about you. My home is on the back end of Kaneohe Bay. I'm sitting on my seawall as we speak."

"Oh, that sounds nice," she said, a musical quality in her voice. "I talked with Viane yesterday," she finally managed to say, "and she's most anxious to meet you. Her hero, as she calls you. I told her we could probably come over for a few hours within the next day or two. What do you think?"

Stone heard her say the word "we" and realized with more than a touch of pleasure that Teri would certainly want to go along, if for no other reason than to be a support for her friend.

"Why don't we go later this morning?" Stone was quick to take advantage of the opening. "We can catch Hawaiian Airlines's eleven o'clock flight. Are you open to short planning, and do you think Viane is?"

She hesitated a moment, collecting her thoughts. Since meeting Stone yesterday, he'd become a constant traveler through her thoughts. Something about him was so easy to like, but she'd been through disappointment with relationships in the past, usually as a result of being too quick to jump in the pond before testing its depth. Yes was all she managed to utter.

It was Stone's turn to hesitate. Her clipped response wasn't what he'd expected, and he felt a little disappointed at not hearing something filled with more enthusiasm—yet she did say yes. *I can't start holding any expectations,* he thought.

He continued, not wanting to allow her time to reconsider, "Why don't you call her back and ask her to meet us at the Empire Café on Haile Street at about 12:45 p.m. That will give us more than enough time to get there. We can talk over lunch." It had been a long time since Stone had an opportunity to enjoy some of Danny's cooking at the Empire. Danny was the owner of the restaurant and also its chief cook. He was adept at performing culinary miracles with Filipino cuisine—one of Stone's favorite ethnic foods. "I'll come by your house around ten if that's all right."

"I'm looking forward to the adventure together, and it'll be great to see Viane again and find out how she's coping after her frightful experience. Oh, and, Stone, if you want to bring a lady friend along, I would certainly understand," she said. "We could all make an afternoon of it."

He smiled at her weak attempt to fish for information. This was definitely a good omen. There was no one special in his life and hadn't been for longer than he cared to think about. He had not allowed himself the time lately nor had he thought about wanting to. *Time* was what he always managed to blame it on—he was very good at rationalizing. He decided to play her game as well. "No, there's no one I would want to have along this time, but please, feel free to bring one of your boyfriends if you'd like. Who knows, I might even get around to tolerating him."

"I'll see you shortly, Stone. I'll call back if Viane has a conflict."

He thought he heard her laughing as she closed the connection.

It was a very fast fifty-minute flight. Conversation between them was easy and relaxed, and they found they shared many of the same values, goals, and spiritual beliefs as well as enjoyment of dancing.

Time went much too quickly as they approached the coastline of the Big Island.

"The shoreline and ponds of Keaukaha are so beautiful, aren't they?" Stone caught a hint of Teri's perfume as he leaned over her to look out the window. He enjoyed the fragrance as well as the closeness. He delayed longer than necessary settling back into his seat.

Teri cleared her throat, feeling a hot flush bathing her skin. His breath in her hair and the subtle scent of his aftershave unsettled her, and she hoped he'd lean over again to look at something else on the ground, but instead she saw him sit back and tighten his seatbelt. She reluctantly did the same.

"It sounds like you know this part of the island." She was finally able to get the words out, keeping her head turned partially away from him so he wouldn't see her flushed.

"This used to be part of my playground growing up. I love this island more than any of the others, and I've been on every one of them. It's still so alive with energy, and the people are so openly accepting of others. The 'big city' syndrome hasn't found its way here yet and hopefully never will."

The airport and rent-a-car kiosk were only a ten-minute drive from downtown Hilo. Stone found parking in front of the Palace Theater directly opposite the Empire Café.

"You really have to love small towns," Stone said as he opened Teri's door and held out his hand to assist her getting out. "Where else can a nickel still buy one hour of parking?"

Teri got out and immediately waved in the direction of the café. Stone turned to see a very attractive and faintly familiar young woman sitting at a table and waving back. The Empire Café has no front wall, being fully open to the sidewalk. When the time comes to close for the night, Danny simply pulls down a metal rolling door that closes out the rest of the world.

As Teri and Stone approached the table, Viane rose, and the two ladies embraced in a hug, as good friends do. Teri reached for Stone's hand and pulled him close beside her.

"Stone, I'd like you to formally meet the nearly drowned woman you pulled from the ocean. This is Viane Koa, my very dear friend." Teri continued, "You've seen her at her worst, and now you can meet her as she really is. Viane, this is Kensington Stone, hero extraordinaire, who chooses to be called Stone." She looked at Stone with an admiring approval.

Viane, a big smile lighting her face, immediately threw her arms around Stone's neck and looked up at him. The wonderful fragrance of the three plumeria blossoms tucked above her ear floated up to him. His senses were being worked overtime by these two beautiful ladies.

"Stone, you are truly my hero. There's no way I can thank you enough for rescuing me. Mahalo a nui. Thank you, thank you, thank you so very much for coming along when you did. You'll always be my hero, my knight in shining white fiberglass." She beamed with happiness and a huge smile, flashing perfect white teeth.

He was being held captive in her embrace, but he really didn't mind. "It's my pleasure to meet you in person, Viane. I too am very happy I came along when I did. I love the way nature brings circumstances into our lives that cause us to cross one another's path just at the right moment. Serendipity at its finest. We were meant to cross paths for a reason. Perhaps someday we may know what that reason was, right? From all outward appearances," he continued, attempting to lean backward in a feigned appraisal of her, "you appear to be unscathed after your soggy ordeal. You weren't in any condition to say very much the last time I saw you." *That was an idiotic thing to say*, he silently reprimanded himself.

Viane finally released him but held his gaze. "I must apologize to you for disappearing like I did. That must have been quite unsettling for you. I was in no frame of mind to understand what was happening or who you were. I simply had to get away to a safe haven, which I did at Teri's place. I hope you understand. I was feeling much too vulnerable at that moment. What a horrible feeling that is. My life is forever in your debt."

"I can't honestly say I know how you must have been feeling because I don't, and I can't put myself into your shoes, but I certainly understand sufficiently to know I might have done precisely as you did under the circumstances."

They sat at a table close to the sidewalk and talked about her family and her life in Hilo as they waited for their lunch to arrive. Stone had ordered his favorite chicken adobo—chicken cooked Filipino style with vinegar, ginger, and Danny's secret seasonings. Teri had asked for the *sari sari*, a pork and vegetable soup, and Viane choose the *dinadaraan*, a Filipino standard of pork blood and meats, one of Stone's favorites and apparently one of Viane's as well.

As Danny brought out their orders, the aroma that came with the food flooded the table. All three, as if on cue, breathed in the multitude of wonderful smells.

"Ah," sighed Stone, leaning over the table to take another deep breath. "This is another reason why I love Hilo so much."

"I come here as often as I can," said Viane. "Nothing beats Danny's cooking."

She handed Stone an old ketchup bottle that was filled with a dark liquid.

"Patis. I love this stuff," he said, accepting the bottle and pouring an ample quantity over his rice and chicken. A popular substance in some communities in Hawaii, it consisted of fermented fish innards and other things best left unknown, but the taste was amazing.

"This is my father's patis," Viane volunteered, enjoying the opportunity to brag about her dad. "He makes the best in the islands. We used to have a steady stream of visitors from all the other islands stopping by our house just to buy it to take home with them whenever they were in Hilo. Unfortunately, that's slowing way down since it's difficult to take bottles of any sort on an airplane now. It's either checked baggage, mailed, or too bad for us. Pops, my father," she said for clarity at Stone's questioning expression, "isn't amenable to creating a website either. Seems that when Pops finally decides to leave this life behind, his wonderful patis recipe will go with him."

As they enjoyed their food, Stone told them the story of his new yacht and its maiden voyage, leaving out the part about the fear that had invaded him in the huge waves—*I have to maintain some sort of hero status*, he thought.

"The curious part," he continued, "is where and how you managed to get off my yacht without being noticed. There's a police officer still thinking about arresting me for fabricating a nonexistent emergency." Teri and Viane laughed at the prospect of him being behind bars. He wasn't so sure he saw any humor in that.

"It sounds to me like we can be thankful for the crappy weather. If you had been in *malie*, flat water, you probably never would have run across her, pardon the pun, but would instead have been roaring toward all points of the channel," joked Teri.

"She's right, Viane. If it weren't for the poor conditions out there, you might be drifting toward California as we speak." They all laughed, mostly to release the frightening image.

"I know firsthand and up close just how bad things were out there." Their laughter quickly subsided with Viane's serious expression.

"Enough humor about my capacity to float," quipped Viane, trying her best to reintroduce some lightheartedness back into their lunchtime. "Let me tell you the whole story, including how easy it was for me to get off your boat, and then we can figure out what to do about it." Stone grimaced at Viane's use of the word *boat* instead of *yacht*, but he let it go. "I understand you're willing to help me retrieve what I lost. It may also keep you out of jail," she said, smiling at Stone.

Viane told about her friendship with Dr. Krivoi Margelese, Doc, and of his alliance with the two guys named Roland and Grey and the deception that took place over the artifacts she had found. It became obvious to both Stone and Teri that Viane was still extremely shaken as she told of the attempted rape and of falling over the railing. She hesitated in her story several times to calm her nerves; the memories were still very vivid.

"The most desperate part was watching the *Whiskey Sea* fade from sight. I expected to see it make a turn at any moment and head back to find me. Apparently, Doc didn't bother telling anyone I had gone overboard, that snake in the grass," she said, anger flaring in her eyes. "He just stood at the railing and watched me drift away." Her anger at recollecting the event was noticeably intensifying.

She told them of the sheer hopelessness she had felt holding the life ring, unable to see anything in the dark, and the immense terror of hearing unseen waves breaking as they rushed toward her before she was tumbled and pulled under with unbelievable force.

Teri reached across the table and took Viane's hand and gently held it after realizing her friend was beginning to shake. Viane relaxed at her friend's touch and sat quietly for a moment before continuing her story in a much quieter voice. She told of unending seconds after being pulled under, then struggling to reach the surface before needing her next breath. The last thing she was aware of, she said, before waking up on Stone's boat, was several waves rolling over her, very close together giving little time to get air before being sucked under again and again. She knew she had swallowed a lot of water.

"That's an amazing story, Viane," offered Stone. "So many things could have gone differently. The way I see it, your friend Margelese, Doc, more than likely thinks you're dead and is probably quite busy covering his tracks. Attempting to rape a student at the bare minimum would get him banned from a professorship anywhere, and the fact that he didn't sound an overboard alarm would probably get him a lengthy stay in the Oahu Community Correctional Center for attempted murder. To confront him at this time would be pointless and perhaps very dangerous for you.

"Also, just thinking off the top of my head, confronting Roland and Grey may push them into hiding or force them to come out fighting, and who knows what they may be capable of doing? They may simply blame it all on Margelese, in which case it would be one word against the other, and the artifacts could be lost forever."

"Your story," he continued, "is also going to be a tough sell. I have a host of friends, not to mention several borderline inebriates, who were at the pier as I pulled into the yacht club, and none of them saw you. Even my police sergeant friend will have to testify he saw no one matching your description in or around my yacht or the club itself. All we have is both our stories and that of an old taxi driver, and according to his log, he thought you were high on something. Our stories have a lot of legal holes."

"Let me ask you something, Stone. What is it you want to see happen? Find the artifacts would be first, I imagine. What else?" asked Viane.

"I think finding the artifacts and keeping you safe is primary. Finding your things, though, will inadvertently have the dangerous outcome of exposing three people who don't appear to have much aloha for their fellow man—or woman in your case. I'd like to see justice done, of course, but more importantly I need to know that both of you"—he looked from Viane to Teri—"are not in any danger as a result of all this. I bring you under that umbrella, Teri, because you know Viane and you know Margelese. That creates a three-way that could jeopardize either or both of you."

Viane broke the ensuing silence. "One thing we must do is keep all of this away from the press. I don't want a rush of people flocking to South Point in search of lava tubes and whatever other artifacts that might happen to be in one of them, and I really don't want reporters bothering my family. And I'm sure neither of you wants to be bothered by nosey journalists either. If that lava tube is a place of significant importance as it appears to be, people swarming through it would be a terrible desecration of an historic place as would be the destruction or removal of any other artifacts it may contain."

"I agree wholeheartedly," said Teri. "This has got to be kept quiet until we see a clear way to go forward. And I think it is advisable for you to stay in Hilo until we can solve a few of the riddles."

Stone didn't know if Viane had heard the use of "we" in Teri's comment, but he did, and he liked the implications.

Viane *had* heard Teri say "we" and noticed that she and Stone were sitting quite close to each other. *It's about time Teri got interested in someone,* she mused to herself. *Maybe this is the serendipitous part of what I experienced.*

"I'm going to stay put for a few more days," said Viane, "but I can't remain here beyond next weekend. I've got to get back to my studies as final exams are getting much too close."

"We," said Stone, looking at Teri as he spoke through a slight smile, "are going to find out what we can about the *Whiskey Sea* and where it is right now. I'd like to know more about Roland and Grey and where all that wealth they apparently boast of comes from. Also, Viane, I've got to discuss everything with Mike, my sergeant friend at Honolulu PD. I promised to keep him informed. I hope you're okay with that. I think we can trust him to keep this under wraps for now, at least until we know more. He should be fine with that since no reported crime has been committed as far as he's concerned."

As they stood to leave, Viane mentioned her two brothers wanting to help and said they were extremely impulsive and temperamental when it concerned their little sister. "They would just as soon barge in and grab any culprits by the throat and not be too concerned about how badly they treated them."

Stone gave Viane a good-bye hug. "I'd enjoy meeting John and Sonny sometime. Those bullish tendencies of theirs may come in handy at some point, but not just yet. I hope they can be patient."

On the trip back to Oahu, Teri and Stone both agreed to take each step carefully and not be stupid about getting in deeper than they could handle. In the meantime, between studies and work, Teri would act as a go-between with Viane.

Stone suddenly felt the reality of having volunteered to be the centerpiece in unraveling this mystery. He liked the thought of being more involved with Teri, though. He'd have to work diligently to ensure a happy ending for these two ladies, both of whom he was beginning to really care deeply for.

It was late afternoon by the time Stone delivered Teri back to her home and made his way over the Pali Highway. They had made a date for lunch the next day.

Bert was sitting on top of the lava rock wall by the entrance gate to Stone's yard as he pulled into the carport. *Poor little girl's probably hungry,* he thought. He picked her up off the wall and carried her up the short flight of stairs and into the kitchen—she purred all the way.

"I guess I had better call Lloyd, Bert, and let him know how the day went." He put the cat down beside her food dish, opened the refrigerator and extracted a bottle of Corona, and unscrewed the cap with its accompanying *pssssst*. "On second thought, I think I'll wait 'til morning. Let's go sit on the seawall and enjoy the evening. I want to think about what I've put my big foot into."

Chapter Fourteen

The earliness of morning gradually shed its light on a low tide expanse of beach fronting Stone's house. It also shed its light on Bert fully engrossed in her endeavor of extracting a small crab from under an exposed rock. Stone walked out to the seawall with his morning coffee, cordless phone in hand, found his usual comfortable perch, and called Lloyd.

"Hey, Lloyd, how-z-it this morning?"

A sleepy voice responded, "And you woke me up at daybreak just to ask how-z-it? Are you sleepwalking, or did you wake up to find a beautiful wahine in bed with you and couldn't wait 'til daylight to tell me? It better be the first one 'cause I don't want to start thinking of anything else yet."

"I figured you really wanted to be up but just couldn't find the words to admit it to yourself. I also wanted to tell you that I met with the floating lady yesterday."

"Really?" Lloyd became more alert. "You met her through that Teri woman you went to talk with? What's her name and claim to fame—the floating lady—I mean?"

"Her name is Viane Koa, and she comes from Hilo. In fact, that's where Teri and I went yesterday."

"Teri and you, huh? That ring in your voice sounds awfully friendly. I'm seeing a future for the two of you in my mind's eye—not sure if it's a murky one yet or not. Did you say the floating lady's last name is Koa?" he asked suddenly more interested. "Did she mention being related to Rudy Koa?"

"Yeah, matter-of-fact she did. That's her father's name. What makes you ask that?"

"Eh, brah, rememba I stay one Big Island boy," he said, unfolding his pidgin for effect. "Her father was quite well known around some of the old sugarcane plantations for his homemade patis. From what my dad told me, he used to show up regularly with the back end of an old pickup loaded with a supply of patis in whatever bottles he'd been able to get his hands on, anxious to sell the lot. And most of the workers eagerly looked forward to his coming, it was that good."

"Yeah, I had some at the Empire Café, and it *was* that good, probably the best I've had."

"I'm surprised you didn't know about Rudy's patis since you love Filipino food so much and love Hilo even more." Lloyd had been born in the Honokaa area close to the Hamakua Sugar Plantation and grew up there until his family moved to Oahu. "I like her already," said Lloyd. "So what's her story and how the heck did she disappear from your boat before I got to see her?"

"You mean 'my yacht'?"

"Yeah okay, your big yacht."

"Much better. I feel important again."

Stone told him what Viane had relayed about her adventure. "I volunteered you, me, and Teri to do some fact finding. Actually, Teri enthusiastically volunteered herself:

they're very close friends. We've got to bring this guy Doc to court to face charges of attempted rape and murder, and we've got to find those relics that were stolen from her. They've taken on an extreme importance to her and to Hawaiian history in general. My intuition tells me that Roland and Grey must have some sort of under-the-table agreement with this Margelese character. From the way Viane describes what happened, it sounds like she was set up."

"Mahalo, Stone, for dragging me into this quagmire. I sure needed a couple more have-tos in my life. Why not let Mike and Honolulu PD come up with a solution to the problem? Isn't that why they get the fancy uniforms, guns, and nice cars?"

"We talked about that, and we all agreed that if Honolulu PD were called in, they'd have to open it up to the press, and that means reporters would be swarming all over Viane, her family, me, and the lava tube where the artifacts came from and whatever else they could dig up and expound on, including King Kamehameha I if they knew where his bones were hidden. It could encourage armchair archeologists and antiquities collectors into mass raids of every exposed lava tube and rock crevasse on every one of our islands. That wouldn't help anything at this point. With your connections and my charm, I think we can do some discreet snooping. Teri has inside access at UH, which may prove to be a major help for us."

"You sure you're not volunteering for all this detective work just to get close to this woman?"

"I have to admit she's really quite unique. We'll have to wait and see how that story unfolds, though. For now, how about using some of your contacts to quietly find out about the *Whiskey Sea*?"

"I would be living my life's dream just to do that very thing, Stone. So when are you going to invite me out on that big yacht of yours?"

"When you see Viane and hear her story, you'll understand why I volunteered us. Come to think of it, your son Kawika is about thirty, isn't he? Is he serious about anyone in particular at the moment? Those two could really make a match. Their interests could be very compatible from what I can tell. Didn't you say you were hoping he'd find someone and move out?"

"Stop being a matchmaker and answer my question," Lloyd demanded. "And no, he's not seeing anyone at the moment," he added. "I think he's more interested in building canoes than meeting anyone."

"Let's see what we can find out today and tomorrow and then use Sunday after the christening to head out over the banks for some fishing. The christening is at ten o'clock and shouldn't last more than thirty minutes depending, of course, on how long-winded Hana gets." There were unseen smiles on both ends of the phone line as each nodded in agreement. Rev. Hana Kawai, an eighty-something-year-old *kanaka maoli*, full-blooded Hawaiian and kahuna lapaau, spiritual leader, could talk almost indefinitely if given an audience. His stories were always fascinating as well as mostly fabricated, but people loved to hang around and listen to him.

"While we're out fishing, we can take the opportunity to compare notes and figure out a few things that we need to cover and some people we need to see. Actually, I'm kind of anxious to get back out on the water for some R and R.

Hey, maybe we can persuade Teri to come along with us. It wouldn't surprise me in the least if she loved fishing just as much as we do."

"I need to meet this wahine before you have a chance to spoil her beyond normal recognition," laughed Lloyd. "I'll call you later and let you know what I find out, and yeah, this Sunday afternoon sounds perfect. Let's check the weather on Saturday."

"Mahalo, brah. That's why we're such good friends, we understand each other. I'm going to give Mike a heads-up so he doesn't get too bent out of shape from us not keeping him in the loop. Doesn't pay to get a cop upset even if he is a friend. Also, Teri and I are heading for Canoe's in Waikiki for a late lunch. You want to join us?"

"Probably not but let me see how the morning goes. I've got to flush out the radiator in Pam's car, and then I'll call over to the yacht club and see what I can find out about the *Whiskey Sea*."

Chapter Fifteen

Lloyd drove into the parking lot at Kaneohe Yacht. It was a little before 10:30 a.m. as he entered the office. An elderly woman sitting at a desk with Wilma printed on a name tag adorning her blouse looked up with a bulge pushing at her left cheek. A bagel missing a bite rested on a plate in front of her. Lloyd's arrival obviously caught her unprepared to see a visitor walk in.

After a moment's hesitation as she quickly chewed and forced a swallow, she found her voice. "Aloha, can I help you with something?"

"Aloha, Wilma. Would you know where I could find Kelvin, your port captain? I talked with him a little while ago, and he said someone in the office would be able to point me in his direction."

"Since I'm the only one here, I guess he was referring to me." She stood and walked around her desk to the counter. Lloyd, watching her approach, realized she was an extraordinarily tall woman dwarfing the counter in front of her and bearing a wonderful, open smile. A crumb of bagel remained, holding tightly to the corner of her upper lip.

"You're in luck. I happen to know exactly where he is," she offered, wiping a napkin she'd held in her hand across her mouth. The bagel morsel vanished; her smile returned. "He just called in from someplace out on C pier a few moments ago. He's on his way into the office. Should be just a few minutes. You want some coffee while you wait?" She moved to the end of the counter where a very large coffee urn stood and began filling a mug without waiting for Lloyd's reply. It would have been a yes anyway since Lloyd was known for never refusing a cup of coffee.

Just as Wilma handed Lloyd a coffee mug filled to overflowing, a barrel-chested middle-aged man appeared in the doorway. His face weathered and leathery, his bush of red hair was wind-blown in all directions, and an equally unkempt, full red beard hid most of his face.

"And speak of the devil," volunteered Wilma as the bearded man, with tattered and multi-stained T-shirt and shorts obviously cut from a pair of blue jeans, approached the counter. "Here he is in person."

Lloyd, balancing his coffee mug, carefully put his hand out. "Aloha, Kelvin, my name is Lloyd Moniz. We spoke earlier."

Kelvin grabbed it and shook it vigorously, coffee splashing over the rim onto the floor. "Yeah, Lloyd, I'm Kelvin Frances, but then good old Wilma here already broke that news to you." Large coffee-stained teeth showed through the spaces between the mustache and beard as Kelvin stood there grinning, no outward sign of releasing Lloyd's hand. Apparently, he hadn't finished his greeting.

"Wilma, pour me a mug of that stuff you call coffee if you would but don't fill it to the brim—I see you got enough on the floor here to clean up as it is."

Kelvin turned back to Lloyd. "Bring your coffee, Lloyd," he said as he pulled on Lloyd's hand in the direction he aimed to head before releasing it and grabbing the mug Wilma held out to him. "Let's go into the bar area to talk, it'll be a little more private since it's not open yet. Not to worry about the spill on the floor. Wilma will get that, won't you, girl?"

Wilma mumbled something, but the door closed before Lloyd could tell what she was saying. He assumed it wasn't a cordial "see you later."

Lloyd called Stone when he got home. "The *Whiskey Sea* is owned by a couple of guys with a Port Townsend, Washington, mailbox address. Their yacht, and this really is a yacht according to the port captain, is magnificent. It's even documented, that's how big this yacht is. Did you say that yours was documented, Stone?"

"Keep it up, and I'll leave you floating around out on the banks when we go fishing. So what else did you find out?"

"Maybe we should talk about that fishing thing first, as in when that might happen. You said Sunday after the christening, right?"

"Funny. We'll get out there immediately afterward just as soon as we're *pau* helping Viane. Speaking of finishing helping her . . ."

"Okay, okay. Two guys, Roland Pratt and Greyson Giani, are the owners according to the yacht club registration. They showed up four weeks ago, and according to Kelvin, they're due to pull out any time. They paid for five weeks but gave him an indication that if they were to leave early, he was to donate any refund to the club's bar flies. I didn't get a look at it because it wasn't tied up while I was there. The port captain said it's almost always there and was surprised that it wasn't. He said the few times they actually leave, they're usually back within hours. He told me they stay pretty much to themselves and don't seem willing to let anyone get too close to them. He's never been invited to go aboard, would you believe that? From the impression I got, not inviting the port captain to come onboard is a real no-no in the yacht club world. My instinct tells me something is a little *pupule* with these guys."

"Thanks for going over there and checking things out, Lloyd. I talked with Mike, and he's agreed to keep Honolulu PD out of things for a while but insists we keep him up to speed. We'll have to do as he requested, but for now let's keep this bit of information to ourselves until we get more information about them and their yacht."

"I called UH after talking with you this morning," continued Stone, "and tried to set up an appointment with Margelese, but they said he wasn't there, and they weren't sure when he would be back. That's a little strange for a university department head, isn't it? I'll ask Teri at lunch today if she'll do some detective work and see what she can find out since she knows some of the department staff. By the way, are you coming down to join us? If you do, we'll be at the Chart House instead of Canoes. I'm not in the mood to fight Waikiki traffic."

"I wish I could, Stone, but I can't do it. Pam and I have some errands to run, and then I want to clean up the barbeque grill and get it ready for your boat christening, since you asked if you could borrow it. Come over to the house when you and Teri are *pau* lunch."

"Oh, and by the way," continued Lloyd, "Kelvin isn't sure whether to be miffed at you or pleased. Said he had a hell of a time getting that cargo net you towed in hauled out of the water. He had to get the club's Boston Whaler and drag it over to the boat lift. Then he didn't know what to do with it once it was out of the water. Apparently, it's taking up space in their dry storage area, and the club's commodore isn't very happy about it."

"Perhaps I should have left it floating around out there. Maybe the commodore's boat would have been lucky enough to find it."

Chapter Sixteen

Teri and Stone arrived at the Chart House, jockeyed their way through the Friday lunch crowd, and edged into the overcrowded lounge. A man and woman appeared preparing to vacate their table, which sat in a small alcove next to the railing and overlooked the boat harbor and the ocean beyond—a perfect, out-of-the-way spot to sit and talk. Apparently, none of those standing three deep at the bar had spotted the soon-to-be-available and often all-too-difficult-to-obtain table, or perhaps they all chose not to be that far away from the bartender.

Stone smiled at the tourist couple as he held the chair out for the woman as she got up and continued to hold it for Teri. He had to chuckle to himself. It was so easy to spot tourist couples in a crowd: they were the ones in matching aloha shirts and muumuus, often with an abundance of very bright red or yellow hibiscus flowers or birds of paradise printed all over them. If children were tagging along, they too would be dressed in the same bright-colored prints as the parents, only in smaller versions. The popular notion of the bright family-matching outfits was promoted by clothing manufacturers to "help" tourists blend in with the locals. It actually had the opposite effect but yet made tourists feel more absorbed into the island culture.

Stone guided Teri quickly to the table. A waitress coming by to clear the table took their order for coffee—it was much too early for a glass of Mondovi Cabernet Reserve, although Stone was tempted. He was experiencing a lighter mood at the moment after all the uncertainty of the past few days and was enjoying the opportunity to get to know Teri on a deeper level.

From their table, Stone could see the launching ramp in front of the Harbormaster's office where he had been just three days before as he took the first step aboard his new yacht.

The lounge was unusually busy this early in the day. He attributed that to the fact that the boating community was preparing for the upcoming Trans-Pacific Yacht Race, which officially finished at the Diamond Head lighthouse; but in reality, here in the boat harbor were all the parties began.

The horseshoe bar in the center of the lounge was rimmed with stools, and all were occupied. People stood two and three deep behind friends fortunate enough to have acquired a place to sit. It was a fun bar and a good mixture of locals and visitors alike. The head bartender, Grant, had been behind this bar for years, as well as his second in command, Jason. A lot of locals made this their home away from home just because of them.

Stone looked over at the Harbormaster's office. "Hard to imagine the amount of *stuff*," he emphasized the word *stuff*, "that can take place in just a few short days, isn't it?"

He pointed to the boat ramp by the office. "That's where the journey began that brought Viane, you, and me together." He looked at Teri, who was taking in the peaceful setting of the harbor. "That reminds me of something I wanted to ask you before we get too engrossed in telling each other our likes and dislikes—business before pleasure, so to speak. A geology department person at the university told me that Margelese was not there, and they hadn't seen him the past couple of days. Does that sound odd to you, or is it just odd to me?"

"It sounds very odd," responded Teri, her calm expression giving way to one of concern. "He teaches class every day, so he should've been there. Why don't I see what I can find out when I'm there later this afternoon?"

"If you can do that without drawing any unnecessary attention. If he's not around, do you think there's a way I can snoop through his office without setting off any alarms?"

"If you're with me, it should be okay," she said, her smile was mischievous. "Let me check things out first."

They sat in silence for a few moments, looking at one another, then out over the field of boat masts swaying with the currents in the harbor. The clanking of ropes gently glancing off masts broadcasted a pleasant and relaxing sound. Their view matched their mood: all was generally well in the world, or at least will be when Viane's situation was resolved.

"I don't know if this has a bearing on anything or not," she said, "but I thought you'd like to know. I talked to a friend at Bishop Museum this morning who was really upset. She told me they discovered several valuable pieces of their collection missing from their basement archives, nine items so far, but they're still looking. Only museum officers and research people are allowed down to those storage vaults. For some reason, I asked if Margelese ever showed up there. And guess what she told me?" Her eyebrows rose in mock surprise. "Our Dr. Margelese has been a frequent visitor over the past few weeks. Being a university professor and head of a department, he has open access to their basement collection, supposedly for research. Funny thing, though. He's a geologist. What interest would he have in a bunch of ancient Hawaiian artifacts?"

"My guess is he's getting tired of looking at a bunch of rocks and wants a change of venue. Do they suspect him of being involved in the disappearances?"

"They don't know what to think since there is a swarm of people with authorized access. They're still doing an inventory, which could take a couple more days. She said they're trying to push it and would keep me posted. She was very interested to hear that a friend of mine had some personal Hawaiiana-type artifacts stolen from her. I didn't go into any details with her, but I know she'd like to know more. In particular, she really wanted to know what the items were and where they came from."

"The plot thickens, so the saying goes," said Stone. "My gut instinct about all this is heading toward the dark side. In the meantime, to lighten our moods, I'd like to suggest we take a boat cruise around Kaneohe Bay this afternoon. Maybe a stop at the sand bar outside Heeia Kea for a swim," Stone said with a devilish grin.

"It seems you chose not to hear what I said a few moments ago. I have to be at the university this afternoon. I've got to be there before four," Teri said, an apologetic look formed as she quickly glanced down at her watch as if having reminded herself of the time. "And that's approaching fast. I've got to be on my way soon. We'd better hurry and eat if we don't want to carry doggie bags to the car."

"So you're going to eat and run and leave me sitting here by myself, are you?" He allowed a sad "puppy dog" expression to unfold and looked at her.

It didn't succeed; she just laughed.

She reached out and rested her hand on his arm. Whatever had been in her thoughts, however, escaped her as her hand picked up the warm sensation of his skin. His eyes fixed on hers as he waited to hear what she had been about to say.

Stone saw a momentary change in Teri's expression—it seemed to be mirroring his own sensation as her touch sent a warm awareness coursing through his senses.

Teri quickly regained her train of thought but not before she cataloged that sensation in her mind file of Desirable—Need More of This. "Poor man, you're lacking friends, are you?" She moved her chair closer to his. "There's a rather beautiful woman sitting on the stern of that sailboat over there, and she appears to be alone," she said, pointing in the general direction of the boats but at no one in sight. "Why don't you ask her to join you when I leave? I can catch a cab home. Who knows, maybe I'll be lucky and get that taxi driver who seemed so interested in my anatomy and wearing apparel the other night."

Stone forced a scowl, saying, "I'll have to find that taxi driver and set him straight." He reached and put his hand over hers to keep it from being pulled away. "I have a feeling we're going to at least have a little fun looking into Viane's situation together, even with the dark end of things looming." Stone's manner became serious, saying, "Viane's lucky to have you as a friend."

Their lunch passed too quickly for either of them. Stone drove Teri to her home. She'd have just enough time to drive back to the university for her appointment.

He drove to Lloyd's place and found him standing on the grass fronting Lanikai Beach, wire brushing his stand-up very large stainless-steel homemade barbeque grill. Abandoning the work, they took a couple of lawn chairs out to the edge of the beach and sat where they could look out over the waves and the Mokulua Islands offshore. Pam brought out two tall glasses of iced tea for them, drops of moisture racing down each glass.

"Hey, Stone," said Pam, "have you found your mystery lady yet?"

"Hey, Pam, and yes, I have. I've also met and dined with her very attractive friend."

"Oh? That sounds interesting. Any possibilities there? It's about time you met someone. You've been living in that beautiful house by yourself for much too long. I hope she likes cats."

"Don't aim me down that 'togetherness' path too fast, Pam. We've only just met. Who knows, she may snore like a battlefield sergeant and probably has ten boyfriends signed up on her dance card. With her looks, that number could easily be double. Besides, Bert may get jealous if the same woman starts showing up too many times in a row, and then I'd have to make a choice between the two."

"Is that the way it goes? And who would you choose? Never mind, I think I already know the answer—poor woman." Pam turned and headed for the house. "I've got work to do," she said. "You two enjoy your view. I see several skimpy bikinis parading around on the beach."

Both Stone and Lloyd quickly glanced in both directions and found to their delight that she was right. "Ah, the pleasures of beach gazing," said Stone.

"I had a good meeting with Kelvin, the port captain at the yacht club, as I told you on the phone," he said as he sipped his iced tea and gazed at a very skimpily bikinied brunette swaying past. "He's quite a character. If he had a patch over an eye, a parrot on his shoulder, and a wooden leg, he'd be the perfect picture of a dreaded pirate. Our mystery yacht still has a week to go on its slip rental, but Kelvin's gotten the impression that it may pull out at any time. Their yacht wasn't there, so I'm wondering if they've already gone."

"You know, from what I'm piecing together," replied Stone, "I have a nagging intuition that all the bananas in the tree aren't ripe yet."

"Huh?" asked Lloyd. "What the heck does that mean? What bananas you talking about? Sometimes you don't make sense, Stone."

"I don't know, and sometimes I don't have to," Stone said and smiled as he reached for his glass. "I just know there's something going on with all this that we're missing and that the people involved aren't what they seem to be. You know what I found out? Bishop Museum has discovered some sacred pieces have been pilfered from their archives, and our university professor is a frequent traveler through those very same archives. That's all I mean." He sat back and put his hands behind his head as he watched a young couple, hand in hand, both oblivious to the rest of the world, walk past. "Ah, this is the life God intended us to live, Lloyd."

Lloyd sat back as well. "You sure you want to be mixed up in all this? Be real easy to call Mike and lay it all on his desk. Then you and this wahine could go off and do things you're probably both thinking about eventually doing."

"That would be easy, Lloyd, but I've promised both Teri and Viane to see this through to the end, and I'm counting on you, buddy, to help me out."

They both sighed as another bikini drifted past.

Chapter Seventeen

The *Star Advertiser* was devoid of any news of bodies washing up on any of the islands over the past few days. Neither Roland nor Grey was surprised. They knew there was a better-than-average chance the girl's body as well as that of Margelese's may never reach any shore. A body floating around in the ocean, they figured, would eventually attract the attention of the surrounding marine life. Small fish would gravitate to its shade and the hiding spaces it offered; bigger fish would be seeking their meal of smaller fish and instinct would lead the way to the floating body. Larger predators wouldn't be far behind, and a feeding frenzy in the food chain would ensue.

The men had spent their entire day Wednesday and the two nights on both sides of it cruising back to the yacht club. They pulled in a little before 10:00 a.m.—they hadn't hurried.

"It really would take a miracle for that wahine to wash ashore," said Roland, "but then again it's only Thursday, and anything could happen. If she's destined to float up onto a beach, it will take a few more days at least. As for Margelese, he'll be riding the circular current west of the Big Island until he disappears into the belly of a fish. Either that or he's bouncing along the ocean floor toward Japan as we speak."

Since tying up to the pier, he and Grey had been busy wiping down all the bright work along the port side of their yacht. Moisture and the inevitable salt spray that accompanies any journey away from the dock robs the yacht of its beauty and eventually its value if it isn't properly cleaned.

They finished the port side and moved around to begin on the starboard and were immediately greeted by a waving hand from Chuck, their neighbor, whose boat was moored beside theirs. He had a Budweiser in hand and was wearing a tank top that advertised a fish market across the front, the words and picture faded from many washings. Volumes of grey hair stuck out from around the neck, back, and arms of the tank top. He had wandered over close to the gangplank and was standing beside it on the pier.

"How-z-it, neighbors," he spoke much too loudly. "It's good to keep our toys looking their best, ain't it? Lotta work, though, especially now during the heat of the day. I have some spare time, be glad to come aboard and lend some elbow grease." His hand was on the railing of the boarding ramp, and he was in the process of taking a step in that direction.

Grey wasn't about to let that happen.

"Thanks, friend, but we're pretty much finished here. We have some other needs that must be attended to. Tell you what though, sometime next week if we're here and you have some time, we'd love to have you aboard for a cold one and a walk-through. How's that for a plan?"

Chuck stepped back onto the pier with a puzzled look and let go of the railing. The only words he managed were, "That sounds like a . . . ," but both men had disappeared through a doorway, closing it behind them before he could finish his sentence. Chuck could see that the starboard bright work was still encrusted with salt spray and knew they had cut their work short. *Must have some pretty important plannin' to do to leave that salt all over the place,* he thought as he headed back to his own boat for another beer. *Not my problem.*

Once inside, Roland retrieved a beer for each of them from the refrigerator behind the bar, and they both stepped out onto the port side deck looking out toward the center of the bay and away from Chuck's prying eyes.

"I think it's still in our best interest to be on our way Saturday instead of delaying anything, especially with our friendly, always-present Chuck watching over us. Besides, doesn't our slip rental expire next week?"

"Yeah, it does, and I agree. It would have been nice to spend a few days in Waikiki before heading for Seattle, but that damn Margelese screwed all that up for us."

"Since we have to take on fuel and supplies before we head out, if we leave here Saturday, we can refuel at the Ala Wai Marina instead of using the local gas dock—what is it, Heeia Kea? We could still spend Saturday and Sunday night moored at the transient dock, enjoy some Waikiki nightlife, get our business out of the way, then move out early on Monday. A couple beers at the Chart House would be a good parting aloha to our adventures here anyway."

"You know, Grey, I think that's a good plan to follow," said Roland, leaning against the railing, enjoying the gentle trade wind breeze moving past. "We haven't talked about Debra yet, and that would solve a dilemma that's been bothering me. We could have her meet us there late Sunday, do the deal, and be on our way early the following morning. Less risk and exposure getting it done earlier, and I'll bet she'd rather meet us in a more populated spot than having to traipse all the way over the mountain to this place. Besides, we'd have a hell of a time moving stuff along the pier and onto the yacht with our *niele* neighbor, Chuck, always on the lookout witnessing the parade. He's sure one nosey son of a gun. Sunday night is looking better and better."

They'd never met Debra Shinn even though she was the primary reason they were in Hawaii. Several weeks prior, a friend and their major contact into the black market, Loren Bucke, had set up the meeting between Roland, Grey, and Debra to arrange shipment of several artifacts she was planning to smuggle into Hawaii from Japan, but she'd called Loren at the last minute to say she couldn't make the meeting and offering no reason why. The call did not sit well with Loren who, like Grey, disliked change of any sort. Roland and Grey were now planning to meet with her themselves and carry her smuggled property with them back to Loren—for a healthy fee, of course.

Loren ran a large and successful black market operation out of the back of the Wong Mai Chinese restaurant in Seattle. He always claimed to have Chinese blood, having been left an orphan in Beijing by a British tourist who had fallen in love with a Chinese woman, a maid in his hotel, as the story went who, in turn, didn't want the baby either. Loren claimed to have never met his father but said there was a connection with the family that ran the restaurant, from the mother's side, as he was always quick to point out if he thought you needed to know. The fact was he had no idea about the truth of his story or who either of his parents were.

He was a man of zero integrity and even fewer friends. The few people who resembled any form of friendship included Roland and Grey, dating back to high school when he was a larger-than-life schoolyard bully. He didn't mingle well with the Chinese students, the white kids, or anyone else, for that matter.

Loren dealt mostly with stolen artifacts and antiques from around the world. If you wanted the original statue of Venus de Milo and could afford his "suggested" price tag, which separated the merely rich from the ultra-wealthy, you could count on it being delivered to your door within a week, probably hidden inside a very large piano or some other non-relevant and unwanted item. He would even arrange to have the piano hauled away for an additional sum if it was in your way. It would invariably find a use camouflaging some other treasure being delivered elsewhere in the world if it hadn't been too damaged in the first go around. He always liked to save pennies where he could while spending millions.

Roland and Grey had helped Loren on several such deliveries and were always eager for more involvement with him as a way of obtaining the obscene amounts of commissions that Loren was willing to pay for discreet work. Handling this sort of undertaking for him fit well with their general view of life and fed their lavish appetite and their overall disdain for the rest of humanity. They thrived on excitement and weren't averse to doing whatever it took to achieve it.

After meeting with Debra and taking her merchandise onboard, as the plan now stood, they were to take their time cruising back to Seattle to rendezvous with Loren. It was originally a good plan.

Inadvertently, however, they had met Krivoi Margelese at a bar in Waikiki when they'd first arrived. After a few drinks and a long conversation, they learned of Margelese's eagerness to dispose of several items he had acquired from the Bishop Museum in the off chance he'd be able to turn them into cash to supplement his meager salary as a geology professor. They, being quick to seize a golden opportunity, had offered to help relieve him of his treasures, after first spending literally hours on the phone convincing Loren it was a good move. They'd managed to convince him and to guarantee a substantial additional commission for themselves.

Plans with their cash-hungry professor were moving along easily and would have been a perfect scheme were it not for Margelese's stupidity in attempting to rape one of his students on their yacht. His actions threatened exposure to not only Roland and Grey themselves but to their plans for meeting with Debra and ultimately to Loren himself. *Stupid man.* And to further compound his stupidity and their involvement, he heaved her off the stern.

Grey called the number Loren gave them as a contact number for Debra. She agreed to meet them at eight o'clock Sunday evening at the Ala Wai transient dock. She said she could pull her car adjacent to their yacht for an easy and quick transfer. Grey then called Loren and told him of their plan change but didn't explain why. They knew he would become hostile on learning the reason for the change in time and location, so Grey didn't bother to tell him.

They'd done all they planned to do for the moment. Walking down the gangplank onto the pier, they both waved to Chuck and headed for Biggies Lounge in Kailua.

Chapter Eighteen

Teri wove in and out of the parade of cars on the H-1 freeway as she headed toward the UH campus. Viane had returned to Oahu on Hawaiian Airlines's early morning flight, and Teri had met her at the terminal to shuttle her back to her dorm.

"Where do you suppose all these people come from?" Teri voiced into the air, expecting no reply. She disliked heavy traffic and was inclined to get a little grouchy when entangled in it. "I swear if this island gets any more cars weighing it down, it'll sink back into the ocean by the end of tomorrow. Why aren't they all at the beach or sitting at a desk someplace?"

In an attempt to get her mind off traffic, Teri glanced over at Viane who sat in quiet contemplation. "You're not thinking of going back into Margelese's class, are you?"

Viane was staring blankly at a Tamashiro Market truck taking up most of the view in front of them. She'd been thinking about that very thing. She shook her head. "No," she said, almost too forcefully. "If I never see that weasel for the rest of my life, I'll be happy. But the next time I do, I may have to rip his eyes out and shove them one at a time up his penis!"

Instantly feeling a blush take over, she looked at Teri, and they both burst into laughter. "Where'd *that* come from?" she said, wiping away a tear that was rolling down her cheek. "Guess I'm no longer the sweet girl Pops thought he raised. He'd be so hurt if he heard me say stuff like that." They laughed more.

"That man deserves everything he's going to get. I'm not too sure about you shoving his eyeballs up his penis, but it's a great picture—I really needed a good laugh. We have to nail him for what he did to you, and I'm going to help make sure it happens. I'll even buy the nails."

"I suppose I'll have to go back to his class sometime. It's too late to pick up another class, and I need the credits. Also, since he's head of the department, I wonder what damage he will do to my doctorate degree application?

"I guess I should report everything that happened to the dean. Margelese can't be allowed to get away with this, should he?" She looked at her friend for an answer.

"Wait a few days to report anything to the dean. From what Stone told me and the way he's feeling about all this, he's determined to get to the bottom of it quickly and make sure Margelese pays for all his sins. But getting back to your original idea, I'd be willing to hold Margelese down while you mangle whatever part of him you manage to get hold of."

They both laughed again, getting even more inventive about what they could do to various parts of him and, inevitably, men in general. Teri had long forgotten all the traffic hassles as she swung right off University Avenue onto

Dole Street and down the half mile to Frierdon Hall. She pulled next to the curb and stopped.

"Why'd you come back so soon, anyway?" Teri asked. "I thought you were going to stay in Hilo for a while."

"I was getting frustrated. Hilo's wonderful, but you know how laid-back it can be. It was like being in a beautiful flower garden without a sense of smell. I need to do something about this mess, Teri. I need to find those things that were taken from me if for no other reason than to put them back where they came from. Besides, Sonny and Pops were treating me like a piece of precious beach glass that had gotten damaged, and it was driving me bananas. I guess my days of being at home are fading behind me."

"You know what I'm thinking?" asked Teri. "I'm thinking I'd like to get a good look inside *Whiskey Sea*. There might be all kinds of incriminating evidence sitting around that'd string all three of those jerks together into a dead flower lei. Maybe I'll go over there and pay them a visit. I can pretend to be a yacht club greeter or something."

"Don't you dare go near that boat by yourself," exclaimed Viane, frightened to think her friend might really do that. She grabbed her friend's arm, which still held on to the steering wheel. "They're crooks, and they're dangerous, Teri. Like Stone said when all of us first talked, who knows what they would resort to if they become cornered? Besides, Margelese knows you, you'd be in instant danger. You better promise me, Teri, promise you won't take a chance like that." She tightened her grip.

"I promise I won't do anything that will put *watashi*, me, in danger. Okay?" Teri reached out with her free hand, placing it over Viane's, which still held on to her arm. "Thanks for being so concerned about me."

Viane shook her head in resignation as she climbed out of the car. Holding the door open and looking back inside, she said, "Your promise sounds pretty weak, but I'll take it. So are you going to see Stone anytime soon?"

"We've got a date tomorrow afternoon. He wants to take me to the Royal Hawaiian's poolside bar. He said they have great live Hawaiian music there to accompany the sunset. Romantic, huh?" She straightened up, an impish look replacing her smile. "We seem to be hitting it off, who'd have thought. He's very open and honest and seems willing to talk about things most guys I've dated wouldn't even think about. Besides, he's got a gentle, corny sense of humor; he's interesting, smart, and has a big boat. What's not to love? What's that line guys always laugh about, 'send picture of boat'?" She giggled self-consciously at her words as she drove away.

The urge proved irresistible. Teri found herself heading over the Pali Highway toward Kaneohe and the yacht club. She told herself she just wanted to *see* the boat, feel what her intuition picked up from viewing it.

As she reached the club, she saw that the security gate was open. *They're making it much too easy for me,* she thought, as she drove through the gate and parked. Heading around the clubhouse she walked out onto the pier that Viane had said the *Whiskey Sea* had been tied to. The only boat of any huge proportions was tied up broadside to the end of the pier. As she drew closer, she saw the name *Whiskey Sea* prominently displayed on a brass plaque above the gangplank. From its age and all the beautiful wood craftsmanship, she didn't need the nameplate to know this was the infamous yacht,

An elderly man wearing shorts, with bare feet, a tank top with clumps of hair finding release all around the openings, and a baseball cap that claimed to be Built Ford Tough covering what appeared to be a bald head, was busy polishing the chrome railing of his sail boat on the slip next to the *Whiskey Sea*. His dark tan spoke of many hours spent in the sun as he looked up and beamed a huge smile at her as she passed.

"Your friends left about an hour ago," he said, moving to the railing adjacent to the pier Teri was on, obviously intent on not letting a chance to talk with someone pass by, especially a beautiful woman. "I'm Chuck." He reached over the railing and offered his hand.

"Hi, Chuck," Teri replied, shaking his hand, intentionally not offering her name in return. She had a difficult time extracting her hand from Chuck's grip.

"They usually disappear this time of day," he offered. "I think they go into Kailua to Biggies Lounge from what someone told me. I saw them a couple weeks ago coming out of that place. They sure don't seem to have much aloha spirit in them, do they? Hey, I'm sorry," he said as an afterthought. "Sure hope my loud thinking don't offend you and your friends. They've been here for several weeks and have yet to invite me aboard. Even offered to give them a hand washing down yesterday after they returned from their three-day trip, but they didn't give the appearance of wanting any of my help. They close friends of yours? Say, do you want to come aboard my boat? I have some coffee already brewed down in the galley, and I can put a drop of something special in it for you if you know what I mean." He winked at Teri and turned to lead the way, obviously unconcerned about any answers she may have offered to his questions, fully expecting her to follow him down the finger pier to the short gangplank and onto his yacht.

"Thank you, but no," she said, loud enough to stop him from proceeding with the invitation any further, "and no, you're not offending me. They aren't friends; actually I've never met them. We've only talked by phone," she lied, realizing her newfound friend was probably the yacht club's walking gossip columnist. She would have to be careful. "There are a couple things I need to talk to them about, that's all." Teri turned to continue toward the yacht not too sure what she'd do with Chuck watching her.

"If it helps a'tall, they usually show up again around six, not that I stand around watching, you know, just notice things is all. If I see them, I'll give them a message for you. Have to be tomorrow though. I gotta get home to the wife pretty quick since it's her birthday and all. What'd you say your name was, missy?"

Teri turned back to him, ignoring his question but seeing an answer to her dilemma. "No, mahalo for your offer, though. Instead of waiting for them to come back, I think I'll catch them sometime during the week. I appreciate you offering, Chuck.

"Take care," she called back over her shoulder as she walked back along the pier toward the parking lot. "That's a beautiful boat you're working on."

"Hey, missy," the old man called out, "next time you come down to the pier, let me show you her insides—she's a beauty."

Teri gave him a wave over her shoulder as she moved out of earshot. She got into her car and waited, hoping that he'd been serious about leaving soon. There appeared to be just one way on or off the pier, and Chuck was obviously a very observant gatekeeper, so she waited. Ten minutes passed before she saw him slowly walking to an old green Ford pickup. He drove out the gate and turned left along Kaneohe Bay Drive and disappeared from sight.

If those guys won't be back till six, then I have some time to take a look around, she thought. She'd promised Viane not to get herself into trouble. *If they're not coming back for a few hours, there won't be any trouble to get into.*

She walked back down the pier and, with boldness, walked up the gangplank. *If you're going to do something stupid, do it with great intention, and no one will ever question your motive.* She'd read that once in a psychology textbook.

On deck, she turned right and arbitrarily opened a door, left unlocked to her pleasant surprise, and went in to begin her search.

"If you guys want another beer, now's the time. I'm closing up early. Got some damn funeral I gotta go to. Maybe a quick one for the road?"

"It's not even two o'clock!" Grey was irritated. The order of things was out of line with his plans, and that usually was a source of irritation for him. He didn't embrace changes as they tended to move him out of the control he generally planned on having, and that represented a threat to his perceived well-being.

"No, thanks, we're fine," replied Roland, taking the edge off the moment. They'd already had two. Turning to Grey, he said, "We need to go back to the yacht anyway and sterilize it just in case someone decides to get nosey. I don't trust what Margelese said about not telling anyone, and who knows what that girl might have said to friends about where she was going for dinner."

"I put the girl's relics into the vault. Nobody could find them, so we're safe as far as those two things go."

"Yeah, now let's make sure there are no telltale signs that either of them were there. We'll need to replace the missing life ring, and it should be one that has *Whiskey Sea* printed on it. If anyone were to look, that missing ring would be noticeable by its absence. Good thing it was the cheap blank one that went over the side with the girl. What about that rope we used on Margelese? Did you pull it off the bulkhead or out of the storage compartment?"

"I forget," said Gary becoming irritated again. "Things were happening quickly, so I grabbed the closest one. What difference does it make anyway? It's not like we buy tailor made rope." His irritation was digging into him.

"Might make a lot of difference if a piece of it is ever matched to some remnant we have onboard. Let's go back and get everything squared away." With that, Roland slid off the bar stool anticipating that Grey would follow him. He did.

They both walked out of Biggies and got into their rented Corvette parked along the side street. It was a short drive back to the yacht club. They pulled into the parking lot, parked, and headed around the clubhouse toward the pier.

Teri stood in what she imagined was the lounge Viane described. She stood staring at a beautiful jade carving of Buddha. She'd never imagined a carving with such intricate detail and so tall. *Must stand at least two feet—it's incredible!* She loved jade and always seemed to be drawn to it but knew she could never consider purchasing something of such enormous beauty.

She looked at her watch and realized she'd been there over an hour already and began feeling anxious. Quickly searching as much of the yacht as she could, she was careful to move as few things as she dared, for fear her presence would be detected. Feeling somehow cheated out of finding anything, she sat heavily on the leather couch, removing the leather pillow that was stacked behind her, absently tossing it aside—it rolled to the floor. She had been so certain she'd find something incriminating but realized that unless she actually found Viane's artifacts, everything else would surely have a reasonable explanation for being there. In frustration, she leapt up and went out the door and down the gangplank to the pier.

Just as she was passing Chuck's boat, she saw two men coming around the corner of the clubhouse heading toward her. Their size and general physical shape fit the description Viane had told her of the two men who owned the yacht. Swiftly moving onto a small finger pier beside Chuck's boat, she crouched down behind a wooden storage locker. *Even if it's not them,* she decided, *the mantra 'it's better to be safe than sorry' was appropriate right about now.*

They were talking softly as they approached, and she was able to pick up part of their conversation.

"At least we won't be bothered by Margelese any longer . . . need to come up with a plausible alibi in case him or that girl in the water . . . bodies . . . someplace. Those two are going to be missed, and the cops will be looking for answers."

Grey was more or less talking to himself, and Roland was simply listening. Grey was good with details, so Roland thought it best just to let him ramble on until he arrived at his own inevitable answer.

They strode up the boarding ramp onto the deck and into the lounge to pour a drink before getting to the detail work of inspecting and wiping away any telltale fingerprints that may be lingering. Grey sat down on the couch, swirling the ice around the deep rich amber color of the okolehao he'd just poured. He absently reached for the leather pillow to put behind his back but instead saw it on the floor partially shoved under the table. His questioning mind immediately started nagging him for answers as to why it was out of place: his world didn't tolerate *out of place.* He readily admitted to being anal about the order of things that affected his well-being. He reached down and grabbed it and stuffed it behind his back, his face etched in a concerned and displeased look as he settled back. *Why are things so out of order today? Something's not right.* He couldn't shake the unsettling feeling, and he didn't like it, and it did nothing to soften the irritation he brought back with him from the bar.

Teri stayed crouched behind the dock locker until she was certain she could leave without being noticed. She'd heard them mention "bodies" and "not being bothered by Margelese any longer" and "girl in the water." *Whose bodies, and why aren't those two men going to be bothered by Margelese anymore?* She knew they were referring to Viane when they mentioned the "girl in the water." Suddenly, she was very frightened and needed to get away from there as rapidly as possible.

The thought of calling Stone and telling him what she'd overheard crossed her mind, but she chose to drive to his house instead, since she was so close: she was in need of a comforting hug anyway. *I've got to give him this information in person,* she easily rationalized. She decided she liked having an excuse to show up at Stone's house, and this was a primo excuse. She quickly walked back to her car, relieved to be getting away from the club. She turned on to Kaneohe Bay Drive, making a right turn toward Kaneohe.

Chapter Nineteen

"You ou went on their yacht? By yourself?" he demanded, exasperation quite evident in his voice. "Are you just crazy, or do you have some desire you haven't explained about experiencing reincarnation firsthand? I mean . . . you know what I mean." He was agitated and almost shouting.

Stone stood in the kitchen leaning over the counter supporting himself by its edge, his head hanging down. The water he was heating for tea was already boiling, the kettle beside him whistling loudly. He straightened up and added a handful of *mamaki* leaves to a teapot and poured the scalding water on top of them. He was puzzled, unsure whether he was angry or just scared for Teri's safety. She was becoming much more important to him than he could ever have realized, and it was surprising him.

Teri sat at the dining room table, just a few feet from the kitchen. He was in her direct line of sight if she chose to look but she was absently staring through the huge windows that overlooked Kaneohe Bay, feeling a deep disappointment that the excitement of her adventure wasn't being shared. *After all, everything turned out okay, right?* Besides, she hadn't given him a chance to give her the hug she'd been so anxious to receive. She'd been so excited she'd gone straight into her story as soon as he had slid the entrance door open for her.

She wasn't sure what she'd expected but knew it wasn't this. Stone's reaction dampened the exhilaration she was feeling from her amateur detective work. And besides that, she hadn't even had a chance to tell him everything she'd heard—there hadn't been sufficient time before he went flying off the handle at her.

Her irritation immediately evaporated, though, as she looked his way and saw him standing in the kitchen, legs and arms crossed, hip against the countertop, grinning at her. Her body relaxed, and she was finally able to muster a smile.

"You rat! I thought you were being serious. I was about to get up and walk out."

"I was being kind of serious. So when are you going to tell me the rest of what you saw during your spy infiltration of private personal property where you shouldn't have been and could have gotten yourself tossed in the can?"

She let out a sigh, got up and joined him in the kitchen, taking up a similar nonchalant pose as he poured the tea into two mugs that were decorated with colorful images of bird of paradise flowers. She relayed the whole story from meeting Chuck to overhearing the men's hushed, but broken, conversation as they returned to their yacht and the fact that while she was onboard looking from room to room, she hadn't seen either of the pieces Viane had mentioned being taken from her.

"That boat is amazing," she exclaimed. "It reeks of money and is decorated like a page out of the *Museum Chronicles* magazine." She paused, looking around. "Speaking of nice places, your home is gorgeous. A full-on, floor-to-ceiling teakwood kitchen. That's quite amazing. When do I get the full nickel tour?"

"Just as soon as we finish our tea and talk." He carried the steaming mugs to the dining room table and set them down. Teri followed and sat back down where she had been sitting previously. Stone sat down beside her.

"It's somehow not too surprising you didn't see Viane's things. They'd be foolish to leave incriminating evidence lying in the open. The fact they talked about Viane being in the water along with someone else certainly implies full knowledge of what took place. Trouble is, nothing is verifiable, and it's all hearsay. There's nothing we can hold on to as actual evidence, and there's nothing tangible that Mike can grab on to either."

They sat in silence, sipping their tea, looking out over the calm water of the bay. Bert gave in to impulse and jumped up on the table, receiving an instant scolding. She moved on to the window ledge adjacent to the table where she stretched, yawned, and immediately took interest in two fishermen carrying throw nets as they walked along the seawall past the house.

"Bring your tea, and I'll give you the grand tour right now." He was very proud of all the work he'd done over the past few years remodeling and upgrading the entire house. They ended downstairs in the bedroom facing a tiled lanai with the calm water of the bay just beyond. Bert tagged along and was sitting by the sliding glass door looking out at nothing in particular.

"I think I better go talk with Mike and let him know what you found out. We could be doing more harm than good by playing secret detective, especially when bodies are being talked about. It might be blossoming into something bigger than we should be playing with—not that there are any 'shoulds' in life. Want to tag along?"

"I'd love to, but I'd better go to the campus and see what I can find out about Margelese. I need to know for sure if he's there or not, and I think Viane needs to know that as well before she barges into his office on Monday and goes off the deep end again, perhaps literally. I'll give you a call when I get there. Wait! If you're not home, I can't call you, can I?"

Stone's moan was audible. He knew what was coming.

"When are you going to get rid of your antisocial syndrome and get a cell phone like every other human being on this planet?" With a resigned smile, she stood looking at him. *I'm sure getting hooked on this guy, and I'm liking the water.* "I'll leave a message on your phone," she said as she headed out the door.

"Don't go climbing on any strange yachts along the way," Stone called out as the sliding glass door closed behind her.

Chapter Twenty

As she drove up the Pali Highway and over the mountains, Teri decided she'd swing past Frierdon Hall and see if Viane was there before checking in on Margelese in his campus office. Her dorm sat on the perimeter of the campus overlooking an old rock quarry. She could park there and easily walk the short distance to the POST Building from the dorm. POST, the Pacific Ocean Science and Technology building, housed the geology department as well as Margelese's office. She rang Viane's room, number 206, from the entry phone. She was there and buzzed the door for Teri to enter.

As she reached the top of the stairs and turned into the hallway, she saw Viane waiting outside the door of her room. Sweat pants, an old T-shirt, and a book dangling from her hand gave the direct impression she'd been in the midst of study. Teri's enthusiasm erupted as she approached. Ten feet away and walking faster, Teri, almost yelling, said, "Guess where I've been?"

They quickly embraced before Viane pulled away, keeping her hands on Teri's shoulders, as a concerned look replaced her smile. They were the same height and stood eye to eye.

Viane guessed the answer immediately. "I knew that promise of yours didn't have any meat on it. You went to the yacht club, didn't you? You made that promise just to appease me, didn't you?" Viane became visibly upset.

Teri's head dropped on her chest with a slow back and forth shake of her head, feeling totally demoralized. She had felt so great about her adventure, but apparently, she was the only one. She'd been on the hot seat with Stone, and now she was back on it with Viane.

She tentatively looked up. "Yes, I did," she said resignedly, "and I wish you could accept the fact that I'm doing what I can to help. I didn't promise you I wouldn't go aboard—I only promised that I wouldn't do anything that would put me in danger, and I didn't. I was perfectly safe, nobody was there, and I'd made sure."

"You actually *went* onboard?" Viane asked hysterically, her arms and hands thrown into the air like she was ready to catch a wayward basketball.

Taking hold of her friend's hands, Teri led her into the room and over to the bed. She sat down and pulled her friend down beside her. Keeping her hold of Viane's hands, Teri turned to face her.

"Yes, I went on the boat, but I knew beforehand the two men weren't there and wouldn't be back for a while." She proceeded to tell Viane about meeting Chuck.

She gave Viane a full account of what she saw and heard and what she didn't see, but leaving out the part about cutting her retreat off the boat almost too close to the men's return—more potentially muddy water. The important thing for her right then was the fact that she didn't need any additional grief from anyone because of her exploits.

"So they think I drowned! *Auwe*." Viane's thoughts momentarily reflected on her ordeal.

"I think that's a good thing," said Teri, bringing her friend's awareness back to the present. "As long as they think you're gone, it may make it easier to get to the bottom of everything and get your artifacts back. Let's make sure they keep thinking you're out of the picture. I told Stone, and he agrees that would be the best approach for us to take for now. The less all three of those men know then the better it is for us. Stone's on his way downtown to talk with his police friend to find out what we could be doing, if anything."

"What'd you think of that boat?" Viane asked softly like there were ears behind the wall. She was calming considerably, her curiosity taking over.

"It's amazing," Teri responded, her voice conspiratorially low to match Viane's. "It looks like a mini palace inside. I'm surprised two guys can do something like that. They must have a primo decorator and very full pockets. I wonder if they have wives or girlfriends? The place didn't 'feel' like it had any female energy in it, it is much too male oriented: too much leather and dark colors."

"If it wasn't for what happened," Viane added her viewpoint, "I could really appreciate the incredible decorating and those fantastic artifacts adorning the place. Those two do seem to know what they like. They didn't mention anyone else, but that doesn't mean anything. That boat's big enough, there may have been twenty-two other people someplace down below, and I'd never have known. Don't you wonder if all those things on display were also stolen? They must be filthy rich."

"What about that guy, Chuck, whom you met on the pier?" Viane asked. "Did he seem okay? Maybe they pay him to be their watchdog."

"I think Chuck is just Chuck," Teri volunteered. "I believe he may imagine himself as attractive bait for any cute wahine who happens to walk past, and maybe he was attractive once upon a time a few decades ago. I get the distinct impression he's harmless as long as you stay clear of his invitation to 'go below.'"

Teri rose from the edge of the bed and moved to the door. She turned to Viane before opening it. "I'm heading over to Margelese's office to see if he's actually there or not. I'll let you know what I find out." As an afterthought, Teri said, "I hope you won't go anywhere near him or even his class until this mess is resolved."

"Want me to promise?" Viane asked, rising off the bed looking at Teri with a smug smile on her lips. "I know how to make promises too, you know." She held out her right hand with fingers crossed but quickly lowered her eyes to the floor in embarrassment and shyly walked over to Teri and embraced her. "I'm sorry. Sarcasm doesn't work for me. I don't know why I said that. I know you're concerned for me, and I really appreciate it. I've got a lot of catch-up study to do since I missed a few days. I'm staying right here."

They hugged for a moment more.

"I'll let you know what I find out," said Teri as she moved through the doorway and let the door close behind her.

Teri wound her way through the quadrangle at the center of the original old buildings of the university, crowded with students enjoying the late afternoon class break, the sun scorching her shoulders and back as she headed for the building that housed the geology department. A hint of cooling mist graced her skin, giving a slight reprieve from the heat. She could see Manoa Valley above the campus shrouded in rain. It could be full sun everywhere else on the island, but Manoa Valley could be counted on to have a cloud halo above it and often an accompanying rainbow. The breeze moving down from the valley was bringing some of the moisture to combine with the sunshine, and true to nature, a vivid rainbow arched across the valley. Full double rainbows were not uncommon.

A student staffer behind the counter in the geology department's office told Teri that Margelese hadn't shown up the past four days. The girl volunteered that fortunately one of the other professors had been able to cover his classes.

"The dean's been unbearable," said the girl. "He charges out of his office every half hour asking if any of us have heard from Margelese yet. Apparently, the professor has never missed a single class before. The dean doesn't handle this kind of thing too well. He hates not knowing what's going on with his staff—*at all times*," she said, a lot of emphasis in her voice on the latter words.

"Thanks, Naomi," said Teri, reading the girl's name tag on the breast pocket of her blouse. "I hope he shows up soon," she lied as she turned and headed for the door.

In the hallway, Teri turned right and walked the length of the hallway and around a corner to the left and approached

Margelese's office door. It was locked. The in box attached to the wall beside the door was crammed with papers. A sign taped to the center of the antique opaque glass of the door read,

PLEASE STAY OUT UNLESS GIVEN
MY PERMISSION TO ENTER!

She called Stone's phone to leave a message, but he answered on the fourth ring just as the answering machine was about to pick up.

"I'm glad you're home, Stone." She felt a small pleasant tingle race up her spine at the sound of his voice. "You change your mind about going to town to see Mike?"

"It's such a nice afternoon I didn't want to spoil it by voluntarily putting myself into Friday rush-hour traffic. I called him, and we did the phone thing. Bert and I were out on the beach burying a dead puffer fish that washed up. Apparently, a novice fisherman speared it for some lame, unconscionable reason. Why do people feel the need to kill things?" He didn't expect an answer and didn't get one. "Where are you and what'd you find out?"

"I'm on the steps of the POST building. Get this"—she was excited—"Margelese hasn't been seen or heard from for the past four days. His in box looks like he hasn't been there for a year and a half, and his office door is locked. I'd really like to look inside, but there's no way anyone is going to give me a key."

"The detective in you is alive and well, obviously. What if I came over and met up with you in the campus cafeteria?

Maybe together we could figure out what to do next. Mike would like us to keep a very low profile on this. He still claims there's been no crime committed as far as he and HPD are concerned. I think, in truth, he admires what we're doing and is encouraging us to keep on it."

"Even my snooping on their boat?" Teri asked in amazement.

"Yacht . . . it's called a yacht," Stone corrected her.

"Okay, hotshot yacht person—their *yacht*," she returned his playful scolding.

"That's better," he quipped, "and remember, my yacht's a yacht as well, just in case I ever gain enough sympathy for you and ask you out for a ride on it. I didn't tell Mike the part about you breaking and entering. I'd hate to see him having to fill in a bunch of paperwork and putting out an APB for you. They'd be on their way to arrest you as we speak after they'd beaten your whereabouts out of me in the meantime. Your being on the yacht uninvited is something Mike would probably not want to know about anyway."

"Thanks for all your theatrics. I didn't realize you were such a ham. I'll give your name to the Diamond Head Theater group as a stand-in for their next comedy show. Now how about getting your handsome body over here? I'll be waiting for you in the cafeteria."

They both laughed as the call ended.

Chapter Twenty-One

Stone walked into the campus cafeteria and spotted Teri sitting at a table in the center of the room. Her back was toward the door, and she was talking to a young man standing beside the table, leaning slightly over her. He appeared to be a student judging by the number of books cradled in his arms, and he looked to be much more interested in Teri's shape than he was in listening to her words judging by his body language and where his eyes were focused. Stone thought of hanging back but instead went over and interrupted.

He moved close, practically standing on top of the student, and offered his hand. "Hi, I'm Stone, and you are?" Stone stood with his hand extended, a wide smile creasing the edges of his face as he looked down past the student and saw Teri's knowing look and slight shake of her head, as if to say, "Men and their need to mark territory."

Jarred from the reverie of his clandestine observations, the student quickly straightened up. He looked somewhat embarrassed and moved back a step to create needed space between himself and the newly arriving gust of wind. He reached for Stone's hand, but before he could speak, Teri said,

"Stone, this is Andrew. He was nice enough to want to keep me company."

Andrew shook Stone's hand.

"Hello, sir."

Stone disliked being called sir with a passion. It made the hair on his arms prickly.

Andrew moved his gaze back to Teri and winked at her, his confidence returning to its pre-Stone level. Stone saw the wink. "I hope I see you around campus again, Ms. White. Thanks for that tip about the book. I'm going to go over to the library right now and see if I can find it. I'll be there for a while in case you find some spare time on your hands." He gave Stone a brief glance and what Stone perceived as a smirk before turning and heading for the door.

"Andrew certainly seemed intent on hearing my thoughts on traditions and their value to family dynamics. He's studying sociology and remembered me from a private session I had with his family a few years ago." She smiled up at Stone and moved an empty chair closer and waited for him to take the hint and sit down. "You seem a little bristly this afternoon. Did you sit on a sharp *kuku* while driving over here, or is there something else rattling around up there in that big globe of yours?"

"Big globe," he exclaimed. "It looked to me like your young protégé was more intently interested in the counselor's globes than in the counselor's words. I couldn't help noticing the way he was hovering above you and gazing down the front of your blouse."

"Whoa, Stone, if I didn't know better, I'd think you were turning a light shade of green. That's flattering, I think, but I should warn you, I don't handle jealousy or possessiveness very well."

"Jealous . . ." Stone gave a small guilty-sounding laugh. "You can put your radar back into its holster. I'll have you know that J word isn't even in my vocabulary, nor is the other one. I was in fact, if you must know, more concerned for him, that's all. From his vantage point above you, if you'd stood up quickly, he may not have been able to get his nose out of the way of your head quickly enough."

"Are you saying I have a big head?"

"Oh, man. We're getting way too familiar with each other, and we've only dated once. Imagine how we'll be after several more."

"And just what makes you think there'll be any more?" she mused, slowly moving her arms closer to Stone who'd sat down and slid his chair close to Teri. Her lips edged into a sarcastic smile as she looked directly into his eyes. "You're so thoughtful, Stone, being so concerned about poor Andrew's nose and my oversized head."

Stone chuckled. His hands moved to cover each of Teri's and came to rest there. "It's piling up pretty deep in here all of a sudden. Let's go take a peek inside Margelese's office."

This late in the afternoon, no one was in the hallway of the geology building as they approached Margelese's door. With the intended purpose of snooping where they knew they had no right to be, anyone hanging around would definitely put a crimp in their plans. Stone moved closer to the door and pulled a credit card from the rubber banded cluster of cards and cash he called his wallet. He wasn't into carrying a normal wallet: he found them much too bulky in his pocket, and the money clips he'd used in the past always seemed to have short lifespans just as he was getting used to them. He liked the idea of using rubber bands that could be quickly and easily replaced—*and in a multitude of colors!*

He gently worked the locked door latch and glanced at Teri with a look of accomplishment, showing off as the locked door came free and drifted open. Her raised eyebrows and questioning look gave him pause.

"What? So I learned a few tricks along the way. Do you want to go in so we can close it before someone comes along, or were you planning to just stand there questioning my many talents?"

He was not so gently, albeit playfully, shoved into the room as Teri followed him in and quietly swung the door closed and relocked it. Stone could see her head shaking, but at least she was smiling.

Glancing about the room, it became glaringly obvious that if they were to find anything meaningful, it would be by the grace of a higher power, not by keen observation. Stone decided that a hiking trail guide would be very useful in finding his way around the room. Every conceivable flat spot and horizontal surface held seemingly helter-skelter stacks of paper and periodicals or boxes of assorted shapes and sizes piled high with rocks, measuring instruments, scales, and several pieces of equipment he couldn't even guess as to what function or use they were intended for.

"What are we looking for?" queried Teri with a puzzled expression.

Stone looked at her and laughed. "I was just thinking the same thing. I'm not sure what we can expect to find." He held her gaze for a few moments in thought. "I guess anything that would enlighten us on his whereabouts or Viane's artifacts. This is the part of detecting that's like a mind puzzle."

Being careful not to disturb anything, they both moved off in opposite directions around the perimeter of the room, dodging the odd pile of fallen rocks littering the floor. Stone moved to the desk set out from two windows overlooking a grassy area to the west of the building and sat in Margelese's chair, visually checking each of the top sheets of paper on the several stacks that cluttered the desk's surface. He cautiously raised some of the top papers and peered beneath. A thick notepad sat beside one of the stacks of paper in the only vacant space on the desk, a pen lay close by. He took it in with a glance and shifted his attention to a glut of notes lying scattered here and there and quickly read each one's general subject matter.

"I'm not seeing anything that might lead us anywhere." Stone straightened up and took in the room looking for anything obvious they might be missing. "This may be a total waste of time."

Teri had been peering in and around any box or pile of rocks she could get to without moving anything. She looked over at him after having surveyed a haphazardly placed stack of chaos on top of the filing cabinet. "I'm not seeing anything either, and I dread moving any of the rock piles for fear they'll come crashing down and end up carpeting more of the floor and bringing a rush of people. He could be hiding anything in behind some of this stuff, including himself if he was so inclined."

"I think you're right." Stone sat back and held Teri's gaze for a few seconds. "It's probably time for a refreshed view of things. We're starting to run around like chickens in a snake pit without a plan. I know the perfect spot to gain some perspective. John Dominis Restaurant may close its doors soon, so let's you and I head that way and discuss this whole adventure and figure out what we need to be doing and the direction we need to be doing it in. Besides, its happy hour, and we hadn't planned a date for tonight. You available?"

"Yes, but what happened to plans for sunsets and Hawaiian music at the Royal Hawaiian? Is your romantic side slipping, or would my big head block your view?"

"Memory like a steel trap—I'll bear that in mind. And I'll inform you my romantic side is firmly attached, thank you." Stone stood for a second, obviously and openly admiring her. "Too much going on to sit and absorb a sunset the way it needs to be absorbed. The lounge in John Dominis will be perfect for some problem solving. Moonlight and music at the Royal Hawaiian will have to wait for our next date."

"What next date are you thinking of?" Teri moved closer to Stone's side. "Could this be considered our second date then?"

"That depends," he answered. "If it was, would you say yes?" He interpreted her silent smile as a yes and took her hand and led her out the door, relocking it as they left.

"I'll follow you to your house so you can park your car. No sense leaving it here and having to come back for it later."

John Dominis is one of Honolulu's exclusive restaurants, sitting on the point of Kewalo Basin and the shoreline. A manmade saltwater stream bisects the dining area and the lounge. Fish of many varieties as well as a few spiny lobsters vie for space in the narrow, four-foot-wide, but lengthy waterway. One could point out a fish or lobster they wished to consume, if they were willing and able to pay the price, instead of accepting what the restaurant already had waiting on ice. The lounge area sits a few feet above and beside the stream. One could sip a cocktail and view the living, floor-style aquarium below, its blue lights making it appear a surrealistic, wandering stream separating the diners from the cocktail crowd. Alternatively, one could gaze out through the entire wall of glass making up one side of the dining room and admire the view of Kewalo Basin and the waters off Waikiki Beach. The illusion was completed by the short footbridge diners crossed to get to their reserved table.

The valet at John Dominis opened Teri's door for her, then quickly moved around to intercept Stone to hand him a parking tag. Inside, the left portion of the lounge consisted of booths adjacent to, and slightly elevated above, the flowing floor aquarium. Stone guided Teri onto a soft leather bench seat in one of the booths and moved in beside her, their thighs gently touching.

They were both feeling the effects of the first cocktail as the waitress collected their empty glasses and wet napkins as well as the empty plate that originally held stuffed pepperoncini, a house specialty. She placed new drinks and napkins in front of each of them. They had both ordered the same thing, a knowing look of recognition at how similar they were in what they liked—Stolichnaya on the rocks, with a twist of lemon peel. Stone leaned over Teri to look at a large *papio* as it swam past in the stream below. As he turned to make a comment to Teri, he found himself only inches away from her, their eyes locked on one another. Neither moved, both feeling the palpable energy. Stone moved an inch toward her and looked down at her lips and noticed them gently part, and he knew he couldn't stop, nor did he want to. They both closed the distance and softly pressed their lips against the others. Stone's hand moved to rest on her slim, firm waist. The kiss deepened as the tips of their tongues touched. The world and the place suddenly went silent as their thoughts fused into one. After a few long moments, they reluctantly pulled apart. Neither moved far nor looked away from the other.

"I certainly hope that wasn't just the Stoli talking." Teri's voice was soft, whispered. She didn't want to break the moment.

"I guess this would not be the time for me to kid around and blame it on the weather or the planets or some other bizarre circumstance," responded Stone, smiling, eyes remaining fixed on hers. "No, I don't think so," he answered himself, his words almost too soft to have been spoken, "and it certainly isn't the Stoli, although that probably lent itself to overcoming any hesitation." He moved toward her again, gently pulling her closer, his hand still held at her waist. They kissed again, both sensing the intentional, demanding, wanting desire their lips were creating.

"You realize," she whispered, "you've just stirred up a potential hornet's nest with these kisses, don't you?"

Stone backed away slightly so he could see her expression clearly. She saw a twinkle in his eyes. "I love a good hornet's nest," he whispered back. "However, right now we're probably making a lot of our fellow drinkers a little warm under their collars. Maybe we should finish our drinks and take a walk on a beach to cool down."

"I think the warmth being generated by our audience is somewhat lower down than their collars judging by the way so many people are trying to look everywhere else except toward us. Let's drive to Kapiolani Park and walk the sand into Waikiki. We can get ourselves lost among the tourists," responded Teri, "and I don't think I'll finish this drink. I may want to do something we'd both be sorry for later."

"Me too. I don't know about being sorry, but I know I wouldn't like to look back at tonight and know that vodka was the beginning of something incredible."

Teri wasn't surprised to feel his hand gently slip into hers as they rose to leave. She sensed his touch had a tender strength, and she enjoyed it. Their fingers intertwined so naturally she felt they'd been experiencing this closeness for a lifetime.

Carrying their shoes, they stepped off the sidewalk onto the sand by Sans Souci Beach at the Diamond Head end of Waikiki and slowly walked, still hand in hand toward the long stretch of beach fronting the Moana Surfrider and Royal Hawaiian hotels. They talked of the tourists they saw and the beauty of the luau torches bordering the hotels and the warm caress of the gentle ocean-scented breeze. Their bodies moved against each other as they walked. Stone guided Teri toward an elevated life guard stand, vacated for the night, and helped her up onto the shoulder-high bench seat.

Without words, they both fell into each other's arms, lips in passion devouring the others. Stone's right hand gently found its way to Teri's breast. Her breath caught with the touch of his caress. He could feel her fullness as her nipple hardened under his touch. He suddenly let go, broke their kiss, and sat back.

"If we don't stop now, I'm not so sure I'll be able to in another minute," breathed Stone, but bringing his lips back to hers and feeling her lips respond.

"Me too, Stone. Thank you for being the kind of man who is willing to honor what we may want to create together in the future. You are a most desirable man."

"Ahhh, mutual admiration. You are a most desirable woman."

"I think we have a mutual admiration thing going on. My admiration started the moment you opened your front door to me last Monday."

"Mine did too, actually," she said briefly lowering her gaze. "Even though I didn't trust or know the stranger standing at my door, my knees felt a little wobbly when I saw you," she said. "I wasn't going to allow myself to imagine there was any heightened meaning to you standing there."

"Let's walk back to the car, and I'll drive you home."

They were putting their shoes on after stepping off the sand onto the cement sidewalk when Stone abruptly stood up and roughly grasped Teri's upper arm.

"Auwe, Stone, what are you doing?" She saw the startled look on Stone's face but didn't try to pull her arm away. She reached her hand up and placed her palm on his cheek. "Are you all right?"

He looked down at her, now holding both her shoulders as if for support. "When we were in Margelese's office, I saw a notepad in the center of his desk that had indentations on it from a note he or someone wrote on the sheet above it. I didn't think much about it at that moment, but my mind's eye just brought an image into focus of the impression of a word. I think it said Whiskey, as in *Whiskey Sea*. We've got to go back and look at that notepad again," he exclaimed.

Chapter Twenty-Two

The sun was casting its brilliant array of colors over the few clouds that hovered over the horizon as Roland stepped out onto the deck, coffee in hand, hair still in disarray from a night's sleep. The soft breeze coming off the bay was warm on his bare chest. He'd seen no reason to put on anything else besides his bathing suit prior to coming up from below deck to make coffee. The sun's heat would soon be overpowering.

He stood soaking in the gentle peacefulness of the small yacht club harbor knowing it wouldn't take long before the scene changed to one of semi controlled chaos, like an army of ants suddenly discovering the body of a dead fly lying close by. The local weekend sailors would soon be preparing their boats for the club's weekly yacht races, and the youngsters would be getting their El Toros in shape for sailing. Everyone would be preparing themselves for the onslaught of preteens to invade the club for their weekly sailing lessons and relentless loud talking and laughter.

It was the perfect day from his point of view, as he thought of what promise the day held for them. The hub of activity on the water within the club's basin would carry the ideal amount of turmoil to distract people's attention away from awareness that *Whiskey Sea* was pulling out into the bay and disappearing from sight through the channel. His and Grey's plans were now in place: they would head straight for deep water and an eventual berth at the Ala Wai Boat Harbor on the opposite side of the island.

Roland heard Grey come out on deck behind him but didn't bother to pull his gaze away from a bird he'd spotted lazily floating on invisible air currents high above him, its wings unmoving, spread full as if being moved about the sky by some invisible giant.

"The locals call that an *iwa*, Roland. It's supposed to be a good indicator of where fishermen will find mahimahi." Grey joined Roland watching the bird become more distant as it slowly drifted out of sight to the north. "Can you imagine a bird with a wing span of almost ten feet? That's huge."

"How would you know something like that?" questioned Roland.

"Hey, give me some credit, Rol. I find things out. Who knows, someday we might be starving and knowing how and where to look for a mahimahi would be a good thing, right? So are you still okay heading for the Ala Wai when all these sail-type people are busy drifting around buoys?"

"Yeah, the quicker we do this whole deal with Debra and get away from the islands the better I'll feel. She claims to be more relaxed about connecting at the Ala Wai instead of here. She's a very nervous-sounding woman. Good thing she doesn't know about Margelese and that girl floating around, or she'd have a whole new set of reasons to be nervous."

"Let's grab a quick breakfast then start pulling in lines before Chuck shows up." Roland turned and headed for the door without waiting for Grey's reply.

"Oh sure, just because you've finished your coffee," grumbled Grey. He looked up, searching for the *iwa* but not finding it before moving to follow Roland through the open doorway. "Speaking of our Pier Gossip, what do you think we need to do about Chuck? He's always there and probably knows everything going on around here. I wouldn't be too surprised if he hadn't noticed Margelese and the girl coming onboard."

"Maybe what we have to do is get to the other side of the island, wait a day or two, then come back here and eliminate him. He could accidentally fall off his yacht and get wedged between it and the finger pier. I think we could manage that fairly easily."

"Things have gotten way too complicated on this gig ever since we met that Margelese character." Grey had followed Roland below deck into their galley. "Are you going to throw some breakfast together for both of us? I'm going to run through our checklist for leaving. We should be on the way by at least nine o'clock."

In the lounge, Grey went to the bar and manipulated a hidden lever under the bar top then watched as the mirrored section of the bookcase slowly glided open to reveal a large enclosure filled with shelves and cabinets. It was their vault: sound proof, light proof, and, best of all, well camouflaged from anyone who didn't know it was there. One look at its contents and structure, and it would not be too difficult for an unknowledgeable person to confuse it with a storage room from a museum—the shelves held what appeared to be an assortment of artifacts and treasures tightly crowded together. Anything susceptible to falling during movement at sea was securely fastened either to a shelf or to the wall. He spent a few moments inside, running a rag over the olivine stone and the wood carving sitting together on a shelf several inches above eye level between two intricately painted vases of ancient Chinese origin. *No fingerprints, thank you.* Wiping down all the items they collected in order to eliminate fingerprints that might be present was a safety procedure they had adopted as a routine precaution.

He took a cursory look around, then left the vault and went to the bar, maneuvering the lever and watching as the mirrored unit swung back in place. It had been a costly room to build but a very necessary one, considering the nature of what he and Roland were usually involved with. The room was so well hidden it would take a wall penetrating X-ray detector to find it.

He went back to his favorite couch and sat down, pulling the cushion into a comfortable spot behind his back. It was too early to make a drink, although he felt like doing so anyway. Something was bothering him.

"I'm curious, Rol." Grey looked towards Roland as the latter walked in the open door carrying a tray with steam rising from its contents. "Knowing how I feel about things out of place, especially these expensive leather cushions, why would you have left one of them lying on the floor yesterday? You know it's a good way to throw me off balance and make me irritable."

"What are you bitching about, Grey? We've both got too much at stake right now for me to be rubbing any of your blisters. Maybe you did that yourself." Although Roland knew that didn't happen, but he had no other response.

"When we came back from Biggies yesterday, this cushion was on the floor shoved under the table. Got there somehow, and I know I didn't do it." Grey's voice was edged with accusation.

"Don't look at me, pal. I know as well as you just how much we laid out for that whole set, and I know full well how overly protective you are of it."

Grey sat up and looked at Roland. He knew his buddy well enough to know there were never any lies between them, that they both took details, even minor ones, very seriously. It was the nature of the trust they had built up and the volatility of their business.

"Someone's been onboard," exclaimed Grey. "They must have been here when we went for a beer yesterday. This cushion was on the floor when I sat down here last night. I wonder if old Chuck isn't more of a snoop than we give him credit for being. Who else could it be?"

"That doesn't feel right. He's an unremitting gossip, but he doesn't affect me as a sneak. Unfortunately, there doesn't appear to be a lot of other choices. You sure about that cushion?"

Both just looked at one another, concerned expressions for several seconds. Roland knew better than to question Grey about anything—the man had a fish trap for a brain. He finally broke the short silence and, putting the tray of food on the bar, said, "Let's eat and then get our butts in gear and be on our way. We can be tied up at the Ala Wai harbor by late afternoon. Chuck's fate can wait for another day."

It was after four in the afternoon when they pulled up to the transit dock in the Ala Wai Harbor and secured the lines.

"Why don't we go grab a couple of beers across the street," said Roland. "Looks like a nice little bar nestled under the Chart House, and it has windows looking out this way so we can keep an eye on things over here."

With all their plans in order, they had nothing to do but wait for their rendezvous with Debra, and it couldn't get here soon enough for either of them.

Chapter Twenty-Three

Flashing red and blue lights from the caravan of police cruisers and emergency vehicles lit up the dark sky on a lonely stretch of highway above Napoopoo on Hawaii. Near midnight on a Friday usually found this stretch of Highway 11 a ribbon of dark solitude devoid of all but the occasional rodent or some other furry creature scurrying across the road. This particular night was not like that, though.

The intense, urgent field of strobe lights gave the area a Stephen King-novel atmosphere. The overabundance of police cars, ambulances, and a solitary fire truck was understandable in the circumstances that were unfolding. Nothing of this nature ever happened around this part of the island. The entire police community, some from as far away as Hilo, if they happened to be off duty, thought it important to be a part of the activities, just for future storytelling opportunities at the family dinner table.

A section of the rocky beach was cordoned off, keeping unnecessary bystanders, although very few in comparison to the number of *officials*, away from investigators as they went about their business, and it was a very messy business.

The body captured in a crevice of lava rock jutting out from the shore was not much more than a ragged mass of flesh and bone with little recognizable shape. Remains of what appeared to be tattered strips of clothing adhered to various parts of the pulpy form. The coroner and his coworkers were doing their best to gather together all the bits and pieces and add them to the existing contents of a large body bag. Two men in aloha shirts and long pants, looking very official, were talking with two teenagers, a boy and a girl, who had discovered the body during their quest for privacy. The investigators were engrossed in writing information in their notebooks, letting their flashlights illuminate what must have been the teens' identification cards.

The excitement was dwindling, and some of the cruisers, the fire truck, and the handful of bystanders began to drift away, heading back into their normal lives, although each individual knew that their *normal* had forever made a slight bend.

Now it was up to the coroner and the investigating detectives to solve the riddle of who it is that they just crumpled into the bag—and the ever-present questions of how the body of a once-living person found its way onto the sharp rocks in such unrecognizable condition and why something so heinous could have happened.

Chapter Twenty-Four

"Good morning, beautiful lady. Did you sleep well?"

"Stone? What are you doing calling me this early? How early is it anyway?" Teri's voice was filled with the softness of sleep. "It's pleasant waking to your voice." She relented with a sigh as she lay back into the comfort of soft pillows and a thick down comforter.

"Did I wake you? It's about six-thirty," he said, sheepishness noticeable in his voice.

"Oh no, Stone, that's much too early. Wake me up again in about an hour," she said but kept the phone receiver held close to her ear. "On second thought, did I ask you what you're doing up at this time?"

"Bert and I are sitting on the seawall, and the world feels full of love and wonder with recollections of last night. It's actually your fault that I had to call this early—my mind wouldn't let me think about anything else this morning. Even Bert knows something's not the same as it was yesterday. She's hovering much too close to me for normal."

"I wonder if cats feel any jealousy? They say animals have a sort of well-developed sense of energy vibrations, and I really believe they do. We'll know for sure if she pounces on me the next time I'm there."

"By the way, it's good to hear your voice as well this early in the morning. And as for Bert pouncing, I'm the one you should be concerned about doing the pouncing—Bert will just have to wait her turn."

"Promises, promises. Had any dreams about lifeguard stands lately?" she asked in a voice filled with a thousand unspoken words. "I think I did. I'm still feeling the warmth and fuzziness of it."

"Last night was quite incredible, angel." Teri smiled hearing the endearment—she couldn't stop herself. "Our lifeguard stand was very romantic. We probably need to revisit that one or find another to sit in sometime soon. Along with being consumed by thoughts of lifeguard stands, though, I haven't been able to let go of that notepad I saw in Margelese's office. We need to take another look at it as soon as possible, like today. Are you willing and able to accompany me for more snooping today?"

"Is that why you're up and calling me this early? How dull. I see we have some work to do with your romantic skills."

"My romantic skills are well, good, and honed to a fine point, as I have previously and recently explained, and some of which you may have observed last night, but *mahalo* for your thoughtful offer of helping me work on them. My skills already consist of a lot of candles and soft music with walks in the moonlight when the opportunity presents itself, along with occasional life guard stand closeness thrown in for good measure."

"Hum . . . that sounds interesting. We'll have to investigate further. Right now, though, you're not giving a girl a chance to get her beauty sleep. I'm both willing as well as able to do some further snooping with you but not quite this early. The campus gets pretty busy on Saturday mornings, so we'll need to wait until later this afternoon, if that's okay with you. Besides, I told Viane I'd stop by for lunch. She mentioned something about going to a small place on Beretania Street that caters to college kids. Sounds kind of funky. I think she called it Komo Mai. Ever heard of it?"

"Would you believe I used to eat there fairly frequently once upon a time? It's inexpensive and plentiful if you like hamburger on top of a mound of rice, all buried under brown gravy, with two slices of bread on the side. What more could a college kid ask for except heartburn, clogged arteries, and the distant anticipation of developing a spare tire around their middle? If I remember correctly, no one worried about that back then, and they probably still don't. Oh, and they had a great pinball machine, but I doubt if it's still there. It's been a lot of years since I last visited the place."

"Actually, your timing will work out quite well. I want to stop by the yacht club and check the lines on my yacht before we go anywhere."

"You mean that big overgrown boat you just bought?"

"Keep talking, lady. Your first invitation to come and enjoy it may involve just standing around on the pier with your hands in your pockets admiring it."

"At least they'll be *my* hands in my pockets."

Stone suddenly lost his train of thought and had to rid himself of the vision that materialized before he could get back to the intended purpose of his call. Also, he wasn't sure of a risk free response to her words and his vision.

"Let me pick you up about three, and we can go find out what that notepad had written on it. If you talk with Viane, let her know what we're doing and suggest she keep it close to her chest for the time being until there's more to know."

Teri's laugh was endearing and held promises. "I'll be waiting for you. Rub Bert's tummy for me."

"I'll tell her the tummy rub's from you, and if she scratches, we'll have our answer about the jealousy thing."

"Well, Bert," Stone said, running his fingertips slowly down Bert's back after disconnecting from Teri's phone, as the cat moved tighter against his leg. "I think that girl likes us. Go figure. I'm going to sit here and finish my coffee and then go see my boat—I mean my *yacht*." He pointed his index finger at the cat, saying, "You better never tell that woman I just called it a boat, or you'll be on bread and water for a week. In the meantime, you can spend your day trying to catch that crab you've been watching since we came out this morning." *Sure hope the neighbors aren't watching me have this discussion.*

"Just walk toward his office like you belong here. No one will question us being here unless we start looking like we don't," Stone whispered in Teri's ear as they walked along the hall to Margelese's office. Teri's nerves were on edge as she kept guiltily turning to look behind them even at Stone's reminders not to.

They had gotten to the POST building about three-thirty in the afternoon and found that the campus was fully engrossed in a craft fair that was obviously quite popular as attested to by the legions of people milling about. The quadrangle was packed with tents and booths, the smells from the various food vendors' delicacies filling the air. He realized he was quite hungry, having skipped breakfast. All the aromas were pulling at his willpower. He saw Teri carefully checking out the various menus as well, as they walked past.

It looked like a lot of the students in the arts department were involved in raising money for a charity called Parents of Autistic Children, or so claimed several large banners. There were people everywhere, including those swarming through the POST building. Teri and Stone worked their way through groups of students standing in the hall, and together breathed a collective sigh of relief as they rounded the corner to find the small corridor in front of Margelese's office deserted.

Stone quickly unlocked the door. They went in and closed it behind them. Everything appeared exactly as it had the day before—even more chaotic than he remembered if that were possible without anyone else having been there.

They moved directly to the desk, and Stone sat down and grabbed a pencil. He hunched over the desktop and began running the lead lightly over the pad that he had glanced at briefly on their previous visit. Teri stood behind him, hands resting on his shoulders.

The impression of words from the earlier message began to show in the pencil carbon.

Whiskey 7p both

x2

750k—1500!

"I'm guessing this was a reminder note." Stone held the pad upright. Teri was close to his side looking at words and numbers showing on the pad. "You ever write the odd word on paper while talking on the phone?" he asked her. Without waiting for an answer, he continued, "I do it all the time—sort of an unconscious reminder of the important parts of a conversation."

"I do that as well," she admitted, "and then a few days later see it again and have no clue whatsoever what it referred to."

"I'm guessing Margelese was talking with Roland and Grey while he wrote this. Look at this." He used the pencil to pinpoint the words on the pad as he narrated a conversation that might have taken place. "Viane and Margelese to be onboard *Whiskey Sea* at 7:00 p.m. The *both* could refer to either both he and Viane or both of Viane's artifacts. No idea what the 750k would mean nor why it's circled so many times, along with the 2x and the 1500, except for the fact that 750 times two is 1500."

He was on a roll, and Teri didn't want to interrupt him to explain what Viane had said.

"They must relate to one another," he continued, noticing Teri rapt interest in his interpretation. "They're obviously important for Margelese to continuously circle both of them unless he was just doodling, but I don't think he was. It doesn't feel that way. He did this intentionally—with importance implied. Look"—Stone pointed at the circle with the pencil—"the circles he made are so pronounced he almost cut through the note paper."

"From what Viane told us"—Teri grabbed Stone's arm in her excitement—"Margelese was to collect money in exchange for her artifacts. Maybe it means dollars—$750 thousand? That's a lot of money for what Viane found, even sight unseen." Stone put the note flat on the desk and sat back against the chair. "We're missing something. I don't think we're getting the full implication of what this note conveys."

Teri half sat, half stood, resting on the edge of the desk facing Stone who was still seated in Margelese's chair. "The name of the boat is evident," said Teri, voice low and quiet—thinking. "The 7p I'm betting is a time to be someplace, like the time to arrive onboard for dinner?"

"I think you're right. Let's get out of here. We can go someplace quiet and figure it out." Stone picked up the pad, pocketed it along with the pencil, and headed for the door with Teri close behind.

"You're taking the whole pad?" she asked, surprised.

"It's easier this way." He momentarily felt guilty as he hesitated and looked at her before closing and locking the door.

They rounded the corner in the hallway and found themselves directly in the path of four men walking their way with a young woman trailing behind. Stone noticed one was a Honolulu PD officer in uniform. Two others, in dark suits, were such massive beings they were living reminders of men who populated the once-popular-now-defunct HPD Metro Squad. Stone had personal history in a memory involving an incident with the Metro Squad as a teenager—it wasn't a good one. He also knew from previous experience that these two men were likely detectives. The fourth man was apparently a campus security guard. All wore dark glasses directly out of the same catalog that made it impossible to see where they were looking or gain indication if their looks were accusatory or not. Teri and Stone both knew, though, the group was looking directly at them. *Is guilt showing on our faces?* They pressed against the corridor wall to let the group pass since it didn't look like any of them were inclined to move out of the way.

The girl with them was quite young, probably a student, and looked as if she was about to cry or perhaps had just stopped. The group turned the corner and headed down the hallway that Stone and Teri had just left.

They turned around and discretely followed the group back around the corner and watched as they stopped in front of Margelese's door. The girl separated a key from a ring she had in her hand and unlocked the door. The men filed past her and closed the door, leaving her standing in the hallway.

"What's happening?" Teri queried the girl as she and Stone walked up beside her. Teri saw Naomi, the clerk who'd helped her the day before in the office, turn toward them.

"I don't know. I think something terrible has happened to Dr. Margelese." She was close to tears. "All I know is one of those big detectives mentioned a court order to open Dr. Margelese's office to search for evidence. I heard them mention the coroner and that he was waiting for some kind of information."

"Whatever's happened, I have this feeling it all fits together somehow," said Stone, directing his comments at Teri. "We need to find out what's been taking place. I've got to talk to Mike."

They left Naomi standing by the door and quickly walked out of the building and headed for Stone's car that was parked along Date Street.

"Let's go back to your place," said Stone, "and I can call Mike and see if he knows anything."

"Why don't we go over there and sit in the grass under the shade of the tree?" Teri was pointing in the direction of a banyan tree in the quadrangle, green grass beneath it with its implied coolness.

Stone looked at her with surprised disbelief.

"Don't look at me like that," she quipped, seeing his expression as she turned and headed for the tree. "You can use my cell phone, and we can save the gas." She lay down, spread herself out like a snow angel, and gave a soft sigh as her body relaxed into the soft, cool grass.

Stone closed the cell phone and leaned back against the tree. Teri remained as she had first settled, lying back watching the clouds move slowly across the sky between the banyan's large limbs.

"Guess you heard most of that." He handed the small phone to Teri.

"Yeah. When does he expect to have any details about the identity of the body? I wonder what led them to think it was Margelese in the first place? What a strange thing to happen. I don't recall ever hearing of a body washing up on any beach in the islands. Do you remember hearing of any? For an island community like ours, it's a rarity."

"That's the thing. Mike said they have no missing person report at the moment, but something must have shown up to tie Margelese to the body. They'd have to know something positive to initiate that warrant to open his office. For some reason, Mike's keeping the information to himself for the time being."

Stone moved closer to Teri and bent down, kissing her gently, followed by a second, more intense and lasting one. He sat up and nervously looked around.

"This is probably not the best place to be overly intimate."

"Are you kidding?" she teased. "Take a look at the students gathered in pairs scattered all over the place and tell me anyone will notice."

"You're right," he said and bent down and kissed her again, then sat back up. "Let's save the best for later. My mind's too active at the moment to get very romantic."

"Pity," she responded as she looked up at him and winked before returning her gaze to the clouds.

"Why don't we go down to the Chart House so we can figure all this out? You could call Viane and have her meet us there, and we can bring her up to speed on the latest happenings."

"Why don't I call her right now, and if she's available, we could swing by and pick her up. Her dorm is just two minutes away from here."

Stone gave her a comical look. "Now why didn't I think of that?"

"You'll just have to leave the important stuff to me, sweetie," she replied with mock authority in her voice.

"I can see part of my future very clearly," mused Stone in a mocking tone. "I'm going to need to think through details before opening my mouth and emitting sounds." Stone smiled as Teri reached up, grabbed his shirt collar, and pulled him down for a quick kiss, which ended up being anything but quick.

"Maybe later we could find another lonely lifeguard stand to occupy." Teri winked at him, and he knew he was fully hooked.

They drove to the dorm and picked up Viane.

Chapter Twenty-Five

The three of them found a table in the Chart House adjacent to the railing and sat down. It was an ideal vantage point to enjoy the harbor and the Hawaiian Village Lagoon in the near distance. It was also a spot conducive to talking freely about Viane's situation without being overheard. A waiter came over and took their orders, and since each wanted wine, Stone took the opportunity to order a bottle of Columbia Crest Sauvignon Blanc, a wine he'd recently discovered and enjoyed.

They talked about Viane's studies and the enjoyment she was gaining from her chosen endeavor with geology. All three had become very relaxed with each other in the short time since they'd met.

They were quiet for a few moments, enjoying not having to say anything but simply appreciating being together. Stone broke the quiet, and he and Teri took turns telling Viane what they knew about her harrowing experience and also what they suspected. When Stone mentioned the note with the heavy circling around the 2x, the 750k, and the 1500, Viane got visibly animated.

"My gosh," she exclaimed. "When I was in Margelese's office last Monday and he invited me to go dine on his friends' boat, he seemed to be very nervous. I thought it was because he felt awkward inviting a student to go to dinner with him. He was playing with a pen and kept going back over and over a circle he'd drawn on a small slip of paper. There were some words and numbers on it, but I didn't bother attempting to read them at the time. I didn't think it was important to what he and I were discussing. Do you suppose that's the note in your pencil tracing?"

Stone pulled the pad from his shirt pocket.

"You took the whole pad?" she queried. "Isn't he going to miss it?"

"Never mind that." He glanced briefly at Teri. "There was a big pile of them—nobody will miss this one." Attempting to bring the conversation back on track, he asked her, "With all the scribbling on it, does it look familiar?" He held it at an angle he figured she'd have observed it.

"Yes," exclaimed Viane eagerly. "That's the note he was playing with. I'm absolutely positive. What do you think the figures that are circled mean?"

"We think they refer to a dollar figure he was being promised in return for the two items you took onboard with you or it may be a total figure that they'd sell them for and use to cut Margelese a commission. It's difficult to know exactly. I bet the 2x refers to both of your artifacts. $750k must denote thousands for one, but if he can get you to bring both, it'd be $1500k, or a million and a half."

The impact of that number stunned them into silence until Stone spoke again.

"That must signify their valuation, not what Margelese's cut would be. If it is his cut, then I'm definitely in the wrong business. Was there any discussion between you about bringing just one of the artifacts?"

"Actually, come to think of it, he was very insistent that I bring both pieces. Originally, I had only wanted to bring the carving because Margelese had made me nervous at his consuming interest in the value of the olivine and not in the overall find, so I had planned to leave the gem at the dorm. He told me both pieces *had* to be kept together."

"He must have had full intention of collecting on both of them at your expense," Stone added his impression. "That's premeditated. If that's not his body they found partly lunched on, he could be put in prison for a very long time when he finally shows up."

"What body are you talking about?" questioned Viane.

Teri looked at Stone, realizing they hadn't told her about the body washed on shore on the Big Island.

"There's apparently some reason they think a body that was found last night in Napoopoo may be that of Margelese," explained Stone. "Mike hasn't confirmed it yet, but we overheard something at the university that points in that direction."

"That would be such a hard thing to accept," offered Viane. "Even if he is a despicable excuse for a human being, he is, was, my friend once upon a time."

"Would you rather we didn't talk about any more of this right now until we find out for sure?" asked Stone.

"Yes, Viane, we could get together sometime tomorrow after we know for sure if . . ." Teri stopped midsentence. A startled expression appeared on Viane's face as she stared out over the railing to the harbor below. Teri looked to see what had caught her attention and reached for Stone's arm, indicating that he should turn around and look as well.

"That's the *Whiskey Sea*," Viane blurted the words as if she was seeing an impossible image appear.

All three watched as the *Whiskey Sea* slowly maneuvered, bringing the starboard side against the railing. Bumpers already hung over her side cushioned the soft impact against the side of the transient dock. A large muscular man jumped on to the dock from amid ship, dragging the spring line behind him and fastening it tight to the dock cleat.

"And that's the guy named Roland!" cried Viane, quickly rising from her chair.

"This is a little bizarre," said Stone as he watched the docking take place.

Viane was moving away from the table, aiming for the stairs when Teri took hold of her arm before she could gain much distance from the table.

"Viane, where are you going? You're not thinking of going down to the yacht, are you?"

She looked down at her friend, her face a mask of anger. "Darn right I am. I'm going to demand they return the two things they took from me. If they refuse, I'm going to call the police. Why shouldn't I? Those things are mine, and they took them without my permission, and I want them back." Her anger was morphing into a look of frustration.

"You can't do that, Viane," Stone spoke up. "They may simply deny everything, which would lead to an argument. Arguing with them would be like arguing with an umbrella stand, it'll get you nowhere and may end up driving them into hiding. Besides, remember they still think you're floating around in the middle of the channel collecting seaweed. Who knows what they'd do if they knew you were alive and well and could testify against them."

"But we've got to do something!" Viane's frustration appeared on the verge of tears. "We can't just let them do this." She relented and sat down, looking from Teri to Stone for direction.

"As long as they're anchored there, we know exactly where they are. I think our best course of action is to contact the Harbormaster and see how long they've booked the transient dock and what, if any, the float plan they may have filed. We should also let Mike know where they are now as well. Besides, he may have recent news for us on Margelese." He self-consciously looked at Teri who had already taken her cell phone from her purse and, with arm outstretched, was offering it to him.

He took it and walked a short distance away from the girls and other patrons. He returned a few moments later.

"Mike's not on duty right now. He'll be back on at seven." He looked at Viane for a moment, and then turned to Teri. "Let's finish our wine and then take Viane back to her dorm. After that, you and I can see about finding Mike. He lives in Kaneohe not too far from my house, so we can swing past and see if he's at home."

The three of them began to stand when an Oriental woman suddenly appeared beside the table, forcing them back into their seats by her mere presence. She looked as though she could be an attractive woman in her mid to late thirties, but the accusing expression crumpling her face diffused any apparent beauty. She was quite slender, with the body type of someone who worked out in a health club and was serious about it. Her eyes implied a sense of alertness, like a cat watching its prey, anticipating the need to move quickly. She was dressed casually, giving the air of a tourist who had enough wealth to make "casual" into something of a statement.

"I happened to see you observing that boat out there." She glanced at Stone, Teri, and then Viane in turn, taking time to register their reactions but saw nothing but a slight frown emanating from the younger woman. She was pointing to *Whiskey Sea*. "Do you know anything about it?" She quickly continued, not waiting for any further response—an action that generally overrides people's ability to think of any response to the initial question. "I'm somewhat of a boat fancier and have been admiring it. Do any of you happen to be associated with it in some manner?" She scanned each face once again, this time anticipating a reply, her features remaining accusatory.

"No," said Stone. *It isn't really a lie, is it?* "I just bought a new yacht, so we've been caught up admiring yachts in general ever since, and it's a spectacular beauty worth admiring. Can I ask why you're asking? Are you familiar with its owners?" It was a polite conversational thing to say, he thought. Besides, her words and body language implied some meaning he was unable to grasp.

Abruptly, she turned away from them and voiced an emphatic no in reply as she hurriedly strode away. She realized she'd get nothing more from them and didn't want to remain face-to-face any longer than she already had. She knew it may have been a mistake to approach them in the first place.

"That was strange," said Teri, looking at Stone with a puzzled expression. They watched the woman disappear around a corner leading into the restaurant's dining area.

"She's certainly no boat fancier," Stone remarked with a slow shake of his head. "Anyone who calls a yacht like *Whiskey Sea* a boat can't know what they're talking about."

"Oh, Stone. Give it a rest already." Teri stood to leave. Viane and Stone followed, smiling at one another.

"That woman's not being upfront with us. I'm betting there's a good story hidden there someplace that we'll probably never learn about."

As they descended the stairs to ground level and walked a short distance to Stone's car, he turned to Viane. "I know you're more anxious that any of us to see this through and get your artifacts back, but let me talk to Mike first. As soon as I do, one of us will call you and outline a plan. You'll be included in whatever takes place, so don't do anything rash, okay? Just be patient and wait for a call from me or Teri."

"It'll be difficult to sit at the dorm and do nothing, but I'll try. Please, please, *please* call me as soon as you know something—anything."

They climbed into Stone's car for the short trip to Viane's dorm.

Debra Shinn watched from her vantage point in the restaurant as the man and both women left the Chart House and walked down the street to a car. The younger woman kept glancing back at *Whiskey Sea*. Her intuition was confirming that something was out of place, but she had no idea what it was or just how concerned she should be about it for her own safety. She was upset for having potentially exposed herself like that to strangers. The line of work she was involved in was getting tiresome; she could feel herself losing her edge.

Teri and Stone drove past Mike's quiet and presently unoccupied house after delivering Viane to her dorm. Stone knew that Mike was a movie addict and, this being Saturday night, figured he had a hot date and was probably at one of the movies in Kailua. They decided to head for Kaneohe Yacht Club and sit on *Wailana Sunrise* and enjoy more wine while they waited for Mike to show and return their call.

Chapter Twenty-Six

Viane paced to the end of the hall fronting her dorm room and turned around. Unable to calm herself, she paced back to the opposite end for the umpteenth time. She'd been doing this unsettled two-way pacing since Stone and Teri had brought her back from the Chart House. She'd much prefer to be in the privacy of her room surrounded by her familiar collection of "stuff," but pacing in the confined space of her room wasn't an option. She had discovered that after accidentally bumping into a stack of books she'd organized earlier in the day. She dreaded the thought of eventually having to restack the mess and reestablish the sequence she'd worked so diligently to establish.

Knowing that *Whiskey Sea* was so close and her artifacts—*her artifacts!*—were so close by kept agitating her, stirring an unspoken demand to do something about it. If she could find a way without being seen, she knew she could climb onboard, retrieve her things, and be gone before anyone knew the difference. Unfortunately, she didn't have a car, so getting to the Ala Wai presented a challenge, and calling Teri for a ride was certainly out of the question:

she'd be going against what Teri and Stone had asked of her. She stopped pacing in front of her friend Ann's room. She'd heard music through the door and knew Ann was busy studying. Ann enjoyed listening to Hawaiian music playing in the background as she studied. She claimed it helped her concentrate while soothing her spirit. Viane was never able to fully grasp the truth of that. She did grasp the fact that it didn't do a thing to improve her friend's grades.

She knocked on the door, and it flew open almost immediately.

"Viane," Ann exclaimed, her too-black hair stacked on top of her head in an unkempt pile and held there, most of it at least, with what appeared to be a purple rubber band—the kind supermarkets use to hold broccoli in bunches. A pencil was skewered into the hair pile. "I was just about to like come to your room to like see what you were up to. I like heard bumping around in there like ages ago. You want to like go to the mall and hang out?"

"That'd be rad, Ann. We could spend some time checking out the new surf shop that just opened, but would you mind waiting until tomorrow? A friend is christening his yacht at the Kaneohe Yacht Club in the morning. You and I could go there and sip some champagne, then head for Ala Moana Shopping Center afterward."

"Like wow, Viv. A yacht, huh? Like I'm there." Ann was of the unvoiced opinion that her friend's name was apparently too *different* so, from the onset of their friendship, she had shortened Viane to Viv, a name Viane didn't care for but never had the heart to mention.

"Right now, though," continued Viane, "I was hoping you'd give me a ride down to the Ilikai Hotel. I have something I need to do but haven't a way to get there except by taxi or walk."

"So like what do you need to do down there, and can I like do it with you?"

"You wouldn't want to, Ann. This is family stuff. I'm meeting my brother," Viane lied. "They just couldn't get here to pick me up but said they'll be able to bring me back." Actually, Viane hadn't even thought about getting back to the dorm afterward and was coming up blank, other than walking. It was a few miles, but the evening would be cooled off by then; and if she was able to get her hands on what she was going for, she'd be able to walk clear around the island and feel great about it.

Ann sensed her friend was not being totally upfront with her. The words weren't matching her body language. *People never like give me credit for like knowing stuff,* she thought. She considered Viv her best friend, so decided to let it slide. *That's what best friends do, right?* "So okay then, like when do you need to like be there?"

"You're so great, Ann. *Mahalo a nui.* We could leave right now if you're okay with that."

"Like sure, let's do it. Besides, this studying thing is like getting to me, and I like need a break." Ann closed the door behind them as they both walked toward the stairwell. "A yacht, huh? How do you like meet a guy with a yacht?"

Ann turned left off Ala Wai Boulevard onto Enid Road and made a U-turn into the drop off area for the Ilikai Hotel.

Viane looked back and waved to Ann as she rode the escalator up to the lobby level. When she saw her friend pull away from the curb, she rode back down and headed for the Ala Wai harbor and the *Whiskey Sea* just a few hundred yards away.

The edge of a cement planter along the sidewalk offered a well-placed spot to sit and observe the boat for a few moments. She wanted to see if there was any sign of life onboard before executing her next move.

Her patience with sitting and watching, though, ran out quickly. She was too anxious to get on with it. She walked across the street and moved close to the side of the yacht. Looking around and not seeing anyone, she leaned in and placed her ear against the hull and listened. There were no sounds to hear except the low hum of a bilge pump someplace in its bowels.

She walked to the foot of the gangplank and, with little hesitation, quickly climbed the gentle rise to the deck. *This is really dumb*, she thought, stepping off the gangplank onto the aft end of the starboard deck with the sudden realization she was on the same deck and at the same spot she had been just a week ago. She had learned so much about people and life in general since that day. She stood, silent, listening, afraid to take another step; but instinctively, she knew she had to move: standing on deck left her too exposed to anyone walking past. She knew the area was popular for both tourist sightseers and other boat owners out for a stroll, so she moved quickly and silently, padding along the deck on her rubber soled sneakers. *Sneakers—what an appropriate name for them.* Turning the handle that would take her into the now-familiar lounge, an unexpected shock coursed through her as the door refused to open to her insistent pulls and shoves. Locked! It was a possibility she'd failed to consider.

She quietly strode around to the port side and tried the door on the opposite side of the same room and breathed a sigh of relief as it swung open. She moved into the room and quietly closed the door behind her. The sun had just set, but there was still sufficient light coming in through the curtained windows with help from the deck lights that showered the passageways.

The lounge was very familiar because of her first visit, and it presented an odd feeling—a foreboding energy, almost palpable, challenging her senses and elevating her nervousness. She knew she shouldn't be here. Everything in the room seemed to be *staring* at her. When she suddenly caught her own eyes curiously looking at her, she came to the very edge of a scream. "Damn mirrors," she muttered to herself.

She looked around quickly, anxious to be back out on deck. The room was eerily quiet and smelled of bar room whiskey, old leather, and the musty odor of antiques.

Now that she was here, though, she wasn't entirely sure what to do next. *I obviously didn't think out this adventure very carefully.* Her olivine stone and wood carving weren't sitting on any of the shelves, bar top, or tables that she could see. She really hadn't thought they would be but had held a distant unacknowledged hope nonetheless.

Standing still for a moment, she took in all the beautiful artifacts decorating the room. She'd noticed them the first time she'd been here with Margelese but had been too excited to thoroughly absorb their richness. She gently laid her hand on a tall jade carving of Buddha, feeling the coolness of the stone against her palm, recognizing it as the one Teri spoke of admiring on her spy mission. *That must carry with it a wonderful story to be told—it's so beautiful.* She pulled herself to the task and began opening the multitude of cabinets along the wall but found nothing unusual in any of them except more very-expensive-looking antiques. She looked at all the books stacked here and there and at the nearly full wall of shelves but saw nothing she had hoped to see.

She moved out onto the port deck and quickly but quietly moved toward the stern, opening the door into the adjacent room. She entered and closed the door as noiselessly as she could. Standing in the center surveying her surroundings, she again failed to see what she so desperately wanted to find. By the appearance of things, it must be a mapping room: Grey hadn't included this room in the tour he'd given her. Stack upon stack of rolled charts filled shelves on both sides of a large flat table centering the room.

As she was about to leave to search another room, something odd dawned on her: she wasn't sure what it was, but a puzzle started forming in her thoughts. The pieces weren't fitting together, though, and it made her very uneasy. She figured her discomfort came from the paranoia of knowing that what she was involved in was very wrong. *Not to mention illegal as all, get out!* She put her hand up against the wall as a brace to allow herself to pull the door open as quietly as she could. As the door opened, a piece of the puzzle fell into place. The wall her hand was on was adjacent to the door, yet she had walked several steps on the deck to get to the door from the other room. *Did I miss a door?* She went out on deck. There was no other door. The lounge's door had also been right next to this same wall but many feet away. How could she have walked so far between doors, yet the walls of each room were adjacent to each respective door? *There's a large space between these two rooms yet no obvious way in,* she thought. *That's what the puzzle is.*

She went forward into the lounge once again. The wall with all the bookshelves was indeed next to the door just as she suspected.

Her excitement began to peak as she softly tapped her fist against exposed parts of the bookshelf's backboard, listening to detect any hollow sound but found it too solidly built to get any substantive results. Short of pulling all the books down, Viane felt a rise of frustration trying to decide how she could find out what was behind the wall of books.

She returned to the map room and its adjacent wall of books and charts. "Auwe! Did these guys also rob a bookstore?" she exclaimed in a loud whispering voice to the wall in front of her. "How can two guys read so darn many books anyway?" She was looking at herself in a narrow floor-to-ceiling mirror that bisected the wall of shelves. Her long hair looked like a tangled mass of fish line. *I'm in desperate need of a brush.* She couldn't help straightening her clothing and running her hands through her hair a few times. *I look the part of a criminal, so I might just as well leave it alone and concentrate on finding what I'm here for.*

She turned from the mirror and headed for the door, unsure of where to look next. As she pulled the door open, she felt the yacht dip ever so slightly. Attributing it to the fact she was on a boat, she gave it no further consideration and moved forward to the lounge once again, opened the door, and stepped in.

The Harbor Pub had filled to overflowing with the usual Saturday evening regulars, and the noise had increased to a level at which Grey and Roland found they were having difficulty hearing the other speak. Knowing one another so well, they didn't need to ask as they both downed the remains of their beer, left cash lying on the bar, and walked out, heading back to their yacht a few hundred yards away.

They walked the incline of the gangplank to the deck and, being creatures of habit following their unspoken ritual, headed for the lounge and the bar it contained. Grey unlocked the door and swung it open, coming face-to-face with a ghost.

Chapter Twenty-Seven

Roland and Grey entered the lounge just as Viane came in through the opposite door. Their intention was to mix another drink and spend the remainder of the evening out on the deck. They had purposely sat in a location in the bar across the street that had given them an unobstructed view of their yacht, yet they had failed to see Viane climb the gangplank and move about the deck, and they knew exactly why: they had become preoccupied with the bartender's attractiveness and were taken in by her charms once, apparently, too often.

The three stood staring at one another for a hint of a second before Viane turned to flee out the door she had just entered. Grey, however, with ultrafast reflexes, was quicker to react and managed to grab her arm in a vise grip before she was able to move beyond the doorway. Roland responded a split second later and grabbed her other arm.

It became a bigger struggle, though, to wrestle her to the floor than they would have believed possible: she was strong, and they were very tipsy. They finally managed to subdue her and bound her arms and legs before placing a dust rag that had been within Roland's easy reach into her mouth. A roll of scotch tape they kept at the bar served to effectively secure it. More than her strength, they had underestimated Viane's will to get away; but by sheer bulk, they had succeeded.

They carried her below deck into a small enclosed sitting area and lowered her roughly to the floor—dropped her, actually—because they were exhausted after their efforts to subdue her. With the door closed and locked behind them, they retreated to the lounge.

"This is the pits." Roland was standing at the bar, an unlabeled bottle of okolehao in hand, an ice-filled glass close by, but he made no attempt to tip the bottle toward it. "This is a nightmare. I thought she was fish food by now."

"We can't leave her down there. She's liable to create a ruckus and attract attention," Roland exclaimed. "There are just too many people around who are nosey enough to cause problems, and we certainly don't need the attention."

"It's essential we keep her hidden and quiet until Monday," Grey voiced his thought. "Once we're at sea, we can dump her anywhere between here and California." He was pacing as he was inclined to do when analyzing all sides of a situation looking for the path that would take them beyond the problem. He was good at it having had ample practice over the years, extricating them both from many tight situations.

Grey walked over to the bar and filled a glass with ice. He held it out toward Roland. "Our treasure vault is sound proof, so later tonight when there are not too many people around, let's move her back up and leave her there until Monday morning. We can move her back below deck while Debra is here if we have to. After that, we'll have a clear shot for heading east. We can dump her a thousand miles of ocean from anywhere while we're on our way. This time, she *will* disappear."

Roland stood in thought, bottle poised over his own glass of partially melted ice.

"Are you eventually going to pour something in our glasses, or are you waiting for some sort of vapor lock to disappear?"

Roland looked at Grey and, with a chuckle, said, "She was looking for her things. If we stash her in the treasure vault, she can lie there and admire her glass ball and statue for the whole day." Roland finally tipped the bottle and poured the whiskey over the ice in Grey's glass, then filled his own.

Holding up his glass, Roland indicated a toast. "To the hidden depths of the Pacific and the many secrets she holds and to those who have yet to sink into her arms."

They laughed together as they tipped their glasses and walked out onto the deck.

Chapter Twenty-Eight

V iane lay in a crumpled heap on the floor, surrounded by absolute darkness. She was very aware of bindings holding her wrists much too tightly behind her. Her ankles were also bound so tightly she could feel her toes beginning to tingle from lack of circulation. As she tried to shift her legs seeking some relief from the discomfort, she felt a searing jolt of pain run through her arms and realized her captors had used the same length of rope to bind both her arms and feet. "Cheap bastards couldn't even afford two ropes," she muttered to herself, feeling a sense of reality return at hearing her own voice. Once, years ago, she'd witnessed a calf being hog-tied at a rodeo outside Hilo and could only sympathize with the poor animal and the helpless feeling those bindings created.

She tried focusing on anything close at hand knowing if she could just see something, anything, the intense anxiety entwining itself into her existence would diminish. But not being able to see anything tangible in her surroundings was beginning to create a fear she'd not felt earlier. Fear was an emotion she had little experience with. Pops raised her to look for understanding in everything that affected her instead of moving her thoughts into fear. He'd taught her that fear brought paralysis in thinking and blocked you from being able to process and reason logically. He'd also told her it was always better to analyze what you feared as simply an obstacle to overcome and thereby allow the body's natural instinct to take over in discovering the way out. *I wish you were here now, Pops.*

At least they had sprung for some soft carpet and good padding, she thought, grasping for the positive. Struggling against the bindings that held her arms and legs, she felt at a total loss. None of the bindings seemed willing to give in, and her struggles were bringing additional pain as they tightened, and her hip bones ground against the carpeted, yet hard, floor. The fear she was fighting against quickly began dissolving into anger. *How dare they just dump me on the floor and then leave. Gutless wonders.* She was also starting to realize how incredibly thirsty she was. *Whatever they stuck in my mouth is sucking me dry.*

Light from a companionway ceiling fixture suddenly blazed into her eyes as the door swung open, and both her captors entered. The darkness that had been hers for the past hours suddenly felt comfortable in comparison to whatever she could envision was coming next.

They briskly lifted her from the floor. Grey held her shoulders, and Roland, his arms around both her thighs, pulled her in tight against his waist like a sack of rice. They carried her out the door with awkward difficulty and very little concern about the bumps and bruises she was receiving from the walls and doorways along the way.

The only light illuminating their maneuvers as they
wrestled her up the narrow stairway and along the
companionway was from the dim glow of a few pier lights in
the distance shedding their slithering glimmer off the water
of the harbor. Viane realized she had little hope of anyone
seeing her and coming to the rescue. She was sure her captors
thought this as well, as they were doing nothing to prevent
would-be onlookers from seeing them carry her.

They brought her back into the lounge, a room that was
becoming much too familiar to her from her overly frequent
and undesirable visits. Viane watched with amazement as
Roland dropped her feet and disappeared behind the bar and
pushed or pulled something hidden from view. His attention
was focused on the mirror centered between the shelves of
books, which immediately and silently pivoted open, revealing
the room that she had suspected was hidden there but hadn't
had enough time to discover.

Unfortunately, too, she saw that she'd soon get a
close-hand look at the room as Roland grabbed her legs once
more and led the way in with Grey and the rest of her body
following along behind.

They rudely deposited her back on the floor but not
before she gave her best effort at wiggling free. The anger she
was holding gave her strength but unfortunately also gave her
a bruised hip and sore elbow. If she hadn't struggled so much,
they may have put her down a little more gently instead of
simply letting go of her. She could only blame herself for
these new pains spreading through her body. Neither man
had said a single word—the outcome had obviously been
discussed and agreed upon beforehand.

Just as the bookshelf wall began closing, bringing impending darkness, Viane happened to spot her wooden carving directly above her on one of the shelves. She presumed the gemstone was close by. Seeing the familiar object was like an injection of needed strength to tamp down her anger and overlook the pain she was experiencing. Her intention and resolve to break free became clearer as she renewed her struggles against the bindings, even before the doorway had fully closed. *I'll find a way out of this, and I'll castrate both of them.*

An image of something else she had seen before the wall fully closed formed in her mind's eye, something on the lowest of shelves to the left of the doorway. It was a samurai sword resting beside an ornate, wood-carved sheath. *More stolen trophies, no doubt.* Samurai swords were quite familiar to her from years of watching old Japanese samurai movies with her brothers when they were all kids. She knew the swords were notorious for their sharper-than-a-razor's edge, easily sharp enough to cut her bindings but also capable of cutting so cleanly and swiftly that it'd be much too easy to do severe body damage before realizing anything was wrong. She could cut her whole leg off if she managed to miscalculate what she was contemplating doing.

Roland and Grey relaxed in lounge chairs on the forward deck, beer in hand, a cooler for resupply just a few feet behind them. Music was drifting down from the bar on the lobby level of the Ilikai Hotel, and a sliver of moon was starting to show over the buildings along the Ala Wai.

"You know, Rol, with that girl being alive, we have a major problem to contend with."

"Yeah, I was just thinking about that same thing. I wonder how many people know she's here."

"There's a good chance that she didn't tell anyone," continued Grey. "She affected me as being quite an honest type of person when we first met her. Since illegal entry is a serious offense, she may not have wanted a bunch of friends knowing what she was planning to do or where she was going. You know, the more I think of it, I'm betting she didn't tell a soul."

"If someone had come with her," Roland added, "we would have known of their presence by now. They would already be knocking on our door asking about her."

Picking up the conversation thread, Grey added, "We could pull out right now and full throttle for the mainland, but that would screw up Debra and our pickup from her, and that would really make our black market man, Loren, pissed as hell. Maybe even enough for him to pull the plug and leave us holding a whole load of hot merchandise, and we can't overlook the enormous amount of capital we've already sunk into this adventure.

"This gets more and more complicated, doesn't it, Rol? She's safe and sound right where she is. If anyone comes looking for her, they'll never find the vault nor are they going to hear her if she decides to make a fuss." They had designed the vault with the very purpose in mind of being able to keep anything they chose to keep totally secret from prying eyes and ears: the place could be entirely closed off from sound.

"Yeah," agreed Roland. "Let's keep our plan as it is and dispose of her when we're out of sight of these islands."

As if signaling an end to that part of their conversation, Grey reached behind him, opened the lid of the cooler, extracted two bottles of unlabeled beer, and handed one to Roland. It was a special home brew affectionately called Trash Can beer that a friend in Port Townsend had given them when they were there for dry docking. The homebrew had come with the accompanying well wishes, For a Special Occasion. It was almost 11 percent alcohol, so they saved the few bottles they were given to mark such an occasion. Grey obviously thought this was one of those. Either that or he needed the wish for wellness that had arrived with the gift.

They leaned back to enjoy the evening. A full canopy of stars stretched out overhead, and the breeze gently caressing all it touched with its warmth. They were especially fortunate in their shared philosophy of life: stressful situations could always be handled by reaching into the beer cooler.

Chapter Twenty-Nine

"Hi, my name's Stone. Can I ask who you are?" queried Stone, walking up to a tall, thin girl with such intense black hair that it made her attractive facial features almost startling. She'd been wandering around the pier and grassy area of the yacht club asking various people who were there for the christening of *Wailana Sunrise* if they knew where Viane was. He'd noticed her ten minutes beforehand as he was introducing Teri to his friend Hana, or more respectfully, Reverend Hanalei, but hadn't had the chance to appease his curiosity about who she was until now.

There were nearly fifty people spread out over the grass and along the pier at Kaneohe Yacht Club, many standing close to *Wailana Sunrise* craning their necks in an effort to peer inside, shielding the reflection from the window glass with their hands cupped around their eyes. Most, however, were either crowded around the various tables loaded with pupus, juices, and water or were lined up at the open bar that the club had set up on the dock to quench the thirst of the club members and guests who had come for the ceremony.

It was 11:30 Sunday morning. Reverend Hanalei, an ordained minister and kahuna lapaau, was in the process of gathering ti leaves and Hawaiian salt in preparation for the formal part of blessing of bringing life to *Wailana Sunrise*. At close to six feet tall and weighing over three hundred pounds, commanding awareness simply by his regal presence, he moved easily and gently as he went about his venerated tasks.

"Like my name's Ann," the young girl explained, showing signs of frustration at not getting anywhere with her search. "You the guy who like own this big boat?"

Stone clamped his teeth in an effort not to be inconsiderate as he curbed his impulse to correct her.

She went on seemingly without taking a breath or waiting for Stone to answer. "I like live in the next room to Viane at Frierdon Hall. She like invited me to this party, but like I haven't seen her since like yesterday. I figured somehow she was with her family all night or her brother or someone, and they like brought her over here and like didn't have a chance to call me or something."

Stone couldn't help smiling at the stark differences between this girl and Viane. *Friendships don't abide by narrow philosophies.* "I don't understand, Ann," Stone responded. "Viane was with a friend and me yesterday afternoon. We drove her back to her dorm around 5:00 p.m. We even watched her go in through the door. What has her family or brothers have to do with where she is right now?" Stone's concern had been heightened knowing Teri had been trying to call Viane's room all morning to arrange a ride to bring her over to the club but had been unable to reach her.

"All I know is like I gave her a ride to the Ilikai Hotel last night, and she like told me her brother would be bringing her back, but like she's not there. I banged on her door like for hours this morning and figured she'd like come over here with her brother and like maybe forgot about inviting me or something."

"Wait a minute," Stone interrupted Ann's story and growing excitement. He felt his own calmness spike with a rush of foreboding. "The Ilikai? Where exactly and at what time did you like drop her off?" He gave himself a silent reprimand for getting caught up in her style of speech. Before Ann could answer, he caught Teri's eye and urgently motioned her over. He held his palm up, hoping Ann would wait a moment before answering.

Teri walked up to him and put her arm through his. "You're supposed to look cheerful. Isn't this the great moment in a boat owner's, excuse me, yacht owner's brief euphoria of ownership? By the way, I still haven't heard from Viane. She's much the same as you, Stone—stubborn. You both hold an absurd idea that you can get by in this world without a cell phone." She looked and smiled at the attractive young woman as if just becoming aware that someone was standing beside Stone. She instinctively pulled herself closer to him—a possessive gesture she was going to refuse to acknowledge.

"Teri, this is Ann. Ann is also a friend of Viane's. Ann, please tell Teri what you just told me."

Teri tightened more but this time more on edge.

Ann, realizing there was a deeper meaning surrounding her friend's absence, relayed the story exactly as she had told Stone, except with a couple more *likes* that hadn't been there before. "It was like 6:30, and I left her off at the escalator that like goes up to the lobby or something. Maybe I should have like stuck around, huh? Course *shoulds* don't like do anything, do they?"

Stone couldn't help but smile at Ann's analysis as he looked at Teri. "Do you know anything about one of Viane's brothers being here, or why she'd go back to the Ilikai Hotel at the Ala Wai? You don't suppose it has anything to do with the *Whiskey Sea* pulling into port while we were there, do you?"

"She didn't mention anything about her brothers being here. I would have told you had she said anything, and she definitely would have told me. Things are much too strange right now *not* to have said anything."

"That's what I figured but didn't want to assume anything. If either of her brothers was coming over from the Big Island, I'm sure she would have said something last night, unless she called them after we dropped her off, and one or both of them decided to make a quick trip over. I sure hope they're not taking things into their own hands. She was pretty upset at seeing the *Whiskey Sea* yesterday. I'm thinking that may be what's happened.

"She may have convinced her brothers to help her retrieve her things and perhaps mess with those characters who own that yacht. The way she described her brothers, I don't doubt for an instant they'd be here in a heartbeat, if she asked for their help.

"They may have gone onboard last night. You and I both know how much she wanted to be here today, so I can't help but feel things have gone wrong somewhere."

"Or," he went on, visibly calmer, "it's possible that having her brothers here overshadowed a desire to be here with us. We should call her dad or whoever's at home to find out who is here and see if they know where we can locate her."

"I hope you're right, Stone. I wouldn't put it past her, though, to do something without thinking it through. I'm going to go find a quiet spot and give her father a call. You better attend to your guests and please tell Hana to hold off blessing your boat until I get back. I don't want to miss anything. Should be just a few minutes."

Stone looked at her and silently mouthed the word *yacht*, then turned back to Ann. Lloyd had wandered over and was standing there looking from Stone to Ann and back in expectation. Stone introduced them.

"Look, Ann. Please make yourself at home. I'm really glad Viane asked you to join us here. I'm sure everything will be easily explained as soon as she shows up. I'll let you know what we find out. In the meantime, why don't you relax and enjoy things? There's lots of food and beer and wine if you'd like anything."

"I'll look after her, Stone," offered Lloyd. "Pam couldn't make it, so Ann and I can watch over each other." He turned to Ann. "That okay with you, Ann?"

"That's like too rad. You're like kinda cute in a like older guy sort of way."

Lloyd turned his head to Stone with an amused expression before taking Ann's arm and steering her in the direction of a table that held a large platter of steamed fish and crab.

Placing Viane to the back of his thoughts for a few moments, Stone wandered among his friends, receiving lots of hugs and handshakes. He made his way over to Hana and was in the process of admiring the long strands of *maile* that Hana planned to drape over the bow as part of the ceremony when Teri joined them. As Hana disappeared to continue his preparations and offer preliminary prayers, Teri moved close to Stone and told him that no one answered the phone in Hilo.

"Maybe the whole family came over to lend Viane a hand. I feel much better with the idea her dad's here as well. I'll bank on the fact he's smart enough to keep all of them out of trouble."

"We'll just have to wait and see if one or all of them show up. I'm going to tell Hana to get started before someone gets drunk and falls off the pier and steals the show."

The ceremony was solemn yet beautiful in its simplicity. Reverend Hanalei invoked several chants and silent prayers as he draped maile leis over the bow of *Wailana Sunrise*, sprinkled Hawaiian salt, and swished ti leaves wet with saltwater over the yacht as well as on many of the guests. The ceremony was short enough to suit everyone as the bar line quickly reformed as the last words of prayer were spoken.

Stone walked around presenting everyone with a ceremonial gift certificate good for a ride around the bay, the timing, he said with as much humor as he could, would be at the discretion and choosing of *Wailana Sunrise*.

As the pier cleared of guests, Stone and Teri invited Lloyd, Hana, and Mike, who'd just made his appearance, as well as a few others to come aboard for a short cruise, as custom would dictate. Lloyd was about to release the lines when Stone motioned for him to hold off for a moment.

Ann was sitting on the grass looking lost, so Stone called to her. "Ann, *hele mai'*. Come take a short ride with us. Teri has her cell phone and will be the first to find out where Vlane got to." Ann quickly stood and walked to the edge of the dock, looking pleased to have been asked.

He turned to Lloyd. "I thought you were going to stick with her."

"Hey, brah. I like stayed like as long as I like could take it, but my brain was like getting like sore. I seriously question how that girl made it this far into the halls of higher education."

Both men had a good laugh as Lloyd went over and offered a hand to help Ann onboard.

They cruised out into Kaneohe Bay and headed across to the Main Ship Channel aiming past Mokolii Island, the small island off Kualoa Beach Park affectionately and better known as Chinaman's Hat by local residents because of the resemblance to an old coolie hat floating on the surface of the water. The seas were fairly calm, and Stone's new yacht rode the water easily. He turned southwest and headed for Mokumanu, the place close to where he'd been on his maiden voyage and not far from where he'd picked Viane up out of the water. He didn't mention this to anyone, though.

The cruise lasted about an hour, and they were back in the bay heading for the yacht club when Teri's cell phone rang.

"Yes, I see. Mahalo, Mr. Koa, for returning my call. It must have been a simple case of miscommunications. I'm sure Viane will call you and tell you the whole story. *Ahui hou.*" She disconnected the call and turned to Stone, gripping his arm to gain his attention.

"None of Viane's family is here. They haven't talked to her since she left them last weekend, other than when she called from my car to tell them she was home safely."

Neither spoke the thoughts each was having as Stone eased both throttles forward to full speed and aimed toward the club.

Chapter Thirty

Stone guided his yacht carefully into his assigned slip at the yacht club as Lloyd busily showed Teri how to handle the lines and attempting to explain what needed to go where, but he got the distinct impression she wasn't paying much attention.

"I get the feeling you're going to have many opportunities to become an expert at being second mate in the not-too-distant future, Teri," he said in an attempt to ease any responsibility she may have felt at having to stand there listening while her mind was obviously elsewhere. "I'll go ahead and finish securing the rest of the lines." Lloyd leaned in close to Teri and spoke in a whisper, "Stone's pretty good with a boat, but he can get flustered at times if things don't go as good as he thinks they should. Know what I mean?"

"I'm enjoying the journey in discovery so far, Lloyd, and"—giving him a knowing smile and gently resting her hand on his arm—"you'd probably be wise not to let him hear the word *boat*."

Lloyd laughed and nodded his understanding and agreement. "Next time we go out, we can spend some time playing with ropes and practicing the word *yacht*. I'll teach you all the tricks of tying knots as well."

Teri gave him a gentle hug in acknowledgment. Her thoughts were indeed elsewhere, and they both knew that—her body had been going through the motions, but her mind had not been present. She knew there'd be time later on to learn the ropes. Right now, she just wanted to grab Stone by the arm and head off in search of their friend. *Their friend,* she thought. *Interesting to think she'd made the transition to a "we" way of viewing their friendship.*

She shared Stone's intuitive notion that Viane was in trouble, more than likely involving *Whiskey* Sea, and they were powerless at the moment to do anything about it. Teri knew each moment spent away from searching could have frightful consequences. While Lloyd went back to securing the mooring lines, rechecking and repositioning the pier bumpers, she moved to Stone, who was talking to Ann. All the others who had been onboard for the very brief cruise were already on the pier walking toward the clubhouse.

Stone turned to see Teri standing beside him and absently put his arm around her waist and pulled her into his conversation with Ann. Lloyd was walking over to join them as well.

Teri felt the warmness of the gesture but let it gently settle as she became aware of the conversation she'd moved into.

"Ann, tell your story again about dropping Viane off last night. I hope you don't mind repeating it, I want to make certain I have everything straight."

Ann slumped down on one hip and cocked her head, giving Stone "the look" as if he suddenly had turned into a clump of dirt she'd been told to reason with. "There's like an escalator, okay, on one end of the Ilikai Hotel, you know, like opposite that parking garage. I think it's Ena Road or something. She wanted me to drop her like at the bottom of that escalator." Ann was slowly getting back into her story once again, her unspoken involvement mounting. "I like watched as she like rode up to the top, and then I left. I didn't like see any reason to stick around. Like now I sure wish I did. Do you think she's like dead or something? Do you want me to like go down there and like hunt around for her?"

"No, Ann, but *mahalo* for offering. I think the most important thing for you to do right now, which would really help us a lot, would be to go back to your dorm room. If she shows up or calls, I want you to immediately call Teri's cell phone."

Teri pulled a card from her pocket and handed it to Ann as they made their way along the pier toward the grass and the clubhouse. Ann gave a quick wave, looking disappointed that she couldn't help more, and headed for the parking lot.

The three of them watched as Ann walked away.

"The way she tells it," offered Stone, "Viane was within eyesight of *Whiskey Sea* when she got out of Ann's car. I refuse to believe she had any reason for going down there other than to go aboard and confront those two men."

"Lloyd, would you call Mike and let him know what's going on? I didn't get a chance to tell him anything about this before he left. See if he could meet us on the dock beside *Whiskey Sea*. Tell him it'll have to be on an unofficial basis as all we have is a lot of guesses and nothing else. Tell him we're probably going to have to go aboard to see if there are any signs of Viane anywhere. His presence as an HPD sergeant will hopefully smooth the way a little and diminish any chance of their acting rash . . . or worse," he added. "I can't imagine those two characters being very helpful, but I'm sure they won't want to cause a problem with Honolulu PD standing in front of them."

"Tell you what, Stone. I'll call him on my way home 'cause I've got to change into something other than a bathing suit and T-shirt, then I'll meet you guys there. Don't go in until I get there. I'll call when I leave home and am heading over the Pali Highway. Wait, I forgot." Lloyd raised his eyebrows at Stone and, with a puzzled but amused seriousness, said, "I can't call you, can I, Stone? You don't have a cell phone."

"Okay, I'm catching all the hints—call Teri."

Teri gave Stone a soft punch on the arm. "Keep at him, Lloyd." She looked up at Stone with a feigned seriousness, duplicating Lloyd's expression of a few seconds before, saying, "What are you going to do when my cell phone and I aren't close by?"

"I've been thinking about that very thing. Maybe you should get rid of your cell phone so I don't get used to having it around."

Teri gave him another soft tap on the same arm, this time, though, not as softly.

"Auwe, that hurt."

"You baby."

"If you two are *pau* playing with each other, I'm leaving now. I'll call you as soon as I'm on my way. Remember, wait for me to get there." Lloyd was halfway across the grass before Stone was able to acknowledge with a wave—both his hands were involved fending off Teri's next playful punch.

"Let's get going. We can stand watch from the edge of the Ilikai Hotel and wait for Lloyd and Mike to show up. In the meantime, we need to come up with a plausible reason why three people and a police officer want to go aboard."

Grey was the first to notice the yacht's swaying motion, suggesting they had unexpected visitors coming onboard.

"What the hell," he exclaimed and jumped to his feet heading for the starboard doorway leading to the deck, but stopped before opening it. "Someone's coming onboard. Rol, grab that piece of jade and the vase and put them into a cupboard out of sight, and I'll go intercept whoever's brazen enough to come onboard without asking."

Roland carefully put Buddha into the cupboard below the shelf it had been sitting on, along with the ornate ancient Chinese vase. Both pieces were part of the haul Margelese brought from the local museum. He closed the cupboard door, grabbed the drink he'd been nursing and a copy of *Yachting* magazine, and sat down on the couch just as the door opened, and Grey walked in, followed by four people. The sight of the police officer almost made him drop his glass, but he quickly recovered his composure. He calmly put the magazine on a side table and stood as the room filled with people.

"Everyone, this is Roland Pratt," Grey said by way of an introduction as he raised an arm and gestured toward Roland. "Rol," Grey continued with eyes fixed on the intruders, "these people claim to have lost a friend and have reason to think the lost girl somehow ended up on our yacht. They apparently don't believe me that there are only the two of us here and insist on looking around. Let's give them the grand tour, shall we?" Looking at Mike, he said, with more than a hint of accusation in his voice, "this good police officer," still appraising Mike, "says he's just tagging along as a friend, nothing official."

Roland, with practiced calmness, looked from one to the other, then held his gaze on Mike.

"Why would you have reason to think this missing girl is on our yacht? And don't you need a search warrant in order to do this sort of thing, officer? What if one of you gets hurt while traipsing around? Will my partner and I have to bear that liability and cost?"

"Is that a threat, Mr. Pratt?" asked Mike. He didn't like doing what he was doing without proper authority and backup support, even for a close friend like Stone, and he was feeling very ill at ease and quite jumpy. He knew he shouldn't have assumed that a threat was being made.

"Don't be absurd, officer. I'm merely pointing out that without a search warrant, Grey and I are left in a very vulnerable position." He was actually hoping they'd take his words as a mild threat—just enough of one that they'd choose to leave—but he could see it wasn't heading in that direction.

"I'd still like to know why you think a missing girl happens to be on our yacht." Roland had no intention of quitting his interrogation.

Stone and Teri had concocted a story just in case they were asked this very question. They didn't know just how close it was to the truth.

"A friend of the girl's saw her standing close to your gangplank last night, and in the few minutes it took to find a parking place and walk back, her friend had disappeared. The missing girl had a fascination for yachts like yours and may have come onboard when neither of you realized it." It was flimsy but the most plausible story they could come up with in a pinch.

Grey caught Roland's eye and briefly shrugged as if to say "They won't find the girl anyway—why cause any undue anger and delay?" Neither could talk about it right at that point, but both caught the implication that it was quite possible that Viane had been seen by some friend. It was another reason to exit Hawaii as fast as they could.

Roland moved behind the bar to refresh his drink. "Can I mix any of you a drink before we scour the yacht for your friend? I'm sure, officer, you'll not accept one. A bottle of water, perhaps?"

Mike had already turned and was heading out the door. He didn't acknowledge the offer. His impression of these two haoles had already been formed, and he really wanted in the worst way to get off the yacht and not have to spend any more time with them. He would stay only because Stone and Lloyd had asked him to, and he wanted to get at the search and get it over with. Besides, he knew he was good at diffusing tempers if any were to get out of hand, so he felt he had a justified reason for being there, sensing everyone's attitudes tightening.

Teri was thinking the two men appeared much too accommodating. If it were her boat being invaded, she knew she'd be close up and tight in the invaders' faces instead of offering them a drink and a tour. She declined the offer as did both Stone and Lloyd, and they all moved to follow Mike out onto the deck.

They spent the next twenty minutes following Grey as he wandered from room to room. They found no trace of Viane or her artifacts. Teri noticed the absence of the jade Buddha that she'd seen when she'd sneaked onboard, but knew she could not ask about it without giving herself away and maybe ending up forcing Mike into a position of having to haul her in for trespassing.

As soon as the group was off the yacht, Mike left them to head back to the station. He'd already spent more time than he had thought he would and knew he was needed on duty.

Stone, Teri, and Lloyd walked over to the old Tahitian Lanai restaurant and settled into a booth. Late Sunday afternoons were busy in the restaurant as tourists staying in Waikiki often found this hidden jewel of a restaurant to be a quiet respite from the hurried schedules of tour companies and diesel smoke from their buses that hustled up and down the streets of Waikiki. This was a place that took you back to the old Hawaii. Too bad it was destined for demolition to make way for another high-rise hotel.

"I'm frustrated," exclaimed Teri, looking from Stone to Lloyd and back. "We saw the whole boat and nothing!"

"No, we didn't."

They both turned in unison like choreographed water ballet swimmers and stared at Stone, waiting for more.

"What do you mean?" Lloyd was the first to ask.

"First of all, we didn't see a boat—we saw a yacht."

Lloyd and Teri caught each other's sigh and their give-it-a-rest look.

"Secondly," he continued, ignoring them, "there's an inconsistency in the yacht. I had a weird sensation when we first started our room-to-room search. Something just didn't mesh. At the end when we walked back into the lounge, I realized what was creating that sensation: there is space that's not accounted for. There is an area not visible behind the mirrored bookcase, both in the lounge and in their map room."

"Is that what you were looking at when you opened that other door and Grey abruptly came back and closed it? He looked very annoyed when he told you we'd already been in that room."

"Yeah, I noticed that. I wanted to settle in my mind that I wasn't imagining it. If my hunch is correct, and it's a long shot, it's entirely possible Viane could be hidden in that space. Also, I wanted to see the bookcase in that other room again. Have you ever seen a yacht with such an extensive library? Books are heavy, and they have two full walls of them—not what you'd normally want surrounding you on something that floats, even something as large as that particular yacht. It wasn't until we came into the lounge from the portside that I realized there wasn't another doorway between the two rooms."

"Stone, if that's all true, we have to get a look behind those walls. Can we get Mike to come up with a search warrant?"

"We can ask, Teri. We'd be treading on libelous waters if we got one, then found the space to be nothing but part of the yacht's superstructure. He'd need something concrete to persuade a judge to issue one, not to mention getting Mike's chief to support the idea."

"You know what we've got to do, and I'd probably be the best one to do this," volunteered Teri. "We've got to hunt down the schematics from the shipyard that built her, if they're still in existence, and see if that is, in fact, part of the superstructure and not a designed hidden space. And we don't have a lot of time to do so. Stone, I've got to get home to my computer. Maybe after you drop me off, you and Lloyd can go down to the station and tell Mike what we think. I bet he'd be happy to learn our time wasn't wasted this afternoon."

"Your enthusiasm is wonderful, Teri, and I don't want to appear negative, but I doubt you'll find any schematics or building plans. That would have been an ideal solution, but many yachts of that caliber and age were built one at a time, and each one is unique. I wouldn't be surprised to learn it was built for a specific wealthy client to unique specifications. Probably a Hollywood type. Hey, maybe it was built for a studio and featured in a movie." He leaned close to her—suggestively close. "You and I need to cuddle up someplace and watch lots of old-time movies and see if we can spot that boat," he said, his wink accompanied a devilish smile.

Teri looked at him in astonishment. "Boat . . . did you say 'boat'?"

Before Stone could respond, Lloyd cleared his throat, a little louder than was necessary. "You two can watch old movies until you're both blue in the face, but right now let's keep on track and see what we can find out, shall we?"

Neither Stone nor Teri said anything, but by their questioning expressions, they knew they had both missed some mysterious or private train of thought somewhere in Lloyd's conversation.

Lloyd found himself embarrassed at his outburst and the surprised look on his friends' faces. He was suddenly missing Pam and realized it. This restaurant had been their secret rendezvous spot many years ago when they first started dating and falling in love. He was feeling the old energy still lingering and didn't need to see it replicated here by his friends—not right now anyway.

Chapter Thirty-One

As Viane's eyes slowly adjusted to the darkness in her carpeted prison, she was pleased to discover it wasn't a total blackout as she at first thought. There was light, albeit dim, filtering in from the adjoining lounge, enough to partially illuminate the confined space. The light was filtering in through the heavily darkened one-way mirror that she knew was centered in the wall bordered by bookcases on the other side in the lounge. It allowed sufficient light to illuminate the shelves on the surrounding walls above her. She could see all the shelves were crowded: a treasure trove of carvings, vases, unfamiliar long odd-shaped things, yet obviously old by their appearance and musty smell they gave to the small room. Everything appeared to be strapped into its own cubbyhole. *These guys apparently took Picasso's words as God's law, "Give me a museum, and I'll fill it."* She admitted that it might not have been Picasso, but she knew someone said it. She'd never seen such an array of artifacts in one place *other* than in a museum. It was stunning.

Rolling over as best she could, maneuvering her bound arms and legs, she was not surprised to find a duplicate one-way mirror on the opposite wall facing the aft map room. A feeling of repulsion shuddered through her as she realized that while she had been tucking her bra strap under the shoulder fabric of her low-neck T-shirt and manually moving her breasts into more comfortable positions in front of that mirror a short time ago, someone could have been hiding in the vault watching her mere inches away, and she'd never have known. *That's really creepy.* She took several deep breaths to calm herself and to override the ill feeling of having been visually seduced, not that there was any way for her to know that, but the feeling was just as real. Now was not the time, though, to be grossed out by something that may or may not have happened since there was nothing she could do about the past anyway. If that were possible, she would have stayed at the dorm with Ann.

She worked at the bindings around her wrists with such ferocity she was sure they'd soon be bleeding if they weren't already, but she didn't care. She felt utterly trapped, and she hated it. Her efforts had succeeded in loosening some of the knots but not enough to give any relief from the pain, nor allow her imagination to conjure up a quick and easy escape.

After an undeterminable amount of time and effort, she relaxed and let her head fall gently to the carpet. The bindings had slackened a bit more, which gave her encouragement. She was devising a plan to use the samurai sword she'd noticed to cut the bindings on her ankles but wasn't quite ready to place her trust in its razor edge just yet. First, she had to figure out how she was going to go about safely accomplishing that maneuver. She realized she had a palpable fear of getting anywhere close to its edge. *I'll be darned if I'll accidentally bleed to death hidden in a trophy room.*

Curbing her fear the best she could, knowing she had to act quickly, she moved her bound legs toward the sword. *Now is the time to see what this blade will do. I can even look over my shoulder and watch while I cut my leg off.* She laughed, realizing she still had some of her humor intact. She worked her way around and managed to get her feet aimed in the direction of the sword and half butt-crawled and half wiggled until she got her feet in a position directly above it.

A strong vibration suddenly rattled through the yacht, coinciding with the low rumble of an engine filtering up through the flooring. The pain of the bindings cutting into the bare skin on her arms was forgotten for a moment as well as any inclination she had to put her legs anywhere near the blade's edge. She lowered and rested them on a shelf and let her head fall back to the carpet. Having the yacht go someplace different than where she had planned for it to remain was the furthest thing from any thought she'd had when she climbed aboard. It presented a whole new set of fears to wade through, but with no choice, she could do nothing but ride it out until they reached their destination. Hopefully then, she could continue to implement her escape plan.

Very quickly—fifteen minutes, no more—both engines stopped, and the yacht became quiet and calm once again.

This is very confusing, she thought. *Where could they go from the Ala Wai transient dock in so short a time? Maybe we've moved to Keehi Lagoon, but there was no rocking motion in the yacht from waves, so we didn't get out into open water. Besides, it would have taken longer than that to get there.* She let the thought go.

She knew she couldn't afford to waste any more time questioning things for which she had no answers. She didn't want to envision what they might do to her or with her if she didn't get her arms and legs free and gain a fighting chance.

Then what? She became conscious of the fact that her escape plan was not well thought out. Even with the bonds free from her arms and legs, she still had no way to escape the vault. Until this moment, she hadn't taken her escape plan any further than getting loose from the bindings. *Maybe when they finally come back in to get me, I can run them both through with that sword.*

She chuckled at the scale of her imagination and began working at the bindings, but the pain emanating from her arms and hands quickly became excruciating, and she laid back. The bindings on her feet were pulling at her arms—her shoulders ached in sympathy. She raised her feet and legs as much as she could bear, turned her head at an angle to the left so she could watch what she was doing. She realized she'd become very comfortable with the dim light. With all her body weight resting primarily on her left arm and hand, grimacing in pain, she resumed her efforts.

She brought her feet down as slowly as possible onto the handle of the sword, her abdominal muscles straining to hold her legs steady, she continued to inch the sword back toward the rim of the shelf and her butt. She wasn't too concerned about making noise. She suspected the room was completely sound proof since they had gone to great lengths putting ultrahigh-quality, one-way glass into the walls, but she didn't want to take any chances. She eased the sword closer to the shelf's edge. It rode out over the lip of the shelf and tilted, the blade tip coming to rest on the carpet, scarce inches from the exposed skin of her thigh. She braced her feet against the shelf and scooted her rear end back a foot. The sword now balanced between the floor and lip of the shelf. She could see there wouldn't be much of the blade's edge exposed to work with, but it would have to do.

She lowered her legs and head to the floor for a moment to ease the burning cramp that had invaded her abdominal muscles. It felt good to rest and to allow her arm and shoulder to relax as well. It gave her a small feeling of pleasure to discover that her fear and anger had abated—pain had a magical way of making almost all emotions fall away. What she was left with was a strong resolve to break free from her trophy tomb and then do everything she could to make sure her captors got their just reward. She resolved that as soon as she was free, she would call her brothers. *They'd be more than happy to deal out some Koa justice.*

She raised her legs once again and began to lower them toward the sword's razor edge, but again she was interrupted by the rumble of the engine reverberating through the hull. She rested again, in frustration, to ride out the boat's motion.

Another brief trip before the engine ceased once more. She could only surmise, from past experiences with her father, that it had to have been a simple trip to a gas pump. She knew the gas dock was a short distance around the end of the piers from the transient dock. Her mind rested in this assured knowledge. Once more, she began maneuvering her legs toward the sword, but suddenly she froze in place.

Out of the corner of her eye, she saw movement in the adjacent lounge. She brought her legs back to the floor and rolled sideways to get a better look. Unfortunately, the shelves protruded so much they blocked much of her view, but she could see feet and legs in pants randomly moving about the room. She had to assume they were that of the two men, but she couldn't be sure as not enough of the remaining parts of their bodies were visible. She silently prayed they weren't coming to collect her.

Unexpectedly, her sideways view of the room began to fill with more legs and feet—too many to count. A woman as well, judging by the obvious difference in physical appearance, entered and joined the rest of the legs. A familiarity struck her. *Was it the way the woman's legs moved? The pose she was taking? Her shoes?* She couldn't tell, but she knew those legs and feet. *Teri. My God, that's Teri, which means one of the other set of feet must belong to Stone.* Her heart raced against her chest in a wave of excitement and anticipation. Then she felt the frustration, fear, and desperation of her predicament.

She attempted to make as much noise as she could, using every ounce of strength, thrusting her feet against the edge of the shelf, ignoring the sword. It was a futile effort at best though, as the noise was barely audible even to her. She didn't have enough leverage to get a decent whack at the shelf, but she kept trying.

She began yelling as loudly as she could, but just as quickly as the feet had filled the room, she watched as it emptied. She lay back consumed by frustration, fighting hard to maintain the resolve and determination that had filled her moments before. Tears flowed as she melted into the carpet and let the feeling of hopelessness she had been pushing so hard against consume her.

Chapter Thirty-Two

Grey and Roland went straight for the bar, mixed doubles on the rocks, and immediately headed for the observation deck. Both were feeling unnerved despite their years and experience of living on the edge within a crime-walled world.

"That was much too close. I don't like having people snooping around, and especially cops. It can only lead to trouble." Roland sat on the edge of the deck chair, elbows resting on his knees, too tense to sit back.

"Relax, Rol. They couldn't spot anything that would give them cause to come back."

Roland couldn't be put off. "That guy Stone was doing way too much thinking. Why do you suppose he wanted to get another look into the map room anyway? Think he suspected we have that hidden vault? He was eyeballing the bookshelf walls in both rooms."

"Yeah, either he's an avid reader, or he suspects something's there," Grey replied. "He's onto something but can't figure out what it is that's bothering him. He's like a person who's very busy *thinking* all the time. His type makes me nervous, as you well know. We need to ramp up our departure even more. I'm going to call Debra and tell her to get her butt over here tonight along with the goods. We can do the deal and be out of here before midnight. I'm glad we fueled up this afternoon instead of waiting."

Grey grabbed his drink from the glass side table, saying, "I'm going to go and call her. Why don't you go through our prep list and get us ready so we can get underway as soon as her feet hit the dock?"

"Better have a good story to tell her about why we keep moving the date and meeting place. If she's at all the nervous type, she's not going to be very accepting of more changes. We may scare her into not showing up."

"Bucke would have our nuts in a vise if we screwed up on this. He already thinks he's overpaying us on this job. Give her your *sugar-sweet* voice, Grey, the one you use to talk all those cute honeys into coming onboard."

Grey found Roland sitting in the lounge as he returned from using the landline telephone in the Ilikai Hotel. It was an unspoken rule between them: never use cell phones on a job—it left a trail much too easy to follow. Roland had a fresh drink resting on the table in front of him as he methodically put check marks on a printout list, which started out with the words, Trouble Happens If You Don't Pay Attention. The first item, with Roland's check mark to the left, read simply, Fuel—Both Tanks?

The list made reference to dock lines, bumpers, food, and water supplies, including beer, and everything else that had to be considered, right down to a warning reminder to check that all personalized life rings, with EPIRB units attached, properly hung on the various ring buoy brackets, were ready to be put into action. The EPIRB, or Emergency Position-Indicating Radio Beacon, was a device that self-activated when immersed in saltwater. It allowed Coast Guard stations around the world to pinpoint its exact location via satellite. EPIRBs have been responsible for saving hundreds of lives since being put into use.

"Debra isn't showing up tonight," Grey announced as he walked into the lounge, his eyebrows creased into a frown. "She didn't give me a lot of specifics but mentioned she had to be in Ewa Beach this evening and couldn't break the engagement. The implication I got from her was that she's got a boyfriend and plans to get some mattress action. I think it was simply a story to stall things. She's got too much money at stake for lame excuses. She didn't sound very pleased with making another change either. Claimed she'd be there all night, so I said okay and told her to meet us at six tomorrow morning at the Pearl Harbor Yacht Club.

"It's a good move for both of us even if she doesn't like it. It's close to where she'll supposedly be, and we need to be away from here as soon as possible, in case those snoops come back for a second look. If they show up here again, all they'll find is an empty dock. If they go looking for us, they'll probably look next door in Kewalo Basin or back in Kaneohe. I'm guessing they'd never think to look out in Pearl. You okay with all this, Rol?"

"Yeah, I got no problem with moving to Pearl Harbor tonight as long as the yacht club has room for us."

"It's all set. I called, and some guy named Bill said their big spot is open, and we can't miss it on our way in. Said it'll be obvious when we pull in. He won't be there to show us since it's going to be so late. He said we can leave a check for the dock fees in a lock box beside the office door if we want to do so before he arrives. I didn't tell him we'd be gone before he gets there."

"That's perfect. Let's get moving then. It's already late, and that's about a two-hour run. We're good on our checklist. I'll see to the tie-ups and the bumpers, and we're set to go. Did Debra give you any idea of what she's going to bring onboard or how many different pieces?"

"Yeah, she said she had five items, mostly small, so they won't be taking up a whole lot of space. Funny, as excited as Loren seems to be, I figured she'd have a whole truckload. They have something to do with an ancient samurai and his personal possessions."

"That's coincidental, isn't it?" observed Roland. "We have a samurai sword, and she has stuff to go along with it."

"I think that's Bucke's interest in getting her things onboard. You know how he is with bringing stuff together in sets." Grey turned to head forward to the control room just as his phone rang.

He pulled it from its holster on his right hip, flipped it open, and answered. "Yeah." It was the only part of the conversation that came from him. He was silent for several moments before closing the phone and putting it back in its holster, a weary look wrinkling the lines of his face as he looked to Roland, knowing his partner was anticipating a comment.

"The man himself. He must have heard us talking about him from across the ocean." Loren Bucke was the only person who had insisted—no, demanded—he has access to their cell numbers. He never honored anyone's choice of not using one when he decided a call had to be made. If it got traced, that was someone else's problem—he personally used nothing but stolen phones. "Seems Debra wasted no time in verifying our dependability. He's madder than a fish swimming in mud. In very few words, he mentioned something about looking for a graveyard on the moon if we mess this up. Apparently, from what I gather, he doesn't care much for Debra. He gave me the impression she's got something over him that's making him run scared of her. It would be great to know what that is so we could use it ourselves if a need ever arose."

"Must be pretty dramatic to have *Cool Hand Luke* Loren uptight. He's vouched for our trustworthiness, so we better get our butts over to Pearl and be ready for her when she materializes in the morning. The impression I get from my conversations with her and from Loren is that she's kind of a bitch to deal with."

"What time did you tell her to be there?"

"Six sharp, and for the record, *she told me* the time she'd meet us. I didn't get the impression there was any room in there to negotiate. Interesting lady, this one. I don't like her, and we've only talked by phone. I wonder what she'll be like in person. Let's make sure our hand guns are loaded and easily accessible."

Chapter Thirty-Three

Her body was fatigued all the way in to her bones. Having spent the past hour with her legs suspended above the blade of the sword, working them back and forth the few inches she was able, her muscles were screaming, and the bindings didn't give any indication of having weakened. She began to feel an urgency building in strength within her core as she forced her legs harder against the blade once again. Her arm and shoulder were shrieking in agony. *If only I could see exactly what was happening down there.* She had no idea whether the binding was being severed by the blade or if she was just going through these motions with all the pains but accomplishing nothing.

Her heart was hurting as well. Knowing her friends had been there, barely a few feet away and likely looking for her, and seeing them all walk out and not come back came close to breaking her will to continue. It should have strengthened her desire to escape, but it had the opposite effect, and she knew her efforts at cutting the bindings had become half-assed at best.

Having rested her legs for a moment and with no other course of action available, she raised them once more and began the back-and-forth movement on top of the blade. However, with the sword lying on its side, so very little of the sharp edge was exposed. She prayed that even a centimeter of blade would eventually do the job. All her doubts, though, were having the effect of pushing her prayers to the side.

Grey turned the key in the ignition and then pushed the Start button to engage the starboard engine. He listened with accustomed pleasure as the engine purred to life. He eased the throttle back to idle. The second button pushed brought the port engine alive as he synchronized it with the starboard engine's rpm's. The telltale vibration sound of two engines not in sync irritated him more than dogs with itchy rear ends. He failed to understand any boat operator letting his engines rotate at different rpm's from each other. It was a waste of power and actually did damage to the vessel over the long haul, not to mention that constant undulating rhythm grating nerves to rawness.

Roland cast off the bow and spring line and moved to the stern to handle that line as Grey threw power to the bow thrusters and edged the yacht's bow away from the pier. Roland knew the precise moment to release the stern line: they had done this maneuver so many times together they could both do it in their sleep. Grey operated their yacht with the proficiency of pushing a toy boat around in a bathtub—it had become second nature to him. Roland had no problem allowing him to do the commanding when he chose to—it made life much easier.

Whiskey Sea slowly made its way along the rows of boats tied to the dozens of finger piers in the harbor. There were boats and yachts of all sizes and shapes: big, small, sail, and power. With all the opulence of adjacent hotels and condominiums, too many of them looked passed over and forgotten. Many gave the quiet impression of waiting for some phantom owner to show up and bring it back into the life for which it was designed. Some were outlandish in their symbols of wealth, but too many others were simply symbols of neglect.

Whiskey Sea made a slow turn to port and headed along the rocky edge of Magic Island toward open water. It was dark. Magic Island was deserted. Only the lonely glow of the lamps spread out along the various deserted pathways in the island park gave any indication of life, albeit asleep at the moment.

Viane's attention to her situation and her surroundings instantly leaped back to her lightless reality with the sound and rumbling vibration of the engines. She'd been so focused on the action with her legs, the sound of the engines turning over surprised her. It came as unexpectedly as the first time it happened. They were on the move once again, but this time it felt different, carrying a menacing feeling with it. She felt the yacht begin to roll, telling her they were moving out into open water. Bringing her legs down to the floor once again, she rested, not wanting to keep them perched over the sharp blade for fear of slicing off more than just the bindings because of some sudden lurch of the yacht as it passed over a wave. During her last leg rest, the lights in the lounge had been extinguished, throwing her small domain into total darkness. She'd lost the precise location of the sword, which made it all the more precarious to attempt anything more.

She pushed against her right foot and pulled with her left to test the bindings for the hundredth time when suddenly, to her utter amazement and overwhelming joy, the binding gave way with a loud snap, freeing her legs. She'd put so much effort into testing the bindings she almost knocked herself unconscious as the binding broke and her knee came charging up, smashing into her chin. *Wonderful—free my legs and loose some teeth.* She couldn't stifle the screech of joy that erupted despite the gnawing pain in her chin and jaw. She was sure she'd managed to poke a hole in something since she could taste blood on her tongue. She realized, too, with a huge relief, that as well as almost knocking some teeth out she'd managed to dislodge the rag that had wicked her mouth bone dry.

With her feet finally free to move, she rolled on to her knees and stood up, feeling the exhilaration of blood flowing freely through her body once again. She quickly sat back down on the floor and, with great effort and impossible body gyrations, managed to get her still-tied hands under her feet and up in front where they belonged. She breathed a long sigh of relief as she stood up, still immersed in the elation of being relatively free to move. It took only a few moments, and not just a little pain, for her teeth to release the binding around her wrists.

She began walking the tight circle, not being too sure of how much floor space she had, before banging her nose into a shelf or stepping on the sword. Rubbing her wrists to regain circulation lost by the tight binding, she felt the positive energy and renewed attitude sweep through her—it felt wonderful. Her spirits were finally on the rise. *Now, if I can stop doing damage to myself, I may actually be able to break out of this prison.*

If the lounge had been lighted, she could have spent hours admiring all the artifacts surrounding her. Unfortunately, with the lights turned off, the darkness didn't allow it nor was it a good use of the precious time that had been given to her while the yacht was underway.

The thought nagged at her that if there was a way to get into this room, there had to be a way to get out. Nobody in any logical frame of mind would build a room in which, once a door was closed, there wouldn't be a handle or button provided to reopen it from the inside. *But where? She had to find it.* Running her hands along the first shelf, she realized the gargantuan size of the task finding a door release anywhere among all these relics. It quickly became obvious she could spend a month and not find it. The construction of the shelves, the mechanisms for holding the delicate antiques and the antiques themselves presented far too many surfaces to challenge her search. She continued, but the resolve to find the release faded rapidly. She would have to think of something else.

Grey guided *Whiskey Sea* west toward distant buoy lights that their chart indicated were the markers for the entrance to Pearl Harbor. The yacht club where they were going to tie up was to the left of the channel entrance and just before the heavily guarded Do Not Cross This Line entrance to the navy's powerfully protected shipyard. They had about an hour's run time before reaching that point. The seas were calm, gentle swells made the dark glassy water rise and fall without disturbing the surface—like a vat of oil. The stars above were brilliant and unending.

"So what's this thing with Debra?" queried Roland, casually leaning his hip against the instrument console, having engaged the autopilot and having set the radar warning signal at Grey's request. The last thing they needed was to run over some hapless fisherman doing some night fishing. "You seem to have come to a conclusion that her story of being 'busy with her stud'"—Roland made quotation marks in the air—"wasn't quite the truth and nothing but the truth. What gives with her do you suppose?"

Grey studied his friend for a few moments. He knew that Roland operated on a very narrow line of acceptance, and if he suspected Debra was up to something, he'd change course immediately and never look back. He'd be willing to accept the consequences of his actions—*their* actions—from Bucke. What he would never accept was the consequences of someone else's actions over which he had little or no control.

"She's hedging on something," he finally volunteered. "Her words said one thing, but I came away from the conversation with the impression she wasn't too sure about the whole deal we've got going with her. Not wanting to show up until the morning was definitely a delay tactic. She disagreed with our thinking that the Ala Wai was too busy to be loading hot goods. I think she just wanted to be disagreeable and bend what she could bend in her favor.

"I suspect she's exercising her form of control over the situation. She didn't seem too responsive to our changing plans, as if we were changing them to suit ourselves, instead of staying ahead of danger. Remember Bucke saying she was a pain in the ass to work with—likes having things done to her best advantage? I'm starting to see his point about her."

"Can't blame her in a way," commented Roland. "She's unloading a lot of valuable merchandise into the hands of two guys she hasn't built any trust in nor ever even met. I'm not sure I'd be too trusting of characters like us under similar circumstances, if I were in her shoes."

"I'm not sure I'd trust her if she didn't do something to ensure her own safety—and that may be to our detriment. We'd best keep a very close eye on how things unfold tomorrow morning."

"Bucke asked us to give him a call immediately after she leaves and we've done the transfer. I'm guessing he needs his own assurances that all of us are holding up our ends of this deal and that she either walks away happy or doesn't walk away at all." Grey held Roland's stare in mutual understanding.

Viane waited out the long journey sitting on the floor braced in a corner between shelves. They gave her something solid for support as well as something to hold on to while the yacht rolled on its way to its unknown destination. She wasn't sure which gave her more cause for concern: her prisoner status or not knowing where they were going. Both were interrelated and equally dramatic in their ultimate consequences.

She sensed, from the yacht's rolling motion, that they were heading in the general direction of either Ewa or Diamond Head, east or west, running parallel to the coastline, but that was as much as she could deduce. At least they weren't going against the seas, which would have meant they were heading out toward the island of Kauai. She allowed herself to reflect on the memory of having been to Kauai only once in her life. She recalled standing with Pops as a young girl of four or five on a beach as he pointed out the distant island of Niihau and told her of the many Hawaiian families that lived there who spoke only in their native Hawaiian tongue. He told her that he knew some of the people living there from having accompanied his auntie on trips long ago. His stories and memories had enchanted many of Viane's young dreams.

Letting go of memories, she sat braced against the shelves, the hilt of the samurai sword she'd managed to find resting across her legs. If those two bozos came charging in, she'd certainly have something at hand to challenge their authority. She sat and waited for the end of the ride.

Chapter Thirty-Four

Debra Shinn couldn't relax and the glass of sauvignon blanc she had poured for herself wasn't satisfying. The wine, she knew, was fine—it was her. Her nerves always gave her fits prior to a hand off. *I'm in the wrong business—should have stuck with real estate sales.* She couldn't buy into trusting her two contacts any more than she could swallow a mango seed, even though Loren Bucke vouched for them. She didn't really care for Loren that much anyway and would gladly rat him out if she had to, just as soon as she had her money. With what she knew about his past, she could put him away for a very long time. Of course he could turn the tide on her as well, so she would have to be content to get her money and disappear.

The apparent indecision of her two contacts and their constant change of plans was a cesspool drain on her innate need to survive—her need for clear, calm, and controlled utilization of time. She didn't like surprises—in fact she despised surprises. Her utopian image of life was one where every second of every hour of every day was thoroughly preplanned, prearranged, or predetermined—by her, at least it had been ever since getting involved in smuggling, which she also despised but had few other options available.

As for the three people she had encountered in the Chart House earlier, she knew beyond any doubt they had been watching the *Whiskey Sea*. She just couldn't figure out why, and that was causing considerable concern, but she couldn't for the life of her figure out what possible connection there could be. They had looked like fun-loving, innocent-type people. Whoever they were, maybe that's why the *Whiskey Sea* was moving again and a new meet location being established. This was definitely not a comfortable situation to be faced with. If she didn't need the huge sum of money Loren was going to pay her, she'd bail immediately and never look back.

In what she determined a desperate need for backup, she picked up her cell phone and placed a call to the Filipino.

Chapter Thirty-Five

"Hey, are you up?"

"No," replied a whiney voice still in the clutches of sleep. "Stone," she emphasized his name with feigned, overacted dismay, "why do you insist on waking me up so early? What time is it, anyway? It must still be dark."

"Listen, Whiney-Voiced Person, it's almost 6:15 a.m., and the birds have already had a field day with the worms."

"I really don't care about the worms right at this point. I'll say a prayer for them later. Right now, I need a very large cup of coffee in order to become civilized and able to engage in meaningful words, which seems to be the direction you're attempting to push me in."

"Do you realize how much I enjoy your early morning, leave-me-alone voice?"

"Are you a sadist, getting kicks out of torturing people you care about? I'm going to keep my eyes on you, buster, for further signs of imbalance."

"Can we talk seriously for a second? We need to get our *okoles* in gear and find Viane."

"I know, I know," she said admittedly. "I'm just giving you reason to think about my sexy, sleepy voice." In Stone's imagination, he saw her lips crease into a smile.

"Who said anything about a sexy voice? Did I say sexy? I don't recall bringing sex into this conversation."

It sounded like she was clearing her voice or maybe mumbling some derogatory word; it was difficult to distinguish over the phone, but he thought he heard her say something to the effect of "I'll get you for that, just wait."

"Listen to what I have planned," she said, her voice suddenly became strong and surprisingly filled with confidence, the sleepiness disappearing and the friendliness returning. "After you dropped me off at home last night, I got on the Internet and located all the shipyards around the Pacific Northwest as well as most of their phone numbers. Remember Viane telling us about seeing the words Port Townsend printed beneath the name *Whiskey Sea* when she was left floating in its wake with Margelese stationed at the railing? That information could be a huge help if we could just find someone who knows anything about that yacht. If it berths anywhere around the Puget Sound in Washington, it would have to have been dry-docked somewhere close by in the past few years. Someone is bound to know something about her."

"I was going to start calling the numbers later this morning, but since I'm now awake, thanks to you," the latter said in her best scolding voice, "I can start as soon as I get my coffee fix. Why don't I call you if and when I find out something or by midday at the latest, whichever comes first? Will you be home, or would you rather hunt around town for a pay phone and call me instead?"

He ignored her jab. "Let me call you. Oh, and I've got some unpleasant news for you. The *Whiskey Sea* is no longer tied up in the Ala Wai where it was yesterday."

"Oh my god, Stone," Teri said, coming instantly present and alert with the news. "How do you know that? We were just there a few hours ago." Surprise mixed with fear flowed heavily through the receiver.

"As we speak," he said, "I'm staring at the very place they were last night. I'm at a pay phone by the Harbormaster's office. I came over early this morning in hopes of seeing something that might help us, but what I found was the empty transient dock.

"We've got to find the *Whiskey Sea*, Teri. I have a terrible feeling about Viane's situation and the danger she's probably in. I'll take a thorough look around here, and if I don't find the yacht, I'll go look around Kewalo Basin, Honolulu Harbor, and then Keehi Lagoon. I talked with Lloyd earlier, and he's going over to Kaneohe Yacht Club to see if they went back there. It's a long shot, but we can't overlook the possibility."

"I'm scared, Stone. Viane must be going crazy wherever she is. She's got a lot of resolve and strength of spirit, but this may be pushing her boundaries. I pray she's all right."

"Me too, angel. She's a strong and determined woman. If anyone can come through this without stepping on kukus, she can. Let's do what we can and compare notes in a couple hours."

Teri heard him call her "angel." A warm contentment momentarily flowed through her but quickly gave way to an overpowering concern that they were wasting valuable time. She'd think about the pleasant aspects of being called "angel" later, once Viane was safely home.

Stone drove as far as the end of Lagoon Drive behind Honolulu International Airport looking at all the shoreline anchoring spots that could handle a yacht the size of *Whiskey Sea* but failed to see any sign of it. He did, however, find a pay phone outside Chunkies Drive Inn.

Half the day had gone, mostly used up in fighting through traffic, and he had nothing to show for the time. He was no closer to finding *Whiskey Sea* or Viane than when he got up this morning. His nerves were starting to form sharp edges as his apprehension expanded. He called Lloyd again to see if he'd had any better luck.

"Eh, Stone, that guy Kelvin is turning out to be a pretty good guy after all." Lloyd had gone over to Kaneohe Yacht Club to see if the *Whiskey Sea* had returned. It hadn't. "I told Kelvin a story about having an important appointment with the two men onboard but couldn't remember what yacht club they said they'd be at. He proceeded to call some of the other clubs for me, and guess what?"

"I'm too uptight to guess, Lloyd. What did he find?"

"The *Whiskey Sea* joined the navy."

"What the devil are you talking about? This is not a good time to joke with me. I've hunted every square inch of coastline from Waikiki to the airport, and I'm a little on the cranky side right now."

"Okay, okay. Keep your slippers on. Get this—the *Whiskey Sea* was scheduled to pull into Pearl Harbor Yacht Club late last night. I mean very late last night, like around 1:30 a.m. this morning."

"How did Kelvin manage to discover that?"

"Like I said, Kelvin's a great guy. He doesn't get to work until nine, so I drove the coastline from Kailua to Hawaii Kai, figuring I might see it anchored somewhere along the way but saw nothing. I got back to Kaneohe just as Kelvin was walking across the parking lot toward his office. He hadn't heard from the *Whiskey Sea* since they left, but as a favor, he called around the places I hadn't looked at yet and was told by the office clerk at Pearl, when he called there, that she had just posted a check for an overnight stay for *Whiskey Sea*. She hadn't gone out to look at it yet but planned to later. Hey, Stone, guess what else? Wait, you don't want to guess, do you? Kelvin told me I was in trouble because I hadn't called Aunt Emily lately. How'd he manage to come up with that, you ask? Turns out he's a second cousin on my mother's side. He didn't connect my name when I was here the other day. I haven't talked with Aunt Emily for years and haven't seen her for many more years than that, so he didn't recognize my face, and I didn't recognize his or his name for that matter. Since he's so much younger than I am, I wouldn't have known his face if I'd run over it with my lawnmower. You know, living on different islands, half the families never see one another. Thanks, Stone, for getting me into this mess. I owe you one—of what I'm not sure yet."

Stone couldn't tell whether his friend was meaning a "happy" mess or just a mess. Family connections had a habit of going either way.

"Mess or not, *mahalo* for getting this information. It could be just what we need to find Viane. I'll tell Pam she has to give you a special kiss for this—maybe even your auntie will get in on the kissing part next time you see her. Where are you now? We need to drive to Ewa Beach and go visit the yacht club at Pearl. Maybe even get Mike to mount a charge on those guys."

"With Monday traffic, it'd take me an hour just to get to where you are. Why don't you head for Ewa, and I'll meet you at the yacht club as soon as I can get there."

"If Teri's available, would you mind picking her up and bringing her with you? I know she wants to be there, and Viane will need her there as well if we're fortunate enough to find her, and I get the feeling we will. I'll call Teri, and if you don't hear back from me in the next few minutes, then assume she'll be waiting for you."

"Why don't you just call me back anyway, Stone? You know I don't thrive too well on these sorts of loose ends."

There was a silence on the other end of the phone before Stone's subdued voice finally responded. "I'm almost out of change for this darn phone, Lloyd, and I don't want to use a credit card for a fifty-cent call. Just go get her, will you?"

Stone could hear Lloyd softly laughing before the call disconnected. *That's it—I've about had enough,* he thought. *I'm either going to have to get a cell phone or carry a couple tin cans and a very long string. Why doesn't civilization take a break from continual change for a change?* He had to laugh at himself and at his ever-present, yet admittedly dissolving, stubbornness.

Chapter Thirty-Six

Two cars slowly moved through the gates of Pearl Harbor Yacht Club a little after five in the morning. The lead car had its headlights on, the car following, far enough back to be undetectable, did not.

The first car through was a Ford Explorer of nondescript color in the early morning darkness. It moved with intention to a spot close to where the *Whiskey Sea* was docked. Debra Shinn knew exactly where to park since she'd had the Filipino scope out the yacht club's layout earlier. He was in the second car.

He circled the parking lot and came to a stop facing the gate through, which they had both just entered. He let the car idle and got out, leaving the driver's door wide open while he went around and opened the passenger door as well. It was precautionary—they had preplanned all of this in the event he and Debra found the need to leave quickly. The interior light bulbs of his car had been removed a long time before, just for covert actions such as this. There had been other times in the past that night stealth and lack of interior car lights had become useful, once even critical, and the stealth move had saved both their lives.

This was the second time this morning that the Filipino had parked in such a manner. He'd spent the better part of the early morning hours parked here in the shadows watching *Whiskey Sea* enter the small harbor and tie up. He had stayed there, vigilant, until the time came to meet Debra and follow her back in. He really didn't like doing the sort of thing he was now being called upon to do. In his mind's eye, he could see himself being an artist, working with all the beautiful types of wood found around the islands. He knew he would like doing that, but he honored Debra with his life in friendship with her and wouldn't think of not being her support.

His name was really Dorteo Aquino. He and Debra had grown up together in Makiki, on the island of Oahu, under the shadow of the Kamehameha Schools, which was upslope, higher on the hillside. They were close friends and had become reliant on one another as one did with close friends since neither had anyone else to call family. Each of their parents, as well as all their siblings, had been killed in the same boating mishap when Debra and Dorteo were still in high school. They had lucked out, if that was the best way to think about it, in having a test at school that day, so neither had joined the two families on the fateful fishing trip. Each had grown with the understanding that they needed one another and needed to watch out for the other's well-being. Dorteo started calling himself the Filipino soon after the accident. It gave him strength when he most needed to be strong and gave him a soul attachment to his father, whom he had worshipped.

His father had been a gentle soul, having been born into a very poor family in Roxas City on the island of Panay in the Philippines. His father had migrated to Hawaii to work on a sugar plantation. His wages, though small, were many times more than his counterparts could earn in the Philippines, and he was able to send money back home for his family's support. It was something Dorteo rarely thought about now, other than during times of quiet meditation when he brought his father's image to mind.

Debra quickly glanced over her shoulder, through her car window, in the direction of her friend. She could just make out the vague image of his car in the darkened shadows. She knew he would be vigilant and would be quick to notice anything out of the ordinary. Of course, transferring illegal art objects from her car to the yacht was anything but ordinary; but in their chosen line of endeavors, it fell in step with much of what she and the Filipino did as a means of supporting themselves.

She sat for a few moments watching *Whiskey Sea*, trying to sense any danger that may be present. Some interior lights were on, which meant her contacts were at least awake. She was early. It was exactly the way she preferred it and the way she had planned it. If anything was amiss, she hoped she'd sense it in time to escape. In the black market business of art and antiquities, vigilance was the only way to keep on the forward edge of survival.

She waited fifteen minutes, assuring herself the Filipino was in place and ready to act, before getting out of her car and walking the short distance to *Whiskey Sea*. She knocked on the hull to announce her arrival.

Roland was lifting a cup to his lips for his first taste of coffee—something he had come to anticipate and which gave him good reason to get out of bed in the morning, hung over or not, the former being the usual. It pretty much gave his body the signal that, in a few minutes, the day would begin to unfold in earnest. He heard the knocking and knew this morning was going to start on its own schedule.

If it was anyone other than Debra, he knew things could get complicated. If it was Debra, then things had already become complicated. They weren't ready for her. *Why in God's name is she early?*

Grey came rushing into the lounge from the opposite doorway away from the dock. "What the hell?" He gave Roland a quick look, who shrugged his shoulders in response. Grey immediately began to undress, throwing his pants and shirt together with his shoes into the corner behind the bar, and then hastily wrapping a towel around his waist. He quickly ruffled his hair and walked out to see who was there.

Roland chuckled to himself. He had to give Grey a lot of credit. The man was always able to rise into immediate action, usually with some amusing outcomes, whenever things moved out of his preconceived notion of order. Whoever was knocking on the outside hull of their yacht would see a man fresh out of a shower and presumably still naked under the towel. It would buy precious minutes with logical excuses.

"Good morning," said Grey, looking down at the Oriental woman standing on the pier next to the gangway.

"Debra," was all she said in response, looking up at the man above her. She'd expected to confront her two contacts with some element of surprise at being early, but the appearance of someone wearing just a towel threw her surprise back at her.

The person she was looking up at wasn't at all the rich, balding, potbellied old black marketer she'd envisioned. She was looking at a ruggedly handsome, well-tanned man, somewhat thick around the middle although not unattractively, with a mat of chest hair that made her knees weak just looking at it. *So much for my having any advantage.*

"You're early," said Grey, holding his anger as best he could. He noticed the effect his fresh-out-of-the-shower presence had on her. He'd seen it a few times before when he needed to gain an upper hand when dealing with overly assertive women. He knew he had gained the upper hand once again but was still ill-tempered that she'd try to throw them off base by showing up early. He figured she'd been in the yacht club grounds observing *Whiskey Sea*, searching for potential trouble spots. It's what he and Rol would have done had roles been reversed, but he had no intention of easing off on her.

"Obviously, you'll have to wait a little until we're dressed. You're early," he repeated, again, "but then I'm guessing you knew that already."

"May I come aboard and wait, instead of standing on the pier?"

"That is most unacceptable," replied Grey. "I suggest you return to your car and drive someplace. Plan to be back here at six as arranged." With that said, Grey turned and walked back into the lounge without waiting for her to respond.

Debra's anger nearly rose to the break point as she turned and headed for her car. If she didn't need to unload the artifacts and get the money Loren had promised her, money she badly needed and Dorteo depended upon, she would drive away and never look back. As it was, though, she knew she had no choice but to comply. She called the Filipino as she closed her car's door. He answered before she heard a ring.

"Dorteo, keep watch. I'm to get lost someplace until six. I'll be back then."

"No sweat, Deb. I have them covered." He didn't need to ask why she was leaving for the sake of thirty-five minutes. She knew her way through these sorts of dealings, and he knew that and trusted her actions. *Never rock the boat—literally in this case.*

Grey walked back into the lounge. Roland had been standing by the door, so he'd heard what transpired.

"We better get the girl moved. Guaranteed that bitch is going to come back before six. Let's put our guest on the floor of the map room and lock the doors. Our business with Debra shouldn't take very long. We can get away from here as soon as she leaves."

Viane's senses quickened. She was aware that something was about to happen but wasn't sure what. She pulled the sword as close as possible to her side and waited. Suddenly, a brilliant light came on overhead, illuminating her confined space and momentarily blinding her.

Roland and Grey stood in the darkened lounge, observing her on the other side of the mirrored glass.

"Look at that, would you," exclaimed Roland. "She's got the bindings off and armed herself with our sword. Resourceful woman. It's a shame we can't keep her for a while. God, I hope she hasn't done any damage to that sword. A scratch would shave a hundred thousand off the price."

"Instead of worrying about that sword, Rol, try imagining what would have happened if we'd just walked in there in the dark without turning on the lights and taking a look first." He looked at his friend for confirmation of the possible bloodbath they barely avoided. Having survived what she'd been through after Margelese threw her overboard, Grey had no doubt about her instincts to survive and probably her ability wielding that sword. He shuddered at the thought.

"This presents an interesting scenario," observed Roland, "but we don't have the luxury of time to mess with her." He looked at Grey with a question-marked expression. "Tranquilizer gun?" It was partly a question but more a statement. He reached to a low shelf behind the bar and came up holding a rifle. He inserted a dart and breached it home as he moved to the bookshelf beside the closed mirror door.

"Okay, open it up, I'm ready. You know it's been a while since we've played with this toy—I hope it still works."

The dart caught Viane squarely in her left shoulder. She immediately slumped to the floor, her face missing the blade's edge by merely an inch.

They quickly carried her to the map room, retying her arms and legs before stuffing a chart rag into her mouth. They roughly crumpled her into a ball, knees against her chest, and shoved her beneath the chart table.

"Let's close the window curtains. If it's dark in here, Debra won't be able to see in through the mirror. This girl will be out for hours," observed Roland.

"Let's hope so, Rol. Remember, these darts are pretty damn old."

Chapter Thirty-Seven

Teri had never realized there were that many places around the Pacific Northwest where one could dry-dock a yacht. She'd been on the phone for the past two hours calling various boat yards in and around the Puget Sound area and Seattle. She was becoming disheartened and beginning to believe her supposed great idea was nothing more than an ill thought-out crap shoot. Several people remembered a yacht exactly like the one she repeatedly described but invariably said the one they were thinking of wasn't named *Whiskey Sea*. Many told her straight out that the yacht she was describing was named *My Mistress* and asked if she hadn't perhaps misread its name. At least this gave her some renewed hope. Her call to the fifteenth yard finally paid off, and she wondered why she hadn't called it first considering where it was located.

The woman she spoke with at a shipyard in Port Townsend, Washington, said she knew the yacht in question and that it had been in her yard just a few months before for regular dry-dock maintenance as well as a renaming. Teri's smile said it all at hearing this confirmation. She was put in touch with a man named Teak who was the shipwright who oversaw all the work on *My Mistress*-turned-*Whiskey Sea.*

"Yeah, I remember that boat. People don't make boats like that anymore. I remember her well. Had the most beautiful and extensive bright work I've ever had a chance to work with. Just the mention of her brings back lots of memories. Was the oddest as well as the most fun job I've ever been a part of. Probably why I remember her so well."

Teak was self-employed and did contract work for boat yards around the Olympic Peninsula. He'd found ample work at the Port Townsend yard and so far saw no reason to move on, so he explained. Besides, he liked the small-town feeling too much to leave—for now anyway, he said. He claimed he was the best of the best as far as craftsmanship and, as a result, only took work on yachts whose owners had no particular need to pinch dollars or shave the quality of materials. "And those two guys, for all their playing around, sure demanded my top-quality work, but they sure paid real good."

His name was Teak, as he explained to Teri, but confessed that his given name was Dick. He didn't bother to mention his last name, and Teri didn't ask. His laugh was deep and throaty with a quality that came from years of too many cigarettes and too much booze. He explained that friends in taverns he'd been in over the years started calling him Teak Dick. "You know," he said, "as in teakwood used on decks? You get that? Soon everyone just shortened it to Teak, and I liked it so I kept it."

"Well, Teak, tell me about the work you did on the *My Mistress* later renamed *Whiskey Sea.*"

"Damndest, oh, sorry about that, darndest job I ever worked on like I just said. Job lasted way longer than any I've ever worked before or since and three times longer than I programmed for, but they paid me good, as I already told you, so guess I can't complain, right, lady?"

"Why did the job last so long, Teak?" asked Teri, eager to keep him talking and find out the information she hoped to gather. "May I ask what you did to her that took you so long?"

"Wasn't the job in particular that took all that much extra time, although those guys had some pretty tight standards and weird requests for me to follow, as I already made mention. Seems I'd go onboard early in the morning to start my work, then along comes those two owners—forget their names now—names ain't part of my memory pattern, you know, lady. Soon's those two showed up a cold beer suddenly found its way into my hand and my work and the rest of the day went south from there. Didn't take long till I couldn't cut a straight line in a piece a wood if my life depended on it. Course if you know boats, you know there ain't many straight lines on 'em to cut anyway, right, lady?" His laughter at his own humor was infectious: Teri liked him already. "Only time I could get my work done was when those fellas didn't show up for a few days at a time.

"Say, why you asking about that boat anyway, lady? What'd you say your name was again?"

"It's Teri, and I'm thinking of buying it," she lied. "They said they had work done, so I wanted to speak to the professional who did the alterations." She hoped she was saying the right words. Apparently, she was.

Teak's voice relaxed a little. For a while there, he'd begun to feel as if he was being interrogated. "You like what I did, do you, lady?" Her name was gone again. "You happen to be in the rare book business too?"

"No, Teak, why do you ask?"

"I figured you may have seen how those two guys did their business and was getting in on the fast money. Must be darn good business to be in, judging by all the dough those two splashed around. You know, that room I built is as completely air, moisture, and sound tight as I could make her—they insisted on it. Said they needed to keep everything from getting in. Said some of the books they find around the world are worth small fortunes."

"That's interesting, Teak. I didn't ask what they did for a living." She was getting more information than she'd hoped for. Teak was finding his own importance in knowing something someone else didn't know and wasn't about to stop.

"Said they hunted the world for rare books for a bunch of museums and collectors. Sort of a hobby, they said. Fancy someone actually collecting books." His laugh came close to sounding like a hacking cough and may have been. "I say that's one hell of a job to have. Sure wish I could figure something like that out. Could just sit around, drink the best of anything, forget work, and just look around for some old books. That'd be the life."

"It's a dream for many of us, Teak. I hope you never give up on your dreams. Could I ask you more about that room? It was open when I looked, so I didn't have an opportunity to see what sort of hardware you used. I guess you used a pretty good door handle since the door looked awfully heavy."

Teak had another good laugh. He was enjoying being able to share some gems of wisdom. He proceeded to tell her about the hidden latch and the air-glide opening and then told her the secret procedure he had devised to unlock it—he was on a roll dispensing knowledge.

"Say, missy"—perhaps a more endearing name in Teak's mind—"if you buy it, you'll have to promise to bring her back here. 'Bout time for another dry dock anyways. We can do the marine inspection for you as well right here, if you like. Say, where are you anyhow? Funny, I remember those fellas saying they'd never sell her. Wonder why they changing their minds."

He wasn't giving Teri any chance to answer his questions—something she was grateful for.

"Say, I forgot to ask. What'd you think of that hot tub? That was one of the most peculiar things I built."

Teri found herself at a loss for what to say, and she didn't want to discourage Teak from telling her more. She hadn't noticed a hot tub when she was onboard nor could she imagine where it might be. "That's one of the most intriguing parts of the yacht, Teak. Who would have thought of doing such a thing? Was it their idea or yours?"

"Well, missy, had that been my idea, I would've scrapped the whole stateroom and put it smack in the middle 'stead of in the forward anchor hold. It's not like they don't have lots of other staterooms. Can you imagine the whole stateroom changed over to an outdoor hot tub garden 'cept it'd be all down below deck? Maybe when you buy it, you and me can think on doing that."

"I'll look forward to the day, Teak."

"What were those fellas' names again? I remember they was a lot of fun until we was all too drunk to remember where our toes met. Sure could drink. 'Bout put me under the bar I built for them every night they was there, and I'm a darn good drinker when it comes to holding my own. Fact, I can hold it better'n most. So what part of my work do you like the best?"

The phone was finally quiet; he was waiting for an answer.

"Their names are Roland and Grey, and they didn't fully explain all the work you did for them, other than the storage room, the hot tub, and the name change." She was reaching on this. "Why don't you tell me all about it, and, Teak, I realize this is taking some of your valuable time, so why don't I hire you for an hour's worth of work while we talk. Does that sound fair to you?"

"Yeah, Grey and Roland, that's them. You know, lady, it's a long story, and we've been at it for twenty minutes now. Maybe we ought to call her two hours. How's that sound to you?"

"That would be perfect, Teak. Tell me all about how you changed the yacht."

It took the better part of an hour. Teak was a man of great detail and long stories, which worked to Teri's advantage. He told her more than she needed to hear as well as more than she hoped to discover. Having listened to Teak describe things, she was really wishing she'd found the hot tub. All she had to do now was find out where a forward anchor hold was located. She ended the conversation, promising Teak he'd have an opportunity to work on the *Whiskey Sea* again if she went ahead with the purchase. She really felt guilty lying to him. Teak sounded like a very genuine and likable soul.

He gave her explicit instructions on where she should mail his money and to whom she should make out the money order. He wasn't into taking checks by mail, he claimed.

She couldn't wait to tell Stone about Teak and his long-winded story.

Chapter Thirty-Eight

Debra walked up to the hull of the *Whiskey Sea* checking her watch. It was precisely 6:00 a.m. She reached down and picked up a piece of drift wood that lay close to her feet, and then quickly glanced toward where Dorteo was secreted. She calmed a bit knowing he was close, giving her the confidence to proceed. For all the determined strength she portrayed as a front to everyone she dealt with, only Dorteo knew that she was actually quite timid by nature.

Drawing in the needed courage, she rapped heavily on the side of the hull of the yacht with the wood. It was a perfect find: it saved her knuckles as well as giving her a degree of satisfaction to vent a bit of lingering hostility on the perfect white-painted side of the hull. She hadn't yet dropped the wood when she noticed two men standing directly above her looking down. This time, though, there was no mistaking the let's-get-to-it aura surrounding them with no curly-haired, bare chest visible to muddle her thoughts.

"Come aboard," said the shorter one, the one her eyes could still envision clearly beneath the shirt he now wore. The other was taller with a playful, carefree-looking face. Both were very handsome, she observed.

She followed them into a room that could be a library or a saloon, depending on one's taste in life.

"Here, Debra"—the hairy-chested one stood, pointing at another small adjoining room—"is where your artifacts will be stored until we release them to Loren. I understand you have five pieces to give us. Is that correct, and how big are they?"

He might have a playful face, but he's all business, she thought.

She held out her hands to describe their size. "As that old saying goes, it's not how big they are but how much they're worth in the pocket." She smiled at herself for the veiled reference that still lingered from her earlier morning vision of him in a towel.

"Rol," said Grey, "help her carry the pieces onboard. I'll prepare a spot on the lower part of one of the shelves."

"I hope you use something stronger than that piece of cut rope." As she spoke, she pointed to the rope Viane had managed to cut to shreds and left on the carpet in the corner. They'd overlooked it when they carried Viane from the room.

"I assure you, your things will be quite safe from harm," said Grey as he picked up the mangled piece of rope. He saw another piece sticking out from under the nearest shelf and brushed it farther under with his foot.

They brought her things onboard in one trip and gently placed them on the shelf Grey had cleared.

"These are quite extraordinary," admired Grey. He held up an object he couldn't identify and ran his fingers along the smooth, obviously very old, wooden piece that Debra had handed him.

"They're ancient," offered Debra. "All of these pieces arc from a very remote part of Northern Japan. The piece you're holding was the cradle on which the Samurai who it belonged to rested his sword, or *katana*, when he retired for the evening. It allowed him to keep it close by his side while he slept. It probably dates to the year AD 900."

"The other piece in front of you"—she pointed at a strange looking hat with horns—"is the helmet he wore into battle. Look at the deep gash along the side." She pointed to a slice that nearly cut through the combination-leather-and-metal helmet. "He was a very lucky man in that one instance."

"All of these pieces are worth a fortune on the collectors' market, a fortune of which Loren still owes me my share. You'll secure them well for the voyage?" she asked. "Loren assured me you are both quite capable of handling these pieces. You won't mind if I watch while you secure them?" It wasn't a question to which she expected a reply. She folded her arms across her chest in a defiant stance with no intention of leaving until she was satisfied.

She hadn't bothered to look around; otherwise, she'd have noticed the samurai sword lying on the shelf where Grey had placed it after removing it from Viane's hand while she lay unconscious. He didn't bother pointing it out to her. He wanted this over with quickly and her off their yacht.

The shelves had a series of sliding clamps fashioned with deep felt-covered foam. The more delicate pieces were clamped from both sides as well as in front and back. Grey, kneeling on the carpet facing the shelf, lowered a fifth padded brace from beneath the shelf above, letting it come to rest on the top of each piece, solidly securing all five from movement in any direction.

As Grey slid the last pad into place over the helmet, with Debra observing the process over his shoulder, the solemn silence that had shrouded the vault was unexpectedly broken by a low, brief rumble from the map room—quite audible and quite recognizable.

Grey and Roland simultaneously realized their oversight. In their haste to move Viane, they had failed to close the small cubbyhole cover in the pass-through between them and the map room. They had opened it to allow air to enter the vault when the girl was tied up and left in here and had totally forgotten about closing it. With it open, their supposedly soundproof chamber was obviously no longer soundproof.

Grey, busily securing the last of the padding, stopped moving his hands—he remained frozen in place as if time had suddenly ceased.

Roland, who had been standing at the entrance to the vault idly watching Grey do his thing, looked at Debra with a stunned expression, not sure if he should laugh, ignore the sound and deny it had happened, or simply turn around and fix a drink. He was inclined to laugh—he saw humor in the oddest places—but one look at Debra's face silenced him.

Debra's eyes were opened wide in stunned disbelief as if someone had just walked up in back and goosed her. Her expression showed a complicated mixture of fear and anger suddenly overridden with accusation. She looked at her two companions in turn. "Who the hell else is here?" she demanded, her voice rising as anger replaced everything else she felt. Anger had always been a justifiable accomplice, saving her on many occasions—she was good at using it to her advantage. "That was a fart I just heard. Who are you hiding behind that glass?" She began to reach for the closest object at hand, a carving of some sort, with the obvious intention of throwing it at the glass wall but immediately dismissed the thought.

Then, before giving any thought to waiting for an answer, she saw the look on the faces of her two contacts, and it became clear she had to get out quickly. She instantly became conscious of being trapped and equally aware she had to summon the Filipino's help. Roland stood in the doorway, essentially blocking her escape.

Everything happened in a split-second sequence.

As Debra began to move, both men recovered their sense of place and purpose and also began to move—Grey came to his feet bounding up like a depressed spring while Roland, who had been closest to Debra, threw his arms around her and raised her feet off the floor, thus immobilizing her.

"Now what?" exclaimed Roland, looking to his friend for some indication of what should happen next. He didn't need to wait.

Debra began fighting him even with her arms pinned to her side, his shins being pummeled by the heels of her shoes. He wanted to punch her to make her stop, but all of a sudden, she yelled.

"Dorteo," she screamed piercingly loud. "Dorteo, I need help."

Roland shifted his arms and clamped a hand over her mouth.

"Holy crap, she's got back up somewhere!" exclaimed Grey, an unusual expletive for him. Now he understood what bothered him about Debra that he couldn't wrap his mind around earlier—she wasn't the least bit trustworthy. He should have listened to his intuition. *The bitch.*

Working quickly, Grey retrieved a length of cord from the lounge and some duct tape they kept on a shelf beside the doorway and went to Roland's aid.

With mouth taped and arms pinned to her body by the cord, Roland busily wrapped her legs and feet with the remaining portion of cord. Grey rushed out on deck on the back side of the yacht away from the club and hurriedly moved aft. Peering around the corner of the cabin area, he scanned the grounds for whoever Dorteo might be.

Since Debra's vocal outburst had been within the confines of the vault and both doors to the lounge had been closed, he wasn't too concerned about her having awoken a slumbering army, but he desperately needed to identify this mystery person and know where he was hiding.

Without much effort, Grey spotted the faint but distinct outline of a car parked facing the club's entrance, its door open. By itself it was obvious, since the car was out of place. It wasn't a spot anyone would choose to park. He couldn't be too sure, but he thought he could see the silhouette of someone sitting behind the wheel. *That must be Dorteo,* he surmised. Dorteo didn't appear to be moving to help his partner. *So much for her bodyguard coming to the rescue.*

It was still early morning, and the club remained quiet, as mornings around waterfronts often are. An elderly woman walking her very tiny dog was all the activity he could see.

Debra's screams hadn't caused many ripples in the serenity of the club's grounds.

"We've got to move—and now," he said as he reentered the lounge and closed the door behind him. "Her bodyguard is sitting in his car by the entrance and doesn't appear to have been aroused by her outburst. I'm going to go power up. You undo the lines from our end but let them lie loosely on deck so they'll fall away as we pull out. Her bodyguard is probably watching, so keep your body close to the deck. Unhook the gangplank as well. We'll have to leave it behind."

Dorteo was getting nervous. He lit another cigarette while admonishing himself for this habit he couldn't break, knowing that every time he lit up he was potentially showing himself to anyone who would be looking. It'd already been too long, and he wasn't sure what he should be doing about it, but the cigarette was helping him think.

He got out of the car, having decided to walk toward the boat as nonchalantly as he could and see if he could hear any voices from inside. As he moved around the back of his car and began walking toward the boat, he became aware of the sound of motors coming to life. As the realization hit home, the boat, with Debra still aboard, began slowly moving away from the dock.

He broke into a sprint, almost bowling over an old lady and whatever it was on the other end of the leash, berating himself on his diminished lung capacity. He hurled himself over the edge of the dock, reaching for the boat's aft railing, hoping to grab it and hoist himself aboard. He'd witnessed it done in movies many times and saw no reason he shouldn't be able to do the same gymnastics. He hopelessly plunged three feet short of the mark and submerged several feet into the yacht's wake and the club's harbor. He resurfaced, banging his head hard on the gangplank, which had been hurriedly allowed to fall away and left to float in the wake.

Chapter Thirty-Nine

Roland stayed low on the deck and watched as Debra's bodyguard leapt into the air, grabbing for anything solid but falling dangerously shy of the stern railing and the churning propellers beneath. Seeing that he presented no further discernible problem, he went forward to join Grey at the helm.

"I have to say, her man Friday has a good shot at winning gold at the Olympics if he ever takes up broad jumping as a sport. He damn near made it onto the deck, but he also damn near fell on the propellers as well. That could have been messy. He's busy swimming for the bulkhead at the moment." They both laughed, more out of relief at having avoided a noisy fight than by the situational humor of it all.

"It appears we have another situation to deal with now—the woman," declared Grey. "I guess if we're to dump one body in the drink, we can just as easily do a two-for."

"Look at the favor we'll be doing Loren," added Roland. "He'll save the money he'd promised to pay her, and since he recently admitted he didn't really care about the woman anyway, she'll soon be out of his hair altogether. Maybe we should ask him for a finder's fee, but in reverse. What would we call it? How about a loser's fee?" They both chuckled at the thought, neither one of them bothered by the elimination task before them—they'd wait until tomorrow for that.

After hog-tying her and running tape twice around her head to keep her mouth shut, they left Debra lying on the floor of the vault and closed the mirrored door. They were careful, though, to make sure she couldn't get herself free of the bonds—their mistake with the younger girl had been lesson enough for them.

"You know, we're actually fortunate she has a bodyguard as it turns out. With him alive and well, we won't have to worry about her car causing concern for anyone," observed Grey. "I imagine Dorteo, or whatever his name is, will do something about it."

"He's bound to," offered Roland. "It's not like we abducted a princess. She's a thief like the rest of us. He'll no more want to get the police involved than I would choose to stop liking scotch, and we both know that's not likely to happen."

Earlier, lying in the dark in the map room unable to move, much less able to use her voice other than a loud throat hum because of the tape over her mouth, Viane watched the action through the mirrored glass as it took place in the vault. More artifacts, probably stolen, she guessed, were being placed on the shelves as Roland and an Oriental woman looked on. She was glad the lights in the vault were bright enough to let her see through the mirrored glass.

She desperately wanted to gain the woman's attention as she figured the woman may be more sympathetic of her situation than her two captors and may actually be in a position to help her escape. She pushed hard against the bindings, but all she got for her effort was a rather large and loud discharge of gas.

Before she could experience any embarrassment, even though there was no one in the room to cause her embarrassment, or to apologize to—Pops was forever on her case about some of her unladylike ways—she watched in horror as Roland suddenly grabbed the woman from behind; and as he fought off her struggles and kicks, he proceeded to bind her arms and legs with tape and a piece of cord. It was a surrealistic movie playing out before her eyes. She watched as the action took place just a few feet away, yet it was all in muffled quietness, like a Charlie Chaplin movie before talkies and color, except a portion of the sound partially penetrated the glass wall. That was confusing. She was under the impression the vault was virtually soundproof. There were faint scuffling sounds as Roland kept control over the gyrations of the woman as they all left the room. The lights in the vault abruptly went out, and the lounge doorway closed, throwing everything, the vault, and Viane's map-room prison, into darkness.

Tears began to flow unabated as the helplessness of her situation became blatantly real. Knowing she was being held captive was one thing, but with a second hostage in the mix, her plight became a degree closer to frightening. At the sudden sound of engines springing to life, the "knowing" that her fate was rapidly approaching its end became much clearer. Instinct told her that any hope of rescue was quickly dwindling—surviving was going to be entirely up to her.

The *Whiskey Sea* made her way out of the Pearl Harbor basin and turned south, steering toward the area off Waikiki and beyond toward the Kaiwi Channel. The mainland was their destination, Washington State in particular, being the eventual target. Loren was expecting them and had their money waiting for them.

Roland and Grey had discussed and agreed that it would be in their best interest to become land-bound for an unspecified amount of time, as this particular "gathering" trip was leaving them both with the desire to disappear for a while and regroup. They were swiftly gaining a large contingency of people interested in finding them, including the recent addition, Dorteo. They were both hoping the same boatswain was still working around the boat yard in Port Townsend. Dry-dock was in order as well as another name change for *Whiskey Sea.* Maybe a complete repainting to change her appearance would be advantageous although they would not want to cover up all the beautiful bright work with paint if there were any way to avoid doing so. As for a name change, they were thinking that *Scotch on the Rocks* may be a good one—neither wanted to deviate too far from their favorite liquid pastime.

Chapter Forty

Stone pulled into the parking area of the Pearl Harbor Yacht Club anxiously anticipating what he was going to do when he finally laid eyes on *Whiskey Sea,* as well as what he'd find when he actually managed to get onboard.

After buying a hamburger at Chunkies Drive Inn, which in truth he didn't want, and getting change for the pay phone, his reason for buying the hamburger in the first place, he'd called Mike, only to have his friend tell him there was still nothing either he or Honolulu PD could do since all they had so far was hearsay. No crime reports had been turned in that he was aware of. He'd taken the opportunity to remind Stone of the need for a missing person report on Viane, which, he said, no one had filed. He told Stone that the fruitless search they had done the day before had not given sufficient reason to do any more. He apologized and hoped everyone understood the problems his superiors would undoubtedly lay on him if they were to discover his involvement in the blind search. He didn't think he should press his luck any further.

Stone was tempted to tell Mike that there was no way he understood, but in reality he did and felt some regret for putting his friend in that kind of position.

Looking around the club's dock area, he felt the beginnings of an alarm. He was not seeing anything that remotely resembled *Whiskey Sea* and began to question just how good Kelvin's information had actually been. He knew he had built up high expectations and was heavily relying on Lloyd's assessment, which was usually right on the mark.

He located a phone in the club's office, as well as meeting a very accommodating Alegra, the office manager. She was young and almost too thin but had an incredibly engaging smile that seemed to brighten the surroundings and forced anyone meeting her to smile in response, Stone included as he returned her smile, while waiting for Teri to answer her phone.

"Stone," Teri said, excitement cascading through her voice when she realized who was on the other end of her phone. "Wait until you hear what I have discovered about *Whiskey Sea*. This'll blow your slippers off," she said. "You were right in thinking there was hidden space between those two rooms. There is." Her voice came close to a joyous shout, she was so excited. "The owners, the now infamous Grey and Roland, had it handcrafted to order while in dry dock in the small town of Port Townsend in Washington State." She relayed Teak's whole story including her own observations of his memory for names. "Did you know they have a hot tub on that boat, I mean, yacht? Sorry."

"From what we're finding out about these two guys, they sound like old-time playboys, so I'm not too surprised to hear that. Certainly unusual, that's for sure."

"Interesting they would choose to change the yacht's name along with all the modifications they had the shipwright make. I'm not sure what implications that carries, but somehow it must be meaningful, although it may have nothing to do with what Viane stumbled into. How'd you manage to get him to divulge all that? Wait, maybe I don't want to know your secrets of bending us males to your will."

She laughed. "Listen to this, Stone, Teak told me the name change came about one night when they ran out of Glenlivet, and it was too late to go buy more. They, apparently all three of them, decided whiskey should flow freely and never run out. *My Mistress* suddenly became *Whiskey Sea,* and they repainted her the very next morning and proceeded to spend the remainder of the day polishing off most of the Glenlivet that Grey had restocked that morning.

"He said he was told that the room he built had to be 100 percent soundproof with hidden releases on the inside and a small, also hidden, pass-through sort of thing for occasional forced-air circulation. He said the walls, floor, and ceiling are close to a foot thick and filled with some sort of special sound-absorbing, lightweight pellets. The one-way mirror is actually three panes thick with compressed air sandwiched between them. Imagine the expense of doing that!

Teak said there's an external lever to open the glass doorway under the top of the bar. Apparently, there's a rod sticking up from the counter. Just pull it up and move it toward you and "presto mundo", as Teak phrased it, "quick as a wink", the doorway glides open on an air cushion so there are no betraying coaster marks left behind on the carpet. Sounds pretty ingenious if you ask me."

"All for collecting rare books, huh? Sounds like a perfect cover actually. You did fantastic, Teri. I'm very impressed with your sleuthing ability, not to mention other abilities I'm discovering about you that we should probably wait for a more opportune time to talk about." He was wishing she was standing next to him. Of course he'd been having those thoughts frequently ever since meeting her. "Teak's story is even more reason to find *Whiskey Sea*, and the quicker the better."

"Is Mike going to help us, Stone?"

"No, and not because he doesn't want to. He says he can't because his hands are tied, but we both know just the person to get them untied. Why don't you call Pops? Be as brief as possible with him but urge him to go down to the Hilo Police Department and file a missing person report. When he goes, he's got to impress upon them that it's an emergency and request that they be sure to attach a copy of it to an email and send it to Mike's attention at the Honolulu Police Department. Once Mike has it in hand, we'll be set to go with an all-out search with his full help and support.

"As soon as you've talked to Pops, call me back at the Pearl Harbor Club office." He read the number to her that was taped to the phone. "Alegra said there'd be no problem relaying messages through her office."

"Who's Alegra?" She could feel the hairs on the back of her neck start to prickle. She felt foolish allowing any form of jealousy to invade, especially at the simple mention of a name; how silly, but invade it did. She definitely had some mental reimaging and confidence work to do on herself. *Just when you think you have all your past baggage filed in its*

*proper folder, along comes a new wrinkle to upset the filing
system.*

"I'll introduce you when you get here. Call me back as
quickly as you can, angel."

There's that angel name again. It had the effect of melting
something in her core, and she knew she'd never get tired of
hearing it. *I don't need to work on any jealousy issues—just
let them go and listen instead to the words actually spoken.*
She let out an involuntary sigh and called Pops.

Stone hadn't wanted to mention the absence of *Whiskey
Sea* from the club's harbor. She'd been so excited with her
discovery he hadn't wanted to ruin that excitement—she'd
know soon enough.

Chapter Forty-One

Teri pulled into the entrance of the yacht club with Pops riding shotgun. It was only two in the afternoon, but Pops' face wore a mask of anxiety that appeared to be several days' worth of pent-up worry, obviously arising from fear and concern for the welfare of his daughter.

Mike had received the missing persons report emailed to him from Hilo an hour earlier and immediately headed to the Pearl Harbor Yacht Club to initiate Honolulu PD's involvement in Viane's disappearance as well as a thorough, HPD-sponsored search for *Whiskey Sea*. He felt good about finally being able to officially step in and knew Stone, and the others would be feeling the same.

Lloyd had arrived moments before Mike.

The assembly of souls officially gathered outside the yacht club's office where Stone told everyone that *Whiskey Sea* had been there and gone.

"Where did Pops come from so quickly?" Stone had pulled Teri aside as the others stood around mildly confused. He needed to soothe any remaining bristles she might be feeling from their earlier conversation and Stone's mention of Alegra's name. She had just come out of the office after meeting her and was enveloped in his hug. Their warmth and strength together were washing away any residual negative energy either of them may have been feeling about everything surrounding them. He asked her about Pops being there so quickly.

"When I called him," she replied, voice muffled against his chest, "he was on his way out the door heading for the airport and a flight over here. He instinctively knows Viane's going to need him when we find her. I think he really needs her as much or perhaps even more, judging by some of the things he told me in the car after I picked him up. It seems that Sonny called the dorm early this morning, but instead of reaching Viane, he got Ann who became hysterical when asked if she knew Viane's whereabouts."

Family and friends' connections with one another in the Islands are very close because of the closed communities inherent in island life. "Pops told me the police chief in Hilo is an old friend, having both grown up and moved through the years of school together. He did the paperwork and immediately emailed a copy marked Urgent directly to Mike Kalama in Honolulu as a personal favor to Pops."

"The chief even forged Pops' signature to the report, but we're not to mention this to anyone. Close communities like Hilo are wonderful, aren't they, Stone? You think you could ever leave this island and move to Hilo?"

"What, and miss out on fighting traffic every second of the day? Are you nuts?"

In truth, for the past year, he'd been thinking of how good it would be to leave the chaos of Oahu behind, to enjoy the gentle quietness of a place like Hilo. He hadn't mentioned any of this to Teri and didn't plan to just yet. There'd be time enough for serious discussions after Viane was safely home.

They walked back to join the others.

Standing in a circle, they brought each other up to speed with their individual bits of information, guesses, and thoughts. As Stone and Teri joined in, everyone simultaneously began drifting toward the water's edge, as if an unspoken urge guided them all in the same direction.

They were all pretty much in agreement on the situation as it presently stood: the irrefutable fact being that Ann had delivered Viane to the Ilikai and the *Whiskey Sea* had also been there and within easy reach. Given Viane's determination to retrieve her artifacts, mixed with the fact that both she and the yacht were not to be found, they all hesitantly agreed that Viane more than likely went onboard. Pops told them that that's pretty much what his headstrong daughter would have thought of doing and volunteered that she was stubborn enough to follow through.

As they stood analyzing this and pondering their next move, a very long-haired small brown dog wandered into the center of the group, an extension tether attached to its pink collar. If there had been a clump of grass at their feet, the dog would have been able to hide behind it, leaving room to spare. At the other end of the leash was a grandmotherly woman with soft brown skin as smooth as a well-loved powder puff. Her flowing long salt-and-pepper hair, thinning with age but still very abundant, was adorned by three plumeria blossoms over her left ear. A *kukui nut* lei circled her neck. She was the quintessential Tutu from the pages of a book on Hawaii's days gone by. She transmitted a sweet, kindly smile, yet one that carried an air of authority and upbringing. Stone figured she must be close to seventy and had probably been quite stunning as a young woman. A good portion of Hawaiian blood showed in her facial features and exuded a gentle presence and proud bearing.

"*Hele mai*, Ichi," she softly scolded the dog, "come here," as she reeled in the leash and gave the dog a gentle tug. "Don't you go bothering these nice people." It quickly found shelter beneath the woman's colorful muumuu. She looked up at Mike and winked. "Hello, Officer Kalama," she said, reading his name badge and then returning her gaze to his face. She briefly glanced at everyone individually, hesitating for a moment on Pops before returning her eyes back to Mike's. "My name's Leilani Davis and this"—taking a small step backward to reveal the furry ball at their feet—"is Ichi. He's just like a little scratch," she said holding her hand to her mouth to shield a giggle. She bent down and took Ichi in her hands and brought the small bundle to her bosom.

"Pleasure to meet you, ma'am," he said. Mike was all business. "Do you have a boat tied up here?" He didn't bother introducing the others—he wasn't here for social graces.

"Oh my, no, Officer Kalama," she said, her left hand going to her cheek as if her answer was an embarrassment. "Ichi and I live in a house just outside the entrance. The club's property is Ichi's favorite place to walk because no one bothers us here. It feels safe. I hope you won't rat us out to the owners." The statement didn't fit the sweet demeanor of the face the words came from. "I'd certainly feel even safer if you were to hang around," she said as she cocked her head at a slight angle and looked up as if waiting for Mike's agreeing reply. He'd obviously cornered her heart or her imagination—one or the other. Perhaps he was a reminder of a long-distant memory of a past close friend.

Mike told her they were here looking for a particular boat and asked if she'd seen a large yacht tied up earlier in the day.

"Now isn't that interesting that you should ask," she said, dropping her voice to a loud whisper. "Why, yes, I did." Her voice lowered more. "I knew something was fishy with those two men. They came in early this morning and left at daybreak. Hardly enough time to dry out. I was out early this morning walking Ichi—I don't sleep a lot all at one stretch. If I do I get this strange feeling, I'll miss something important. I'm kind of *niele*, you know. My curiosity is too big for me at times," she said with a giggle. "Besides, eight hours is a long time to be dead to the world. Isn't that such an appropriate phrase for sleep, Officer Mike? Dead—it's so peaceful, but it's so absolute. I don't want to be that way yet, if I can help it—dead, I mean. That's why I take lots of very short naps."

She motioned to the others with her free hand to move in closer—she apparently had a secret to share. She held Ichi a bit closer as if to emphasize a secret that only the two of them had any knowledge of. "It was just like the *Godfather* movies," she said, her voice becoming even quieter. "I just love movies. Don't you, Officer Mike?" She laid her grandmotherly hand on his arm. He was quickly becoming her best friend and personal confidante. "Where was I? Oh yes, the *Godfather*." Her voice dropped another decibel—everyone instinctively leaned even closer. "I usually walk Ichi around those trees," she said and pointed toward the entrance with an extended finger. "That way, when he does his *necessary* business, I won't feel too badly if I don't manage to pick it all up." She giggled again. "Sometimes Ichi gets a little soupy, if you know what I mean." Her gaze hadn't swayed from Mike's face. Everyone else needn't be there as far as she was concerned. "Sometimes, if it gets too mushy, I pretend I don't notice what he's doing so I won't have to mess with it. Instead, I look up in the trees or out over the water.

"This morning, poor Ichi's business was like a miniature-sized wet cow pie, so I looked around trying not to notice what he was busy making." Another decibel lower. "That's when I saw this man dressed in dark clothes, sitting in a car over there," she said as she pointed in the direction of the entrance. "Both doors were open, but no lights were on." Another giggle at her perceived pun. "I mean no lights were on in his car. I have no idea about the man's lights or marbles or anything else." More giggles. She was enjoying telling her story. "Don't you find that odd, Officer Mike? Don't all car lights come on when their doors are open?"

Mike was reaching the edge of his tolerance to listen. Gently taking the woman's hands in his—leash, dog, and all—and catching her eyes, which wasn't very difficult since they had rarely strayed from his, he said, "Ms. Davis, someone's life may be at stake, so our timing is very critical. Please explain the rest of what you saw as briefly and as simply as you can. We'd really appreciate that," he added. "We'll have time to talk stories later. I'll come and visit after this is all over."

And he would—it was who he was.

She straightened her shoulders and back and with apparent hesitation, removed her hands from Mike's grasp.

"I do have a habit of rambling," she acknowledged. "Poor Ichi has no choice but to sit and listen to me since he can't go off by himself, although goodness knows he tries often enough." She cast a loving glance at Ichi contentedly asleep in the crook of her left arm. Her love for Ichi was quite palpable.

"Okay," she said, squaring her shoulders once again, "let's get to the damn facts." It was close to the hardest thing any of them could do to keep from breaking into laughter, and under normal circumstances, they would have, but the situation kept them somber. Leilani Davis had her special charm.

"This man in the car had his eyes focused on an Oriental woman being escorted onboard the large yacht tied up here at Charlie pier. Ichi and I walked a few trees closer to see what early morning funny business was happening. Ichi was done with his *necessary* so was antsy to move away from it, and so was I. The woman and one of the men came back down the boarding ramp and took several things out of her car. I couldn't tell what the things were, though. They then carried them back onboard and into one of the rooms and shut the door behind them. Ichi was busy sniffing some bushes so I stayed and watched to see what else might happen."

"Did you happen to get a good look at him?" asked Mike. "Could you identify him if you saw him again?"

"Oh no, I couldn't do that. You see, it was too shadowy under the trees where he was parked, and I didn't want to get close. Ichi may have caused a ruckus if the man got out and made any sudden movements, like he ended up doing anyway when he ran off chasing that yacht."

A small feeling of pleasure rolled through Stone at hearing the word *yacht* being used properly but joined the rest in anticipation of what Ms. Davis was referring to.

"Could you explain what you meant by this man's making some kind of sudden movements toward the yacht?"

She put her one free hand up in a gesture of patience and continued as if the question hadn't been asked.

"Don't interrupt, young man. We're getting to the good part," she loudly exclaimed, startling everyone as her hand came to rest on Mike's arm again. "The yacht's engines fired up, and it started to move. They didn't even bother with the boarding ramp. They just let it fall off the boat into the water. Do you think they forgot it was there?" She searched Mike's eyes for an answer but saw none. "They even forgot about the lines holding her to the pier and just let them play out and fall in the water as well. Now, isn't that strange? Imagine leaving their ropes and that ramp behind like that," she said as she took on a disgusted look, hands moved to her hips. "Nobody does that," she exclaimed. It was probably fortunate the two men weren't there—she would have given them both a large piece of her mind for doing such a wasteful thing.

"But then," she continued, reanimated and back to her story once more, grabbing Mike's arm with both her hands as if for emphasis, one arm bent enough to support Ichi, "the man sitting in the car jumped out and ran toward the moving yacht for all he was worth and jumped off the pier with his arms outstretched, flying in the air. Can you believe that? Just like that Spider-Man person, except it didn't end well. He just sort of did a belly flop into the harbor, and the yacht kept on going. What excitement! Even Ichi was jumping up and down like he got bit by a cockroach or something.

"I would have gone over to help the man out of the water, but he was cussing something awful. Ichi gets very upset when someone makes a commotion like that, so I had to pick him up and head for home. Such foul language," she scolded at no one in particular. "It's a wonder he didn't drown with his mouth open so much, and I don't believe that woman intended to go for a boat ride since the trunk of her car was still open when the yacht pulled out."

"Could you tell us what kind of car the man was driving, Ms. Davis?" Mike had a pen in hand prepared to write in his small notebook.

"No," she said as if it was the silliest question she'd ever been asked. "That sort of thing is not very interesting to me. If Ray were still alive, that's my late husband," she explained, "he'd be able to tell you everything all the way down to the size of its tires. I could tell you the license plate number though, if that'd help."

Teri got the question in before the others. "How did you manage that?" she asked, an incredulous look appeared on everyone's faces.

More giggles as she looked down at her dog. "Ichi found something that his nose couldn't get enough of outside the entrance, so I stood waiting for him to finish sniffing when that man drove out the gate in the woman's car, then came running back just a few minutes later. If he saw me he didn't look like he cared very much. Just as I reached down to pick up Ichi—he'd gotten a kuku in one of his paws and was whimpering—the man's car came barreling out the gate. His license, ILY-222, caught my eye."

She looked at Teri, asking, "Do you know what ILY stands for, sweetie?"

"No, I don't think I do," replied Teri, looking questioningly at the woman, "although if I had to guess I'd say something like I Love You." An understanding look spread across her face as she continued. "Too, too, too. I Love You, Too, Too, Too," she exclaimed obviously pleased with her imaginative guess.

"Ray used to say that to me and would write little notes and leave them around the house for me to find. I Love You Too Too Truly. Gave my heart a funny nudge when I saw that license."

Everyone stood quietly in reverence of the special gift of love this woman must have experienced. She broke the silence and the gentle mood that had taken hold.

"Do you think the two men on that yacht are going to have their way with that woman? You think they'll do the nasty, and then dump her in the water? Shame on them." The disgust she exuded was as blatant as it was sudden. She quickly secured the dog in her arms and stormed off as if she'd answered her own question and was blaming the group she was with for allowing such a terrible thing to take place.

Stone looked down at nothing in particular, trying to keep from laughing as best he could. He sensed everyone else was doing the same. When they were sure she was out of earshot, none of them could help but laugh and break the somber mood affecting them, but the common anxiety for Viane's safe return quickly reasserted itself.

Mike spoke, mostly to himself, about the task that lay in front of him. "Now we must consider the likelihood that two women are onboard with double the likelihood for violence." No one commented, each already knew the truth of those words in their hearts.

Pops, who had stood partially behind Teri the whole time the woman told her story, wandered a short distance from the rest. He wiped a tear from the corner of his eye and watched as the woman and Ichi walked away.

"There's a place in my heart that remembers that lady from someplace," he said as he came back to the group. "Can't remember where, though. I know it was a lot of years ago. I wonder what meaning can be placed on having our life's paths crossing again now?" His voice was soft, talking mostly to himself. He looked again at the receding figure of the woman and her dog. "I don't think she remembered me, though," he said, his voice still speaking softly in her direction.

Chapter Forty-Two

Dorteo sat on the wooden bench running his bare feet through the cool grass, letting it caress the toughened skin on the bottom of them. It seemed to calm the anxiety he was experiencing. Deb had asked him to be there as support but also as a measure of security for her, and he had completely failed her. The most upsetting thing of all was not being able to come up with anything he could have done differently to keep his friend safe, other than go onboard with her, and she'd specifically asked him not to.

Man, what a mess. Maybe if I'd have parked ten feet closer to the yacht, I would have had a better chance of snagging that railing and pulling myself up on deck.

His shorts and shirt were starting to dry. His slippers had come off at some point between leaving his car to run after the departing yacht and making that desperate attempt to gain a handhold on the railing, before plunging into the club's harbor. His head still ached from hitting that ramp as he resurfaced.

After pulling himself out of the water, he'd had the presence of mind to drive Debra's car to a residential street close to the club and return for his own. After watching *Whiskey Sea* leave the club, he assumed they would head back to the Ala Wai, and he'd driven like a crazy man to Ala Moana Beach Park and ran out the path to the end of Magic Island hoping to see where they tied up, but instead he had to sit and watch as it went passed the entrance to the Ala Wai as well as Waikiki and kept on going.

It could be headed anywhere, he thought as he sat watching. *All the other islands with the exception of Kauai were possibilities given their current heading, including the mainland.*

He knew that telling the police would only serve to open the cabinet door to a huge collection of illicit and highly illegal activities that he and Deb had been involved in lately. Not telling them, however, could spell a death sentence for her. There was the possibility, though, that they may be planning to pull into any one of the many possibilities along the Oahu coastline and leave her behind. She was extra baggage, and he was sure her mouth would be causing them endless grief right about now. They'd be happy to dump her off and be rid of her. No one involved could squeal to the authorities because everyone was up to their collective nostrils in criminal activities.

Man, what a mess. He was feeling the desperation of fear for his friend—unsettling fear at not knowing what he could do to help her.

He watched *Whiskey Sea* as it disappeared from view behind Diamond Head. He ran for his car and headed through Waikiki toward one of the lookouts on Diamond Head Beach Road so he could continue watching.

From his vantage point on the back side of Diamond Head, he could see all the way to Koko Head. Beyond that, he could make out the faint outline of the island of Molokai nestled in the haze of salt-laden air.

If *Whiskey Sea* was heading for one of the other islands, he'd be able to see its direction from here and come fairly close to narrowing down their intended goal: at least narrowed to the intended island, not that that information would be of much help to him.

He stood and watched, though, as the boat slowly diminished in size and disappeared behind Koko Head Crater. He knew only that they were either returning to Kaneohe Yacht Club or, more likely, judging from their distance out, heading straight for the West Coast.

He figured his best move was to take a run past the yacht club in Kaneohe just to see if by chance they came into the bay, but as he turned back to his car, he was confronted by flashing blue lights from an HPD patrol car that had pulled to a stop and was now blocking his car from leaving. The officer was just getting out of the patrol car, his right hand resting on the butt of his gun.

"Oh no, not now," he said under his breath.

Chapter Forty-Three

Mike had left the group standing by the entrance to the club's office, but in less than thirty minutes, he was returning back through the entrance gate. He found everyone just as they were when he'd left since none of them had known where to go from there or what they needed to do next. Alegra had suspended her filing duties and opted to join the others standing in a loose circle. She'd apparently convinced herself it was far more important to the club to know everything that was going on. She'd satisfied herself the filing could wait until tomorrow.

He parked and walked up to the group and stood there for a moment, not wanting to interrupt their frayed discussions. He didn't have to wait long.

Stone looked at him. "You didn't get very far, did you, Mike? You're looking as if you can't hold something in. What's up?"

Mike stood for a brief moment looking down, gently laughing, and shaking his head. "I just can't hold stuff in," he said as he looked up at everyone. "That's why the department would never allow me to work undercover. Can't play poker worth a darn either, can I, Stone?"

"That's why you're always so welcomed in the poker games, Mike, I thought you knew that," Stone added, matching his light mood.

"I came back to tell you we've found the car belonging to the woman Ms. Davis saw."

The reaction startled everyone. All eyes were on Mike, waiting for more.

Stone finally voiced the silent thoughts of the others. "How'd you manage that? You just left here."

After Leilani Davis' story, Mike told them, he'd called his chief to convince him to begin the full investigation. "The missing person report that Rudy filed on his daughter lent a lot of weight to pushing for a quick resolution. Viane's connection with *Whiskey Sea* added some emphasis as well, but mostly it's Pops' connection to the police chief in Hilo that did the trick.

"Turns out that while we were standing here listening to Ms. Davis's story, a yacht club neighbor was in the process of calling 911 to report something he thought was suspicious. He reported a strange-looking man had parked a car early this morning and proceeded to jump out and run away. The guy got curious, went out, and looked inside the car and found the keys still dangling from the ignition.

"We ran the plates and found it belongs to a Debra Shinn who lives—guess where, Stone?—in Kaneohe not far from your house, in back of Greenhaven Memorial Cemetery. She has a rap sheet that says enough that we'd like to find her for a conversation about several things that have taken place lately. I'm guessing that the man the neighbor saw run from the car was the same one who went for a swim behind the

Whiskey Sea. He probably didn't change clothes or comb his hair after the plunge, so I figure he looked *real* strange running from a car. Also, Shinn's car upholstery was soaked with saltwater from someone sitting there dripping water.

"It's circumstantial right now," continued Mike, "but Ms. Davis's description of the man who jumped for the yacht matches that of the man the neighbor saw parking Ms. Shinn's car and running away. I think we have a 99 percent match."

It was Teri who broke the silence that ensued after Mike stopped talking. "How will knowing about Debra's car lead us to the *Whiskey Sea* and Viane? The info's great, Mike, but the trail to Viane appears vague at best. Aren't we wasting time not getting the Coast Guard out looking or have the police department's helicopter flying around searching for them? It's only been what, six or seven hours since they left here? They can't be more than a hundred miles out, can they?" Her voice was cracking with an up swelling of emotion, matching the pools of water collecting in her eyes. She was hearing lots of words but wasn't seeing the action she expected to see. She moved close to Stone and put her arm around his waist, seeking comfort. Stone's arm went to her shoulder, pulling her close to his chest. She was a strong woman, but he was discovering she possessed a very tender heart when loved ones were concerned, and it needed comforting, especially now. He was glad he was the one she came to with that need.

"Knowing who she is," answered Mike, "won't bring us much closer to finding Viane, but it adds to the only trail we have to follow. As for the Coast Guard or our helicopter, we have no way of knowing which way to go to look for them.

They have a 360-degree choice, and we have no way to divine which direction they took."

"The best I can do, Stone," Mike said, directing his comments, "is to call you when we find the guy Ms. Davis saw. He may be able to shed light on where the yacht's headed. It's the best we can do right at this point until something else breaks."

"Better take my cell number, Mike," volunteered Teri. "If Stone's not home, you can't reach him." With a feigned hopeless look, she playfully poked Stone's stomach, breaking out of her somber mood.

"Rudy's going to come to my place for the night, Stone," Teri said as everyone prepared to leave following Mike's departure. "I've got the space, and I think he feels a kinship with me because of my friendship with Viane." She moved closer to him and whispered, "You'll just have to get along without me for the rest of the day." Then glancing in Alegra's direction, who had gone back into her office to presumably continue her filing, Teri looked up at Stone, saying, "You leave first."

Stone caught the reference and smiled. "You're a very gracious individual, aren't you?" He couldn't resist kidding with her. "Since we can't do anything for Viane right at this moment and since you and Rudy are heading for Nuuanu and Lloyd's already left, I'm wondering if Alegra may need help with all her filing."

The pain in his ribs from her elbow was intense. At times he could be very insensitive when he tried to kid around. He'd have to learn to stop doing that with her or start wearing chain mail for protection.

"I'm leaving," he winced. "I think you broke several ribs. At least Bert's waiting for me, and she never breaks ribs. If Mike calls before I get home, either call Kaiser Hospital or leave a message on my phone."

"Stop being such a baby." She put her hand on the area her elbow had connected with and reached up to kiss his cheek. Quickly becoming serious, moving her hand to rest over his heart, she said, "I really hope we get a call before you reach home. It'd be the best that could happen." Then, letting go of the serious note in her voice, she gestured toward the gate, saying, "You leave first, I'll follow."

Chapter Forty-Four

Viane was rudely jarred awake as the room's door swung open and banged against the wall. She'd had full intention of staying alert, prepared for any opportunity that presented itself to her to escape when they dumped her on the floor, but the exhaustion she felt from the past few days' pent-up emotions mixed with the gentle back-and-forth motion of the boat had lulled her to sleep. She immediately became aware of pain in her hip and shoulder from lying on the hard, albeit carpeted, floor. She felt like she had been asleep for quite a while.

Roland roughly hauled her to her feet as if she was an old cardboard box he was about to discard. She saw the morning light streaming in through the doorway, which sent mixed signals to her brain: early mornings were her favorite time of day, always a part of the day she greeted with joy. Now, she just felt an ominous threat coming to its climax.

Roland removed the binding on her hands, giving her reason for optimism. That hopefulness quickly evaporated as Roland brought her arms in front of her and retied them, then looped the loose end of the rope around her neck.

Putting tension on the rope squeezing her neck, he moved behind her, bent down, and proceeded to untie her feet.

"You're too awkward to drag, girl," said Roland, the first words he'd spoken in answer to Viane's puzzled look. "In case you get any ideas, keep in mind I have a tight grip on the other end of the rope that's twisted around your neck, so walk where and how I tell you, and you won't suffer a permanent lack of air. Now step out the door and head for the stern," he said as he shoved her in that direction. Along with his words came a corresponding tightening of the rope that partially cut off her ability to breathe. She eased her neck back hoping to take the tension off the rope and began to move in the direction she was being pushed.

With her neck angled back and arms tied in front, she awkwardly walked out onto the deck into what would have been a beautiful morning had circumstances been different. She unconsciously pegged it at 8:00 a.m. as she squinted at the sun shining directly into her eyes, being magnified by the water's surface.

As she came around the corner onto the open stern deck, Viane saw the other woman she had watched through the mirror, only now she too was a captive—her hands bound in front and several loops of rope turned around her neck with Grey holding on to the other end.

It suddenly became very evident where all this drama was heading. It sent a chilling dread rippling through every fiber of her being. Her body's fight-or-flight syndrome was rapidly kicking in as she began to frantically search for a way out of the peril confronting them both. The life ring hanging on the railing immediately caught her attention. The EPIRB attached to it instantly pointed the way she knew she had to go, and it was all the incentive she needed in order to act.

Before Roland could react, she swung around to face him and with both hands grabbed the rope he was holding. Pulling him toward her, she planted her knee squarely into his groin. As he went down, losing hold of the rope, she swung back toward the railing and in two steps grabbed the life ring off the railing, hugged it tightly to her chest with tied hands, and flung herself over the rail into the water, praying all the way down that Roland hadn't managed to regain a grip on the trailing end of the rope that still looped around her neck.

"Oh God, here I go again," she voiced as she plunged into the water. Reams of emotions and thoughts flashed through her mind, the uppermost being the nagging notion that this may not have been such a smart idea after all. She felt only partially relieved at her freedom as the turmoil rolling in her mind instantly collided with the good and the bad: she was happy to no longer be in physical danger from the two men onboard and that she had regained some semblance of being in control of her destiny. The grave part of her actions, she knew, was that she was back in an unforgiving ocean, facing a fight for survival once again.

With a personal preservation instinct Debra had always been blessed with and had managed to hone to a fine point, she immediately saw what the girl's intentions were; and in the confusion of Roland's agonizing scream and crashing to the deck writhing in pain, she yanked her rope out of her distracted captor's hands and followed the girl over the railing.

"Shit," was about the only word Grey could come up with, his hands burning from the rope, as he stood in stunned surprise at the hurricane of action that had unfolded—all in the amount of time it would take him to spit.

He looked at his friend curled up on the deck moaning, feeling a small amount of relief it wasn't him. "I guess they didn't want to wait for the ceremony, did they?" Roland was oblivious to his partner's stab at humor. "It could be said truthfully that they committed suicide, so it appears we're off the hook for their demise." Grey was seeing nothing but the positive side of events although it was a desperate effort. He bent to help Roland uncurl and get to his feet when his attention was abruptly drawn to the absence of the life ring. He'd apparently missed seeing it leave the railing during the turmoil.

Startled, he grabbed Roland by the shirt and pulled him around, ignoring the painful protest, so he could look into his face, "The life ring is missing. Did that girl grab the life ring on her way over?"

"Hell, I don't know. I was more concerned with the condition of a certain appendage and making sure both nuts were still in the bag. That girl has some strong legs, I'll say that for her." He looked at the railing, trying to remember. "Yeah, there was a life ring there, so either she grabbed it or it fell overboard during the commotion." He sat up suddenly ignoring the excruciating pain that radiated down both legs.

They both began talking much louder than was necessary as if by voice alone they could make things change for the better as a realization came to light for both of them.

"That life ring has our name on it," exclaimed Roland. "If its floating free and she gets her hands on it, we'd be specifically identified with her." He sank back against the bulkhead with an expanding awareness. "Oh man!" He looked at Grey and saw the knowing look as his friend shook his head with a similar recognition. "We have a much worse problem than that, don't we? If she's got the life ring, she's also got that damn EPIRB that's attached to it. It's probably already broadcasting its call for help. Oh man," he repeated, quieter, more to himself.

"We've got to go back and retrieve it and hope neither woman knows that the life ring's in the water and have managed to get their hands on it. Hopefully, they've both sunk to the bottom. I got a bad feeling, though, Grey."

The *Whiskey Sea* had been on autopilot since they passed through the Kaiwi Channel during the middle of the night. In the time since the women went over, they had been continually widening their distance from them. Backtracking was going to be a nightmare, and both men knew it, and they also knew they had no choice but to try. A homing beacon onboard tied to the frequency of the EPIRB would guide them back to within a matter of feet to the life ring. Even at that close distance, in rolling seas, seeing anything floating on the surface was going to be a challenge at best.

Grey went into the control room and turned the autopilot off as he swung the helm hard to starboard to make as tight a turn as was possible. Roland had switched on the homing beacon and instantly began receiving a signal. "Looks like it or they might be about three or four miles back. This shouldn't be too difficult."

"Would have been a lot less difficult if you hadn't insisted we untie their legs. 'Give them a fighting chance to tread water,' you pleaded. What the . . ." He couldn't finish, he was becoming frustrated. "You're a softhearted fool at times, Roland, you know that? If we'd left them bound up and simply threw them over, we wouldn't need to backtrack just to hunt for a needle in a wet moving haystack. I swear one of these days I'm going to slip a potion into your scotch along with the cubes and turn you into a Border Collie."

"Quiet down, Grey, and stop grumbling. We'll be on them momentarily. I'm going out on the bow and watch for them. Put both hands on the wheel and follow my signal."

Chapter Forty-Five

"Hey," yelled Viane as loudly as she could. "Hey," she repeated, "over here, over here." Her mouth was dry from having the gag in it for so long, but the saltwater was quickly taking care of that. The impact of hitting the water had blown the rag out of her mouth. *Thank you, God.*

Before she landed in the water and her thoughts had screamed loudly, "NOT AGAIN," she'd had the presence of mind to grasp tightly to the life ring and had caught a glimpse of the other woman splashing into the water not far away. Memories of her last episode in the ocean were quickly forgotten as she frantically sought the other woman's attention. She knew there were only moments available to get the life ring within the other woman's reach, and if she wasn't a good swimmer, with tied hands and rough water, she would quickly go under. The red light on the EPIRB was blinking out its calling signal. Viane knew help would rapidly be on its way.

Thank you, Pops, for all the knowledge you gave me. Help me make it through this ordeal.

Even on his small boat, Pops had always carried an EPIRB. The waters off Hilo were much more unpredictable than most found around Oahu, and the danger of being swamped by a rogue wave, or rolling over in a trough, were always present. The EPIRB, he had told her, would save the day if that were to happen—he was trying to put his little girl's fears aside. He explained that if he were to find himself in the water after flipping his boat, the EPIRB would immediately begin to send a distress signal. The saltwater, he explained, activated it; so even if he were unconscious, it would tell the Coast Guard where to find him and would even tell them who it was that needed help "by name," he had explained, since it was personally coded with his identification. Viane always hated to hear Pops talk like that, but she knew the common sense it imparted and knew he didn't want her to ever fear for his return. He'd always promised to be there whenever she needed his help. In her heart she knew, even now, that Pops would somehow learn of her plight and would be finding a way to get help to her.

There was no doubt in her mind that without Pops' love and guidance and his forethought in teaching her how to survive, she may not have even thought of grabbing the EPIRB and jumping over. *Always take the door that's open for you. Mahalo, Pops.*

She was puzzled why her captors had changed the bindings the way they did. Had they left them the way they originally were, she had little doubt she would have gone straight to the sea floor. "Dear God," she exclaimed as a reality became clear. "They may have planned to brace the end of the rope when they threw me overboard. I would have broken my neck before hitting the water." Even though conjecture, it confirmed her notion of just how sleazy her captors were.

"Help me," the woman said, her voice weak. Surprised out of her thoughts at hearing the voice, Viane pushed hard on the life ring, aiming in the woman's direction.

As soon as the life ring came within her reach, Debra, as near to exhaustion as she'd ever been, lunged with her remaining energy and caught hold of it. They both stayed silent for a time as Debra caught her breath and regained some strength, before they both silently began working at untying the other's ropes binding their wrists.

"God, I'm freezing." Debra leaned back in order to focus on this other woman. "Who the hell are you, and where'd you come from, and what the hell were you just mumbling to yourself about?" she demanded when she'd drawn enough air into her lungs to speak. "You're the cause of all this. Damn it. I would have been sitting having a martini at Duke's in Waikiki if you hadn't made that confounded noise. Who farts when they're all tied up like I saw you were a little while ago? What business do you have with those two?" Then Debra's lights went on amidst her unending barrage of accusations and questions. "I've seen you before. Son of a bitch! I knew something was wrong, and I didn't pay attention to my own intuition. I wish I had a cigarette." She looked across at Viane like she'd love to reach over and punch her, if she could summon up enough strength.

Viane's relative happiness at having company to share her circumstances was quickly evaporating at the rank drivel coming from the mouth of her life-ring companion. If she didn't have a deep sense of compassion and love that she held so dearly for fellow beings, she might have happily told the woman to go find her own life ring.

"Look, I don't know who you are or what rock you've been hiding behind, but shut the hell up." *I'm sorry, Pops. I'm becoming a gutter mouth, but sometimes compassion needs to give way to the rough edges of reality.* "You're holding on to a lifesaver, thanks to me; and if we're to get out of this mess and cause those two guys some hurt, we've got to work together. The first step is to conserve energy by concentrating on staying afloat and keeping alert instead of letting all your trash flow free. You're welcome to return to being the person who you think you are after we get to safety."

"Look, kid. The way I see it, we're in the middle of this godforsaken ocean, holding a piece of foam that's about as big as my toilet seat, and you're spouting off about staying alert. You can look at the damn glass half full all you want but get your fool head out of the sand. And if your feet kick my shin one more time, I'm going to pop you one in that toothy smile of yours. Are we clear? And if you can see a way out, other than calling on Jesus to help us walk back over to land, then I'll become a goddamned minister and saint."

Viane closed her eyes and took a deep breath in hopes of finding an avenue of thought that would color the situation a better shade of caring. She opened her eyes and looked at the woman, hoping a form of reverse logic would be helpful. "Let's reverse sides for a minute. I don't know what you were doing with those two, but from my recent history with them, I can only guess that you were there because you were being duped out of something, or, and I'm getting a clearer picture of this, you are a part of what they represent, and things went wrong for you. I'm guessing the latter, since you're out here with me, and I saw you in their vault helping to secure some treasure of yours or theirs. So that probably makes you about as big a thief as I know they are.

"When this is all over and we're rescued, I'm willing and, quite frankly, will be pleased to forget we ever saw one another, but until that time, you had better stow your superiority and lend yourself to working together, or we're both doomed." Viane surprised herself by the well of assertiveness that sprang up out of some hidden place within her. She liked knowing this resource was a part of her makeup and could be accessed if and when the need arose.

"And what makes you so darn certain we'll be rescued? I don't see any of your friends rushing out here to pick you up and carry you to safety." Debra, for all her harsh words and abrasive nature, was beginning to see their need to cooperate. She was way out of her element and knew it, so she was inclined to start listening. Besides, she found herself admiring the gonads that sprang to life in this young Hawaiian woman. She could see a memory of her younger self in this woman, before she'd come to know the struggles that life had dished out to her as a young girl. She'd withdrawn into a shell that had protected her until she and Dorteo, in his own protective shell, had each helped lift the other out of the cocoon they'd both been forced into.

The two clung to the ring and looked at one another, finding themselves appraising the other.

"What did you mean by your comment, 'I've seen you before'? What are you referring to?" asked Viane.

"At the Chart House a few days ago. You were sitting with two other people, and all three of you were staring at *Whiskey Sea,* even though the man with you denied it."

Viane vaguely remembered seeing the woman. At the restaurant, she had briefly glanced in the woman's direction having been more interested in the *Whiskey Sea* at that moment than paying much attention to the conversation taking place.

"I was sure you were all scrutinizing it for a reason, but I let myself believe I'd imagined it. Are you a part of those two on the yacht? And if you are, why are you out here with me? I'll come clean with you if you'll come clean with me. It's not like we're going to get saved by your imagined friendly rescuer. Right here is where we both bid aloha to life, so there's nothing to be lost, is there?"

"Okay," replied Viane, playing along, "you go first."

"What the hell," exclaimed Debra in resignation. "I had some merchandise that those bozos were going to cart over to the mainland for me. I was to collect some major cash in exchange and with it start a whole new life for me and a friend. After you farted, you sorry excuse for a woman, all hell broke loose for reasons that I still don't understand, but here I am—with you."

"So who's Dorteo? I heard you yelling his name. Is that the friend you just mentioned?"

Debra lowered her eyes and took in a breath as she smiled to herself, as one does at fond memories. She replied softly, "Yes, he's a very dear friend. Perhaps the only friend I've ever had. He was watching over me from shore—my self-proclaimed protector." Debra's seething anger was leaving her at about the same rate that her body temperature was dropping. She had forgotten about poor Dorteo and wondered what he had done when he saw the yacht leaving with her onboard. She hoped he was all right, wherever he was. She knew he must be going crazy wondering what to do. Viane could see the softening taking place in Debra's face and wondered what had triggered her to suddenly let go of the hostility she'd so repeatedly displayed.

"Were the things that you were so intently watching get secured to the shelf stolen from somewhere?"

Debra appraised her life-ring mate for a second, saying, "You're very direct, aren't you, girl? Matter-of-fact they were, and they were worth a fortune, and that's all you need to know. What makes you so perceptive, anyway? And while you're at it, what evil did you perpetuate to find yourself sharing a life ring out here in our large wet paradise?"

"Those two 'bozos,' as you call them, I have much stronger names for them, stole some artifacts from me, and I climbed aboard to retrieve them. Unfortunately, I misjudged the timing, and they returned to their boat earlier than I expected and found me."

"So what were you and your two friends doing spying on the yacht from the restaurant? Planning your attack? Are they floating somewhere out here with us?"

"No," Viane spoke in an almost apologetic voice. "I came by myself. They had warned me about taking things into my own hands, but I didn't bother listening to them. We'd gone to the restaurant to make plans of what to do about getting my artifacts returned. We were all surprised to see the yacht pulling up to the pier since the last we knew it was still in Kaneohe at the yacht club."

Yeah, I know, thought Debra.

"Aren't we a pair? A crook and a straight, both going under for the final count together. Sort of makes you think about the strange twists of fate in life, doesn't it? We're two opposites on a spectrum of good and bad, yin and yang, being put in the same grave. I wonder if that balances the scale in God's eyes? My name's Debra, by the way. What's yours?"

"Viane, and with a little positive belief on your part, neither of us is going to be put in any *grave* together. Help should be on its way fairly quickly, so all we have to do is survive until then."

"Okay, Vi-ane," spoken with accusatory inflection, "what makes you think help is rushing our way? What do you know that I am failing to notice? Help me out so I can be a believer as well."

"Ever hear of an EPIRB? I suspect not. You don't strike me as being too boat smart. We happen to have one attached to our life ring, and that, my dear Debra, is what is causing the rush to our side. Ever hear of one?" she repeated. Debra's blank stare was enough of an answer. "Stands for Emergency Position-Indicating Radio Beacon, and as soon as it hit the water, it began telling the world we needed help. Also tells the world exactly where we are, and if the bozos bought the best one they could buy, it's also telling the world who it belongs to and where they keep all their furniture. The Coast Guard should be heading our way right now."

"The Coast Guard is not the only one who's heading our way, and I'm not too sure which one I'd prefer would get here first."

Viane turned to look in the direction Debra was staring and immediately felt her heart sink as the bow of *Whiskey Sea* appeared rising over the waves, bearing down on them.

Turning back to Debra, Viane frantically yelled, "Quick, take off your blouse." Viane began to struggle out of her own.

"What the hell are you doing, and why should I take mine off?" Debra had started to give Viane credit for her awareness and levelheaded thinking, but this seemed on the edge of being too bizarre; but without further hesitation and not waiting for a reply, she took off her blouse and handed it to Viane whose hand was outstretched waiting for it. Viane threw it over the white life ring and the blinking red light of the EPIRB. Her shirt had disappeared below the surface, leaving both women wearing only their bras and a layer of goose bumps.

"Help me hold your blouse in place. If I'm right, your blouse is almost the same dark color as the water, so it'll help camouflage us. My white one would be like waving a flag for them to see. Now, we need to make ourselves invisible. Keep the life ring between them and us and get as much of your head under water as possible. Chances are, in this water, they will be looking for the white coloring of the life ring. That's why they're white by the way—makes them easier to spot. Pops and I spend a lot of time on the water, and I know that things can be extremely difficult to see, especially if they blend in and particularly in this rough water. All we need to do is remain invisible until the Coast Guard arrives."

"This Pops character sounds like a walking book of common sense. You're fortunate to have had someone like that in your life. Sure wish I had!" Debra was rapidly gaining a whole new respect for this young woman. Placing herself in Viane's hands was becoming easier by the second. She sank down low in the water trying to keep just her nose above, which was proving difficult as the waves kept dumping water over them, making them both cough when it found its way up their nostrils.

"Pinch your nose and breathe slowly through your mouth," said Viane as she spit out the water that had trickled in.

Viane didn't know if it was going to work as she planned or not, but she grabbed the EPIRB and held it upside down, clamped between her feet, as far under water as she could reach with the flotation cord attached to it. *It may not stop sending, but with luck it may distort the signal enough that they wouldn't get a strong signal to track in on.*

They watched as the yacht passed by them a few times. They knew their camouflage idea was working. Once, though, she thought they'd been spotted as the yacht had been so close, almost on top of them. Apparently, the men were looking elsewhere and didn't see them just a few feet to starboard. An overriding fear now was of being chewed up in the propellers if the yacht passed by any closer.

"Where are they, Rol?" Grey was yelling through the glass windshield. "According to the signal, we should be right on top of them. That life ring can't be that difficult to spot."

"Make another swing around. We've apparently passed them." He was staring at the water so intently he was close to becoming hypnotized by its motion.

"Come on, Rol. Keep your eyes open for Christ's sake. You know we can't turn this thing on a dime, and this is the third pass. We've probably run over them already if they're still above water."

"Maybe we have, Grey. The signal just stopped. Let's give it a few minutes to see if it starts again. If not, let's get the hell out of here."

"The signal stopped?" Maybe we *did* run over them. We can be sure the Coast Guard has intercepted the signal and will know someone's in trouble. Hell, they'll know *we're* in trouble—that EPIRB will have already broadcasted our ID."

"Remember the ID in that EPIRB refers to *My Mistress*. We bought it before the name change, remember?" Grey was bringing the helm hard around for another pass.

"Yeah, that's right. You know what we could do?" exclaimed Roland. "It may sound crazy, but it might work. We could dump a couple garbage cans of jetsam overboard; maybe it would make it appear that *My Mistress* went down. That would at least keep the Coast Guard busy until we're far enough away. Don't we have some stuff lying around that still carries the old name?"

Chapter Forty-Six

The sun had yet to break over the horizon above the Kaneohe Marine Corps Air Station on the far side of the bay. It was still too early, only 5:30 a.m. Stone sat on the seawall absently looking at the brightening orange-red skyline as sunrise approached. As often happened when he was lost in the world of thought, the moment the sun decided to show up over the dark silhouette of the low hills, its appearance would pull him back to awareness, hopefully with some enlightenment on puzzled thoughts.

He'd been unable to sleep, other than short spurts during the night, because of a steady montage of apprehensions. Concern for Viane was uppermost in the unending kaleidoscope, but his deepening feelings for Teri generously shared his restlessness.

What he had struggled with most over the past hours was the disturbing notion that if anything happened to Viane, he was not sure how that would impact his deepening relationship with Teri. Would there be constant reminder over the loss of their friend in the face of the other every time they looked? The idea of not having Teri in his life was quickly becoming one he chose not to entertain, but he found himself doing just that, and it agitated him. His one consoling notion, and the one that finally brought a smile to his face as the sun made it presence known, was that their relationship was new and needed time to mature and gain time-proof understanding. Whatever happened, Viane would always be a bond, not a division, between them.

"Lots of rocky road in a budding relationship, Bert. Better be cautious if that tom cat next door starts to put the moves on you."

Bert, whether sensing Stone's mood or simply being what nature made her, had been lying in the groove formed between Stone's legs for the better part of an hour, head erect but eyes closed, lost in the absentminded stroking she was receiving.

Tranquility such as this, though, is subject to immediate and startling change as the phone rang. Stone jumped up, and Bert went flying onto the grass suddenly wide-awake.

"Stone, we may have a break." Mike's voice sounded hopeful. "Unfortunately, we don't know whether it's a good break or a bad one."

"What gives, Mike? Any break is better than none at all—let's go for the positive side. What have you got?"

"It'll be a few hours until we have much more information, but the Coast Guard has just called in an alert. It's a procedural thing they do when they scramble to send out a search and rescue vessel. They know we need to be informed—kind of a courtesy thing on their part. From what I gather, they've just started receiving an EPIRB signal from a 130 miles east of Oahu. The signal is originating from a device registered to a vessel named *My Mistress*. Didn't Teri tell us that the *Whiskey Sea* was originally named *My Mistress*? I'm thinking the signal is directly tied to your situation with Viane." Stone noticed it was still "your," not yet "our."

"Yeah, Mike, she said it was changed last time she was in dry dock. A signal coming in, though, could mean a lot of things, couldn't it? The yacht may have sunk in a storm, or someone may have fallen or, even worse, *been thrown*, overboard. Someone might have stolen the EPIRB off *My Mistress*, and it's just now doing its thing." He was thinking of Viane's original episode of falling off the *Whiskey Sea*. "Maybe a life ring simply fell off the deck and self-activated, and they have no clue that it's calling us," he said, his voice trailing off in thought. Stone was grasping at straws, and they both knew it.

"Either good or bad, Stone," continued Mike after letting Stone run the range of his opinions, "we won't know which until the Coast Guard arrives at its location and gets a visual of the situation. Since the signal is only 130 nautical miles out, I suspect they'll send their chopper out ahead of the USCGC *Kuokoa*, so we might get our answer within an hour or so. The radio operator is a friend and has promised to keep me up to speed on developments. You going to call Teri on this, right? You'd save me some time if you would. Of course you probably don't need a reason to give her a call, do you? I'll leave that in your hands to take care of. I'll call when I hear more."

"You're a good friend, Mike. *Mahalo*. I'll call Teri right now and tell her what we have. Probably no need for me to ask that you call as soon as you hear anything more, right?"

"You got it, Stone. Call you back real soon with good news, I hope. Oh, I almost forgot to tell you, we picked up Debra Shinn's accomplice yesterday. Dorteo Aquino, by name. Nothing there yet as he's decided not to talk to us. Just keeps shrugging his shoulders at all our questions. Only temporarily, though. We'll open him up."

"*Mahalo*, Mike, for keeping me posted. I'll let Teri know what you've told me."

Stone called Teri and relayed everything Mike had told him. They discussed not telling Pops for fear of upsetting him with the uncertainty of the situation but finally decided that he would be more upset by having information kept from him. Pops, with his easygoing attitude on life, appeared on all accounts to be the kind of man who needed to know about any event that surrounded him, especially those that affected his family.

"Tell him everything, and if he has any further questions, I can answer him when I get there."

"You're coming over?" she asked, an obvious smile in her voice. "I'll have some coffee waiting."

Chapter Forty-Seven

The front door flew open before Stone had a chance to knock and found himself immediately surrounded by Teri's arms. It felt wonderful and reminded him that they had had very little chance to be alone the past few days. At least it seemed that way, even though their moments shared in the lifeguard stand and those wonderful kisses seemed like it had been just yesterday. So much had happened in such a short time. Maybe that was the underlying cause for the nightlong discussion he had had with himself.

Both moved easily, facing each other and allowing their lips to briefly meld together. It could have gone on forever were it not for the sound of a male voice being cleared. It came from the entrance to the kitchen.

Stone looked over Teri's shoulder, saying, "Good morning, Pops." He felt foolish having been so absorbed in Teri that he'd forgotten that Pops was also there. As he released Teri to shake Pops' hand, he saw that Pops was just standing in the doorway to the kitchen, making no effort to come any farther into the room.

Stone absently wiped moisture off his cheek and realized Teri had been crying and had left a tear resting where her face had been. He looked at her and saw her eyes were red and cheeks moist with recent tears. "What's going on?" He looked from Teri to Pops and saw his dark chiseled-cold expression and unsmiling face and immediately knew he'd missed something somewhere between home and Teri's place.

Moving into the center of the living room, he said, "One of you needs to start filling me in. I came over the Pali Highway feeling good positive vibes about the way events are unfolding." He looked expectantly at Teri and waited to hear what had dumped these two spirits in the sand and brought Teri to tears.

"Just after you left your house," she said, her voice muffled behind a tissue, "Mike called to tell us the helicopter heading out to intercept the signal can't locate it because it's not making any noise now. Apparently, it suddenly went quiet before they had gotten very far.

"They initiated a five-mile grid pattern search but said that with so many white caps it will be difficult to spot anything and the grid search is going to take several hours. The pilot said something about the view looking like a spilled bag of popcorn on a blue carpet. They had just started their search when their commander ordered them to break off the grid search and instead go intercept a vessel spotted in the area, presumably *My Mistress/Whiskey Sea* since the signal device is from her.

"According to Mike's friend, a satellite image shows a vessel close to where the signal had been coming from. They figure whoever's on that vessel may have retrieved the EPIRB. She told him it was the Coast Guard's reasoning for the signal to have stopped sending its signal."

Teri moved into Stone's arms once again, seeking his consoling. "Oh, Stone. I was hoping it would be a simple matter of finding Viane and bringing her home." Her voice was soft, almost too quiet to hear. "I'm so worried for her."

"There could be a multitude of reasons why the EPIRB signal would stop," volunteered Stone, attempting to put her and Pops at ease. "I think we need to maintain our positive outlook on events instead of letting ourselves drop into a lava pit of worry. If we do enough worrying about it, we'll end up manifesting the reality of that worry."

"What?" Teri looked up at him through returning tears as if he'd just announced he was planning to climb Mount Everest tomorrow.

"Something I heard recently that, strangely enough, made a lot of sense."

"You think?" she commented, her face finding a resting spot buried in Stone's shirt.

"That's got to be that darned *Whiskey* boat out there with my girl." Pops' voice was that of a loud growl. "I'd like to have my boat out there right now. I'd know what to do with those haoles." He turned back into the kitchen, returning a split second later with a mug of coffee, steam circling his face, and making his already angry features appear ghostlike as he took a sip. He sat down on the couch that Viane had slept on only a few shorts days before, but he didn't know that as Teri had thought better of mentioning it.

With Teri's face cushioned against his chest as they stood by the front door and Pops on the old couch looking like he could peel the outer layer off a dozen rocks, Stone forced some upbeat music into his voice. "You two are acting like the last star in the sky just winked out. If you let your thoughts sink into the doldrums, you'll end up doing nothing but dredging up every negative possibility that exists. As I just said, let's start concentrating on the positive side of all this. Look," he continued, "the Coast Guard helicopter will be on top of that vessel very soon. If that's the *Whiskey Sea* out there and it's still in the area where the signal was, the USCGC *Kuokoa* will be on site within a short time and will be able to secure whatever's going on out there. I say we hold as much positive energy as we can muster for finding Viane safe and sound.

"Pops, you know your daughter. How would she expect you to be acting right about now?"

Pops began slowly shaking his head from side to side. "You know," he said, looking up from his coffee mug and appraising Stone and Teri, who'd pulled apart in order to look at him, "she'd think I'd gone and soaked my head in vinegar. She'd be expecting me to be the last one on earth to cave in on a positive outcome. Funny how you can be so strong on every front and face into any wave that God pushes in your direction until you see that wave coming at you, and it has the name of someone who's an intimate part of you written across its surface. It's difficult to find that positive train of thought in all this, but I agree that it's essential we all do just that. *Mahalo*, Stone, for speaking true."

"Okay, Mr. Positive Guy," said Teri, leaning back to look up into Stone's eyes, her tears having dried. "I'll buy some of that positive substance you're dishing out. So what now? It appears we can't do much until Mike calls with further information."

"Actually, there is one more thing to do—something more for me to do. Sort of a 'reminder' step to make sure it's not overlooked."

He picked up Teri's phone and dialed.

"Could I speak to Sgt. Mike Kalama, it's important that I speak with him as quickly as possible." He waited a short time before hearing Mike on the other end. "Mike, it's Stone. Teri filled me in on the latest. That other yacht that's in the vicinity, if it turns out to be the *Whiskey Sea*, they'll need to do a thorough search for the women, at least I hope they will. Good, that's at least reassuring. Make sure they also know about that hidden room that's amidships aft of their lounge. If push comes to shove, have the Coast Guard call and speak with Teri. She's got the secret lowdown on how it can be opened."

"What's the *reassuring* part, Stone?" asked Pops after Stone had closed the connection with Mike. "Something positive I hope."

"Mike told me the Coast Guard commander has been made aware that *Whiskey Sea* is suspected of a crime and is aware there may be two kidnap victims onboard."

They became silent. Teri remained cradled in Stone's embrace. Pops slowly sipped his coffee, deep in thought.

"Pops," Stone suddenly exclaimed, breaking the quiet, causing Teri to jump, "you made that coffee sound good. Is there more in the kitchen?"

"Almost a whole pot full. Teri knew I liked my coffee, so she made plenty this morning. It's darn near as good as mine." He gave Teri a quick wink.

"I'd like some too, Pops," said Teri, with no energy to
return his kidding. "Let's all go sit in the kitchen instead of
being so mopey out here."

Before any of them could move, though, there was the
distinct sound of a car door shutting just beyond the front
door, followed by a sudden and insistent knocking.

They broke apart as Teri apprehensively reached for the
door handle and pulled it open.

None of them could have been more surprised to see
who was standing on the other side, big smiles on their faces,
knowing full well the impact their visit would have as a taxi
pulled out of the yard.

Chapter Forty-Eight

"Are you thinking of inviting us in, Auntie, or do we need to call that taxi back?"

Teri was momentarily too surprised at seeing Viane's brothers on her doorstep to respond—she just stood, almost in shock. Only two minutes before Stone had arrived, she and Pops had been discussing the possibility of his sons coming over to help. She'd been a little unsure of having so many people involved. Truth be told, she couldn't imagine where she was going to house the Koa family and had decided maybe it'd be better if the boys didn't come over to Oahu just yet. Pops, though, was of the opinion, and he voiced it more than once that 'the more hands in the pot, the better the stew.' Obviously the decision about the boys coming over from Hilo had taken its own path.

She gave them both hugs as they came into the living room, tears starting to form in her eyes again, but now with joy. It suddenly felt right having Sonny and John join them in the search for their sister. A place for them to stay could always be figured out. She knew Stone had room and would gladly offer it.

Pops had come over and stepped in when Teri motioned them into the room. Without words, he embraced both his sons in one grand hug. "Good you boys came. I thought you would."

Stone joined in their welcome. He realized by their smiles and nods to him from over the top of their father's head that they were appraising him, in light of the closeness that Teri, their calabash auntie, standing with her hand casually resting on Stone's arm, was obviously demonstrating. He had become part of Teri's life and therefore, seemingly, a part of theirs as well. They both briefly embraced him as their father relinquished his hold, so he figured he'd gained their approval on some level.

They weren't there for pleasantries, so the subject of their sister rapidly became the center point of conversation.

Stone told the brothers everything the group knew up to that point. Both Pops and Teri were filling in the holes in his relaying of events that he had inadvertently left open.

"So all you really know for certain," summarized Sonny, "is that you don't really know where Viane is right at this moment." He hesitated while looking at each one before continuing. "Well, I know where she *was*." He knew how to capture their attention with his emphasis on *was*. "There's no way she could resist climbing aboard that boat, so that's exactly where she is . . . or was," he added, looking around the room.

Stone didn't feel like correcting him on the boat thing. He let it slide and saw Teri's quick wink and smile at understanding his reluctance to correct Sonny.

Sonny was continuing, "The only question I can see is whether she's still on the boat or not. If an EPIRB signal's been detected, then my money's on her being where the signal's coming from, which is back in the water. What do you think, John?"

"If those two things she found and was so excited about finding, believing them being so darn important, and if they're on that boat, then that's exactly the place she would head for. She wouldn't be resting without first trying everything she could to get them back, and if they dumped her off that boat once, I'm betting they wouldn't hesitate to dump her again. Why the signal device is in the water could mean a struggle happened, and we all know she'd be in the middle of it, hopefully on the end that includes the signal."

Everyone quietly voiced their mixed reactions to John's somewhat dismal appraisal of the situation as a palpable dark cloud descended and cast its shadowy gloom across the room once more.

Chapter Forty-Nine

The *Whiskey Sea* was ready to come about and make its sixth pass. They had initially made a mistake, and each of the men knew it, but there was no going back for a do-over. They were experienced enough to know that backtracking to a precise spot in the ocean could be a daunting task with the absence of reference points. Add that to the ever-present ocean swells that easily hid things from view, and they knew they were in the proverbial haystack. One of them should have gotten a GPS reading marking the exact spot the women went over. *Should have . . . should haves are always so darn clear in hindsight.* Roland had been in no condition to even think properly, and Grey's anger had overshadowed any rational thoughts. Had they gotten a GPS fix, they would be pin-point on the spot and not be relying on the EPIRB's signal to lead the way, which it was no longer doing.

Roland's anxiety to find and silence the two women was easing with the growing certainty they had either drowned or were ground up in the propellers. He was willing to concede to one of those outcomes and also willing to accept that the EPIRB malfunctioned for some unknown reason. Too old, perhaps. He wasn't even partially electronics knowledgeable, so it was virtually a guess.

Roland walked into the control room where Grey stood, one hand on the helm, apparently deep in thought, gazing out the forward window while pondering their next step.

Neither felt secure in the notion that the women were indeed gone, but without any sign of them or the EPIRB's signal, there were scarce few options left to consider.

"What are you thinking, Grey? Cut and run or do a few more passes?"

"Without that signal, we could be a few yards away from where they went over or a mile. It's like throwing darts in the middle of a football field in the dark and wearing a blindfold. Our chance of seeing them if they're still floating is rapidly approaching zilch. What are you thinking?"

Roland was standing by the door he'd just entered, his back to the room, looking out over the water. "Oh man," he exclaimed, "we might have guessed. Looks like someone else noticed the signal and has come to join the party. Our fun just never stops."

Turning to Grey, he said, "I think our future choices are diminishing by the second," deflated tones in his voice as he raised an arm and finger and pointed. "There's a helicopter approaching, and by the markings on its side, it appears to be the Coast Guard coming to pay us a call. I'm betting they're responding to the EPIRB signal and are probably just as confused as we are about why it stopped."

Grey looked quickly in the direction Roland was pointing, saw that the helicopter was still several minutes away but approaching fast, and quickly swung the helm hard to port.

Roland almost fell out onto the deck before grabbing the doorjamb to steady himself.

"Your turn to act, Rol," Grey responded with obvious tension. "Drop the port deck ladder over the side and get yourself soaked. Here's your story." He was working up an idea—Grey was good at improvising. "You slipped off the ladder while you were trying to retrieve a life ring that had fallen from its rail holder. You're guessing it went under the props. Go now," he hurriedly exclaimed.

Roland always marveled at Grey's quick thinking. Without hesitation, he headed portside, away from the approaching helicopter, dropped the ladder over the side, tied a safety line to his waist as well as to the deck rail, and jumped in.

He was stepping back onto the deck from the uppermost rung of the ladder, dripping wet, as the helicopter began to hover directly over their bow. *Perfect timing. They are now witnesses to my story.* He stepped over the gunwale onto the deck and moved out of sight of the helicopter, dropped what he had found against the bulkhead, and then walked to the doorway of the control room to join Grey.

"Ahoy, *Whiskey Sea.* Cut your power and stand by to receive personnel."

"Damn," exclaimed Roland from outside the control room, "their megaphones could wake up a dead fish. You're doing what they want, right?"

The engines went silent as they waited for Coast Guard personnel to be winched down to the aft exposed deck. It was an extremely dangerous maneuver with the yacht rising and falling with each passing wave. *Maybe they won't be able to make it and will have to go away,* mused Roland as he and Grey walked out onto the deck to greet their two new uninvited guests who were thirty feet up and quickly descending on two winch lines.

They made an expert landing on the deck as if they did this maneuver every day before lunch. Their lines quickly retracted into the helicopter as they both moved the few paces to where Grey and Roland stood waiting. The helicopter moved fifty feet away from the yacht but remained close in order to maintain observation.

"I'm Chief Petty Officer Chamberlain and this"—indicating the woman standing next to him with a slight nod in her direction—"is Petty Officer Third Class Samson. Thank you for cutting your engines as requested. We would like your permission to inspect this yacht."

Without waiting for a reply, each of the officers shrugged out of their life jackets and top portion of their flight suits, the latter were cinched around their waist—performed with almost perfect, practiced synchronization. It gave Roland and Grey an unobstructed view of the heavy side arms they were both equipped with. It also implied a warning in case there was any doubt about the seriousness of the occasion.

Chief Petty Officer Chamberlain was a tall man carrying massive shoulders and vein-ridged arms. They were virtually hairless and looked like huge wooden clubs dangling from the too-small short-sleeved shirt of his uniform. His face, pockmarked from a youthful battle with acne, showed a calmness mixed with undeniable authority, all framed in a stern, humorless sort of way.

Grey and Roland both instinctively knew they'd have to tread carefully with this man. They had no doubt he'd be able to lift and throw them both far from their yacht without effort, if he chose to do so. The woman, Petty Officer Third Class Samson, was his direct opposite. She looked like a teenager in a uniform that didn't befit her mousy demeanor. Her solemn features gave the impression of a person trying desperately to be assertive, but had so far found it eluding her abilities.

"Looking for anything in particular?" Grey responded inquisitively, attempting to smooth the way for the Coast Guard's speedy exit off their yacht. "We could save you time and show you around, show you where all our life jackets are as well as our safety equipment."

"That won't be necessary, sir, we know our way around yachts." Another nod toward Petty Officer Samson followed his words, this time apparently meaning for her to lead off and begin the search. Instead, she stood statue-still with a fixed stare resting on Roland.

"May I ask you, sir, why you were in the water, and are you all right—not hurt in any way?"

"Thank you for asking, miss"—Roland wasn't big on military-type rank names—"I'm fine." He continued to explain without waiting to be asked—he knew it would be her next question anyway. "We lost a life ring overboard and didn't know it was missing until our EPIRB signal indicator came to life. We decided to come back for it. Life rings are expensive, you know, especially those with the EPIRBs attached. I thought I'd spotted it and was reaching for it when I slipped on the low rung of the ladder and fell in. Luckily, I had thought to attach a lifeline. The life ring and EPIRB must have floated into our propellers." His excuse sounded lame, even to his own ears, but it was already spoken.

"Sir, you were holding something white when you stepped over the gunwale onto the deck. May I ask what that was and where you placed it, since you no longer appear to have it in your possession?" She had apparently managed to bypass any difficulty she may have experienced with being assertive. Her unblinking and accusing stare compelled a response.

The hesitation in Roland's reply was obvious—he was caught without having a reasonable answer, not thinking they even knew he'd found something. Grey held his gaze on Petty Officer Samson, not wanting to look at Roland for fear any facial expression he may convey, no matter how bland, could hamper his partner in arriving at a plausible explanation. Besides, he really wanted to hear what Roland had found and, at the same time, totally in fear of hearing what he would say in response.

"Oh that," he finally responded, trying to brush the question into the "Oh, you were serious?" category. "Just a piece of cloth that happened to be floating past when I fell in. You know, 'keep our oceans free from debris' and all that."

"We'll take it off your hands, sir. That will save you the trouble of disposing of garbage, it's the least we can do." With a quick nod, she indicated he should lead the way to where he'd stashed it. Grey decided they must teach head nods at Coast Guard school.

With no choice available that he could quickly see, Roland led the woman the short distance down the portside deck.

She quickly moved ahead and retrieved it off the deck before Roland could bend over to reach for it. With arms raised, she held it up and spread it out.

"This appears to be a woman's blouse and doesn't look to have been in the water very long." She glanced at her partner to be sure he was looking at it as well. Roland caught the knowing eye lock that passed between the two officers.

She proceeded to roll it up and stick it, wet, under her right arm. Grey's respect for the woman was upgrading by the second.

"We'll proceed with the inspection now, sir," said Chief Petty Officer Chamberlain, alternating eye contact between Grey and Roland to make sure they both understood. "We'll find you when we're finished." Another nod to Petty Officer Samson, and they both moved through the adjacent door into the lounge, apparently knowing precisely where they were going.

Grey and Roland followed, but instead of shadowing their guests, they went to the bar and pulled out a bottle of Glenlivet and reached for ice. The Coast Guard pair exited the lounge through the starboard doorway.

The men were on their second refill when Chamberlain and Samson came back into the lounge. The woman's entire right side was now wet down to her waist and probably beyond, but that part of her was covered by the lower part of her flight suit. The blouse remained trapped under her arm.

"We've notified our ride to pick us up," offered Chamberlain as both zipped up their flight suits and shrugged into their life jackets in preparation for the chopper's retrieval lines to be lowered. "As soon as we clear your deck, you're free to continue on your journey. Thank you again for allowing us to inspect your yacht."

As if we'd had a choice in the matter. Grey suspected they were being overly courteous since they apparently had found nothing incriminating.

"That's quite a hot tub you gentlemen have. First time I've seen what is normally a bow anchor hold made into one." Roland sensed a shift in attitude in Samson, realizing she appeared to be a little turned on, which surprised him. It shouldn't have, really. It was a similar reaction he and Grey often noticed from women they'd brought onboard.

"Apparently, she really likes hot tubs," he observed, after the two officers had been winched back onto their chopper.

Chapter Fifty

Viane had to marvel once again at the ocean's ability to hide its victims. She and Debra were less than two hundred yards off the *Whiskey Sea*'s portside and watched as the Coast Guard helicopter approached the yacht and hovered over its stern. They had been in Roland's direct line of sight just moments before and had watched him, to their astonishment, hurriedly throw a rope ladder over the side and proceed to jump the railing into the water.

"What on God's earth do you suppose he's up to?" Viane had no logical answer until she saw him climb out carrying something that looked much too familiar. She felt around the waistband of her shorts and realized her blouse was no longer tucked into it. She had little doubt that was what Roland now carried as he ascended the ladder.

Over the past several hours, each time *Whiskey Sea* passed them, they dreaded that they would be spotted and hauled back aboard to be subjected to something unimaginable. They'd huddled closer and closer seeking warmth, attempting to bolster the other's spirit, but their efforts were failing miserably.

Seeing a Coast Guard helicopter had suddenly filled them with renewed reason to believe they would at last be safe, and their spirits decisively began to soar, their bodies warming to the thought. They speculated the two people landing onboard were there to find them and lead them to safety. All they had to do was wait a bit longer.

They tried to call out but realized their voices were no match against the helicopter's rotating blades. Besides, they were to the point of being too exhausted to yell much above a soft speaking voice. They weren't going to be heard.

In stunned silence, after waiting for what seemed to them a very long time, they watched as *Whiskey Sea* began to stir back to life as their would-be rescuers were hauled back up and into the helicopter, which immediately rose into the air, slid sideways into a sharp turn, and began moving quickly away.

"For God's sake, Viane," shrieked Debra, "we've got to do something. Everyone's leaving us." She waved her free arm and screamed as loudly as she could, "HELP . . . HELP US . . ."

"The EPIRB," Viane shrieked in response to Debra's hysterics, "we forgot about the EPIRB's signal." Debra stopped her frenzied antics and stared at Viane, waiting for what came next.

They'd been avoiding *Whiskey Sea* as best they could and forgot about the signal device not sending out its signal. Viane had hidden it below the surface; its cord wrapped around one of her legs, trapping it upside down with her feet. She quickly loosened the cord and let the instrument float back to the surface. As it floated onto the surface, they nervously checked and found the small red light blinking once again, presumably alerting the world that they were still desperately in need of someone's help.

Chapter Fifty-One

Grey watched the helicopter recede into the distance and disappear into a dust spot on the horizon. He powered up both engines and pushed the throttles forward into a slow, near-idle speed. Roland's discovery of the blouse meant the two women were close, or at the least had been close, if they were in fact still above water. He intended to have one final look now that the helicopter and its crew were no longer a threat. Leaving the area for the mainland without first knowing for sure whether the women had sank to the bottom or not was almost too unsettling for him to consider, so he deemed a final quick search was needed.

Roland strolled into the control room with two frosted glasses of okolehao on the rocks and handed one to Grey. They'd managed to find two cases of the local whiskey that they hoped would carry them through the two-thousand-five-hundred-mile trip to the Washington coastline.

"That was too close. I think we're still in hot water with that blouse I found, but I can't imagine where it could lead anyone—not as if they can tie it to one of our women."

"Stop calling them 'our' women." Grey was feeling the anxiety of the moment. Roland smiled at his choice of words. "They kind of *were* 'our' women there for a little while. Anyway, that was lousy timing that the Coast Guard showed up just in time to see me carrying it out of the water. That Samson girl must have the eyes of a sea hawk. Should have left the damn thing in the water."

"No such thing as *should have*, Roland, I've said that before. It's only *what is*. We just have to adapt to the situation and proceed forward."

"You sound like some kind of a new-age guru, Grey, with your 'No such thing as *should have*' mantra. Whatever happened to your old mantras, 'Live for the moment' or the one that went, 'Each moment comes at you only once'? You make this stuff up as you go along, don't you?" he queried as he took a sip of okolehao.

They were both beginning to relax from their run-in with the law. Their relaxation often took in a lot of back-and-forth banter.

Grey began smiling as he looked at Roland. "Wonder if someday we'll see that Samson woman coming onboard for a soak. I think our hot tub really got to her."

Roland wasn't paying attention. Instead he was looking at the EPIRB signal indicator flashing coordinates. "The signal's come back to life, Grey. It's apparently reactivated itself after whatever it was that stopped it earlier. Those women must have been able to temporarily silence it somehow, or else its age is beginning to show. I wonder if this means they finally went under and the life ring has floated free of them? We better go take a look before that helicopter decides to come back for a second look. My intuition is telling me *our* women are still out there holding on."

"That's what we're in the process of doing, Rol."

"Swing hard to starboard, Grey. I think the signal's not much more than a hundred yards away from us. We should have a visual on the location real quick."

As Grey swung the helm into a turn, Roland went out on the bow once again where his view of the water ahead was unobstructed, totally determined to find at least the life ring, if not its former occupants. He wasn't sure how he felt about seeing the women—either alive or gone. He was leaning heavily toward hoping they had disappeared on their own and could no longer create trouble for them.

The *Whiskey Sea* moved slowly. Roland's eyes swept the water from side to side. He could *feel* the women's presence: his gut instinct told him they were close and, unfortunately, very much alive. Given enough belief in one's intuitive ability, the energy behind what was being looked for became very strong. *Darn Grey and his guru stuff—it's rubbing off.*

"There," he shouted pointing a little off to his left. "I see them, Grey. Both women are still holding on to the life ring. Swing two degrees to port. They're about forty yards out."

"I got them," shouted Grey. "Get the ladder down and the gaff hook ready. Pull them both in like you would a fish if you have to, but don't miss getting them back onboard."

"Run them down, Grey. It'll be faster and a lot less messy than using the hook."

Grey moved the yacht's wheel a degree to the left, bringing the bow directly in line with the women. Another few minutes, and the propellers would grind them into fish food. Roland grabbed the fishhook with its dangerously sharp pointed hook and held it ready. It could sink into flesh without the least effort. He was going to keep it close at hand—just in case.

With body temperatures dropping rapidly, the women knew something must happen, and soon. They watched for the helicopter and prayed, something Debra had done very little of in her life, when suddenly they sensed a shadow moving over them.

Quickly glancing over their shoulders, they were stunned to see *Whiskey Sea* a mere thirty yards away and progressing slowly toward them. It had quietly slipped up behind them while they were concentrating their vision and their hopes on the opposite horizon.

Roland had lowered a rope ladder and stood looking down at them with a fishhook on a long pole held in his hands.

"You ladies have three choices," he said, his voice loud, almost yelling, in order to be heard. He'd changed his thought and decided it would be better for him and Grey if the women were onboard. They could then make absolutely sure the threat ended. "Climb the ladder immediately, or if you choose, I can help you aboard impaled on this hook. The last option is probably one you don't want to choose. Grey is quite willing to run you over and change you into minced fish food. You have one minute to start moving."

In a few precious minutes, the women would be within striking distance of the gaff hook—he wasn't going to lose this opportunity to finish this thing.

Chapter Fifty-Two

Mike pushed his chair back and began to get to his feet when his desk phone rang again. He'd just hung up after checking on the progress of the interrogation involving Dorteo Aquino, learning that he still refused to answer any questions: he hadn't said anything since he was brought in.

"I don't think he's playing dumb, Mike," said the other officer, "it's more like his thoughts are totally someplace else."

Mike decided to pull records on him and see what the guy's history looked like before getting involved in the questioning. He sat back down to answer the phone.

"Hey, Mike, it's Robin." PO1C Robin Jaffers was Mike's friend and the Coast Guard's radio operator at the station on Sand Island. He and Robin had struck up a friendship the year before, after Mike responded to a break-in call from the station. Robin had discovered an abandoned gate, the padlock cut off and lying on the ground with the gate wide-open. They didn't discover anything damaged or stolen after their exhaustive search, but they did find they got along quite compatibly as friends as well as becoming aware of an attraction that was developing between them.

Neither desired nor had time for a committed relationship, so they chose instead to spend off-work time together whenever time and responsibilities permitted. They frequently met in Davey Jones' Locker, a bar under the Reef Hotel on Waikiki Beach, to enjoy a drink. The bar was a fun place to meet and watch swimmers in the hotel pool who didn't realize the bar had a viewing window below the water line that looked into the deep end of the pool. They found it could be quite entertaining and generally added an element of humor to their need to relax after particularly long, energy-taxing days.

"I wanted to keep you abreast of the action on our end," she said. "The physical search of the *Whiskey Sea* didn't turn up anything other than a woman's white blouse, which was found by one of the yacht's owners. Our guys think he was trying to hide it, but that was all they got, and it doesn't appear to mean much. I know it doesn't help much, Mike, but there was little else they could do except head back to the original grid pattern and continue the search. The USCGC *Kuokoa* isn't too far away and is going to rendezvous with the helicopter. The cutter's coming home from its routine patrol around Niihau and Kauai and should be at *Whiskey* Sea's location soon. Sorry, Mike. Wish I could tell you something more positive."

"Yeah, me too, Robin."

"Chief Petty Officer Chamberlain said they did as thorough a search as they could and said the yacht's owners did not try to interfere. Sounds clean to me. There were some interesting comments made about a hot tub onboard, but they weren't being too specific about it. I think they were just trying to make me jealous."

"*Mahalo*, Robin. Not sure where this takes any of us, but I need to pass the news on to the missing girl's father. Can you find out if the search team looked into what is believed to be a hidden room aft of the lounge? If they didn't know about it, they may have missed an important element of their search."

"I'll find out what I can and get back to you. *Ahui hou*."

Mike made some notes of the call and pushed his chair back to go look into Dorteo's history with the law. The man held the only key to understanding the chamber of intrigue that Viane and now HPD had inadvertently stepped into, but before he could rise two inches out of his chair, his phone rang again.

"Follow up to our conversation, Mike." It was Robin again. "Our guys say they have no knowledge of any hidden room. Said there were bookcases and mirrors on the aft wall of the lounge. They still claim to have done as thorough a search as they could but are ready to go back if further information warrants it."

"Mahalo for checking that out, Robin, I'll pass the information on, but I think the chopper crew needs to go back and open that room. Where's USCGC *Kuokoa* right now?"

"About ten miles east of *Whiskey Sea*'s location. As I mentioned, they're going to . . . hold on, Mike. Something's coming in, don't go away." The phone was put on hold, but she was back on the line in less than a minute.

"Mike, you still there?"

"Yeah, what do you have?"

"The chopper pilot reported the EPIRB signal just reactivated, so they're doubling back to take a closer look see. Said it's coming from the very spot where they just were.

USCGC *Kuokoa*'s now going to rendezvous with them at the signal's location. Should be there pretty quickly."

"Hey, Robin, have the skipper of the cutter call a woman named Teri White. She's at 521-0168. She'll give him the details on the exact location of that hidden room and how to open its door. Another physical search will be needed in order to examine that room."

"I understand what you're saying, Mike, but you know that might be a hard sell after having already conducted a search. A second one without documented support could put the Coast Guard into a risk of liability. Let me see what I can find out."

Chapter Fifty-Three

Mike didn't waste a moment before calling Teri's house to relay the information he'd learned from Robin. He knew they were all there and anxious to hear any news he could share.

Teri answered her phone as the men continued dissecting Viane's probable actions.

"That was Mike," she said as she emerged from the kitchen, excitement dancing in her eyes. "That signal has started doing its thing again, and the Coast Guard helicopter has been instructed to get back there as quickly as they can. He also said the USCGC *Kuokoa*'s not far away." She automatically folded into Stone's arms like it was the most natural thing to do. The rest noticed her comfort with Stone and smiled their approval and nodded at the same time as if the news had been expected.

"That's her," said Pops. "I can feel her there." Looking at Stone, he asked, "How do we get out there, Stone?"

"Pops, short of renting a helicopter or one of those cigar boats if we knew where to find one, I don't think we can. Our best action would be to wait for word from the Coast Guard or from Mike, then make whatever move we need to make, based on what they find out."

Pops looked down at his feet in resignation, knowing Stone was right. He disliked not being able to be actively involved in some way—it wasn't his nature to sit by and wait for an outcome. He was about to say so when there was a knock on the front door. Before anyone could react, it opened.

"Eh, you got one party going on that I wasn't invited to?" Lloyd, full grin creasing his face, stood in the doorway, looking around at everyone. His gaze briefly took in Sonny and John before stopping on Stone.

"Lloyd, it's good to see you, my friend." Stone grabbed his friend's hand and embraced him as he pulled him into the room in a single smooth motion.

"Everyone," he said, "this is my best and dearest friend, Lloyd Moniz." He introduced him to Pops and the two boys saving Teri for last.

"And this beautiful lady is Teri."

"Teri," he said, taking hold of both her hands. "Stone told me you were beautiful, but then he has a penchant toward major exaggeration, so I wasn't too sure until this moment. It's quite obvious he was not."

He let go of her hands and looked around at everyone, settling on Pops. "Pops," he said, "you and me will have to have a talk about your famous patis after Viane's safely home. You know I'm a Big Island boy from Honokaa. I remember you coming to the plantation peddling it a long time ago. My dad would wait for you to show up and always moan about not buying enough the last time you were there whenever he ran out."

Pops, obviously touched, just nodded in the pleasure of past memories. He pointed at Lloyd and smiled, saying, "I have a couple bottles at home just for you, Lloyd, next time you go back to the Big Island."

"So what's the latest?" Lloyd said to no one in particular. "Where do we stand as it applies to our missing girl?"

Stone began telling him the latest information they had when they were again interrupted by the ringing of the phone. Teri ran to the kitchen as silence descended on everyone, in anticipation.

She stood ashen-faced in the doorway after hanging up. "Mike's friend said the helicopter crew has spotted two women in the water and is close by, but that there is a major complication of some kind that she couldn't divulge to Mike at this time. She said she'd call him back when the situation was resolved. She said she couldn't tell him anything further until cleared to do so."

Everyone stood in quiet contemplation. Teri burrowed back into Stone's embrace. He could feel a growing apprehension descend over everyone. He wished Mike hadn't called just to tell them that. It was like telling them they were in the path of a bus but unable to move out of its way. The feelings in the room sank rapidly.

"Stay positive, everyone," voiced Lloyd, surprisingly upbeat. "Let's not bring any more negative energy to this than we came with. Mike will call as soon as he hears more, so let's keep some positive thoughts going here." Despite his attempts to be lighthearted, he could tell everyone was depressed.

Stone was pleasantly surprised by his friend's words. They were his thoughts as well. *Now all we have to do is wholeheartedly believe Viane is all right.*

Chapter Fifty-Four

Lloyd had heard Stone mention his positive outlook on life so often and for so many years that even *he* was surprised by his own comments about everyone staying optimistic.

He had not always been upbeat in his thinking—close to the opposite in many ways and for too many years. He was frequently inclined to grind thoughts down into the smallest of pieces, dissecting them to the point that there was no positive or negative aspect, just a whole lot of independent and oft-times unrelated snippets of events to contend with. It was his way of coping with life. Maybe he was finally accepting the positive side of life instead of the pessimistic point of view as being the true reality.

Since he'd last talked with Stone a few days prior, he'd been deeply involved in research into artifacts similar to those Viane had found—at least what he guessed she'd found, having not seen them. Stone had told him in broad terms what they were and the general area she had found them.

If in fact they were discovered deep inside the lava tube at South Point, then they probably were of great historical value, not to mention the monetary value a collector would see in them. If they related back to prerecorded history of Hawaii, they were more than just historical because they could connect directly to the very core of spirituality brought in with the first inhabitants.

It was well known that the ancient Polynesians had many gods surrounding them, governing all aspects of their lives. Of utmost importance to the ancient travelers were the gods that protected them on their journeys across the ocean.

Through his research and his own connection with the islands dating back many generations, he knew Viane's artifacts must be found and, above all, returned to where they were meant to be—exactly where she had found them.

He hoped above all else that Viane would be found safe, along with the two artifacts and that she would have enough appreciation for her own culture to want to see them returned to where they were meant to be. He was certain that she did.

Chapter Fifty-Five

From Grey's line of sight, the bow of *Whiskey Sea* was directly in line with the two women. He reached for the throttles and increased their speed as well as increasing the rotation of both propellers. He was aiming to cut directly over the center of the life ring, sending each woman into one of the two propellers. He was becoming irritated that Roland was not being more of a guide. From his body language and arm movement, it appeared he was actually negotiating with them.

He was about to call to catch Roland's attention when suddenly his vision was totally obscured by the appearance of a Coast Guard helicopter, probably the same one as before, that had swiftly dropped down into view and was hovering barely a few feet above the water's surface and directly dead center on his bow and between the boat and the women.

"Roland," he yelled, "why didn't you warm me?"

"It must have come in pretty high and dropped fast. I didn't even hear it." They were both yelling to each other to be heard over the beating sound of the chopper's blades. Both men knew they should have heard it, but neither did.

"Reverse power to your engines immediately and come to a stop," bellowed a voice from the helicopter. The helicopter crew had little doubt about the men's intentions as they watched the action on the approach and drop-down. Coming in from a height had worked as planned, but all of them knew their advantage from their surprised drop could dissipate suddenly.

This was definitely not going the way Grey had planned things. He was getting angry. He was also experiencing a kind of fear he'd never experienced before—that of being trapped. His brain was sending conflicting signals to both increase power and hope to disable the helicopter by hitting it or pull back to a stop and talk his way out of this.

He pulled the throttles into reverse, brought the yacht to an abrupt stop, and proceeded to cut power to the engines. Talking and attempting to reason made much more sense than taking a chance on the yacht being disabled by ramming the chopper and having a bunch of armed and angry people climbing onboard.

He felt that, with any luck, he may have already run over the women. Roland wasn't in a position to give him confirmation. Their exact location got lost in the turmoil, but he presumed the bow was split seconds away from engaging them when the chopper appeared. If he'd managed to run them down, he'd be able to talk his way out of that as well. *After all, wasn't the helicopter interfering in a legitimate rescue attempt?*

Roland stood frozen on the bow where he'd been directing Grey's aim. He faced the stare of the Coast Guard personnel in the chopper as the face-off proceeded between them and Grey. He was afraid to turn his back on the chopper for fear they may not be paying too close attention to where the chopper's blades were rotating and inadvertently allow one of them to get too close to his head. The wind from the blades was fierce. He let the gaff hook slide to the deck hoping his body had shielded anyone from noticing he'd been holding it.

Chapter Fifty-Six

Viane was struggling to keep her head above water and continue to hold on to the life ring against the indescribable force of wind beating down from the helicopter's blades, scarce feet above her and Debra. It was a horrible feeling to be just a few feet from the bow of the boat as it rose and fell on the waves in front of them while, at the same time, having the wheels of the powerful helicopter close above their heads together with the incredible force of wind. She saw Debra struggling as well, the expression on her face giving the appearance she was on the verge of panic. All she could do was pray that the wind didn't push them both under or a large wave didn't roll past, bringing the bow of the boat down upon them.

The good thing, and there was always a good side to bad things as Pops had continually taught her, and usually added that you may have to look really hard to find it, was that the helicopter's downdraft was keeping the water's surface fairly flat. That would help immensely in their rescue. Viane moved her body tight against Debra's, as the other woman responded and did the same. She needed to impart reassurance to Debra but was also looking to gain some herself through the sheer closeness of someone else. The situation was frightening and the outcome clearly not one to celebrate, yet.

Chapter Fifty-Seven

Petty Officer Chamberlain was keeping a watchful eye on the two women directly below as the pilot moved the chopper into a good recue position. It was easy to see the precarious situation the women were in—trapped between the yacht's bow and the strong downdraft caused by the helicopter's blades. If anything were to go wrong, he had situated himself in a position to be able to call the orders. He and Petty Officer Third Class Samson were wearing their survival suits and other necessary gear and knew there would be no hesitation from either of them to jump to the women's rescue were it necessary to do so. Both he and Samson knew that if they had to jump before proper conditions were established, both would be putting their lives in jeopardy, along with the women, but that was part of what they were expected to do, and they accepted it.

A small self-inflating raft and a harness were at standby close at hand, ready to be deployed when *Whiskey Sea* backed off and gave them room to proceed with the rescue. The pilot had issued an order over the loudspeaker for the skipper to restart the engines and slowly back away twenty feet. They were all watching to see if he'd comply.

As Chamberlain watched, his curiosity became awakened at seeing both women wearing what appeared, from his distance, to be only their bras. It was very difficult to get a clear view, but since he was watching them, he couldn't help but wonder about the explanation that was sure to come. He'd pointed that out to Samson, who was also watching, but just got an "I don't know" shoulder shrug. They had already figure out that the blouse found in the water came from one of these two. Chamberlain unexpectedly noticed the dark blue material draped over the life ring. A smile of new admiration showed in his features. He wasn't sure he would have thought of doing something like that if it had been him in the water—he hoped he would have been smart enough, though.

The chopper increased altitude ten feet and moved slightly off to one side so the raft that was about to be deployed wouldn't drop directly on the women. The yacht was backing away slowly. That meant rescue operations could begin momentarily. The rescuers rechecked each other's equipment—it was standard procedure—as they would both be in the water to help the two women climb into the inflatable raft. The plan was for the two rescuers and the two women to climb into the inflatable raft and be pulled over the boarding platform of the cutter. The chopper would then immediately head back to Sand Island station.

Chamberlain noted the USCGC *Kuokoa*'s arrival as it slowly moved broadside to the yacht. He knew the sequence of events that was about to begin and was concerned for the level of shock the women may be in and whether they could summon the presence of mind to not resist rescue efforts.

It was not unheard of for people being rescued to fight off rescuers, having let their minds go in a multitude of directions in a mixture of panic and shock.

With the chopper in position, the pilot gave the okay. Chamberlain and Samson gave him the thumbs-up signal—they were ready to begin. The self-inflating raft was deployed into the water, falling fifteen feet away from the women, and immediately sprang into inflating itself—all in less than a minute.

Both Chamberlain and Samson jumped and landed close to the inflatable. They maneuvered it to the women and proceeded to help them into the raft, neither woman creating any difficulty but instead did their part to assist themselves. Chamberlain stayed in the water so he could give the women a helping boost, and Samson, having already climbed into the raft, helped them over the gunwale pulling on their arms at first, then grasping them around their waists, and tugging up and over until they were securely seated on the flooring.

A line was cast from the cutter and attached to the raft so it could be pulled to the cutter's extended boarding platform where people were assembled to help bring everyone onboard.

Chapter Fifty-Eight

Since Mike's phone call moments before, alerting them to some problem involving Viane's rescue, he hadn't called back to explain any more about what was being done, if anything, and everyone had become subdued and quiet—waiting to hear. Even Lloyd, after his verbal expression of the need to remain positive, had pulled into himself, quietly leaning against the front door.

Stone had settled onto the arm of the couch centered in the room, legs extended out in front, arms folded across his chest. He found himself staring at a spot on the carpet directly in front of him, but not really seeing it.

The others had followed Teri into the kitchen with the prospects of a fresh pot of coffee. Just to be doing something was a huge release from their building apprehension. She had whispered into Stone's ear of their prospects of a long evening of uncertainty before leading the others into the kitchen. He didn't like it but had to agree with her.

Stone wanted to call Mike back and demand to know what was happening, and it was taking all the intestinal strength he could scrape into a pile not to do so, knowing his friend would call when there was something to pass on.

"Hey, everyone." He'd decided someone had to break the somber silence as he got up and walked into the kitchen. "I don't know about the rest of you, but I can't sit here any longer. I'm feeling too helpless, not doing anything. I feel like a broken spoke on a wheel. I think all of us need to drive down to the Coast Guard station and wait there for any new developments. We'll be right next to the horse's mouth or the mongoose's chatter—whatever turns your clock—and I know for me, it'll make me feel a whole lot more like I'm involved, instead of sitting out here in the wings. We'll end up there no matter what happens, so we might as well be there now rather than stay here acting like misplaced automatons."

His words were an attempt to raise morale. He didn't know that everyone had been thinking the very same thing as they all immediately embraced the idea and rushed for the door.

"Teri, please call Mike's office and ask them to relay our change of location to him, in case he needs to reach us before we get there. Better leave your cell phone number with them as well." Teri lifted an eyebrow and looked at the back of Stone's head—like duh, as she followed him out the door, smiling to herself.

Thirty minutes later, Stone's Explorer with everyone onboard except Lloyd, who opted to drive his own car, and Sonny, who had wanted to keep Lloyd company, approached the gates to the Coast Guard station on Sand Island.

As they stopped at the gate, a very tall, as well as very large, guard came out of a small shack and slowly made his way to the cars. Stone identified himself and the others in his and in Lloyd's car, which was close behind him.

"Ya'll here because of that rescue that's happening right now, right?" Rescues at sea were obviously big deals around the station, and everyone knew what was taking place almost as it was happening. "I was told to watch for ya'll and aim ya'll toward that building over yonder." He was pointing to a large gray building sitting close to the water's edge. "They'll bring all ya'll up to speed."

Pulling up to the entrance of the building, they parked next to a police cruiser that was already parked there. Running his hand over its hood as he walked past, Stone could feel the heat of a very recently arrived vehicle. Lloyd, who had pulled up on the other side of the HPD car, was now holding the building's door open, waiting for everyone to enter.

Chapter Fifty-Nine

Seeing the small inflatable coming toward them, knowing that in a few moments they'd be safe, both women hugged and squealed in sheer happiness. If they were on land, they'd be jumping up and down together like a tetherball finally loose from its pole. It was all Viane could do to keep from letting go of the life ring and swimming out to meet the raft but thought better of taking the risk. The glassy look in Debra's eyes told her to stay close by and not trust the other woman's strength to navigate to it, nor to trust her own.

They gladly released their handhold on the life ring as their rescuers, one in the water and the other already in the raft, reached out for them. The intense heat of the sun-drenched neoprene of the raft felt incredible against Viane's icy cold skin as she was pulled out of the water and over the inflated gunwale.

"God, this feels heavenly," voiced Debra, who immediately responded to her rescuers' helping hands into the raft. "I want to just lay here draped over the side like this for the next several hours. It feels so good!"

Chamberlain retrieved the life ring and handed it up to Samson. He climbed in just in time to catch the monkey fist and accompanying rope thrown from the *Kuokoa*. He attached it to the raft and knelt on the raft's floor waiting to take hold of the cutter's platform when they got close.

Onboard USCGC *Kuokoa*, a young woman, smartly dressed in uniform, introduced herself as PO Renee Martin and led the way below deck to hot showers and dry clothes, albeit Coast Guard uniforms. Either one of them would have changed into anything handed to them just as long as it was dry, and there was enough of it to keep them warm.

"Relax as best you can," a sympathetically smiling Office Martin told them, "but stay below deck until the commander comes down and talks with you. He's got paperwork that unfortunately must be filled in, but he's also said he'd prefer neither of you come up on deck just yet anyway, in case there's any unforeseen trouble. I'll bring you something warm to drink, and I'll roust the chef and have him put together some food for you."

They more than readily agreed to stay put below deck as they hurried to strip off their wet clothes and head for the showers and steaming hot water.

Chapter Sixty

Roland and Grey had always found their soft leather couch in the lounge very comfortable in the past, but it was anything but right at this moment, under these conditions. Grey shifted his position as he looked for some relief from the pressure the handcuffs were causing in the center of his back. He couldn't move his arms in either direction to get them out of the way. He was extremely uncomfortable and rapidly becoming annoyed. Roland was squirming around next to him, apparently equally uncomfortable, and probably becoming just as ill-tempered.

Two Coast Guard sentries stood at attention by the lounge doors, one on each side of the room, rifles held at high port. They were a picture of perfection in military bearing and equally as fear inspiring if one wasn't accustomed to having loaded weapons close by—neither Grey nor Roland were. Both guards were vigilant for any escape attempt yet obviously confident that there would be none. Neither spoke. Both simply held a seemingly contemptible stare at Roland and at Grey like they were nonentities within the dredges of humanity.

The guards stare didn't help to make the men the least bit more comfortable, and of course they weren't meant to.

Chief Petty Officer Chamberlain walked in and said something to one of the guards but spoke so softly that Grey couldn't understand what was said. Chamberlain nodded at the guard, either in understanding or acceptance of whatever was discussed before turning to face his captives.

Grey had had enough—his irritability was changing into hostility. It was time to get out of this mess—it was time to take charge of the situation.

"Sir," he said, being as formal as he could under the circumstances, not wanting to antagonize the man too quickly before he'd laid the groundwork. "You must know you're detaining my partner and me illegally and are trespassing on private property without just cause. Coast Guard or not, you do not have legal right nor any cause to be holding us like common prisoners. I'd like to see your commanding officer and get this matter settled so we can be on our way as quickly as possible. If you'd just undo these demeaning handcuffs, we can get on with it."

Chamberlain stood looking at him, his face expressionless, letting him rant.

Misreading his stare for attentive listening, Grey continued, upping his feigned control, "He has our permission to come aboard, or better perhaps, why don't you lead the way to where he's keeping himself. I'll speak with him in person."

Chamberlain was amused and actually smiled but remained standing in the center of the lounge observing Grey with an amazed expression framing his facial features. His head began to move side to side, the smile unchanged.

"Legal rights, huh?" he finally said, the smile slowly disappearing, his words taking the form of a challenging accusation. "Those two women probably think they had a few rights of their own before you two tried to grind them into fish chowder. They had a few legal rights you gave little regard to, and all your threats won't change my mind from what I saw, and have reported, as being your implied intentions." His expression relaxed into amusement once again. "Actually, you ought to feel lucky we have you safely sequestered apart from them right now. I overheard one of them mention tying some green Buddha to an appendage of both of yours and throwing it and the both of you overboard. Your actions apparently lit up one of those women's burners real good."

"Look, those two women stowed away on this yacht. Probably looking for a free ride to the mainland at our expense. They are the ones you should be putting handcuffs on, not us. We offered to help them, but they chose to jump overboard. Granted, we may have acted too quickly and scared them into thinking they'd be better off overboard, but come on, they were stowaways. How do you think they got the life ring for God's sake? We threw it to them and were about to pull them from the water when your chopper interfered. I think we have a legal right to charge the US Coast Guard with interfering in the progress of a rescue at sea."

Roland had been sitting quietly, content to let Grey roll out a story, but he found he needed to say something in support. "Listen to him, *sir*," putting emphasis on the *sir*. "You saw me on the bow. I was getting ready to throw a line to those women so I could pull them to safety. I already had the ladder over the side so they could climb back onboard. You and that Samson broad were in the chopper, you must have witnessed all that."

Chamberlain swiftly moved in toward Roland and bent over him, bringing his face as close to Roland's as it could get without touching. "What I saw, *sir*," he said, his voice loud, enunciating each word, "was you on the bow with a gaff hook, not a line ready to throw—there's a distinct difference in intent between the two. I witnessed the position this boat was moving in relationship to where the women were and I also saw your hand gestures to your buddy as we were dropping down on you. Further, I've talked with the women and saw the telltale rope burns each has on her arms and neck as a reminder of your hospitality. I don't believe for one minute that you intended a rescue nor will anyone else.

"And," he said, his face moved a degree closer, forcing Roland to move the back of his head backward into the cushioned couch, "between you and me, I'd also watch my use of descriptive language around Petty Officer Third Class Samson. She happens to be extremely proficient with very sharp objects and dislikes being called a *broad* more than anything else." He stood straight, shaking his head in disgust, all semblance of humor gone.

"I'll ask one thing and one thing only, and I'd appreciate a direct answer," he said as he stood looking from Roland to Grey. "Where is this hidden room I've been instructed to locate and how do I open it? Cooperation is the key word at this point, gentlemen."

Grey saw that the challenge of talking their way out of this was going to be more difficult than he originally anticipated. "There's no such room on our yacht," he said, trying to slough off the question as ridiculous. "Why would a hidden room be built on a yacht of this caliber? It's a myth probably perpetuated by those two stowaways."

"Yeah, I can see that," humored Chamberlain. "I guess that's why they both wanted to come over and break some mirrors. I'm guessing they were referring to the mirrors on this wall," he said, pointing at the vault's mirrored door. He turned and walked out the door onto the deck closest to the *Kuokoa*, returning moments later followed by Petty Officer Third Class Samson, who walked straight for the bar, went behind, and began systematically searching for something. She straightened her back, her hands working at something beneath the bar top, and then watched, as they all did, as the mirror in the center of the book shelves began to glide open.

"Well, look here what you found, Petty Officer Samson." Chamberlain glanced quickly at the two men in mock surprise, then back at the vault. "Looks like a really big treasure chest, don't it? Only thing missing is the proverbial pile of gold and a couple of mummies." He and Samson looked approvingly at one another with a slight nod of "job well done." Chamberlain moved to the vault opening as he pulled a small flashlight from his shirt pocket and peered around at all the shelves filled with artifacts. "I don't suppose either of you would be inclined to tell me where the light switch is? No," he answered himself, glancing over his shoulder, appraising the hostile glare he was receiving from them both, "I don't suppose you would since you didn't even know this room was here a minute ago. That's okay."

"Tell you what, boys," he said as he turned fully to face Grey and Roland sitting quietly on the couch, expressionless, as they looked at the room they had just lied about. "I think you both need to have some alone time in order to enjoy your treasure room while we sort things out and get underway."

Grey and Roland were moved into the vault and made to sit on the floor with their handcuffed wrists held over their heads as they were tethered to one of the shelves above and behind them. Samson returned to the bar and triggered the lever, then watched as the mirror glided closed with Grey and Roland sitting helplessly in the quickly diminishing light.

"Samson, look around under the bar top for the light switch. We need to be able to see through this mirror." She easily found it and turned the lights on inside the vault illuminating their prisoners.

"We have a long journey back to base. I'll take the first two-hour watch. Okay, Samson?" Chamberlain set up the two guards in the control room so they could relieve each other at the helm as they began the easy duty of guiding *Whiskey Sea* back to home base in Honolulu Harbor.

Finally underway tracking behind USCGC *Kuokoa*, Samson, a devilish smile aimed in Chamberlain's direction, moved toward the starboard deck. "I'll be checking out that hot tub down below deck for the next couple of hours. Don't come looking for me," she warned with a friendly yet firm look.

Chamberlain was no fool. He wouldn't dare venture below deck even if his life depended on it—*well, maybe*, he thought. Sometimes he got the distinct impression that she thought she outranked him.

Chapter Sixty-One

The inside of the gray building on Sand Island that the Coast Guard called headquarters appeared almost sterile. The central large operations room had ultrahigh ceilings painted white to match the concrete block walls. The cement floors were polished to a deep luster, and not a shred of paper appeared out of place on the surfaces of any of the several small gray desks strategically placed about the cavernous room. Panels of glass enclosed several small offices on the perimeter of the room, obviously for the higher-ranking individuals. The glass partitions had been cleaned to as near spotless as humanly possible—housekeeping was apparently a big thing here, true of most military installations.

Mike stood talking with a thin older Japanese man in the open doorway of one of the offices. He looked over as Stone's entourage entered and waved them over.

"I'm really glad to see all of you here. I was about to call and suggest you come." He stood looking at each of their expectant faces, an obvious smile beginning to crease his face, like a child who can't wait to divulge a secret. "First, though"—he became serious with required formality—"I want to introduce all of you to Seichi Takemoto. Takemoto-san is in charge of security at Bishop Museum. I've been supporting him in the investigation of the theft of artifacts from the museum over the past few weeks. He anxiously agreed to come down and identify any of the museum's things that may be in that hidden room onboard *Whiskey Sea*. Chief Petty Officer Chamberlain radioed in a while ago that the room looks like a showcase you'd expect to find in a museum, only the customary descriptive cards are missing. We're hoping some or all of Bishop Museum's things are in there."

Everyone politely but hurriedly greeted Seichi, anxious to get to the reason they were all there—to be informed of what they all hoped to hear. Stone returned Mike's look with a questioning expression that yelled, "Stop stalling and get to it."

"Okay," Mike said after a few moments hesitation as he waited to capture 100 percent attention from the group which wasn't difficult. As if orchestrating a symphony, he waited to gain eye contact with each—more theatrics as evidenced by the pleased look on his face. He was playing with their emotions. It would be different if the outcome wasn't what they were so hopeful of hearing.

"Viane is safe, sound, and on her way home."

He watched as everyone instantly assimilated this information and erupted in spontaneous shouts of joy. Pops, Sonny, and John, almost in unison, made the sign of the cross before resting their heads against each other, arms wrapped over the other's shoulders in a huddle, talking loudly as they playfully jostled one another.

Stone was more subdued as he returned Teri's embrace, who'd immediately flung her arms around him. Mike's words had been music to their ears.

Tears showed in everyone's eyes as they all acknowledged one another, patting and hugging whoever was close.

After a few moments, Mike, also watery-eyed, motioned them all to regroup around him. "She's onboard USCGC *Kuokoa*, and from all I've been told, she is in high spirits and anxious to arrive home. She's had a hot shower, been given dry clothes, and is in the process of finishing a healthy meal. It will be early tomorrow morning before they dock."

As the tumultuous joy became relatively calmer and after all the questions were exhausted, the group slowly spread out as each sought their own way to let the news sink deeper into their hearts. Mike came and stood beside Stone.

"Debra Shinn is also onboard with Viane, and from the reports I've received, she's being very cooperative. We're fairly positive this Shinn woman is the one responsible for the theft of several extremely rare items from a small museum in Northern Japan. From everything we've been able to put together so far, she got fixated on the Japanese Sengoku period, about AD 900. The small museum specializes in artifacts from a battle during that time when thousands of samurai warriors were killed. Debra Shinn successfully *borrowed* several priceless relics, hid them in her garments and backpack, and walked out of the place. They caught her on camera but weren't able to work fast enough to catch her before she left their country."

"Well, that doesn't make any sense. Why didn't they catch her before she boarded an airplane, since they had her on camera?" asked Stone.

Mike continued, "Something about the authorities there, without the aid of a photo, looking for an American and not realizing they should have been looking for a Japanese-American: the surveillance film was not good quality. I don't know, Stone. The museum people there are not too adept at this sort of thing. Apparently, stealing is almost unheard of in that remote region. They were slow to react and not too good with details. That's how we believe Shinn was able to get her hands on things so easily. If she had been able to carry it all, she probably would have grabbed everything that wasn't nailed down.

"Anyway, we have a description of what she took, and we also have Takemoto-san who, in his spare time, has become one of the foremost authorities in Japanese antiquities. We have a physical description of those items as well as everything missing from our museum."

"When do you expect to be able to take a look at all these artifacts?" asked Stone.

"The *Whiskey Sea* is following *Kuokoa* to the harbor. They called in about two hours ago and informed the station commander that they're encountering some rough water, which is slowing them down. That's why they won't dock until early tomorrow. We won't know anything until they tie up and we're able to go onboard."

"What about the two men? What happens to them now?" asked Sonny. He'd been standing there listening to Mike and Stone, waiting for a chance to ask questions. "Any chance John and I can have a few moments alone with them out behind this building?"

"Only if you want to follow them to jail, Sonny. They'll be headed to trial for antiquities theft, kidnapping, attempted murder, and perhaps first-degree murder, if we can successfully tie them to the body found floating in Napoopoo on the Big Island. We believe they are also tied to a black marketer named Loren Bucke in Seattle whom the authorities there, along with the FBI, have been covertly tagging along behind to see who he's involved with and who else they can catch in their net. The names Greyson Giani and Roland Pratt came up in connection with an international black market group tied to him, as did Debra Shinn's. We have to wait to see how that pans out and whether we add additional charges to their list of felonies."

"You've been busy, Mike. I hadn't realized you were so intimately involved with all this intrigue. You let me believe that Lloyd, Teri, and I were alone in this mystery."

"You think I've been sitting around on my *okole* for the past two weeks, warming an office chair? This stuff has been building up, Stone. Sorry I couldn't tell you about it. The black market for antiquities has been expanding at an exponential rate ever since Iraq, Saddam Hussein, and the ransacking of the museum in Bagdad. Many people around the world have a lot of money to invest in these kinds of things, and Hawaii is the central clearing spot for this stuff moving between Asia and the US mainland. I couldn't open that up to you until now.

"I knew there was something going on since I first went on your yacht looking for the mermaid you rescued. We tied Roland and Grey into that Seattle character shortly after learning their names. The Feds were about to bust Bucke and his setup, but it looks like he got wind of it and left home without posting any forwarding address. At least we have these two and the woman to play with."

Chapter Sixty-Two

"I'm starved. Let's go someplace and celebrate Viane's safely being home, even though she won't be until early tomorrow morning. We can have an early dinner. How does everyone feel about going over to the Halekulani?" Stone was intent on getting everyone moving toward the door of the Coast Guard station and ultimately to the parking lot. He saw weariness in their faces, especially in Pops'. It was a well-earned exhaustion but was now necessary for them all to relax for a few hours and unwind from all of the pent-up anxieties. When Viane finally pulled into the harbor in the morning, they would be in a good frame of mind to welcome her safely home.

There was nothing any of them could do until *Whiskey Sea* arrived anyway. They'd been assured their daughter, sister, and friend was being taken care of and the *Whiskey Sea* was returning in the safety of Coast Guard control.

Seichi's anxiety over the past two weeks of having let his employer down was easing with the prospect of having the museum's property returned to safekeeping. As head of security at the museum, he had been humiliated by the theft of artifacts he had been expected to safeguard. He was still unable to fully relax and wouldn't be until the contents onboard the yacht had been verified as actually being the missing property. He declined Stone's offer to accompany them to dinner and instead opted to return to the museum. He'd be back in the morning with a picture file and complete listing of the things his museum was missing.

Mike declined as well, and everyone understood the inappropriateness of a police officer sitting down to a dinner at the Halekulani while in uniform and on duty. Besides, he told everyone, he needed to check the forensic report on the body that had been discovered. He had a strong hunch everything the group was involved in related directly to the *Whiskey Sea*, its illicit cargo of treasures as well as the body that had been found.

Checking the forensic report was, in reality, simply the reason he gave for not going to dinner: he withheld the main reason. There were a couple loose ends he wanted to check on but was making more out of that than he needed to. It would take all of ten minutes to review the findings if the ME department had done their job—if not it could take a lot longer. Their report would have a direct bearing on how the *Whiskey Sea* was greeted in the morning, which was definitely of critical importance. He and Robin had also agreed to meet later, after they had both finished their work, at their usual spot for a glass of wine.

Dinner at Orchids, Halekulani's oceanfront restaurant, sitting at a table overlooking Waikiki Beach, was exceptional, and everyone rose to the celebration of the moment.

They left Orchids and wandered into Lewer's Lounge to sit in on the entertainment, have some dessert, and enjoy the relaxing atmosphere that had grown among them. Loretta, Stone's favorite singer as well as friend, happened to be singing as they walked in. The celebratory mood of the group had given way to a quiet thought-filled and thankful calmness as each let their hearts fill with gratitude.

Chapter Sixty-Three

Stone and Teri stood back as lines were thrown and cleated, securing USCGC *Kuokoa* to the Coast Guard dock. Pops, Sonny, and John stood close by, anxious for the boarding ramp to be maneuvered into place, anxious for Viane to make her way off so they could wrap her in their love. She was standing at the railing and appeared close to jumping for it and not bothering to wait for the ramp.

When the cutter first pulled into the harbor and came into view, Viane was visible on the deck jumping up and down, waving her arms wildly and shouting names that could just barely be heard over the distance. The docking procedure was almost painfully slow for everyone waiting on the dock. Viane's energy and excitement during the procedure had slowly evaporated as emotions claimed her. She stood looking down on her family and friends waiting to welcome her safely home.

With the boarding ramp finally in place, Stone stood back with his arm around Teri's waist as they watched Pops, Sonny, and John rush to Viane's side and bury her in hugs, an obvious reinforcement of the love a family can bring to one another without a need for words. He absentmindedly pulled Teri a little closer.

He also saw the familiar face of the woman who had approached them days ago when they had all been at the Chart House. She was standing with her back against the bulkhead, neither smiling nor showing any other emotion, an armed guard standing close by her side. He assumed this was the Debra Shinn who Mike had referred to. He looked to see where Roland and Grey might be but couldn't see any sign of them.

He suspected they were being kept onboard their own yacht, which remained stationary in the middle of the harbor, waiting for the cutter to finalize docking. The sound of approaching traffic brought attention around to Mike as he drove in through the gate with a host of unmarked police cars and a prisoner transport vehicle following close behind. They quickly pulled to a stop behind everyone standing at the edge of the dock and, with their cars, formed a curved ring around them and the dock, virtually sealing the space against any escape attempts. Mike's passenger, Seichi Takemoto, remained in the car as uniformed officers began piling out and gathering around Mike. He'd obviously stopped at Bishop Museum on the way to retrieve Seichi for the ride to the Sand Island station.

Action happened quickly as Debra, now handcuffed, was led away and placed into one of the cars. *Whiskey Sea* had pulled in and was being secured behind the cutter as officers stood by to go onboard and place Roland and Grey under arrest.

In a show of compassion and generosity, HPD had arranged a suite at Hawaiian Village for the Koa family in exchange, so they claimed, for Viane's testimony. She would have given her testimony quite willingly and freely, but this was a very nice gift she quickly accepted. Pops suspected his friend, the police chief in Hilo, had a hand in this and probably was footing the entire cost himself, but he was not going to question the nature of the gift.

Mike also made arrangements to have them driven to the Hawaiian Village after assuring Viane her artifacts would be safe under Seichi's watchful eye. With so much attention being placed on Viane, the Koa family was anxious to get to the hotel for an opportunity to be alone, together.

Stone drove Teri home as they both had obligations that needed tending to. Later that evening, he took her to the Royal Hawaiian Hotel's beachside cocktail bar for some relaxation and a glorious sunset. He and Teri were both feeling the euphoria of having done all they had done seeing Viane safely home. It was now their time to enjoy one another.

Chapter Sixty-Four

Two weeks later

It was a small room and felt crowded. The heaviness of the subject matter being discussed made it seem even more cramped than it actually was. There were four people facing a large wooden desk. Three were seated while the fourth hadn't decided whether to remain standing or to sit down. Mike Kalama was ready to propose an idea he hoped the man they all faced would accept and figured he'd be able to speak more sincerely standing rather than sitting—the uniform lent itself to that as well and was much more authoritative at full stature.

Viane and Teri, sitting against the wall farthest from the desk yet merely a few feet away, were attentive as Mike explained the police department's proposal to Judge Joe DeSilva. Mike had earlier explained to them how relieved he was that DeSilva was the judge hearing the case. Judge DeSilva was usually amenable to the police department's requests, knowing it was staffed with exceptional people doing extraordinary work. He'd been a police officer himself many years ago prior to becoming a judge. It was during the younger part of his life when he lived in Hilo.

Debra's face was downcast, as Mike looked at her but continued talking to the judge. She didn't want to look up. If she didn't look, she thought, things wouldn't appear as bad as they would were she to look.

"I don't want to make less of the crime of smuggling that Ms. Shinn has voluntarily pleaded guilty to. She's proved herself an exceptionally skilled smuggler in her exploits at evading arrest up until now, and that's precisely why we're here. But I want to impress upon Your Honor that her difficult life's circumstances played an excessively large part in bringing her to this cross point. She has expressed a desire to change, if given an opportunity to do so.

"We've heard the unsolicited confessions of Ms. Shinn as expressed to Ms. Koa while the two faced terrifying sentences of death from their captors.

"What I propose is this: instead of placing Ms. Shinn behind bars for the next ten years, I am asking Your Honor to place her in conditional probation under the guidance and oversight of the police department."

Debra abruptly looked up at Mike, astonished at the words she'd just heard. She had been prepared for the worst and didn't want to place any hope in such a reality, yet she couldn't help notice her heart's increased pulse as she looked at the judge to see if she could read his reactions; but all she saw was an expressionless, stoic face giving no indication of the direction his thoughts might lean toward.

Viane gripped Teri's hand tighter at hearing what Mike proposed. She wanted desperately to speak up or yell in affirmation of the idea, but both she and Teri had been instructed—warned—not to speak unless in response to Mike's or Judge DeSilva's questions. Their ordeal had given Viane an appreciation of what Debra had faced in her life. She wanted to see this woman given a chance to change and, perhaps, even become a friend.

"Judge DeSilva," Mike continued his plea, "Ms. Shinn has unique experience that is lacking in the department. She could be of immeasurable help working undercover and in liaison between the department and customs officials in putting a tighter squeeze on smuggling."

Debra couldn't understand it but was suddenly filled with hope for an image of a better future. In all the questioning over the past days upon days, neither Mike nor any of the others had even hinted at this possibility. She was sitting forward on the very lip of her chair, willing with all her heart that the judge would say yes.

She was amazed at the way circumstances in life could take such dramatic turns. This time two weeks ago, all she hoped for was that Dorteo would find his way without her and that she wouldn't drown—she couldn't think of a worse way to die. Then after her rescue, she had searched for a way to escape, to find Dorteo, and maybe together disappear somewhere and make a new life for both of them.

In the time she'd spent with Viane hanging on to a life ring, she'd glimpsed a life in Viane's enthusiasm that she wanted to experience and be a part of but couldn't envision a path in front of her that would allow that dream to unfold. Now she saw a door that could open and through which that might all be possible.

"Hawaii is a central clearing hub, Judge," Mike was explaining. "Smuggling, especially in the antiquities market from the Orient, flows through here bound for the US mainland and Canada. Debra Shinn can help stem this by working from the inside and feeding information out. I have a firm belief that she wants to change the conditions in her life." He caught her eyes and saw tears begin to shine.

He'd said all he could. It was up to the judge now.

"Ms. Shinn," the judge said as he leaned forward implying a more personal touch to the conversation, although his face remained resistibly unreadable. "Do you have anything to add to Officer Kalama's suggestion?"

She really wanted to leap up and surround him with a hug in hopes of swaying his thinking, but instead she remained calm, looked up at Mike, who remained standing, then back to the judge.

"This would be a life's dream for me, and I can't think of anything I'd rather do more. I could finally climb out of the pit of hell I put myself into, welcome the chance to resurrect some of the self-esteem and respect I left behind long ago. If you were to say yes, Judge DeSilva, I can promise you that you would never regret the decision."

"Could I add one thing, though?" She again looked up at Mike's face before continuing. "I would ask that you allow Dorteo Aquino the same avenue. The two of us would be perfect as an undercover couple, even though we are just very close friends. We work together and rely on each other. Divide us, and you will only have the lesser part of a dynamic possibility and potential failure."

It came down to a question of who was more surprised by Debra's request. Viane sat startled, as did Teri. How could Debra place her freedom on the line like that? They could see their hopes for this woman dashed without question. DeSilva was a compassionate man, but there were limits to which he would allow himself to go.

Mike looked astonished as he looked at the judge and slowly sank into a chair close behind him. This wasn't going the way he thought it would, but he was also finding himself thinking of the further possibilities this would open for everyone.

The judge sat staring at Debra, still leaning over his desk, elbows supporting him. If anyone just happened to glance at him, they may have thought he was about to pounce on an unsuspecting bug.

He'd already familiarized himself with all the charges against Debra as well as Dorteo Aquino and had a fairly decent handle on what direction these two people's lives could take, depending upon what he said. He knew life. He knew the criminal mind. He knew who would falter and bend to pressure and return to a former life of crime. He also knew those individuals who were where they were because of the pinball experiences that moved them through their lives, giving them little choice in the outcome that befell them. He also knew people who had an innate desire to reverse the tide of their lives and become someone better. He saw this in Debra.

He sat back in his chair and looked at Mike for several moments, saying nothing. He looked at Viane and saw what he knew would be there—compassion and hope staring back at him.

He didn't smile when he finally looked back at Debra, but his facial expression had softened, probably to the limit his face ever allowed.

"Ms. Shinn, I am inclined to rule in favor of Sgt. Kalama's suggested proposal. Your own plea, though, gives me pause for concern." He remained motionless as if someone hit a Pause button—the room stood still.

Debra's heart was sinking. She couldn't do any of this without Dorteo, her foundation and only friend.

Finally speaking, he looked first at Mike and then back to Debra. "I'm going to rule in favor of Sgt. Kalama, and I'm also going to rule in favor of your own plea, but understand this"—he pointed his finger as if he were a scolding father—"there will be an exacting set of conditions that you, Dorteo, as well as the Honolulu Police Department must follow."

He looked again at Mike. "Sgt. Kalama, I want you and Ms. Shinn to remain here while we go over the details of how this is going to pan out." He looked at Viane and Teri sitting close, holding each other's hands. "You ladies may leave now. Thank you for being here. The strength of your support, Ms. Koa, on behalf of Ms. Shinn was a major part of my decision."

Unable to contain herself, Viane wrapped her arms around Debra's shoulders in a hug before starting to leave.

As they were about to close the door on their way out, Judge DeSilva called to Viane, "Ms. Koa, please tell your father, Rudy, I send my aloha. I'll be on the Big Island soon and will stop by your house to catch up on some old memories."

Everyone was a little stunned by the judge's intimate comment. It was a reminder to all of them, though, that family and friendships throughout the islands went generations deep and crossed all lines.

Chapter Sixty-Five

Stone felt very pleased with Mike's forethought. He knew in advance what Mike was planning, and he enthusiastically agreed with the idea. They had been talking two days before and bringing each up to date on events that surrounded them over the past two weeks when Mike confided he was going to ask the judge about his, or rather the police department's, taking charge of Debra's future. He also knew Mike had a pretty good chance of succeeding in having his request granted since he'd often overheard Mike talk about Judge DeSilva and the support the department often received from him. He didn't know Debra, other than what Viane had told him about her, so he really had no opinion to express other than knowing it was always better to open up a chance for someone to change as opposed to slamming a cell door on their future, thereby virtually guaranteeing *nothing* would change.

In talking with Viane, he knew she held an elevated impression of Debra's sincere desire to distance herself as far as possible from the lifestyle she and Dorteo had found themselves in. This was certainly going to be her opportunity to do just that.

He was sitting on the seawall, simply enjoying the late afternoon sun. Bert was nowhere to be seen. He figured she was someplace close to Teri who, with head bent down, was wandering the beach examining the sand at her feet. She was engrossed in a slow search for anything unusual that the high tide may have washed ashore during the night. He was coming to know her well and knew this form of *mindless* wandering was becoming an integral part of how she was able to release stress from her mind: a walking meditation. He knew she was coming to love his house and this part of the bay as much as he did: the quiet beach in front and the beauty that presented itself in every direction you looked. He loved having her here, and apparently Bert did as well. She had bonded with Teri instantly, and she and Stone both knew it was the fingernails along her spine, fluffing up her fur that had rapidly garnered Bert's affection.

He was reflecting on the past two weeks since Viane's safe return and the way circumstances in life triggered an avalanche of far-reaching changes—a ripple across society—touching people who were seemingly independent from the other.

Viane may have drowned had he not picked up a copy of Boating *magazine while sipping a latte at Manoa Coffee House a few months earlier and decided to buy a yacht. Had he not decided to do so, what, he wondered, would have been Viane's fate? What if he'd shown up a few minutes earlier or later? What if Lloyd and Kawika had accompanied him, and they went in a different direction? It was all hypothetical. The reality of life was the sequence of events that* did *happen.*

He observed Teri engrossed in something she'd picked up and was turning over and over in her hands. *I wouldn't have met her had I not gone to the coffee shop in the first place, or had reached for a copy of* Honolulu *magazine instead of the* Boating *issue.*

Maybe I would have! Maybe events in life play out no matter how the sequence of events gets started. Maybe outcomes in life are preset and just the path to get there an option.

What he knew for sure was that he was happy. Teri was in his life, hopefully for the long term. Together they had both deepened their friendships with Viane and Mike, and Teri had come to know Lloyd, and he knew this friendship would grow as well. They had Viane's family in Hilo who professed eternal friendship toward both him and Teri for all they had done to ensure Viane's return.

"Life just doesn't get any better," he said as he looked up at the sky as if answering an unspoken question.

"Hey, who are you talking to, and what great mysterious garden are you letting your mind wander through?" Teri had come off the beach and walked over beside him. "You look like your mind was in the clouds above your head." She sat down on the seawall beside him and let her legs dangle over the edge. It was low tide, so there was only sand beneath the wall.

He bent close and kissed her cheek. "I was just playing with mind dominoes and watching them fall against each other in a repeating and almost unstoppable cavalcade. I was thinking about how interconnected we all are. How everything we do, no matter how insignificant we think it might be, has such a tremendous impact on so many others' lives." He leaned against her. "And I'm also getting much too philosophical, sitting here by myself."

"Didn't Jimmy Stewart make a movie about that very thing?"

"*It's a Wonderful Life*. That was a great movie, I'd forgotten about it. Find anything interesting on the beach?"

"Just this cross-shaped bone that's as sharp as a needle on the long end." She held it up for Stone to see.

"That's a quill from a puffer fish. You don't want to ever hit your foot on one of those guys when he's swimming around close by your feet. You'll feel the pain for weeks."

She closed her hand over the quill and looked at him. "You like what happened to Debra and her friend, don't you? Me too," she said, not waiting for a reply nor expecting one. "She's going to do great. Viane said she's very anxious to take her over to Hilo to meet Pops and her brothers. I think she sees a deeply connected friendship in the making. It would be interesting to know what she and Debra talked about while they were clinging to that life ring. She won't tell me much about it, but I know it must have been powerful and evidently private between the two."

"I can only imagine that almost drowning side by side would create a pretty tight bond between two people and that some dynamic changes would have to occur as a result."

Bert appeared and began rubbing herself against Stone's back. "Ah, back again are you, Little Girl?" It was a nickname he had been calling Bert since finding her, as she had been so tiny and looked so helpless at the time.

"Mike called while you were beachcombing," he said, absently rubbing Bert's neck. "Between the note we found and having Margelese's fingerprints all over *Whiskey Sea*, they have enough unanswered questions to hold Roland and Grey for further investigation into the floating body, which, by the way, they have identified as being the late Dr. Krivoi Margelese. The nail in their coffin is going to be that black market guy who was picked up in Portland, Oregon, a few days ago. Mike figured he'll implicate Roland and Grey and their involvement with Margelese as soon as they offer him any sort of deal on a sentence reduction. They already know all of them are mixed up together in the same poi bowl."

"You have some funny expressions." Teri's head was resting on Stone's shoulder as she spoke.

"So I've been told. Do you know what else Mike told me?" he asked her, humor in his voice. "That jade Buddha you saw when you snuck on board was actually theirs. They had a bill of sale for it. They actually bought it—who would have guessed."

"Uh-huh." She was too relaxed in the warmth of the sun for any greater response.

"Are you up for a boat ride? I figure it's about time I showed you the ropes about handling the ropes."

"Did you hear that?" She'd turned to the cat. "Did you hear that, Bert?" she repeated. "He said a *boat* ride," she said as she turned back to Stone, bringing her lips very close to his ear. "What if I wanted to go for a yacht ride instead? Huh?"

Chapter Sixty-Six

Pops was standing at the base of the escalator in the Hilo terminal, waiting, smiling, as they made their way down to greet him. Viane, Teri, and Stone had caught the early bird flight on Hawaiian Airlines from Honolulu so they would have the entire day to do everything they had been wanting and needing to do.

For Viane, returning to Hilo carried emotions and remembrances of the last time she arrived, only this time she wasn't running from anyone nor seeking the sanctuary that her home offered. She was happy and thrilled to see Pops' loving smile, arms outstretched, waiting for her. She was pleased to have Teri and Stone beside her for their support in helping her return the artifacts back to the lava tube where she knew they belonged.

She'd hoped Debra could come as well, but she and Dorteo had to leave for a training school to which the state government had agreed to send them. Viane was pleased her new friend was embracing her new life with such determination and enthusiasm. Meeting her family could come later—everything in its appropriate time.

It was to be a day of celebration as well as one of reverence. They had all eagerly agreed to be a part of the ceremonial reburying of the olivine and carving, but that was going to be later in the afternoon. Seichi Takemoto had asked an elderly Hawaiian couple, knowledgeable in such matters, to accompany them to be sure everything was done in a proper, historically accurate fashion. A kahuna lapaau was coming as well to accompany them.

It was still early, just minutes past 7:30 a.m., when they strolled into Ken's House of Pancakes, the eating icon of Hilo, to find Sonny and John waiting for them at a large booth. There was a lot to catch up on, so Pops proposed they all eat and then head for their Kinoole Street house to wait for Seichi's group.

"Stone, Teri," Pops began, leaning in their direction over the table in a gesture of confidentiality. "You remember Leilani Davis, the woman at Pearl Harbor with that tiny dog? I got her number from Mike, and I called her. I knew something was familiar about her, and I was right, and it took a while for us both to recall things. She and I had a thing for each other back when we were about fourteen years old. We had sworn eternal love to each other. It didn't last long, and I had forgotten all about it."

"Pops," exclaimed Viane, a look of shock on her face. Sonny was patting her hand, waiting for their father to continue.

"Relax, kuuipo. That was way before your mom showed up." He looked down at the table and started to smile before looking up at Viane again. "We have a date next time I go to Oahu or she comes to Hilo. I may want to fly back with all of you when you go." His face had already lit up with the prospect.

Breakfast was almost finished when Stone moved close to Teri and whispered, "Let's you and I go our own way for a few hours. We can be back here by noon in lots of time to head for South Point and the lava tube ceremony." She smiled and took his hand as he slid out of the booth, pulling her along. Turning back to the group still seated at the table, he said, "We'll see all of you around noon back at your house. Viane, you and your family have a lot of being together that needs to be done, and our presence would only distract from that." He winked at her and saw a knowing look that told him she could see through the flimsy reasoning. They quickly left.

Stone drove out to the small town of Kea'au, turned, and headed for Pahoa and beyond to Kalapana, a beautiful black sand beach. They were both pleased to see the beach totally deserted, the black sand shining in the morning sun and a gentle surf breaking against the shore.

"Here," said Stone, reaching into a backpack he had brought along and pulling out Teri's bikini, holding it out to her. "You can go by that string of palm trees and change," he said as he pointed at a huge grove of coconut palms lining the head of the beach, "no one is here to see but me, and I promise not to look."

"Stone," she said with an amazed expression. "How did you get my bathing suit? I was wondering what you had in that backpack. Do you have yours?" she said in a singsong sort of voice, a devilish yet shy smile forming.

"Viane helped me get your suit yesterday when we were finishing plans to fly over here, and yes, I have mine as well," he said as he reached into the pack. "I'll forget to bring mine on some other occasion. In the meantime, I have this thin blanket for us to use." He held up a tie-dyed green piece of material. She laughed gently and headed for the coconut trees to change.

Stone, not one for being very modest, changed right where he stood and was folding his shorts into the backpack as Teri moved out from behind the trees and walked toward him.

"You are an incredibly beautiful woman, Ms. White. Have I told you that before?" He was actually stunned by her extraordinary beauty and her fit, trim, and very shapely body as she walked toward him. *Thank you, God.*

His expression must have given his thoughts away as he could see she was blushing as she came close.

"And so do you, my handsome one. You don't think I was going to miss an opportunity to see you do a striptease out here on the beach, do you?"

Chapter Sixty-Seven

Seichi was followed into Pops' front door by the elderly Hawaiian man and woman, instantly filling the room with bigger-than-life energy, aura and generous size. Naturally polished *kukui nut* leis adorned both. The woman, in a striking red-and-dark-orange-yellow mu'umu'u, also had a strikingly bright yellow lei of *o'o* feathers, from an extinct native bird that flourished a century ago. It's storied that Kamehameha the Great, when having a large cloak made for himself from the feathers of this bird and another one, would only allow his gatherers to pluck a single feather from each bird they captured, before releasing it. Whether the woman's lei was real feathers, which would make it quite old and undoubtedly very rare or made to look real, didn't distract from its incredible beauty.

The couple was introduced as representatives from the Hawaiian Heritage Foundation and would act as overseers for the return of the olivine gemstone and the wood carving of Keahimauloko, who had been identified and was storied to be one of the ancient gods for travelers through the Polynesian archipelago and the only carving known to exist.

412

Reverend Hanalei followed the couple into Pops' living room, moving in his slow purposeful way, completely at ease. He wore a *lei poo* of maile on his head and long strands of the vine draped over his shoulders, their ends almost touching the floor.

Seichi introduced Reverend Hanalei, to those who didn't already know him, as the kahuna lapaau who would be at the *replacing* ceremony, as Seichi had been calling it. Hana was there to spiritually intercede, if the need arose, and for his general guidance.

Seichi gathered everyone in Pops' living room to lay out his plans.

They would all drive to the general store in Naalehu, meet up with Stone and Teri, and then caravan down slope to the lava tube entrance. Once inside, he told them, they would carefully make their way to the exact spot the artifacts were initially found. Viane would be their guide.

Seichi reminded everyone that part of their task would be to search for bones that were sure to be close by if they were still intact.

"From then on," he said, looking around the room, "just our two foundation volunteers, Reverend Hanalei, Viane, and I will proceed. Everyone else will follow the small strobe lights that will be placed to mark the way back to the entrance. Reverend Hanalei will decide on the final resting place."

During the twenty minutes Seichi took to lay out his plans, Pops had been busy carrying platters of food from the kitchen to a large wooden table that rested against a wall nearby. He made a production out of carrying in two bottles of his precious *patis* and put them on the center of the table. Danny, from the Empire Café, had been asked to put together a feast for the celebratory gathering. Pops had planned on Stone and Teri being there but knew their developing relationship needed time away from everyone, and what better place to find solitude than on the Big Island. There would be food enough left over for them before beginning their journey back to Oahu.

Stone moved his arm out from under Teri's neck. It had been feeling numb for the past ten minutes, but he had not wanted to move and chance interrupting the serene mood they were both experiencing. They had been dozing in one another's embrace for the past hour, simply enjoying feeling their togetherness.

"Let's move the blanket up into the shade," he spoke softly. He'd also regretted breaking the special silence they both had been enveloped in, but besides his numb arm, the sun was reaching a high point, and its burning rays were getting uncomfortable—they needed to move.

They walked higher up the sand and spread the blanket out in the cooler shade of a large coconut tree just as Teri's cell phone rang. She reached in and brought it out of the small bag she carried and looked at the caller ID.

"It's Pops. I gave him my number so he could let us know what we were missing. Here"—she handed the phone to Stone—"you need to become familiar with these new inventions." She couldn't help smiling as she rubbed the hint a little further under his skin as she knelt to straighten the blanket.

His humorously disgusted look told her it was working. She also saw something that caught her breath at the realization that, besides being able to rib each other good-naturedly, they were beginning to understand one another on a much deeper, more heartfelt level.

When he handed the phone back, he said, "We're all right for another hour unless you're hungry, in which case there is a mountain of food at Pops' place, but we'd have to leave right now."

"And if I'm not?"

"Then we can return to what we were doing for another hour, then head for Naalehu to join the parade down to the lava tube. It sounds like Takemoto-san has everything under tight control.

"And guess who the kahuna lapaau is who will be hiking into the tube with us?" he asked, his voice excited with the news. "It's Hana," he exclaimed. "I have to give that man a lot of credit. Either that or he doesn't know what he's gotten himself into. Hiking into a lava tube isn't a walk in the park. With all the rocks and boulders that litter a cave's floor, carrying his bulk up, over, and around those things could take a toll on his physical abilities. You and I will have to watch out for him."

They lay back and spent the next hour entwined around each other, enjoying the sound of the surf rolling in and gently breaking across the black sand.

After meeting at the general store in Naalehu, everyone caravanned down to the lava tube and carefully made their way into its forbidding depths.

They discovered human bones scattered around, as had been predicted, and not too far from the spot Viane pointed to as being the original location of the artifacts. The Heritage Foundation couple, who had spoken very little the entire trek, went about gathering the bones and wrapping them in the lauhala, the leaves of the *hala* tree they had brought with them, and then proceeded to wrap Keahimauloko together with the olivine gem. Carrying the bundles in their arms, the couple fell in line behind Hana, along with Seichi and Viane, as he led the way deeper into the cavernous tube.

Pops and his sons led the way back to daylight with Stone and Teri following behind. Their journey out of the tube was in silence, as they all felt a mixture of reverence and honor at having been a part of this small piece of history that would probably never be made public.

Hana led the small group farther into the cave until he felt with certainty that they had reached the proper place. With hands raised, he motioned for everyone to stop as he continued a few paces farther and, with a soft voice, sang a chant before returning to where the others waited. In silence, they placed the three bundles together in a spot that would be hidden from any casual hikers brave enough to venture this far, then they began the journey back out.

Unexpectedly, as if someone tapped him on the shoulder, Hana turned and went back to the bundles, bent, and picked up the one containing the bones. He held it close and bestowed a special blessing on it. Perhaps the long silent spirit of Hanalei, one of the first to step on to this land and carry that name, had awakened and beckoned to the Kahuna for awareness. He replaced the wrapped bones and turned to leave with the others.

As they retreated, the two Heritage Foundation members carefully walked backward sweeping the ground bare of their footprints using palm fronds they had carried in. They continued sweeping back to where Viane had initially found the artifacts—it was a long process.

The bones of Hanalei, now connected in spirit with a modern-day namesake and kahuna lapaau, were resting once again with the spirit of Keahimauloko.

Chapter Sixty-Eight

Three months beyond

It was a perfect evening. The air had cooled from the day's heat, letting the scent of plumeria blossoms float free. A blanket of stars glistened in the dark clear sky as Stone and Teri walked hand in hand along Waikiki Beach, shoes dangling from their free hand. With the return of the artifacts to the lava tube, this part of their experience was now a memory.

Debra was due to start work with the Honolulu Police Department in a few days' time, so Viane had taken time off from her studies to bring her to Hilo and show her the sights and spend an evening with Pops. Both women had wanted to renew their friendship before Debra and Dorteo, having completed their three-month training course, got immersed in their new careers.

As Stone and Teri walked past a lifeguard stand, the silent sentinel of their secret, they squeezed each other's hand a little tighter in unspoken recognition, but they didn't stop. They were slowly making their way toward the restaurant at the Colony Surf to celebrate the three-month anniversary of their first meeting.

"I wonder if they have our reservations?" queried Stone in a strangely humored voice. "We should probably call them to make sure, what do you think, angel?"

"It's probably a good idea," she said and started rummaging in her purse for her cell phone. She stopped searching when she heard Stone speaking to someone and looked up at him.

"Aloha, this is Kensington Stone. We may be about ten minutes late arriving. Is that any problem?"

He stood looking at her, a mile-wide grin creasing his face as he held his new cell phone to his ear. He loved her surprised expression and playful laugh.

THE END